PAINTING THE LINES

ASHLEY R. KING

CITY OWL
PRESS

PAINTING THE LINES
Aces of Hearts, Book 1

CITY OWL PRESS
www.cityowlpress.com

Cover Design by MiblArt. All stock photos licensed appropriately.

Edited by Charissa Weaks.

For information on subsidiary rights, please contact the publisher at info@cityowlpress.com.

Print Edition ISBN: 978-1-64898-003-9

Digital Edition ISBN: 978-1-64898-002-2

Printed in the United States of America

Praise for Ashley R. King

"King debuts with a delightful, character-driven rom-com, *Painting the Lines* about two underdogs working toward redemption… an expert at balancing chemistry and tension to create a couple readers will root for. Fans of slow-burn romance will be swept away."
— *Publisher's Weekly*

"*Forever After* is SUCH a fun read-the perfect blend of paranormal and contemporary romance with a side of mystery. The unique premise of a vampire reality show hooked me instantly, and the descriptions and details from the confessional booth to the coffin beds kept me absorbed in the fantastical world that Ms. King created."
– *Kat Turner, author of Hex, Love, and Rock and Roll*

"*Painting the Lines* is a fast-paced, chemistry-filled, feel good sports romance! Who knew tennis could be so sexy? Game. Set. Match. You'll fall for Amalie and Julian in straight sets, guaranteed."
— *USA Today Bestselling Author Natasha Boyd*

"Lovely characters, smart dialogues and a great romance! Both characters were lovable, and I couldn't get enough of them!"
— *Read More Sleep Less*

"The characters in *The Wilde Card* are so sweet and their connection is so so genuine. I cried and I laughed, and I laughed until I cried. My heart is so connected to this story, and I'm honestly blown away."
— *Colby Bettley, author of Christmas at the Grotto*

"I really cannot wait to see what Ashley comes up with next! There was absolutely no hesitation in deciding to rate this book five stars, it's truly well deserved!"– *Naomi, This Ginger Loves Books Blog*

"I love Autumn. I love Oliver. I love the whole concept of this book. I loved it all so much I got a paperback so I can read it all over again. If you want to read a paranormal romance with memorable characters, a clever premise, and a compelling mystery, you *need* to read *Forever After!*"
– *Gabrielle Ash, author of* The Family Cross *and* For the Murder

For my heart, Jared. This book would not be possible without you. I love you more than you'll ever know and am so thankful for your love, support, and jokes. Thank you for being you.

Chapter One

AMALIE

AMALIE SCANNED THE BAR, LOOKING FOR ROMINA'S RAVEN HAIR BENEATH THE dim lights. For a Tuesday night, quite the crowd had gathered inside Oakley's, a trendy hangout in midtown Atlanta.

"Can I get you something else?" Bryan, the cute bartender, asked with a boyish smile.

Amalie looked at her watch again. Romina was already fifteen minutes late. Tonight of all nights, when Amalie needed her best friend most.

Amalie's father, mega-billionaire Andrew Warner, had just dropped the hammer with his latest ultimatum, and Amalie needed Romina's sage advice, help, magic—*anything* that might help her figure out what to do. Her father had been pushing her to work for the family business, something she had no interest in doing. If she didn't, she'd be disowned and disinherited from the great Warner Hotel fortune. To some that might not be a huge deal, but to Amalie, who had no back-up plan, it was everything.

She sighed and took one last sip of her daiquiri. "No, that'll be all. Thank you."

With a quick nod, Bryan moved to the other end of the bar, where a seat had been claimed by a man who, even sitting down, was still taller than most. Amalie couldn't help but give him a once-over. He had a powerful frame, even if soft around the edges, like the forgotten build of an athlete lived under his skin. But something else snagged her attention.

Amalie watched with interest as the bartender seemed to contemplate cutting the guy off for the night even though it was only eight o'clock. The man bristled, spine stiffening, fingers tightening around the empty tumbler before him. But in a half-second, his eyes flicked up to one of the flat screens suspended behind the bar and he leaned forward, completely enraptured, his face oddly serene.

As a writer, or well, washed-up writer on the hunt for her next idea, Amalie was captivated by this guy's body language. One minute it looked like he might shatter his whiskey tumbler with his bare hands, and the next his eyes were glued to the television.

Amalie glanced at the screen, surprised to find a replay of the US Open tennis finals from several years ago. She knew enough about tennis to know the names of the Grand Slam tournaments and some of the cute players (hello, Rafael Nadal), but other than that, she was clueless. Her father, who loved tennis and watched it religiously, had tried to inspire a love of the sport in her, but…it just wasn't there.

Her eyes slid back to the enigma at the end of the bar. There was a catlike tension in the way he studied the battle between Rafael Nadal and Novak Djokovic, his entire focus narrowed to the game, his muscles twitching with restrained energy. Her writer instincts screamed that there was far more going on here than a bar patron watching the rerun of an old match. Cheering and clapping erupted on the screen.

"I could've done that! *Easily!*" The man pounded his fist on the bar and exploded from his seat with such force that his barstool tumbled backward. He was just as tall as she imagined, well over six feet.

Amalie gasped and took a step back. The man downed his drink, slamming the empty glass onto the bar with a thud, wiping his mouth with the back of his hand.

"Another," he growled at the bartender.

He shifted slightly and when he turned, she caught sight of his lovely eyes in the dim light, but they were marred with heavy bags beneath them.

"Hey, man. Julian, come on. You've got to chill," Bryan pleaded.

Julian. Amalie rolled that name around in her mind, tasted it on her tongue. She supposed he looked like a Julian, though to be fair she hadn't met a single Julian in her twenty-eight years. She studied him, his calves and thighs muscular beneath his khaki shorts. Yes, shorts, despite the cold. Even his arms looked like they had once been powerful, but judging by the slight beer gut he was rocking, Julian had missed a workout or two. He was ridiculously attractive, though, even if Amalie struggled to reconcile that fact with his brutish behavior.

She studied him further, imagining his story and committing his features to memory, a memory she would later take out, dissect, and piece together into one of her fictional heroes. Romina always teased that Amalie was more voyeur than participant in life. Perhaps that's why writing was so important to her.

Julian's burnt umber hair fell in unruly waves across his tanned forehead, his nose almost too flawless. But no, when he turned, she noted a slight bump, perhaps hinting at a fight at one point in his life? Or maybe, if he was like Amalie, a pretty nasty run-in with a suspiciously transparent sliding-glass door.

Julian's profile, with his sulky lower lip, was a thing of beauty, and she found herself wondering why such loveliness had been wasted on a staggering mess of a man.

As if feeling the levity of her gaze, or rather her judgment, Julian met her stare. Now *that* was completely unfair. His eyes stood out against his dark skin, a stunning green that reminded her of lush trees in the spring, and there were tiny lightning strikes of sparkling gold darting from the pupils.

Wait…

Holy crap, she was standing directly in front of him, having gravitated toward him without even realizing it. It didn't matter how hot he was, how *big* he was, she didn't want any part of this.

As if he heard her thoughts, he raised a perfect, dark eyebrow, a quirk she was sure was meant to be sexy and had probably worked on dozens of other women, but at that moment it only came off as sloppy and awkward.

"Like what you see?" he challenged. His sultry voice would've made her panties melt if not for the slur accenting it.

Amalie recoiled, cheeks hot as she leveled the behemoth with a sneer. "Excuse me?"

Julian tilted his head, studying her with a drunken intensity that made her squirm. "I said, do you like what you see? My place isn't that far…if you think you can keep your hands off me that long."

Bryan snickered as he shook his head, pretending to be mesmerized by the cleanliness of the beer mug in his hand.

"Can you believe the balls on this guy?" Amalie hooked a thumb toward Julian as she looked to Bryan. For what, she had no idea.

"A filthy mouth, too." Julian shot her a wink and sat back down at the bar. "My *favorite*."

"You are out of control." Amalie huffed. "I can't help it that I naturally gravitated toward *this*"—she waved her arms around, motioning and flailing at Julian—"train wreck. I thought I might've had my next book idea. But yet you disappoint, something I'm sure is very common."

There. She hated to be a mean girl, but he'd totally asked for it.

Julian reared back as if she'd slapped him but quickly recovered. "Enough of the spoiled little rich girl act. It reeks."

She faltered, the sting hitting home. "You don't even know me."

"Right, and you don't know me either, princess."

Princess? Anger burned inside her as she poked her finger into his surprisingly hard chest. "You have no idea who you're messing with, mister."

He puffed up, straightened his broad shoulders, and gave her a scalding once-over. "Yeah, I'm shaking in my boots. Listen, I'll have you know that you're looking at a US Open contender." He leveled her with a hard glare, daring her to argue.

Interest piqued, Amalie remained in place, her finger falling away. "*You're* a tennis player?" she asked through gritted teeth while mentally berating herself for continuing this conversation.

Julian paused a beat too long before answering with a shrug. "You could say that."

"Okay…" Amalie stretched the two-syllable word into three and cocked her brow as if to silently say, *I call bullshit*.

Julian blinked, but his gaze was still hazy as he responded with a surprising amount of vindication in his voice. "Actually, I'm going to qualify for the US Open." His eyes widened, as if his words were a revelation to him as well.

Interesting. Amalie's nails tapped the bar in an easy rhythm as she assessed him. "So I gather you used to play?" She almost mentioned his fading physique, but he was being oddly civil now, and she feared an observation like that would bring out the pig in him, *again.*

Julian averted his gaze, studying his hands, which now gripped the edge of the bar. He gave her a tight nod, then he seemed to slowly deflate. "I used to be the best. Before it all went to shit. Now I'm just a has-been, stuck selling pharmaceuticals day after day. I had everything I ever wanted right here"—Julian lifted a hand, palm open, his stare searing into his own flesh—"then I let it all slip away."

It was a surprisingly coherent statement, one that echoed and mirrored things Amalie felt about her own life. But before she could dwell on it, electricity hummed in her veins, the wheels in her head spinning wildly.

A tiny spark of sunlight filtered through the cracks of the prison that had slowly become her life as an idea quickly formed. Ever since New Year's Eve, she'd been mulling over goals, and writing a book was at the top of her list—this was perfect. The threat of having to work for her father receded as she pulled in a deep breath and let the realization settle over her bones. *This* could be her next hit, a novel that chronicled the rise to the top of a former tennis great. Hadn't her agent, Stella, recently hinted that sports romances were making a comeback? Besides, everyone loves a good underdog story. She could see the headlines now: *Washed-Up Tennis Player Makes Run for US Open.*

What were the odds that he played the only sport she knew even a little bit about?

Right now, it didn't matter that she hated tennis. It didn't matter that her father always rubbed it in her face that her older sister, Simone, was such a great player. It didn't matter that he'd tried to force Amalie to take lessons even though her instructor was the meanest person on the planet and cut her down every time she made a mistake.

Her past with tennis was exactly that: *the past.* An opportunity had presented itself, and she was hellbent on taking it. Stella had been adamant that Amalie write something "real and honest," something more along the lines of her debut, *Breaking the Fall,* the story that shot her into the next-big-thing stratosphere at the ripe age of nineteen. Of course, Amalie didn't want to let her down. Stella Frenette of Frenette Literary had been a hard win after Amalie lost her first agent for being a little twit high on fame and her own wealth. She'd bailed on so many commitments and haggled over stuff so stupid it made film and book people walk away. Yeah, film—that's how close she'd been to the big time.

Somewhere along the way, Amalie also lost the gift of natural storytelling. Every time she set pen to paper or fingers to keys, it felt forced. Her words read like *See Jane run. See Jane jump. See Jane suck at writing.*

Her last two novels fell flat because the characters weren't realistic. To fix the problem, Stella suggested Amalie study real people. Her bestseller had centered around a heroine based on none other than her sister, Simone. The intimate knowledge shared by sisters had given Amalie the means to create a three-dimensional character readers adored, which was really no surprise. Who didn't love Simone?

Amalie's follow-up books hadn't had that benefit and suffered because of it. She struggled to craft characters who leapt off the page, and she had no doubt the reason was because, other than Ro, she hadn't let anyone get close. Not even her ex-fiancé, Maxwell. Not really. Amalie failed at human connection because people broke hearts, and her heart already had enough cracks. It couldn't survive another quake.

She cringed as she thought of her early writing days, trying to reconcile that person with who she was now. Sadly, though she was ready to write again, the human connection thing was still a problem. But maybe Fate had given her a workaround. Readers—and Stella as well—would love that this novel was based on a real tennis player—one who was gorgeous and, with some training, would have muscles popping by the time the tournament rolled around. It would be so easy to capitalize on his looks and to even use the momentum of his rise to the top for promotion of the book.

She couldn't let fear get in the way of her dream this time. She just needed to get this Julian fellow to the US Open.

Just as Amalie was about to open her mouth, Julian slumped over the bar, passed out cold. The bartender dipped his head and smiled. "From what I hear, he does this all the time. He's pretty popular with the ladies, so usually he's already secured one or two to go home with. Looks like he didn't get that far with you." He had the audacity to smirk.

"Hard to imagine that he's popular with the ladies when he acts like a Neanderthal."

Bryan leaned forward on the bar conspiratorially, his voice hushed. "He was different tonight. Besides, I think you got under his skin because you called his bullshit. But hey, that's just my opinion."

Amalie sized up the situation *and* Julian, her mind calculating a million possibilities at once. "Was he really a great tennis player?" she asked Bryan, needing to know for sure before she made her next decision.

Bryan nodded. "Hell yeah. You never heard of Julian Smoke? They called him 'The Smoke' in college because he was a beast. He was even pegged as the next tennis great of his generation."

Amalie studied Julian's face, willing herself to remember him from one of her father's endless tennis ramblings. "What happened?" she asked, bringing her gaze back to the bartender.

"That's his story to tell. You'll have to ask him."

Amalie drummed her fingers on the smooth surface of the bar one last time before releasing a deep breath and making a decision she was sure she'd regret. "Help me get him to my car, will ya?"

Chapter Two

AMALIE

WHY DID THE ANSWER TO HER PROBLEMS HAVE TO BE A TALL, HEAVY, stumbling drunk?

"God, can you at least try to walk straight or, ya know, hold your body up a little more?" Amalie panted as Julian's increased weight made her stumble, her legs burning beneath the pressure. The faint hint of sandalwood cologne wafted beneath layers of alcohol, and his skin felt hot beneath her touch. She had one of his enormous arms draped across her neck, and each step made her grunt with effort. She was too small and too out of shape for this. A burst of freezing air sent a shiver over her body. She'd left her jacket at home so her sexy off the shoulder sweater would be on display.

The door to the pool house was in sight. So close, yet so far away.

Julian startled at her words. His eyes opened and then his head lolled, his body slumping over, so he practically engulfed her.

Amalie tried to ignore the contact, because this was the closest anyone had been to her in a minute and it felt good. *Nope. No, don't think that.* It didn't feel good at all. This guy was unbelievable.

As if to prove her unspoken thoughts, Julian leaned further down and took a deep sniff of her neck, his nose tickling her skin, startling her with an even more keen awareness of *him*. Had his lips accidentally brushed her pulse?

His head snapped up and a faint little dimple popped in his cheek, his eyes glassy as he pulled away. "You smell nice. What is that? Cupcakes? I like cupcakes."

Ugh. Why'd he have to be so cute, but such a jerk? The Julian from the bar was a no go.

Amalie shook her head, the movement brushing against his solid bicep. "It's none of your concern, and I'd thank you not to sniff me anymore."

Finally, they were at the door. She blew out a breath as she tried to unlock it while keeping Julian upright. He mumbled unintelligibly, but as soon as the door swung open, he magically regained usage of his legs. She watched as he staggered like a baby deer into her home, all kinds of cuss words flowing through her mind.

"You couldn't have used your legs earlier?" She slammed the door behind her, still trying to catch her breath.

Julian stopped in her living room and did a slow spin, causing him to stumble this way and that. Her eyes did a quick scan and immediately started to shove the coffee table out of the way in case he fell.

"Did you take me to a hotel room?" he asked. "This is a nice hotel room. It's big, but little all at the same time, like a *teensy, wittle* baby house. It's so cute and small. Not like me. I mean I'm cute, but I'm *not* small."

His voice had gone to a lilt, and he looked so young that it quickly chased away Amalie's foul mood. She pressed her hand over her mouth to suppress a giggle. She didn't answer him as she continued moving other possible hazards out of his way.

"Where are we? Are you going to seduce me? I'm telling you now that I'm on board with that. I think you'd like it. I know *I* would."

Amalie straightened. "Not gonna happen, buddy."

Apparently, that was a challenge because Julian started to sway in some kind of pseudo-seduction dance, and then he reached to take off his shirt.

It didn't come off easily. He got stuck in it, maybe even freaked out about it.

When Amalie finally stopped laughing long enough to catch her breath, she took pity on him and moved over to help him pull the tee over his head. He took a deep gulp of air and then his eyes met hers, panic dissipating.

She bit her lip as her eyes betrayed her, roaming over his nakedness. He was so beautiful. When she looked at his face again, those star-flecked eyes studied her, like he could see to her soul.

Amalie hung transfixed in his spell before finally shaking her head and taking several steps backward. She needed to get him to the couch, for him to sit there and not move. She let loose a small yelp when she realized what was still splayed across the cushions.

Julian followed her gaze to a pile of clean laundry, underwear that she still hadn't put away.

"Sexy panties," he said, lumbering toward the couch like a hot Frankenstein, hands outstretched to grab the scanty slips of material.

"Oh no, you don't." Amalie rushed forward, one arm out to sweep her undies into her other hand. "Those are not for you to see."

"*Yet.* But I will eventually. Sexy undies for a sexy lady." He snagged the lone pair that didn't make it into her hurried grasp.

Amalie dropped the underwear onto a kitchen chair and came running back, trying to get the thong out of his hand. Julian was too tall and lifted it so high that she felt like a chihuahua nipping at his heels.

He dipped his head as he pocketed the undies. "I'm so sleepy."

Amalie pinched her lips together at the sight of her bright red thong sticking out of his pocket. She made herself remember the reason for all of this, the reason she was even putting up with this mess. She knew Julian was drunk, but there was something she had to ask.

"Hey, how badly do you want to get to the US Open?" She edged closer to him, hands wringing.

He propped a hand on the back of the couch, his eyes even heavier lidded than before. "I...I want it more than anything, but it's impossible," he slurred.

"What if I can get you there? What if I can make it happen?" She cocked her head to the side, realizing she was quickly losing him. He was minutes from passing out. *Again.*

"You can't. You live in this *tiny, itsy bitsy,*" he held his pointer finger and thumb together, "house or hotel or whatever this place is. Tennis is expensive, more than I can afford." He shuffled to the front of the couch.

"But what if I *could*? What would you be willing to do for me?" She regretted the words instantly.

A sexy smirk tilted his lips, and then his hands went to the button on his jeans, his thumb tracing that sexy trail of hair right above it. "Are you propositioning me?"

Amalie forced herself to look away.

"Oh, no you don't," she said while blindly smacking at his hand, ignoring that little bit of drool pooling at the corner of her mouth from his impromptu show. "You are not about to completely undress here."

Suddenly her hand smacked at emptiness and she turned to see that Julian had fallen onto the couch haphazardly, one hand still on his fly. He was out cold. She growled in aggravation as she dug her underwear from his jeans, careful to keep her eyes averted even though those traitors wanted to look their fill.

After rearranging him as best she could, she looked down at his unconscious form, still feeling a little breathless. She'd found out what she needed to know. Julian could be bought.

"You don't know it yet, but you're going to save me from a life I don't want, Julian Smoke."

She stepped out of the pool house into the cool night air and wasted no time seeking out her father.

Nausea churned Amalie's stomach as she lifted her clammy hand to knock on her father's office door.

"Come in," he boomed.

She squeezed her eyes shut before twisting the door handle.

Andrew Warner's study had been off-limits since she was little. As a matter of fact, as she stood in the immaculate room completely overwhelmed by dark wood, she realized she'd only been in there maybe twice in her life. She wasn't surprised, however, to find Simone standing near the fireplace, one hand on the mantle, the other holding a glass of water.

Simone was tall, taller than Amalie by about five inches, slender and willowy where Amalie had curves. Where Amalie's hair looked like a curtain of fire, Simone's was a short ebony wave, cut in a cheek-grazing bob and fringe that fluttered atop her lashes, making her look like silent film star Louise Brooks. What Amalie loved most about her sister was not that she put actual supermodels to shame with her beauty, but that she was even more gorgeous on the inside. Simone Warner-Lennox loved fiercely and protected vigilantly, but she was also the most giving soul. As part of her "heiress training," she demanded that Andrew Warner get more involved in worthy causes and donate more often to charities. Lord knows they had the change to spare. Amalie imagined her father as Scrooge McDuck, swimming in a pool full of his gold. He only gave if there was something in it for him—a return—which made what Amalie was about to do all the more difficult.

Amalie dared a glance at her father, who kept rapidly blinking at her intrusion, a scrunched-up look on his face. Immediately cowed, her gaze moved to her sister.

Simone's head drew back in surprise. "Amalie!" Quickly recovering, she placed her glass on the mantle before moving to gather Amalie in a tight hug. "I was going to drop by and visit tonight."

Amalie's heart swelled as her sister's perfume, one that reminded her of days at the beach, tickled her nose. She adored her sister, even though they couldn't be more polar opposites. Warner Hotels CEO had always been Simone's dream, whereas Amalie couldn't get far enough away. Because of that fact, it was beyond obvious that Simone was their father's favorite. Andrew had always been an absent father, but things shifted after their mom left. He'd become more business- and Simone-oriented than ever, while still trying to control Amalie. He liked to remind her of her failure as a writer, saying that maybe it was time to settle into the "real world." Through it all, Simone was there, ready and willing to help Amalie pick up the pieces.

"Enough of that, girls. Amalie, I have business to discuss with Simone, so whatever this is, make it quick," Andrew snapped. His gray-blue eyes were shrewd as he took a slow sip from the whiskey tumbler in his hand. He sucked his teeth afterward, a habit her mother used to despise. He didn't care, of course. If it didn't deal with money, it didn't particularly matter to Andrew Warner.

Amalie steeled her spine and lifted her chin, even though it was the opposite of what she felt. Andrew had coached his girls not to show emotion, not to cry, to essentially be made of ice. Amalie was anything but that, yet in his presence she had to pretend, even if it felt like killing a piece of herself. "I've got a new idea for a novel—"

Her father's scoff cut her off, but Simone quickly stepped in. "Hear her out."

"Fine. Continue." He gestured with a disinterested twirl of his fingers, his eyes still studying the documents spread out before him.

"I've met a former tennis star, and he wants to compete for the US Open. I thought...I thought this would make a great idea for a novel, fictionalizing his attempt."

Her father's head snapped up. "I can tell you right now, that idea will fail. You know nothing about tennis."

Amalie flinched as she silently cursed herself for showing weakness in front of this man.

Simone scowled but turned her attention to Amalie. "What do you need to make this happen? Money? Maybe I can help."

Amalie nodded. "Definitely money—"

"No," their father interjected. "If anyone finances this, it'll be me. Now tell me what you need money for." Amalie knew he wouldn't dare be overruled by anyone, let alone one of his daughters. *Well played, sis.*

"I need enough financing for a trainer, a coach, entry fees for tournaments, travel expenses..." At least that's everything she'd learned from the internet before walking over from the pool house.

Andrew leaned forward, hands clasped on his desk. "Name?"

Amalie shot a quick glance at Simone, then back at her father. "Ah, Julian Smoke."

Cruel laughter filtered through the room as her father tilted his head back. He made a show of wiping nonexistent tears from his face when he finally calmed down. "Julian Smoke? He's a joke. He's what, thirty? Tennis players retire when they reach their thirties, unless they're one of the greats..." Andrew sat up straighter, his eyes flashing. Amalie knew that look. She'd seen it countless times when he was being ruthless with competitors—all flashing teeth and condescension. "Actually, I have an idea, Amalie. I think we can form a financial arrangement that suits us both. You know you have a decision to make. Work for me at Warner

Hotels, or you're on your own. Your head is in the clouds, you're a daydreamer—you're not a Warner, not where it counts."

Ouch. Amalie sensed Simone move closer to her, placing a steady hand on her back. That gesture alone was nearly enough to send the tears falling.

"This adventure will fail, I know," he continued. "I have a knack for this kind of thing—"

"Then why finance it at all? I know you hate wasting money." Amalie surprised herself by speaking up and was proud that her voice hadn't cracked like everything else inside her.

"I'll consider it charity work. But when this falls apart—and mark my word, it will—you'll see that you aren't a writer, that you are nothing more than a one-hit-wonder who got a lucky break early in life, and you'll come to work for me. No more of this back-and-forth, finding-your-bliss talk. You will carry on our family legacy, and you will be proud to do it, just like your sister."

Simone stiffened. "I wish you'd leave me out of this."

Simone hated being the barb thrown down in a fight, but this was Andrew Warner, and that was what he always did. Besides, Amalie was still trying to sift through the other slight, the one where he reminded her of the day her dreams shattered, the day she became caged.

Not wanting to give her father a chance to draw Simone into it any further, Amalie said, "So that's it? That's what's in it for you? A big fat I-told-you-so? A way to bring me to heel?"

Andrew nodded sharply. "Amalie, you might not believe it, and I know I might not have the best way of showing it, but I do love you. You're my daughter. I only want what's best for you, and a writing career isn't it. Do you know how competitive that industry is? Do you know how few authors can actually feed themselves off a writing career alone? You're chasing a pipe dream when you have a job waiting for you at Warner Hotels, a job that comes with automatic status and a regular, dare I say handsome, paycheck. It's security, Amalie. Security is everything. I can give you that."

Yeah, but in exchange he'd be clipping her wings.

She nearly asked if this had something to do with her mother. Simone mentioned that maybe he'd changed because he was scared of being alone. Amalie was sure it had to do with the fact that their mom once had dreams of being a writer, and that part of the reason she ran off with the yoga instructor was because he supported said dreams. She'd overheard her mother yelling at Andrew one night, saying that she was tired of the debutante schtick and wanted something more. In that way, Amalie supposed she was more like Katharine Warner than she thought, and that probably scared the shit out of her father...probably made him wonder *when*, not *if*, she'd leave.

Either way, here was her chance to finally prove she was worth more than her last name. She was worthy of so much more—of love and respect, not constant ridicule.

She took a nervous step to shake her father's hand, all while praying this would work. If not, she'd be stuck doing what she'd been trying so desperately to avoid all these years.

With all the confidence she could muster, Amalie looked Andrew Warner in the eye and said, "Then you've got yourself a deal."

Chapter Three

JULIAN

Julian woke to a foreign sound: the rattling of pots and dishes. The smell of bacon tickled his nose, but the pounding in his head captured the majority of his attention.

Damn, how much did he drink last night?

He cracked one eye open with no idea where he was. He sat up slowly, like a vampire from one of those old black-and-white movies, his hands scrubbing down the stubble of his face, the sound loud enough to drown out the frantic beating of his heart. He was no stranger to waking up in random girls' homes, but this? This felt a little too domestic after a one-night stand.

Then it registered—if it was a one-night stand, then why the hell was he covered by a blue quilt on someone's couch? He stood hesitantly, letting the quilt drop to the floor, only to realize he was still fully clothed.

His brow wrinkled. So, a definite *no* on the sex, which intrigued him even more. He considered himself a good enough flirt and an even better lover, so he couldn't quite wrap his mind around the situation. Seriously, where was he?

Julian made it a point to be quiet as he tiptoed to a mantle laden with pictures. Each photo had the same common denominator: a really *freaking* hot redhead with wild wavy hair. Her eyes were a strange, misty gray-blue, and her heart-shaped mouth…tantalizing. And yet he'd failed to land her?

He squeezed his eyes shut, as if that would help the memories grow clearer. He'd gotten way too drunk last night, but it'd been a rough day and the bartender, Bryan, wasn't as tough as the other guys. Then he remembered the girl and her sneer. But most of all? He remembered that he couldn't stand her.

His memory wasn't great, but he did remember her spoiled-little-rich-girl "you're just a piece of gum on the bottom of my shoe" attitude. He'd seen that exact sneer countless times before, because when you're a poor boy playing a rich man's sport, well, it's bound to happen.

Amalie was entitled and reminded him of the members at the country club where he and his dad once worked. They were condescending and rude, thinking their money made them better, that Julian and his dad were nothing more than servants. Like the rest, this girl didn't know anything about him or what he'd been through in what felt like a lot longer than his thirty years. His life had three parts: BT, Before Tennis; DT, During Tennis; and AT, After Tennis. The AT years all seemed to run together in an endless path of nothing.

His chest ached, and he brought his fist there to massage away the pain. The sound of a microwave beeping reminded him that he needed to get the hell out of this situation.

He did a quick survey. Okay, house, not apartment. It was a really nice house that overlooked an incredibly well-kept tropical paradise of a pool.

"Oh, you're awake," a cool voice greeted his back in the same kind of tone that could've said, "Oh, thank God he's dead."

Slowly, Julian turned to find the girl in the pictures standing in front of him. She was a tiny thing, dressed in skinny jeans that did wonders to accentuate her curves, topped off by a half-tucked white tee shirt and a black blazer with black motorcycle boots. Her red hair was down and wild around her face, and a silver coin necklace hung around her neck. In each hand, she held a plate of bacon with two waffles perfectly layered in butter and syrup.

Julian dragged his gaze from the extended plate of food and back to the smoky blue eyes currently assessing him. God, he already despised that snooty know-it-all expression, so he shot her a bored look and headed for the door.

"Yeah, look, it's been nice, and I still have no clue how I ended up here, but I don't know you, so…"

Just as he reached for the door handle, the woman spoke, her icy voice freezing him to the spot.

"Don't you dare walk out that door, Julian Smoke."

He tensed at the usage of his full name because hell if he knew hers.

"Yeah, I know who you are," she said, "and you better believe I didn't haul your heavy ass all the way into my living room just because I thought you were cute or would be a great lay. Because I didn't."

The fire in those words burned enough to make Julian turn around. He hated to admit it, but he was impressed; that fiery attitude was a huge turn-on.

But it didn't change the fact that there was just something about this girl that rubbed him the wrong way. He knew it last night, and he knew it this morning.

Julian crossed his arms over his chest, which was now a sad shadow of what it once was, much like his entire life. He raised an eyebrow and said, "Fine. Then who the hell are you, and why did you bring me here?" He thought for a minute and then added, "And where am I?"

The redhead placed both plates on an immaculate wooden coffee table with books stacked at even angles. She rolled her shoulders as she stood back up, her pretty face scrunched in obvious disdain. He wanted to tell her the feeling was mutual, but then she placed her hands on her curvy hips, cocking out one foot as she said in a no-nonsense tone, "I'm Amalie Warner. No need to worry, you're perfectly safe. You're in my home. I live in the pool house on my father's estate."

Julian let loose a mirthless laugh, followed by a sardonic twist of his lips. "*Pool* house? This is a freaking pool house?" He took in the ornate fixtures and open spaces of the whitewashed room. He was no stranger to luxury, especially at the height of his career, brief as it was, but this was profuse.

Amalie clicked her tongue. "You're here because, despite the fact that I find you utterly ridiculous—"

Julian bowed, his eyes fluttering as he said, "Why, thank you. The feeling is one hundred percent mutual."

She didn't even flinch. She merely shrugged. "You're welcome. Anyway, last night you said you wanted to qualify for the US Open."

Julian's world tilted, and he found himself moving away from Amalie and taking a heavy seat on the couch.

"I said that?" The words were like cotton in his mouth.

Amalie sat next to him, pushing a glass of orange juice into his hand, acting strangely civil. She'd probably poisoned the OJ.

Seeing him eye it, Amalie scoffed. "It's not spiked or anything. Drink it."

Julian lifted a brow. "And isn't that exactly what someone who is poisoning someone would say?"

An unimpressed look settled on Amalie's face. "Wow, okay. Anyway, you did say you wanted to qualify for the Open, whether you recall it or not." She took a breath that looked like it pained her and then said, "Look, I did some research on you last night—"

"You what?" Julian, totally thrown off his game, drank the poisonous orange juice because damn if that statement didn't make his throat constrict.

Amalie rolled her stormy eyes. "It's called the internet. But I'm guessing there's something you don't want me to find, since you're drinking my poison juice."

The glass froze halfway to his mouth, and he skewered her with a glare. "Guess you'll have to get daddy to bail you out of this if it's really poisoned."

Her hands clenched and unclenched at her side, nostrils flaring. Her voice went tight when she finally spoke. "Look, I'm a writer, and you could say we've had similar lots in life." Julian looked around the pool mansion and snorted, but the woman, God bless her, kept right on talking. "I need a bestseller, or I'm done for. You need to qualify for the US Open or…" Her brow furrowed as if trying to think of the right thing to say. "Or you go on being the drunken mess you are. Here's where we can help each other out."

She leaned closer to Julian, close enough that he caught a whiff of her vanilla perfume. "I'll bankroll everything," she continued. "A physical trainer, a coach, your hotels, your entry fees to the tournaments, your equipment, your gas, *everything*."

Now she had Julian's complete attention, poisoned orange juice be damned.

Money was one of the many things that kept him from returning to the game he loved. There was a reason tennis was called a rich man's sport, and he didn't make enough selling pharmaceuticals to pay for all it entailed. He *could* make enough, if he actually enjoyed his job. At least he had enough vacation and sick time to take off for training and matches. If he really wanted this, this was his shot, something his dad would've told him to jump on immediately.

At the thought of his father, the ache in his chest grew. It had been nine years, but the man's death still felt fresh, like it happened yesterday.

"How are *you* going to pay for all of that?" he asked, desperately trying to banish memories of his father. "Especially since you live with your parents?"

Amalie flinched at his words, and for the briefest moment, he saw a chink in her armor.

Julian had the gift of knowing exactly where to aim for people's weaknesses—both on and off the court. He should've felt bad, but he didn't. A few more memories from the night before had resurfaced in his mind, and she'd hit him where it hurt, too.

He watched as Amalie smoothed a hand over her denim-clad thighs and then quickly cleared her throat, her tone devoid of emotion. "My father is Andrew Warner, perhaps you've heard of him?"

Julian jerked his head back in shock before he could get a grip on his carefully constructed, emotionless facade. Suddenly everything clicked into place. Spoiled little rich girl had been a more than accurate assessment, and to be honest, the realization of who Amalie was made him dislike her even more.

He glanced around, choking down a disbelieving laugh. He was sitting in Andrew Warner's pool house being a prick to his out-of-touch-with-reality daughter. Amalie's dad was a billionaire, making his money from the worldwide Warner luxury hotel chain. Amalie's older sister, Simone, frequently graced the cover of the society pages since Atlanta was enamored with her, their most famous heiress and claim to fame. Julian's mom followed the family like a fangirl, but he didn't recall much mention of Amalie at all. Hell, he didn't even know that Andrew Warner had another kid besides Simone.

Careful to wipe away his shocked expression, he rested his elbows on his knees. "All right, rich girl. I'll play, but first tell me what you need me for."

Amalie's eyes sparkled with a hint of excitement. "I write fiction, and I want you to be the main character in my next book."

"You want to write about *me*?" He almost felt flattered. Almost. But something told him Amalie Warner wasn't the flattering type.

"Well, you but not really you. It's fiction, so it's kind of going to be based around you, about a loser who's down and out—"

"What?"

"I mean, a guy who's...well, a guy who's going to try for the unthinkable."

"Wow, your belief in me is overwhelming. Really. It's enough to bring me to my knees." Julian clutched his chest like he was actually overwhelmed by her words. What the girl didn't know was that he'd pretty much do anything short of becoming a gigolo to have another shot at his dream. Despite that, he couldn't help the impending word vomit that trailed out of his mouth. "Why don't you just get one of your father's tennis buddies to help you? I don't see why you need *me* specifically?"

Amalie brought a slim, pale finger to her necklace, an absent look in her eyes. "My father's tennis buddies don't have the underdog vibe I need. You do. Besides, I feel like your success will equal my success."

"Meaning?"

"You had a gazillion fans and most of them still love you and still talk about how they wish you hadn't quit the game. They'd love to see your comeback. I can totally see it now." Her hands stretched above her in an imaginary line, "*Based on the comeback journey of Julian Smoke.* It would sell because you already have that built-in fan base."

"Will your writing make it sell?"

"Since I'm writing about a real person, yes, it will. That's where I do my best work." Her voice was smug, her head held proudly.

Julian rubbed his chin. "So you're thinking you'll get the bestseller you need? And you can guarantee that you'll be able to fund my run for the US Open?"

Amalie responded with a sharp nod.

He shouldn't trust her. He knew that. Her kind of people—people with more money than God—repulsed him. For them, money could buy anything. Even other people. And there he was, on the brink of being bought.

Julian stared at Amalie. Her eyes were crystals, as impossible to look away from as two glaciers. Damn. He was probably going to regret this, but he extended his hand anyway. "I'm in," he said. "But I still don't like you."

Amalie gave a wry smile that convinced him she was used to getting her way, then she wrapped her tiny fingers around his larger ones in a surprisingly firm shake. "The feeling's mutual."

Chapter Four

AMALIE

"*HELL NO. THERE, IS THAT A BETTER RESPONSE?*" ROMINA BIT OUT, VENOM drenching every word.

Amalie sipped her sweet tea. "You do realize you owe me since you stood me up at the bar? This is kind of your fault after all."

Romina scowled as she tossed her glossy, black hair over her shoulder. "Amalie, that was *one* night, and you're asking me to do this for…"

"Oh, you know, seven months," Amalie replied with a pretty-please smile.

"He's an ass. I've heard that from so many people. He'd be a nightmare to train." Romina shuddered at the thought.

"I know he's…unpleasant."

Romina's dark eyes focused their bullshit-detecting stare on Amalie. They'd been friends long enough to see through each other's lies. It'd been love at first sight when they randomly picked each other as project partners back in their Agnes Scott College days.

Amalie winced. "Fine. I hate his guts. He's an arrogant jerk who thinks he's God's gift to humanity thanks to all these people online who think he's the sexiest guy walking this earth. And apparently, from what I heard from Bryan the bartender, so do the women at the bar."

Romina grinned around a bite of pizza. "Now that's more like it."

"But think—you could punish each asinine comment with an extra push-up or mile. Or if you *really* want to be mean, make him run suicides for two whole minutes."

Amalie knew she was being evil, especially since she was depending on Julian for her success. It was a foreign feeling and one she didn't particularly like, especially given that she didn't know a lot about him— just that he'd made it to the pros and things had bottomed out pretty quickly. But at this point, she was up for anything that could get her away from her father and all things Warner Hotels. Simply speaking, Julian was her ticket out of hell. But if they were going to give this a shot, Amalie wanted nothing but the best on their team, and Romina Arroyo was the best fitness trainer in Georgia.

"My dad's paying for everything," Amalie added. "You'll be getting paid as if you're training a pro tennis player."

Romina's eyes went round. Amalie had eavesdropped on her father's "heiress in training" lessons with Simone more times than she cared to count. One of the most important lessons was how to broker a deal that couldn't be refused.

Romina blew out a breath. "Fine. I'll do it."

Even though Amalie was relieved, a familiar worry slithered into her mind.

Romina stretched one hand across the table, the other still holding a breadstick. "Hey. Don't go there. Accepting this job is about me liking the idea of sticking it to that asshole dad of yours, but it's also about being a good friend and helping you catch that dream you've been chasing. Okay? So wipe that look off your face. I'd still be your best friend even if your last name wasn't Warner."

Amalie's eyes darted around the tiny restaurant, to her plate, everywhere but to Ro. Romina had a talent for slicing right to the heart of a matter, and sometimes it made Amalie squirm because, well, she wasn't used to talking about her feelings. But like it or not, Ro had read her plainly. Too many people saw Andrew Warner's money when they looked at Amalie, instead of seeing her for the longing-to-be-independent woman that she was. It had poisoned her with enough doubt that she'd just questioned her best friend's motives.

"Warner, look at me, damn it," Romina growled, putting down her breadstick.

Amalie met her friend's stare. "Must be serious if you're laying down the carbs."

Ro leaned forward. "It is. Now say it. Say that I'm your best friend no matter what, and that who your daddy is don't matter one bit to me."

Amalie sighed. Ro would sit and hold her hand in a death grip while giving her an equally unsettling stare until Amalie did as asked. "You're my best friend no matter what, and you don't care that my father is Andrew Warner."

Apparently satisfied, Romina sat back, releasing Amalie's hand from her numbing grip.

Eager to avoid discussing any more of her hang-ups, Amalie asked Romina one question that the internet couldn't answer. "Any idea *why* Julian quit? I read that he was amazing. Brilliant. Until he...*wasn't*."

Romina quirked an eyebrow. "I'm not sure but, whatever it is, maybe it'll help you write something like Stella requested. Secrets always add interest."

Amalie leaned back in her chair, mulling Ro's words. "You might be right."

"I'm always right, my lovely." Romina winked before scanning Amalie's plate. "You plan on eating the rest of that?" She motioned to a half slice of greasy pepperoni goodness.

Amalie pushed the red plate over to Romina and sighed. "Enjoy. I need to get home and outline questions for my introductory interview with Satan. I'm supposed to meet him at Morgan Falls Overlook tonight."

With a mouth full of pizza, Romina deadpanned. "What an interesting event that will be." Amalie wrinkled her nose, but Romina continued. "Tell His Surliness to be at my gym at eight a.m. *Sharp*. Each minute he's late, I'm tacking on another mile. He seems like the type who doesn't care about anyone's time."

Amalie stood from their table, pulling on a jacket before throwing her black Prada bag (a guilt gift from her mother, who she hadn't seen in eight years) over her shoulder. "Oh, this is going to be fun."

Seven o'clock turned into seven-ten, which turned into seven-twenty, and finally seven-thirty, and yeah, Amalie was pissed. Julian promised he'd meet her, but he was nowhere in sight.

Amalie closed the book she'd been reading and released a pent-up sigh. She scanned the park beneath the cotton candy sky, bouncing from the lake to an old man walking his chihuahua to a harried dad chasing after his little girl. Getting stood up seemed to be Amalie's new normal, and she wasn't having it *at all*. After fishing her cell out of her purse, she gathered her book and once-warm coffee and dialed Ro.

Romina picked up on the first ring. "Let me guess, the prick didn't show?"

Amalie slid into her car, turning the heater on blast. "You would be correct. Any idea where a former tennis player might hide out? Bars? Strip clubs? Country clubs?" Amalie asked as she pulled out of the slowly emptying parking lot.

"How about a tennis court, love? Drive around. Check out the nearest courts. I'd bet my gym you'll find him there."

Amalie smacked her forehead. "Well, I'm an idiot. I'll ride by the courts I know and then pull over so I can look up others. You're a genius, Ro."

"I know, I know. Now go find your victim, er, um, subject." And then the line went dead.

Amalie stuck her tongue out at her phone and muttered as she drove around looking for the nearest tennis courts. "Directions, thou art my enemy," she groused, but then slowed when she noticed the bright lights of a tennis court and the sign for the Thornbriar Tennis Center. A familiar bear of a man was on the court, hitting ball after ball to no one. Amalie pulled her car into a parking spot hidden by shrubbery, turned off the engine, and crept out for a better view.

Amalie stood there, huddled in her jacket and boots, while Julian danced around the court in shorts and a tank. A glowing sheen covered his arms, accentuating every curve and cut. He also wore black shorts that showed off pretty decent calf muscles.

Amalie rolled her eyes. Fine, they were more than decent. As were his sculpted thighs. As much as she hated to admit it, her initial assessment from the bar was correct. He was...hot. The man had once been—and maybe would be again—a machine, in possession of a body built for vigorous activities.

She swallowed hard, shoving thoughts about Julian's body to the darkest depths of her obviously desperate mind, but the noise coming from him drew her attention—the grunting when hitting a shot hard, the cussing when it didn't land where he wanted.

A tingle traced up her spine and her mouth fell open on a breathless sigh that was as mind-boggling as it was annoying. She was supposed to be throttling him, not ogling him.

Any response Julian had drawn from her quickly faded when she noticed his intensity increasing at a stunning pace, as if he were being chased by some inner demon. He hit shot after shot without pause, serve after serve. His arm had to feel like it was about to fall off. Really, what was the purpose of this? Why was he working himself so hard?

Amalie's heart raced as she watched him run himself down, his grunts becoming more ragged with each slam. Her hand went to her necklace as she remembered her initial intention to give him a piece of her mind. She was still angry, yes, but it looked like Julian was working through something important. She could wait and yell at him another day.

Just as she was about to return to her car, the automatic timer lights went off, and the court and everything around it descended into darkness. Amalie stiffened. Surely she'd been caught, but no. The *thwack* of Julian's racket hitting the ball continued to echo alongside the sound of his tennis shoes slapping the asphalt. It was poetry in motion, a symphony of agony. But how long was he going to torture himself? Mesmerized, she stood there partially concealed by shrubbery as he played in the darkness for another ten minutes.

Amalie squinted as her eyes adjusted to the lack of light, the nearby parking lot lamp allowing her to just make out Julian's form. He hit a crappy serve, and then his racket slammed down on the court.

Quickly on its heels was another practically inhuman sound—part animal howl, part anguish—as Julian fell to the ground, head in hands, his entire body shaking.

Amalie's chest tightened. She was clearly trespassing on something she was not meant to witness. She still disliked Julian, and she was still mad that he stood her up, but she wasn't completely made of stone.

Not wanting to intrude, Amalie tiptoed back to her car, making sure she closed the door without a sound. She'd text him later about meeting Romina at her gym. After all, tomorrow was another day. But tonight? Tonight was his.

Chapter Five

JULIAN

LAVA RAN THROUGH JULIAN'S VEINS AS HE SAT SHAKING ON THE ASPHALT. Sweat fell in rhythmic splats on the court where he'd collapsed. Breathing felt like a thousand knives stabbing his lungs, but he'd gotten it out of his system, whatever *it* was. At least for now. Damn it.

Truth was, he'd never stopped playing tennis. It was ingrained far too deeply in him to ever think about quitting. For him to stop playing, whether for fun or money, would be like cutting out part of his brain.

And his father. More than anything else in his life, Julian clung to memories of his father. When he thought of his dad, that salt and pepper beard, the crinkled green eyes that genetics had passed on, it felt like stepping into a puddle of water surrounded by downed power lines. Julian's downfall was never Oliver Smoke's fault. Everything had always been and would always be his own damn failing.

"The Smoke, my ass." Julian panted through ragged breaths as he tried to get up from the court, his hip making noises as he stood.

Welcome to thirty, ladies and gentlemen, where you fall apart overnight.

Hearing his old nickname, the one everyone called him on the pro circuit, as short-lived as it was, sucked. It just reminded him of all the things he didn't do. Those thoughts were the kinds of things he should be sharing with that redhead. *Amalie*. The name suited her—intriguing and beautiful but altogether more trouble than it was worth.

Digging into his past was the last thing he wanted to do. His regrets, guilt, the thoughts and feelings that perpetually haunted him, would rise up and bite him in the ass.

That's why he stood Amalie up. He'd been on his way, dressed as his alter ego, the guy he absolutely loathed: the Clark Kent of pharmaceutical sales. *That* Julian walked through life like a zombie. *That* Julian wore khakis and button-ups and sleek black suits, mimicking the rich guys he fucking despised. Talking to Amalie, helping her research, being her novel's not-so-fictitious subject suddenly felt suffocating. Which was why he'd pulled into the Thornbriar Tennis Center instead of going to the park.

Julian conjured an image of Amalie sitting on the wooden swings overlooking the river, forlorn and lonely. It was almost enough to make him feel guilty.

Almost.

After drying his face with the hem of his sweat-soaked shirt, Julian gathered his stuff. His eyesight in the dark was pretty good thanks to years of practice. He and his dad used to train at the Otter Pines Country Club after hours, and sometimes the lights would go out. The first time it happened, Julian fumbled around the court, tripping over tennis balls and cursing, but his dad had moved with stealthy grace. Within seconds the balls had been gathered in the hopper and handed off to Julian. He'd looked at his dad in utter confusion. It was then that Oliver taught him to rely on the feel of the court, on the sounds of the ball striking the asphalt, on the *whoosh* of the racket instead of sight. It took months, but eventually Julian could see in the dark as clearly as his father.

"Why do I need to learn to play in the dark?" Julian had asked.

His dad slung an arm around him and said, "If you can play in the dark, you can play anywhere, including the US Open."

The US Open, once a pipe dream, was closer to becoming a reality. After his stellar run at the University of Georgia with three national championships under his belt, he figured his career in the pros would go similarly. Obviously it didn't, and that's where he had to swallow his pride.

He *wanted* this now. Wanted a different life, not some cracked half-life.

He wanted to know what he was capable of without a shady agent, without Nadine and her betrayal, without anyone or anything distracting him from the dream he'd been born to achieve.

After throwing his tennis bag into the trunk of his Altima, a remnant from his college days, Julian climbed in and rested his head against the driver's seat. Scrubbing a hand down his face, he grabbed his phone from the glove compartment, scrolling to Amalie's contact info, info she'd put in herself that morning.

His fingers hovered over the screen. Regardless of how he acted, deep down lived a Southern gentleman. His mama would have his hide if he just texted a girl, anyone actually, after standing them up. So he got ready for ball-busting as he pressed the call button.

"I'm assuming you're calling to grovel?" Amalie's smug voice filtered through the phone. "Well, I hope you're on your hands and knees, because I need to make sure you really mean it. Maybe you should FaceTime me."

This girl was something else. And because it was so damn fun pushing her buttons, Julian ignored thoughts of his mother's disapproval and played dumb. "Grovel? For what?"

Silence. Shuffling. A puff of breath so loud that Julian had to pull the phone away from his ear.

"Damn, you practicing those fire-breathing skills?" he asked.

"Actually, I am. Maybe if I learn to breathe fire, you'll take this seriously."

He fought an eye roll. A root canal would be easier than dealing with Amalie. "You done?"

"With you? Almost. I don't like having my time wasted, Julian."

A tiny seed of fear blossomed in the back of his mind. He couldn't afford to let his own stupid decisions get in the way of things again. God, he hated having to eat crow. His dad used to tell him he must like the way it tastes because he ate it more than anyone he knew.

"Fair enough. Let's move on to the next phase of whatever this is. You said I'd get a trainer and a coach, right? When does that happen? I'm not about to answer all your questions before you deliver on your end of the deal."

A pause, then, "Was that an apology, Julian Smoke? If so, it was the worst one I've ever heard. You need to try again."

"Listen—" He started to tell her where she could shove her money, but he closed his eyes, pinching the bridge of his nose instead.

Money made the world go round—he knew that better than anyone.

He remembered the day he overheard his dad talking to the head tennis pro, begging him to give Julian lessons. The guy, in front of his rich friends, looked down his nose at Oliver and questioned whether or not he could afford the sport for his son. Even called it a dead dream. Determination had raged in Oliver Smoke's eyes at that. Julian could still see him, fists clenching and unclenching. Anyone who wanted to make it in the sport started young, took private lessons, and went to an expensive academy.

That was the day Oliver Smoke began training Julian himself, like a pro.

Julian's blood boiled all over again, recalling how rich people treated his father, how they'd always treated him. That was how Julian lost his money after he went pro—a rich sleazeball taking advantage of him. Now? Now he wanted to go out there and make his dad proud, make his sacrifices and hard work for his son worth it after all these years. Julian would prove that just because he didn't grow up with money or train in an academy, he was still valid. That all those country club assholes were wrong.

But Julian had already burned his bridges. Sponsors wouldn't touch him, so it was either sit there and apologize to an entitled rich girl or lose his shot, forever.

Julian finally got the words past his lips. "Fine. Sorry."

"For?" Amalie's voice turned patronizing.

Just who exactly did she think she was? She was so caught up in herself that she didn't even realize what a gift that one "sorry" was.

Julian couldn't help the words that came pouring from his mouth. He'd spent the majority of his years being pushed around by people just like her. No longer. "Take that apology or you can find someone else. If you even come close to having any of your future characters resemble me in any way, and I'm talking about the hair color to the flecks in their eyes, I'll sue you for so much that your dad will be calling me Boss."

An intake of breath and a long pause. "Fine," she replied. "We'll pretend you apologized with flowery words and praises and I forgave you, with hesitation, of course. A girl can't just forgive right away, right? It'll make you think you can run all over me. And Julian?"

He grunted out a grizzled, "What?"

"You can't. You may have got one in this time, but you can't expect me to do all the work here. This is a working relationship, and I want it to be successful for both of us, regardless of our mutual distaste of each other."

"Loathing, detestation, abhorrence is more like it."

Laughter filtered through the phone, and Julian couldn't help but join in. He couldn't stand her, but their banter was the most fun he'd had in a while.

"Yes, those are more apt descriptors," Amalie replied. "So, you're supposed to meet my friend Romina at her gym, Precision Fitness, at seven in the morning. Afterward, she'll text me, and you and I can meet at the Thornbriar Tennis Club, where I'll introduce you to your coach."

Julian pressed his lips together. A coach who wasn't his dad. A coach who...never mind. Just a coach he had no say in picking. He wanted to bitch but decided to keep his mouth shut. Instead, he blurted out one of the most random things he could think of. "Favorite tennis player?"

Without missing a beat, Amalie answered, "Rafael Nadal."

"I'm more of a Sampras man myself. So I'm guessing you follow tennis?" His stare roamed over the dark court outside his windshield. He knew why he loved it there so much. It was *home*.

A scoff, then, "No. I hate tennis."

Shocked at her answer and a little bit offended, Julian said, "You've got to be kidding."

"Not kidding. Not everyone likes tennis. Jesus, what is with everyone trying to shove this sport down my throat?"

He imagined his earlier comment about her breathing fire, because she sounded one step away from it. What did she look like when she was that pissed off? Was it anything like he saw last night at the bar? Wait, why the hell did he care?

When he spoke, his voice and words were way too smug, but he didn't give a shit. "Hit a nerve there, did I?"

A hiss. Did she have a cat? He hadn't seen one when he was there.

"This book is about *you*, not me," she said. "It doesn't matter if I know tennis or not, because what I need to know is *you*, you whom I'm basing my character on. And if you haven't noticed, I'm trying to get to know you, you arrogant ass."

"Actually," Julian said, his words filled with unrestrained glee, "you *do* need to know tennis. How else are you going to write a book about a tennis player? You're going to have to write about matches and make it sound accurate, not like you're pulling stuff out of your ass."

He stifled a groan. He did *not* need to think about her ass.

"I'm a professional, that's how," she said." I know what I'm doing. I don't have to jump out of an airplane to be capable of writing about it."

"Well, I'm the pilot on this flight, and I say you have to jump. Jump or it's a no go."

Amalie stuttered and stammered, and Julian wished he could see her, mainly so she could see the huge grin overtaking his face.

Finally, she forced her words out in normal order. "You wouldn't."

"Actually, I would, and I will. It's time to get to work and start learning the difference between a volley and a lob, rich girl. I'll be at your pool house at six-thirty in the morning. That's where we'll begin your tennis education. Hope you have a decent pair of tennis shoes."

Without another word, he hung up. He put his phone on silent to ignore any of her attempts to call him back. Damn. Getting a rise out of Amalie Warner felt good. Way too good. He smiled. "See you tomorrow, princess."

Chapter Six

AMALIE

AMALIE FLOATED ON A DREAM-SPUN CLOUD, HER BODY WRAPPED UP NICE AND burrito-esque beneath the sheets. A sudden banging pulled her out of that cozy, toasty world.

"What the...?" She added a few choice curse words under her breath. The sound came again, rattling the front door of the pool house.

"Amalie, open up!" It was Julian's smooth-as-molasses voice.

More grumbling and cursing erupted from Amalie's mouth before she opened her eyes. The bedside clock read 6:30. Who got up at this ungodly hour? And most importantly, *why*? The haze cleared from her sleep-addled mind and she remembered what Julian said before he hung up on her last night. That asshole.

"Am-a-lieeeeeee," said asshole sing-songed. "Wakey!"

"Hold your damn horses!" she shouted back as she made her way to the living room with her comforter wrapped around her shoulders. The cold January air had filtered through the pool house and settled, despite her kicking the heater up as high as it would go. She opened the door and squinted to find Julian looking like a real-life sportswear ad. "What the hell? I didn't think you were even a little bit serious."

His mid-thigh shorts showed off gorgeous muscular legs topped off by a white long sleeve shirt. He looked really good, even more attractive than normal. He also smelled heavenly, like sandalwood and mint mixed with morning dew and his own earthy musk. She would pay to have that scent bottled, for the sheer reaction it stirred in her. But never mind that. He'd woken her up, damn it, and he needed to pay.

He crossed his arms and leaned against the doorframe. "Time to get dressed, princess. We're going for a run."

Amalie clutched the comforter to her body, a shiver chasing across her skin. "A *run*? In this weather?"

Julian nodded with a glint in his eye. "Yes, Amalie, a *run*. And it's not even that cold. Once you get going, you'll warm right up. See, I'm even in shorts." He kicked out his beautiful legs for inspection as Amalie stared at him, unblinking. He didn't wait for a response. "Like I said yesterday, if you're going to write this book, your life has to be as much about tennis as mine. By the time this is over you'll be eating, sleeping, and breathing tennis."

Seeing this conversation wasn't going to be over soon, she grabbed his wrist and dragged him inside rather than standing there freezing their butts off. The warmth of his skin took her by surprise, but she soldiered on.

"I don't even own workout clothes," she admitted.

Julian quirked a brow. "Seriously? Nothing?"

She tilted her head and narrowed her eyes as she thought about it. "I have some yoga pants and capris."

"See, there you go. Go put on a pair. Hurry. I don't want to be late for Romina."

"But I've never worn those for working out. They'll get all sweaty and gross."

Julian chuckled, low and smooth. The sound slid over her like velvet. Her gaze shot up to his face, and of course the image of him laughing was even better than the actual sound. The dimple in his left cheek popped with the movement and the corners of his eyes crinkled.

Ugh. She hated that he was so damn pretty.

"Well, believe it or not," he said, "there's this fantastic new invention called a washing machine. You should try it."

She growled. "Shut up."

Julian made a shooing motion. "Go! Get dressed."

What sort of terrible choices had she made where she was now having to run (for *fun* and not from dinosaurs) and, on top of that, basically immerse herself in a sport she despised? An image of her father floated through her mind, causing her to scowl as she stalked into her bedroom and found her favorite black capris. She mourned the loss of them being solely loungewear while simultaneously detesting the fact that running was now a *thing* in her life.

"Let's go, Amalie," Julian called.

Well. She was planning on brushing her teeth, but since he wanted to be all rushy-rushy he could just deal with her stank morning breath. She hurried into her outfit, threw her hair into a ponytail, and then made a begrudging appearance in her living room.

"You look good in athletic stuff." Julian's gaze raked over her in a lazy head-to-toe perusal.

She stiffened, trying to get her game face on. Those eyes though. She'd never seen anything like them, especially in the morning light, their green offset by golden stars. Damn. If she let herself, she could get lost in them.

Amalie extended a hand to stop further comments. "I'll take that as the compliment I hope it's intended to be, but know that I'm not a morning person. I apologize in advance for any threats of bodily harm."

"What was your excuse before?" he joked.

She stuck out her tongue. "Let's go before I change my mind."

An hour and a half later, Amalie had been thoroughly tortured. She'd never, not once in her life, worked out—not for fun, not because she had to or should for her general well-being, and definitely not for a man.

Julian held the door to Romina's gym open, his lips kicked up in a taunting smile. "Wasn't that fun?"

Amalie pushed past him. She didn't enjoy herself on the run, didn't care for the way her capris chafed the crap out of her thighs, or for how she now smelled like a locker room. Her hoodie was soaked in sweat, which made her cold now that she wasn't exerting herself. On top of that, the rat's nest of tangles at the nape of her neck made her shudder.

Still trying to catch her breath, Amalie attempted to speak. "So…I've done my…part. Right? Now I just…watch you train, take notes, and… video it?" She winced at how hopeful her voice sounded.

Julian followed her inside and laughed, the sound full of sarcasm. Not the least bit winded, he said, "Oh no, princess. You're training, too."

Before Amalie could respond, Romina appeared from her office. Her expression was all business, but Amalie didn't miss the curious expression that flitted across her face upon seeing her anti-gym friend in enemy territory. She'd offered to train Amalie for free countless times, harassed her to do a 5K, pretty much anything in an attempt to get her butt off the couch.

Amalie eyed the torture chamber with unease, her gaze bouncing from the elliptical and treadmill (cardio, yuck) to the weights area. It was kind of funny that it was a book that finally got her into a gym.

"Good morning. I'm Romina Arroyo. You're on time. I appreciate that." She stuck out her hand, her voice firm and flat, a tone that let people know this was her gym and you played by her rules.

Julian shook her outstretched hand, turning on the charm. "Julian Smoke. Thank you for training me. I was thinking we could start with—"

Romina cut him off with a curt shake of her head, her high ponytail swinging. "I've already got your exercise plan drawn up. I've done my research, and Amalie has filled me in on a few particulars. Once you begin working with your new coach we'll alter as needed."

Amalie fought to tamp down the sheer delight of watching Romina manhandle Julian's ego. The woman dealt with divas of all shapes and sizes, so she'd practically perfected the "don't argue with me" persona.

"I've never done things that way," Julian argued, a polite yet absolutely fake smile teetering precariously on his face.

"Smoke," Amalie butted in, just in time to see the vein in Romina's forehead throb. "Romina knows what she's doing. Let her do her job and then once we speak with your coach today we'll switch up whatever needs to be switched up."

Julian made a face that looked like he'd sucked on a lemon, but there was still something immensely attractive about him—the way his eyebrows furrowed, the cute little number-eleven lines there. It was sickening really. All that beauty wasted on such an arrogant man.

As if sensing her thoughts, he shot her a cold stare and took a step closer. "Amalie, I know what I'm doing, too. I'm not some hotheaded athlete who needs to be coddled."

She took a step closer, too, and glared up at him. "Actually, you're acting like one—"

"Am not." Julian's body shifted into a defensive stance, bringing his chest within inches of her face.

Without thinking, Amalie placed a finger against his lips, surprising them both. It was too late to turn back, so she continued onward while desperately trying to keep her expression blank. God, it was hard to think straight. His lips were as soft and full as they looked. "Just shut up and let the woman train you," she said. She caught Romina's proud expression before meeting Julian's death stare. Apparently, the shock of her touch had worn off for him.

He grumbled in protest as Romina led them deeper into the bowels of the torture chamber surrounded with mirrors to better highlight all their inadequacies.

"Amalie, want to grab a seat on the yoga mat?" Romina asked as she handed Julian a tiny notebook that detailed not only their training plan but nutrition details as well.

Without lifting his eyes from the book, Julian said, "Amalie's training, too."

Romina slid a worried glance toward Amalie. It very closely resembled an expression that screamed, "Blink twice if you're being held against your will." And while Amalie wanted to blink, wanted to say forget this entire impulsive idea, she said nothing.

This book idea had brought a spark to life inside her, the spark that had nearly flamed out, reminding her that she'd been a success before—family name or not. If she was going to get the most accurate information for her Julian-esque character, then she had to do this thing. *Really* do it. She couldn't phone it in like everything else in her life. "Just know I haven't worked out in twenty-eight years, Ro," Amalie said, voice dropping to a murmur followed by a brittle laugh.

Romina looked entirely too pleased. "Now *this* will be interesting."

Thankfully, she took it easy on Amalie despite Julian's protests. He whined as he gasped, pointing an angry finger, asking why Amalie didn't have to work out as hard as he did. Each time he did it, Romina made him run suicides, which made Amalie shake with sadistic laughter. By the fourth time he complained, Romina had had enough.

"Amalie isn't the one trying to get into the US Open," she said. "You are. Besides, I need her to still be able to walk so I can help her pick out a dress for her sister's party in March. Everyone knows all the best dresses go early."

The mention of Simone's party put Amalie on high alert. Her sister wasn't the issue, nor was her precious two-year-old niece, Tallulah. Her brother-in-law, Damien, was a different story, but that was a tale for another time. What she really hated was hobnobbing with a bunch of people she didn't like, especially knowing her ex-fiancé would be among them. She'd heard the things said behind her back at those soul-sucking events: "Poor Amalie couldn't handle the pressure, but look at Maxwell, top lawyer at his firm, with such a gorgeous fiancée. You could say he definitely dodged a bullet." It made Amalie want to vomit, and on top of that, her dad would be there, his face proud as he watched Simone easily navigate their social stratosphere. Amalie would always be the screwup, the one who ran back home from NYC with her tail between her legs, everything ruined.

Thankfully, Romina's phone rang, pulling Amalie out of her spiral and cutting off the major pissing contest going on between Ro and Julian.

"Amalie!" Ro called out, pressing a hand against the speaker of the cell phone. "Fill in for me while I take this call."

"Fill in?" she said at the same time Julian growled, "No way."

Ro held out her hand to silence her athlete, focusing on Amalie. "Yes. He's going to do sit-ups on the ball, and I need you to watch his form because it's been a minute since he worked on his core and—"

"Hey, I'm right here you know." Julian crossed his arms and cocked a brow.

Ro was undeterred. "You'll need to kneel beside him and make sure he keeps steady on the ball, his neck straight, and chin up. If you see him struggling, make those minor adjustments for him." She didn't even wait for Amalie to nod or salute or say anything—she just turned and headed to her office, phone to her ear.

Amalie turned back to Julian, who mirrored her glare. "Welp. I guess that's it, then."

She hopped up from the weight bench and headed over to the exercise ball she'd spotted earlier. Julian followed, reluctantly, and sat his rather shapely backside on the ball. With his hands behind his head and feet planted wide, he began the first set.

Amalie knelt beside him, catching another whiff of his cologne, mixed with sweat. It was almost too much, along with the fact that his body was laid out before her like a smorgasbord, muscles flexing and tightening. And those grunts. Jeez. They didn't help matters, because they sounded like they belonged somewhere other than a gym. *Ahem.*

It was hard not to look at him, not to drool at the way his hair was plastered to his forehead, bits sticking up here and there, and then a girl's best friend…gray cut off sweat shorts. Whew, mercy.

"You gonna check my form or what?" Julian's voice bit through her haze.

"I *am* checking it." She totally wasn't, so she tried to actually focus on the areas Romina pointed out. Every once in a while his neck would come up, straining. She pressed light fingertips to the spot where his hair curled at his nape. In an attempt not to meet his eyes, she turned her attention to his legs, watching the powerhouse beneath his skin, those thigh muscles popping and shifting. She cleared her throat in an attempt not to show how impressed she was.

The *ding* of a text jerked Amalie to attention, so she reached into her hoodie to check her cell. It was Simone. Just as Amalie was about to reply, Julian released a loud sigh of exhaustion, and in a dramatic gesture, flailed his arms, smacking Amalie in the face. Her knee jerked, slamming into the ball, knocking it right out from under Julian's ass.

With a quick bark, his hands flung out, desperate to find purchase. That purchase happened to be Amalie's sweatshirt. His fingers grazed her boob before pulling her on top of him in his collapse.

Her face hovered inches above his, those bewitching eyes studying her with a quiet intensity. His hand tightened at her hip, this thumb creeping beneath her hoodie and searing her skin. Without her permission, a tiny gasp squeaked out, her lips working for some kind of reply, but she was transfixed by the beautiful man that she was currently straddling.

Oh, God. She was straddling him, and what she'd been eyeing in those shorts, well, it was definitely awake and pressed against her.

Her body came alive, but her mind was screaming at her to get the hell off him. So she did the most graceful thing she could think of and fell over sideways like a drunken crab.

Julian, having woken from the very same stupor, coughed into his fist, his voice still husky when he spoke. "Really, princess? What are we doing? If you wanted to feel me up, all you had to do was ask."

Her face burned, but she refused to let him see how much his sheer physicality had affected her. She made a *psssh* sound and waved him off, even though he was standing now, and she was still akimbo on the floor. "You wish."

A wicked smile tilted Julian's lips, that damn dimple in his cheek nearly disarming her as he reached toward her. "Here, let me help you up."

"I may not know how to spot, but I know how to get up, thank you very much." That may not have been totally true as she moved onto her knees, keeping her gaze trained away from the bulge that happened to be staring her in the face. She had a shred of dignity left and was hellbent on keeping it.

"Doesn't look like it to me." He laughed, keeping his hand extended.

Finally, she got up just as Ro appeared from her office. "I see this went well." Julian and Amalie said nothing as they bowed their heads like kids being scolded. "I think that's enough for today," Romina added as she moved the exercise ball back to the mat.

"Come on, rich girl," Julian provoked, amusement crinkling the corners of his eyes. "We've got to meet this coach you've dug up." He even winked at her as she dusted off her butt, his gaze totally checking out her assets.

She gave him a syrupy smile and shot him a bird.

Romina looked between them and shook her head. "Julian, I've got to speak with *Amalie*." Romina made sure to emphasize Amalie's actual name and not Julian's nickname. "If you need to go ahead, I can always take her to the tennis center."

Julian didn't miss a beat. "I'll wait." He grabbed his water bottle, refilled it, and then met Amalie's stare. "I'll be outside." He hitched a thumb toward the doorway of the gym, then turned to Romina. "Nice meeting you. I'll be sure to bring the coach's notes tomorrow."

Romina gave Julian a sharp, wordless nod as he swaggered out the door into the morning light. Without hesitation, Ro grabbed Amalie's hand and dragged her into a tiny but extremely well-organized office. Once the door was shut, Ro turned the lock and then leaned against it, her eyes looking a little wild.

Amalie raised a brow. "What?"

Romina held up a hand to silence her. "You did *not* tell me he was hot. Asshole? Yes. Hot as hell? No."

Amalie laughed, a nervous tittering thing she'd only read about in books, and yet here she was tittering all over the place.

"He's so *not* hot," she argued with a hollow laugh, her gaze roaming all over the office unable to meet Romina's eyes. That girl was a human lie detector.

Her friend gave her a knowing look as she tightened her ponytail. "Whatever. If that's the story, then why were you struggling to drag your eyeballs away from his ass during those squats I made him do? Which were for your benefit, by the way. You're welcome."

Amalie shot her friend an incredulous look. "Just because I like his ass doesn't mean I like his face, thank you very much. He made those shorts look like a million bucks. I've never seen anything so...grabbable." She made grabby hands in the air. "So yeah, that's why I was struggling. Natural instincts and all that. And thank you for giving me the ass show."

Romina's voice dropped. "Y'all have this super-hot tension going on. It's almost like...foreplay."

"What are you talking about?" Amalie's words tangled as they came out of her mouth. She was totally thinking about his sweat shorts, his muscles, his dimple, his...

Ugh, she had to get a grip.

Ro tapped a glittery purple nail against her tan skin. "The tension between you two is strung so tight it feels like it might snap any second. I bet you'll sleep together before it's all said and done. I mean with the love/hate thing—"

Amalie piped up, her nose scrunched and mouth twisted at Romina's words. "Hate. Most definitely one hundred percent hate,"

Romina waved away her interruption. "The sex would be *fantastic*."

Amalie's jaw dropped, and she quickly screwed it shut. Those words, the thoughts they provoked—nope, nope, *nope*.

"I see I've left you speechless," Romina teased as she pushed off the desk. "You should invite him to Simone's party. He'd be great eye candy, and imagine that *bootay* in a suit." She fanned herself, fluttering her long lashes. "Maxwell the third would lose it."

Amalie toyed with a rogue paperclip on the desk. "Maxwell wouldn't care. He's engaged to that model or whatever, and besides, I despise Julian in a totally non-sexual way." Though she didn't mind the idea of that ass and those quads in a suit.

Ro pulled back, the force of her stare nearly knocking Amalie over. "Take Julian. *Please.*"

"No way." Amalie shook her head. "As you saw today, he can be kind of a jerk."

"Yeah, but I think, maybe deep down, under all those walls of his, he's got a soft spot for you—and don't even think of arguing with me about that." Romina's eyes twinkled mischievously as she walked toward the door and opened it. "You've got a meeting to get to, so you'd better scram, but hey..." She paused, making sure she held Amalie's attention. "Seriously, ask him."

Amalie groaned as she left the office. "Yes, mother."

Plot twist: Amalie had no intention of asking Julian for anything more than she already had.

Chapter Seven

JULIAN

As Julian sat in his car, his mind wandered back to the feel of Amalie pressed against him, the sight of her ass in those tight black capris. If she were any other woman, he would've already asked her out because he couldn't deny the fact that he wanted her—hell, his body had blatantly alerted him—and her—at the gym to that fact. As it were, he despised her perfect upturned nose, her sarcastic remarks, her know-it-all attitude, and her rich-girl upbringing.

Something clenched in his chest, arguing the opposite, but he shoved it down. She was just a pretty face, and he had a penchant for those. That's all it was.

Amalie opened the door and slid into the seat, startling him from his daydream. "You ready to answer some of my questions?"

His shoulders slowly crept to his ears, the tension in his neck appearing immediately. There were some things he didn't want to discuss, and he was pretty sure those were the things Amalie was most interested in.

Not even caring that he hadn't answered, Amalie dug a notebook out of her purse. Noticing the car hadn't moved yet, she cut her eyes over to him. "Well? Are you going to drive, or do you know how to teleport?"

"Always so feisty," he fired back. "I'm going. Did you want me to start rolling before you put your seatbelt on?" Amalie snapped her seat belt into place and then made a show of batting her lashes. "Aww, you're worried for my safety."

Julian snickered as he pulled out of the parking lot. "I'm worried about the ticket I'll get if you don't have your seat belt on."

He saw Amalie stiffen out of the corner of his eye.

"Harsh. *Anyway*." She held up her journal. "Tell me how you got into tennis."

He didn't even try to hide his sigh of relief. Okay. That was pretty tame. He could answer that. "That's easy. My dad."

Amalie scribbled something in her notebook and then said, "Your dad. He coached you. Tell me about him."

That tension from earlier? It ratcheted up a few notches as a buzzing sound filled Julian's head. "No."

"No? What do you mean 'no'? I need this—"

"No." He sliced a hand through the air between them. "My dad is off-limits. Next question."

Silence.

Julian was almost afraid to look at Amalie, but his curiosity got the best of him. She was sending little hate daggers into him with her eyes.

"Fine," she replied. "*For now*. Tell me what it feels like when you get on the court. I saw you the other night—" She stopped, and the rest of her sentence ended in a garbled mess before she turned her face toward the window.

"What do you mean you saw me the other night? Where?"

Amalie shrugged; her notebook suddenly became very interesting.

"Oh, so I have to talk, but you don't? Where did you see me, Amalie?"

With a drawn-out breath, she leaned back in the seat, shielding her face with her notebook. Why did that endear her to him? It was cute as hell.

"Fine," she said. "I saw you at the tennis courts playing in the dark."

His skin felt unnaturally tight. There was a lot he wanted to say, because that night, *that night*, he'd been working through some serious demons, and that was something he wanted kept private. To know she'd been there?

His hands tightened on the wheel. "That wasn't for you to see."

Her entire body slumped forward on a sigh. "I know." She tapped her knee and then the rest of her words came out in a rush. "I wanted to leave,

I did, but you were so passionate that it was hypnotizing. I'm really sorry, Julian. I shouldn't have intruded, and I promise it won't happen again."

He glanced at her hunched form, her slender fingers now picking at something on her capris, her mouth a straight line. He hadn't missed the force of sincerity in her voice—she'd meant that apology, and now she looked absolutely miserable. He drummed his hands on the wheel. He knew the perfect way to break the tension.

"You're a lot of things, Amalie Warner, but I never took you for a stalker."

Her eyes narrowed, but there was a smile glinting in their depths. "In your dreams."

"Yup. And you're always the star, ever since that night at the bar," Julian teased, though if he was honest, it wasn't a lie.

He was rewarded when he turned to find her face had gone beet red.

She rolled her eyes. "You're impossible."

He chuckled and turned into the tennis center. Once parked, neither of them moved. He noticed Amalie had a hair stuck to her lip and, of course, his hands had a mind of their own and reached out and pulled it away.

That was a terrible idea, because the touch of her lips on his finger? It caused all kinds of images of her mouth, and none of them were in G-rated territory. He wanted to rub his fingers against her lips again, slower, so that he could catalog the dip of her upper lip.

He couldn't help but think of when she'd touched his mouth at the gym, even if her reason was to shut him up—it'd worked, but it also made it difficult to concentrate on anything else but her. Did she feel like that now? Was she affected by his touch?

God, he hoped so.

When he looked up, Amalie was completely still, so still that he actually wondered if she was still breathing. "You had a, uh, hair," he explained lamely, realizing he'd leaned halfway over the console.

Amalie blinked a few times before moving away and shoving her notebook back into her purse. "Well, that was enlightening," she growled as she practically tore the handle off the door to get out as fast as humanly possible.

"What? How fast you can actually move when you want to?" Julian snorted as he unbuckled his seat belt and rounded the car to the trunk.

Amalie glared at him, her expression nothing short of fierce. "Look, I'm hoping I get more from you soon, because at this point all I know is that my main character is a giant ass."

Julian bit his lip to keep it from tilting upward. Messing with her was so much fun, giving back just as good as she gave. There was something about her when she was angry, the way her lips tightened, how she cocked her hip, putting her hands there. Sexy as hell. When he didn't say anything, she huffed, threw up the hood of her sweatshirt, and dipped down to grab her tote bag.

Julian held up his hands in wordless surrender, the first she'd ever gotten out of him, before grabbing his racket bag out of the trunk. That bag housed his most prized possessions.

His heart drummed wildly, in time with each step he took toward the court. It was a bittersweet moment, and all he could think about was how badly he wanted to pick up the phone and call his dad. He still did that way too often and wondered if the instinct would ever go away. Nine years was a long time, but apparently not long enough.

"Hey." Amalie snapped her fingers in front of his face, doing her best to keep up with his long strides. Julian blinked a few times, surprised that he'd zoned out so easily. "I need you to focus, all right?"

"Yeah, yeah, I got it." He waved her off as they stepped onto the court, the hard surface familiar beneath his shoes. He sighed. On the tennis court, he felt whole again.

"There's Paul." Amalie pointed to a short, rotund older man carrying a ball hopper onto the opposite side of the court. His white polo was crisp and bright, clinging tightly to his form. Paul had a gray beard covering most of his tanned face and wore a hat rocking the Roger Federer logo, a mess of salt and pepper hair escaping beneath it.

This guy couldn't be for real. You never saw a tennis coach that out of shape or that old in any of the pro players' boxes.

Julian turned to Amalie, his voice sharp with agitation. "Who is this guy?" Paul hadn't yet noticed them hidden in the shade at the far end of the court as he waddled around, busying himself with cones.

Amalie lifted a brow, mouth pinched. She had yet to figure out that when she looked at him like that, well, it pretty much egged him on.

Her voice was all business. "He used to play."

Julian laughed, disbelief causing his eyebrows to jump up to his hairline. "On *tour*?"

Amalie nodded slowly. "Yeah, for a few years."

Julian scrubbed a hand down his face. He was already tired, and now he was getting irritated. He should've known Amalie would set him up with a hack job. He should have insisted that he pick his own coach instead of this penguin wearing a human suit.

"How am I supposed to learn from this guy?"

"Hey, he used to be a pro. No offense, but nobody wants to coach you. I had to practically bribe Paul to do this."

Julian scoffed. "What are you paying him in? Donuts?"

A deep voice with a Brooklyn accent interrupted their argument. They both turned to Paul as he said, "Okay, wise guy. Get on the court. Let's warm-up. Or do you even know what that is, cupcake?" Amalie buried her mouth in the neck of her hoodie, but Julian knew she was laughing as Paul winked before warning, "I won't say it again. Get on the court."

Julian dropped his bag and grabbed his racket, struggling to conceal his frustration. He'd do one practice with the guy and then he'd tell Amalie either he picked the coach or the whole thing was off—dream or no dream.

The first thing Paul did was have Julian work through a series of dynamic stretches—the usual arm circles, ab twists, high knees, and jumping jacks.

"You ready to do a few warm-up drills?" Paul asked before shoveling two pieces of Juicy Fruit gum into his mouth.

Julian lifted his chin, feeling his attitude flare. "I've *been* ready."

Paul pointed at him with his racket. "The lack of a tour card says otherwise, boy. You forget only one of us on this court was pro for longer than a couple of months."

Julian winced at the low blow, even though he deserved it.

Without another word, Julian let Paul lead him through a series of warm-ups—backboard drills, medicine ball catching, and throwing at the service line. Then they moved into mini tennis drills like serves and volleys, cross and alternate hitting. Paul was a beast, not even out of breath as they switched to lobs and overheads.

Paul broke everything down, explaining as they moved through each drill, even though Julian was already familiar with the moves. Julian admired how Paul was a big server like him, rearing back as he tossed the ball, hitting it with a good, solid smack.

A cell phone alarm went off, causing Paul to straighten. He gave Julian an evil little smile as he walked to the bench, shut off the alarm, and drank a few sips of water. "Twenty minutes is up. Ready to hit for real?"

Julian tried not to roll his eyes as he walked to where Amalie held out a water bottle for him. The kind gesture shocked him, and if it hadn't already been sealed, he would've checked for poison because, well, that was their thing.

"Yeah, let's do this." He gave Paul a stony look as he passed the water bottle back to Amalie, who was surprisingly silent.

Paul's serves started off soft, despite what he'd done earlier, and Julian was able to hit them back over the net with ease.

"Is that all you got, old man? I thought we were training here?"

Yeah, he was a cocky and arrogant asshole, but he didn't exactly have a lot of time to waste, with the US Open only seven months away. It took place the last week of August and ran into the first week of September. Seven months would fly by.

Paul's brown eyes narrowed beneath his Federer cap, and Julian felt his balls shrink a little. That look, coupled with the way he reared back to crush the ball, was, in truth, terrifying.

But Amalie was watching, and Julian couldn't suck because his pride would be shot. Then there was the fact that she'd probably find someone else, someone she actually got along with, to help her write her book. He knew his main appeal was the fact that he had former star power, a ready-built fan base, and she believed he could do it again. He didn't think there were a lot of washed-up tennis players within her grasp, but even so, he didn't want to jinx it. So Julian pulled from some long-lost reserve and played lights-out tennis.

Paul ran him all over the court while yelling, "There you go, kid, letting your mind get in the way," or "Tennis ain't for the faint of heart."

Finally, after what felt like the longest rally of Julian's life, Paul hit an incredible winner. The sound of the ball smacking the asphalt echoed through the small court.

Julian froze, eyes wide with shock, mouth hanging open as he stared at the older man. "What the hell?" he muttered under his breath as he looked at Paul and then to where he'd landed the ball on Julian's side of the court. He didn't even have a chance; there was no way he would've been able to get to it in time.

Amalie bounced on her toes at the sideline, clapping wildly, pen clamped between her teeth. Her eyes were bright as two stars as she ran to meet Julian and Paul at the net.

Damn, was that a sight to behold. The day had warmed a little, thanks to the South's mercurial weather, so she'd shed her hoodie and now wore a fitted long sleeve tee that didn't do one fucking thing to hide her absolutely delicious curves.

Jeez. He had to get a hold on his hormones, something that proved easier to do than he imagined, because when Amalie arrived at his side, she only gave him a quick once-over, as though he were an afterthought.

"That was amazing," she gushed at the coach. "I don't even know what you did there or what it was called, but it was killer."

"You're gonna have to learn about tennis if you're writing a book about it, Amalie," Paul said. "You'll need to describe matches in detail. Go into my office and grab the book on my desk, will ya? I'll let you borrow it for research." Paul dug his office keys out of his pocket and handed them over to Amalie. With a quick point in the direction of his office, he sent her on her way. Then he turned his full attention on Julian.

Before Paul could say anything, Julian stuck out his hand. "That was some good tennis, Paul. I'm sorry for doubting you. It's obvious I don't know what I'm talking about."

Yeah, it was like chewing nails, and each word was a tiny stab to his ego, but he'd decided in the final moments of that rally that Paul Mercado was no joke. He would be a damn good coach who could teach Julian a lot. And he would keep him in line. A small part of him knew Paul reminded Julian of his dad. Oliver Smoke never took any of his son's crap, on or off the court, and didn't hesitate to call him on it if it'd make him a better player, or more importantly, a better man. He sensed the same in Paul.

A familiar ache rose in Julian's chest as he imagined his father clapping him on the shoulder one last time. He'd do anything for one more pointer or one more "Good game, son."

Paul gave Julian a curt nod and shook his hand. "Anthony Fox was your manager? After your father?"

Talk about another punch, this time to the balls. Julian wished memories were like trash—that you could get rid of the ones you didn't want anymore, the ones that rotted and festered in your mind.

Julian croaked out a small, "Yeah."

Paul unwrapped two more pieces of Juicy Fruit and pushed them into his mouth, never breaking eye contact with Julian. "Anthony Fox is a 'yes man' who only cares about money and endorsements. He doesn't give a hoot about this sport or its players. He whores out both, but I'm figuring you already know that, don't you?"

The man's steady gaze bore into Julian, causing him to squirm a bit, but shockingly he was able to find his words. "Yeah. I know all about it."

And that was one hell of an understatement. Anthony Fox was flashy and had dollar signs in his eyes ever since they'd first met. He'd precipitated Julian's demise in the tennis world.

"And I know Anthony let you do whatever you wanted because you were his number one moneymaker. Before we do this, you need to understand that I'm nothing like that lowlife. I'm going to call you on every little thing you do, on and off the court. Got it?"

Julian swallowed the lump in his throat as he nodded, his hands gripping the net.

Paul looked over his shoulder where Amalie had disappeared and then turned back to Julian. "Man, I actually know a lot about you. I used to tell people, 'That kid's going to be the next Roger Federer.'"

Julian squeezed his eyes shut, trying to contain the emotions swirling around inside him. When he opened his eyes, Paul continued. "But then I saw you play in one of your first big tournaments, and I knew by the look in your eye that you didn't have it there mentally, that you weren't ready. I can tell you have more talent than most players out on the tour now, but if you don't love tennis, love the struggle, then you're never going to be truly great."

Paul studied him as he let those words settle. Julian knew everything the old man said was the truth because his father used to say the same thing. Somewhere along the way Julian lost himself, lost the love for the sport and the appreciation for the game. It became a mindless blur of money and entourages and popularity, but this, *this* was what he wanted more than anything now. He didn't care about all that superficial stuff anymore. He just wanted to play, and to win.

"I want to fall in love with tennis again," he admitted.

"And I can be the one to help you do that. I'm gonna teach you how to start painting the lines again."

Painting the lines. How long had it been since he'd been able to do that, been able to hit the ball on the line, anytime he needed to?

Across the court, a door slammed behind them and a frustrated Amalie appeared. She ran a hand through her wavy red hair.

Even though he could see she was flustered, Amalie was nothing short of polite as she handed Paul's keys back over to him. "I looked all over that office of yours, Paul. I couldn't find that book anywhere."

Julian found himself entirely too entranced by the way her lips formed words and how cute the freckles high on her cheeks were, like little constellations. He shook his head to clear those thoughts. He needed to get laid but, sadly, tennis was the only mistress allowed for now.

Paul nodded thoughtfully before bursting out with, "Oh! That's right. I have it in my bag. Here, let me get it for you." He looked over the top of her head and gave Julian a wink.

That sneaky bastard.

Chapter Eight

AMALIE

A ROUTINE FORMED OVER THE NEXT MONTH AFTER JULIAN DROPPED DOWN TO part-time at Madison Pharmaceuticals. Amalie and Julian would meet at her place and run the trail to the pond behind her dad's mansion. No one really visited the pond anymore, since it had once been her mom's pet project. She could still remember the day Katharine Warner teetered around the water's edge in her red-soled Louboutins, directing where she wanted the benches, gazebo, and flowers.

"Amalie? You stretching or daydreaming?" Julian called out, a playful tilt to his lips as he pulled his quad back in a stretch. They were both bundled in sweats and beanies, since Georgia decided to try its hand at a real winter. "I'm a writer. I'm always daydreaming." Her mind roamed again as she attempted a few half-hearted stretches. She thought about the pages she'd just written and the two protagonists she'd created, Jax and Penelope. Penelope was a good mix of Romina and herself. Definitely the strongest character she'd written so far, which made sense. Who else did she know better than herself and her best friend? Penelope got shit done, and she didn't take no for an answer, something Amalie had been trying to channel into her own life.

"You ready, princess?" Julian's voice cut through the reverie. His hands were cupped in front of his face as he blew his breath into them.

"Might as well be," she offered with a weak smile.

Julian led the way, and as she watched him break into a jog, she couldn't help but think of Jax. Every time she wrote a line that came from Jax's mouth it was Julian's smooth, rich voice that said it. It was Julian's fingers that lingered over her, um, er, *Penelope's* lips, not hers, totally not hers. She shook her head at the thought.

But even though Julian had given her that instant spark of inspiration, he'd failed to give her anything else. She wanted to know more about tennis and how it felt to be an athlete. What did it feel like to win a hard-fought match or to lose one? That's what she was after today, and that's what she intended to get.

"Julian," Amalie called, her words breathy. Had he picked up the pace? "Julian," she said again. His eyes were on the path ahead of them, but the pace increased a little more.

Aggravated and maybe channeling her inner Penelope, she popped his headphones from his ears. "Julian!"

A flock of birds erupted from the field at the sound.

"Damn, what the hell?" He yanked his headphones down, careful not to break stride.

"I've been trying to get your attention, but you keep running faster every time I say your name. Coincidence?" She would've tapped her chin and done this whole head tilt thing, but she was really trying not to die. She dodged a rock in the path, careful not to trip because that's all she needed—another coordination fiasco in front of Julian.

A chuckle escaped Julian's perfectly plush lips. "Whatever you want to believe, princess, but I don't like talking on runs. Thought we established that on day one."

"Why don't you like to talk? Because you're ashamed of your vocabulary? I have a dictionary that can help you with that," she joked, playing into the jock stereotype because she knew Julian couldn't stand it.

He clenched his jaw as he shook his head, and then looked back at the wooded path. There were a few low-hanging branches, and they wouldn't hesitate to smack a careless passerby in the face. "I don't like to talk because I like to focus on my breathing and pacing. Nothing to do with vocabulary, I can assure you. Although I'm pretty sure if you'd let me, I could teach you a few new words followed by my name. *Loudly.*"

Oh. Oh, wow. She bet he could teach her a whole set of new words—with his lips on hers, trailing down her neck, dipping to her collarbone, going lower…

"You got some serious sex eyes going on right now." Julian laughed. Deep. Rumbly. Hot.

"Do not," Amalie protested, wishing she'd worn her sunglasses. Julian's stare pierced the side of her face and there was nowhere to hide as they ran side by side.

"It's cool. I know you want me. Only a matter of time." His breath clouded in the air.

Amalie blew out a long, agitated breath. "I see you're delusional as usual today."

"Honest is a better term, wouldn't you agree?"

"Like you don't check out my ass every chance you get," she snarled.

"Like you don't love it when I do."

"Just…just shut up," Amalie sputtered, holding up a bouncing hand.

"Thought you wanted me to talk?"

She *could* just say forget it, but she needed this. Most of her life she felt helpless, and this one last shot actually gave her power. If she could do this, never again would she have to worry about her asshole father manipulating her life. She could still hear his insult echoing through her mind, that she wasn't really a Warner. Well, maybe not, not in the way he wanted her to be. Either way, she would prove she could get shit done by simply being Amalie. She'd show the world she was meant to do this, meant to write. Those thoughts fueled her desire to fight for details from Julian.

"I need information for the book, Julian, and today you'll give me something." Her feet pounded the earth in determination as she kept pace with him.

His heated stare flicked to her mouth. "I could give you something you'd like. That pretty blush on your cheeks tells me that much."

Denying the ache snaking through her belly, she feigned offense when she was pretty damn intrigued. "God, you're the king of deflection. I mean, it's the coldest morning of the year and I'm out here running with *you.* You'd think you'd answer at least one of my questions."

He didn't answer, just picked up the pace, enough that it was a struggle to talk and breathe.

"Tell me how you get your mind right for a match. How do you stay focused?"

"Well," he began, "to get in the zone, you listen to music with a good rhythm. You know, drums and bass to get you pumped."

Careful not to scare him back into his shell, Amalie asked the next question softly. "I get that. What about during the match?"

Julian wiped his brow with his sweatshirt, revealing his abs that were slowly coming into being, and Amalie had to quickly look ahead so she wouldn't trip over something. Thankfully he wasn't looking at her, so he couldn't see the drool forming at the corner of her lips.

"You have to stay focused on each ball and fight the whole time," he said. "You have to keep your mind on that goal—fighting for each point. If you do that, you'll win a lot of matches, but if you don't, you'll start worrying about who's in the crowd, what the score is, and you should *never* worry about what the score is. You only worry about the next point, that's it."

Amalie's brows lifted. "See, that wasn't so hard...was it?" They navigated their way around the pond, her eyes drawn to the mist rising off of its surface.

"Kind of, since I just want to concentrate on the run."

"Smart-ass. Okay, now tell me about coaches. What do you look for in a coach? What did you like about your dad's coaching style? How did he motivate you?" She knew she was pushing it on the dad issue.

"I told you, I'm not talking about my dad right now."

"But he was your coach. How can you talk about tennis and not talk about him?"

"Look, do you really need to talk to me to get your tennis stuff right? Can't you just watch me and write it down and make it sound pretty?"

"No. I need to know you in order to know Jax."

"Who's Jax?"

"Jax is you."

"Jax is me?"

"Yeah, you. Jax is you in my novel. So, I need to talk to you so it can be authentic. I don't know how to get that through to you." She stumbled but quickly righted herself, trying to find the rhythm of her feet again. She really wanted to ask him about a certain gorgeous model named Nadine Merriweather who'd popped up in some of her internet searches, but something told her today was not that day. Instead, she went a different route. "If you won't talk about your dad, then maybe tell me about that Fox guy. Didn't catch his first name, but I heard you and Paul talking about him the other day."

"That's a big hell no."

"Julian. You *will* talk to me about one of them." Amalie panted as the pace increased yet again. Damn it. Her legs were screaming at her to quit.

"Nah. I'm pretty fast, so not today." With that Julian took off down the dirt path, dust kicking up at his heels. That biteable ass in those sweats.

"Julian Smoke, get back here!" Amalie yelled, but he'd already disappeared.

Amalie sat on the courtside bleachers, notebook in hand, bundled in her sweats, raincoat, and a blanket she'd found in her car. She kept blowing warm breath into her scarf to thaw her nose. The chilly air had grown damp with the threat of rain, which would equal hell. For a minute she even contemplated watching practice from her car, but this was her dream. She'd promised herself to do whatever it took to make it happen, even if it meant freezing her butt off.

She glanced at the court just as Julian hit the last shot before Paul called it a day. She'd asked Paul to torture Julian for leaving her on their run, but Paul just shook his head, a grin stretching wide beneath his mustache, and training went on as usual.

Her eyes followed Julian as he sauntered over to his bag, talking to his weekend training partners—players from the UGA tennis team. Julian's schedule was tough and would only grow in difficulty the closer they drew to August.

On a normal day, Julian trained with Paul twice, Romina once, and during his ever-dwindling downtime, Paul had him watching tape for two hours. It was busy and exhausting, but Julian never once complained, even on days when he had to squeeze all of that in on top of work. He did bark at her here and there, and occasionally they even had an amicable moment, but he never once said he wanted to quit or that it was too hard. It made Amalie take stock of her own life as she sat night after night, staring at a blank page. Stella, her agent, had asked for new chapters, but after those initial pages of banter between Penelope and Jax, Amalie had nothing.

She slumped over her gray notebook, the one that had become like a third limb. Her inability to write wasn't the only thing bothering her, though. She couldn't figure Julian out. One minute he was civil and halfway decent and the next he was condescending and rude and, well, *Julian*. It was clear that if this little venture of theirs was to be successful, then it would have to be up to her. The "rich girl" barb was one he'd cleverly crafted to get under her skin, but what she had to do, or at least *try* to do, was appear unaffected. So lately, each time he threw that one out there, she turned to stone—no expression or line of emotion aside from boredom, which she now plastered to her face as she heard footsteps approach.

God. Her skin flushed, and she struggled to look unimpressed. Julian shouldn't look that sexy drenched in sweat. He'd shed his sweatpants in favor of shorts, and his long sleeve tee clung to his body like a second skin. He ran his towel over his thick, wavy brown hair and then slung it over his shoulder as he shot her a lazy grin. "I see you've got that notebook with you again."

"Well, I'm a writer so…"

He shrugged. "Just wondered if maybe you miss out on things when your nose is stuck in it. You could always watch the practice and then ask me to clarify anything later."

Were there laser beams of straight-up hostility shooting from her eyes? Because it one hundred percent felt like it as she narrowed her gaze on Julian, stupid, perfectly pretty Julian with a dumb dimple on his left stubbly, equally stupid, marble-cut cheek.

He raised his hands in front of him, that dimple deepening. "Or maybe not. You do you."

"Don't mess with my method. I don't tell you how to play tennis, so don't tell me how to write," she quipped.

"Speaking of writing," he said, "I did some internet digging myself and found out about your bestseller. Nineteen is pretty impressive."

Amalie's gaze flicked downward. "Yeah, well, not something I like to talk about. I did a lot of stupid things back then."

"You were a kid. I did some punk-ass things at nineteen, too. Still do today."

"Yeah, but did you pack up and move to New York with your fiancé, Maxwell the third?" Amalie volleyed, her words devoid of emotion.

Julian staggered backward a bit. The surprise written across his face was enough to tip up the corners of Amalie's lips. She wasn't proud that she'd been engaged to Maxwell the third, given his general unpleasantness, but at least it got Julian off the topic of her failure. For now. That damn book was synonymous with just how stupid she'd been, at how much she'd lost.

"I know we live in Georgia, but damn, that's a little young to get engaged, ain't it?" Julian rubbed the back of his neck, studying her.

Amalie resisted the temptation to roll her eyes. "Yes, it's young, but some people do find the love of their life at nineteen."

"Did you?" Julian raised an eyebrow.

Amalie flashed her ringless left hand. "Does it look like it?"

Julian glanced at the darkening clouds, then back to Amalie. "Well, the guy was obviously an asshole."

Amalie stood, clutching her notebook to her chest, ever her lifeline. "What makes you think he was an asshole? I mean, you're right, but just curious, though."

Julian shook his head, his eyes on the court as a tiny smile curled his lips.

"So, you're just gonna keep that one to yourself, huh?" she asked.

"I guess so." After a pause, he looked around the court. Paul was the only other person left, and he stood near the gate, every once in a while opening it and peering out. Amalie assumed he had a hot date or something with the tension that seemed to run through the old man's body. Paul wasn't one to be nervous about anything. Finally, Julian said, "You wanna go grab a bite to eat?"

Amalie choked on her own spit. The shock of his question was too much, and she inhaled wrong and, well, there went that, along with big, fat tears rolling down her cheeks, leaving mascara in their wake.

Julian's hand was warm and solid as it landed on her back. She wanted to say, "Yep, don't mind me. I do this all the time." Which wasn't a lie, either.

Finally, after getting it together, she took in a very careful, deep breath, totally noticing that Julian had moved closer and that his hand was still on her back. The heat of his body tempted her to lean into it, to let it fully envelop her.

She shook her head, her hands fidgeting around her journal. "I'm okay," she said, her voice a little croaky. She was totally not okay.

"You're that excited to hang out with me, rich girl? If I knew it would render you speechless, I would've hit you up sooner."

Amalie opened her mouth to speak, but Julian reached out a finger, lightly pressing it against her lips, something that, no matter how many times it was done, still made her feel like she'd stepped on a livewire. She willed away the blush creeping up her neck, imagining the mockery Julian would put her through if he saw it. He already walked around with a massive ego; he didn't need more ammunition.

"Don't even think about making any smart-aleck comments." He quirked a brow to punctuate his thoughts as he slowly moved his finger away from her mouth.

Amalie fought the urge to lick her lips, to taste where his touch had been. "I wasn't going to say anything remotely smart-aleck at all," she responded.

Julian chuckled. "Yeah right. Now come on, let's go and—" He paused, his hands moving for the edge of the notebook Amalie cradled protectively to her chest.

"Um, excuse me, are you trying to touch my *boob*? Again?" Her voice went a little shriller than intended as she smacked his hand away.

Julian didn't move his hand, just held tighter to the corner of the notebook. "I'm not trying to touch your boob. I wasn't trying to touch it at the gym either. You made me fall, I can't help where my hands went. Jesus."

"Yeah, you better call on Jesus." She tugged the notebook a little harder. Julian was stronger than she gave him credit for.

"Give me your notebook, Amalie. I think you should let me hold it or lock it away somewhere for the next hour or two. You know, so you can actually experience life instead of just writing it down." He leaned down, a cocky grin curling his lips. "I swear I'm not trying to touch your boob, princess. If I wanted to, I'd have already done it by now."

She reared her head back, the notebook temporarily forgotten. "So, what, you'd just reach out and grab my boob, is that it? I knew you were a pig, but I had no idea the level." She wrinkled her nose in absolute disgust.

A growl emitted from Julian's throat. "God, woman, you frustrate the hell out of me. No, I wouldn't just *grab* it. I'd ask permission first, of course." Was he sweating even more than before? It looked like some newly formed perspiration had cropped up around his hairline, along with the slightest tinge of pink in his cheeks.

"Seriously?" she asked, her eyes watering as she giggled. "So, you'd be all, 'Hey, Amalie, can I touch your boob?' Suave."

Julian's entire face lit up, and until then, she hadn't realized just how much he'd been hiding in the shadows.

"Something like that," he said. "But I'd say *pretty please,* of course. I do have *some* manners." He gave her a sexy little wink that sent the most adorable crinkles out from his eyes, but she ignored all of that. Because she didn't like him. At all.

Amalie wiped away the tears that had escaped the corners of her eyes, knowing her eye makeup was thoroughly ruined for the day.

"You want the notebook?" she asked, moving it a safer distance from her body.

Julian nodded. "May I?"

She drew the notebook back to her chest, an eyebrow raised. "Boob or notebook?"

Julian laughed, the blush on his cheeks deepening. "Notebook." His words said one thing, but that dark, scorching gaze of his said something totally different.

Amalie couldn't decide whether to be angry or flattered, although the way her body flooded with warmth and her fingers ached with the need to touch, she was pretty sure which emotion dominated. She blamed it on her dry spell that rivaled the Sahara.

The squeak of the gate swinging open had them both turning around, gaze traveling to where Paul stood. A stunning woman who looked to be in her sixties stood next to him, chatting.

"Does Paul have a date?" Amalie asked. "If so, she's *way* out of his league."

"Hell no, he doesn't have a date, because that woman is my mom."

And with that, Julian took off, his long stride taking no time to eat up the distance between him and Paul—and his mother.

Chapter Nine

JULIAN

"Julian! I didn't teach you to be rude. Now bring that beautiful young lady over here right this instant and stop acting like a barbarian. You were raised better than that."

Julian turned around, jerking his chin at said beautiful redhead. "You coming, princess?" he asked, trying his damnedest to keep it together. He and his mom didn't have any sort of beef with each other...it was just... "I haven't seen you since Christmas," he said.

His mom engulfed him in a tight, floral-scented hug and then kissed him on the cheek. Then she gave him that mom-look, right before she turned her attention on Amalie. Julian stiffened, unsure what to expect when his two worlds collided.

His mom's voice grew more excited. "Now who is this? Your new special someone?" She didn't wait for Julian's response as she wrapped her arms around Amalie.

"No. No, no, absolutely not, no." Amalie made an awkward noise, her face red enough to match her hair. "Nope. Never in a million years. Wrong person. No. I'm just the writer."

"Damn, I think we get it," Julian cut in, his pride taking a hit. She made it sound like being his girl would be the worst thing in the world, and while he knew they weren't close, he hadn't expected that response.

His mom swatted his arm. "Julian Alec Smoke! Language!"

He swore he heard Amalie snicker. Before he could apologize, Paul interjected, "Charlotte, this is Amalie Warner. She's part of the team."

"And obviously not Julian's special someone. Although, son, I'd like to see you have at least one serious relationship. That Nadine really did a number on you, and I worry you won't ever get your heart straightened out."

"Shit, Mom. Way to put my business out there." He hadn't mentioned Nadine to Amalie, and as far as he was concerned, Nadine was dead to him the moment she screwed someone else while engaged to *him*. She'd broken his heart, and yes, he hadn't been the same since, and his trust level definitely could use some help, but Amalie didn't need to know this.

Amalie placed a hand on his forearm, her touch almost distracting. "I know that name. Who's Nadine?"

Julian stammered, but his mom, the steamroller, kept talking. "Nadine Merriweather was Julian's fiancée. When did y'all get engaged? Twenty-one?"

"Fiancée? Twenty-one?" Amalie faced him, arms crossed beneath her breasts. "Well, well, well, that's a little young, ain't it?"

Julian glared at her, pouring a heaping dose of sarcasm into his voice as he said, "You would know, wouldn't you?"

Hating that she now knew this little piece of his past, this tiny bit of knowledge that could hurt him whenever she wanted, Julian sighed and turned to Paul. "Not that I don't like seeing my mom, but is there a reason you called her here?"

Adjusting his hat, Paul cleared his throat, then said, "Charlotte, can you excuse us for a moment? Coach stuff, you know, and then we'll be right back over."

Julian gave his mom and Amalie what probably looked like a grimace, because let's be real, getting a colonoscopy would be more pleasant than this current reunion. He loved his mom, and she'd always supported him no matter what. But he knew they would probably talk about tennis, which would lead to talking about his dad and that was something he wasn't ready for.

Paul led Julian to the gate, his gruff voice hushed. "I know you're not happy about this—"

"I'm pissed is what I am," Julian growled as he ran a hand through his damp hair. "You thought this was a good idea? I don't see what my mom has to do with anything."

Paul took a step forward, pointing at Julian, his face completely stone. "Damn right I thought this was a good idea, kid. You won't open up to me or to Amalie, and it's hard to coach someone who's locked up tighter than Fort Knox. You're battling some demons in there, and I know it all stems from your dad, and I'm willing to bet you pushed your mom away afterward."

Julian's blood turned to ice. His life was none of Paul's damn business.

"Guilt's a funny thing that way," Paul continued. "I want you to work things out with your mom, and I'm telling you it will transmit to the court. Now, it's rude to keep the ladies waiting. Just trust me. That's all I ask. But if you don't trust my coaching methods, then you need to say it now." Paul crossed his arms over his barrel chest, the sleeves of his polo tightening against his biceps.

Julian hadn't remembered how exposing tennis could be. He was sure Amalie had to go through the same thing as a writer. Tackling internal shit was part of conquering the obstacles standing in the way of any dream. His dad had taught him that, and once upon a time, it hadn't been a big deal. But now? Now he thought about telling Paul to forget everything. US Open-level dreams were one thing for a kid who thought he could take on the world and an entirely different beast for a thirty-year-old failure.

Then again, he'd felt good out there on the court. *Alive,* for the first time in months. No, years. Holding that racket in his hand, his feet hitting the asphalt, it felt right. He hadn't completely sucked out there with the UGA tennis players today, although his bones were screaming that he wasn't nineteen anymore.

Finding his voice, Julian said, "I've never talked about it, but I'll *try.* Will that work?"

Paul nodded, clapping him on the back in a way that, once again, awakened memories of his father. "That'll work, son," Paul said.

Julian avoided Amalie's scrutiny as they returned to the women. His mom's expression, however, softened. Her voice lowered as she bent her head closer to his. "I was afraid to get my hopes up when Paul called. Now I know it's true. You're *playing* again. You're really playing." Julian could only nod, especially as he caught that hopeful glint in his mom's eyes. "I'm so glad," she went on. "Your father would be so proud of you, honey. He would've wanted you to keep on playing, you know that, don't you?"

Breathe in. Breathe out.

His mom wasn't saying those things to be hurtful—she meant them to be supportive and loving. It was just that she didn't fully understand how much his father's death had affected him, how it was intertwined with tennis and always would be. As a matter of fact, since Oliver died, they hadn't talked about much besides his job, her retirement, and the weather.

He felt Amalie's stare, waiting, wondering. When he looked up, would he see pity in her eyes? Would she figure out what happened, why he quit playing?

Overwhelmed, Julian squeezed his mom's hand and tried to smile. "I, uh, I…I forgot something in the locker room. Wait right here for me, okay?"

Without looking back, he took off. He needed to get away, just for a minute, to collect his thoughts, to steady his breathing, to quiet everything around him. Once he stepped inside the locker room, he took a deep breath, his hands pulling at his hair. He walked down to the last locker, pressing his forehead against it, allowing the coolness to seep into his bones.

"Julian?" a small voice came from the doorway. Amalie stood there, hands wringing and fidgeting. She moved one foot back out the door, then moved one in, indecision written across her face. "Um, I thought you might want someone to talk to? If I'm wrong, I can… I can just go." She hooked a thumb behind her, her curly red hair swishing across her pale skin. She was so pretty that sometimes it hurt to look at her, but that didn't change who she was or what she represented, that she lived in her perfect gilded cage, untouchable and wanting for nothing, a life he would never understand.

Pushing off the locker, Julian faced her. "Have you figured out that I'm a shitty human being yet?"

Her brow furrowed, but his words didn't scare her off. No, this girl was fearless. She took two steps inside the locker room, and then she took a few more, until she was standing toe to toe with him. She smelled like vanilla and sunshine, and this close he could see the smattering of freckles across the bridge of her nose and her cheeks. It was adorable, which was slightly confusing, because how could a woman be so adorable while also being mind-fucking sexy and yet irritating as hell?

"I don't know what you mean by that, but I do know you kinda ran off the court like lightning struck you. I just wanted to make sure you were okay." She straightened her spine like she was expecting a battle.

He shook his head. What did she know about being okay? "It's not any of your concern, but I am. Okay, that is."

Amalie propped her hands on her hips, irritation lighting her eyes. "First of all? It *is* my concern. We're in this together, Julian. I'm helping you, and you're helping, well, you're *supposed* to be helping me. But are you? No. You and I argue, that's all we do, and so far, all I have are notes of your training. I don't even know where you live. I don't know anything about you except what I learned that night at the bar and what your mom just told me about Nadine."

More guilt heaped upon what was already weighing Julian's shoulders down. He almost slumped beneath the pressure. She was right. He'd done nothing to help her, but he hadn't wanted to let her in.

With a sigh, he plopped down on the lacquered wooden bench. "Don't take it personally. It's just how I am. I don't like to share. But I will help you—I promise."

Amalie didn't budge. "Fine. But I'm staying here until you're okay, because you're totally lying. And don't get me wrong, it's okay to not be okay, but you should have someone around during those times. It usually helps."

Julian met her stare. The gesture should've thawed his heart, but it didn't, maybe because his heart had hardened a long time ago. "I appreciate you being here, Amalie, but you can't understand this. Your life is perfect. You haven't let your family down like I have. My mom's a good person. It's tough for her to be here because she's one of the only people who knows what I've done."

She stalked toward him until she hovered over him, a looming little red-haired bundle of barely-tamed fury. "Listen here," she said. "You don't know anything about me. I've let my family down *plenty*. Why do you think I'm living in my dad's pool house with the threat of having to work for his company hanging over my head every damn day? It's certainly not because it's fun."

Definitely not the response he expected. He took a minute to study the woman before him, her anger-stained cheeks, the glistening eyes, and he saw that maybe his initial assessment was off, but...but she still had both of her parents. She might've disappointed them, but not on the scale that he had.

Amalie's chest heaved—something he really didn't need to be staring at —and it looked like she was trying to calm down, but her anger flared again before she could suppress it. She held up a hand as if to silence any response he might have. "You know what? This was all a huge mistake. I can see that we aren't going to be able to make this work."

And just like that, Julian saw his dream turn to dust, *again*.

His stomach churned at the thought. Without her dad's money, Julian had nothing.

Desperate to keep Amalie from walking out that door, he scrambled to dig his cell phone out of his pocket. "Wait!" Amalie went still, her back to him. "Please," he added, his voice cracking.

And that's what did it. She turned around, her mouth a straight line. "This is your last chance, Smoke. Better make it good."

Julian nodded, his eyes on the screen of his cell phone. His heart raced, fighting against his ribs as he opened his photo album. "You better sit for a minute, then."

Despite the wariness that spread across her features, Amalie took a seat next to him on the bench, her eyes darting to Julian's phone. His hands began to shake, but it was this little piece of himself or his dream. This piece...he didn't need it, did he?

He flipped through a few pictures and landed on one that had always been one of his favorites. His mom had the original and refused to relinquish it, since it sat in a frame on her nightstand. Even though it still hurt to look at it, it felt good to see his father's face, felt good to relive that day again.

Julian handed his phone to Amalie, his voice barely a whisper as he said, "When I was eight years old, my dad took me to the US Open. The Sampras/Agassi final."

Unable to help himself, he leaned over and looked at the picture again, too aware when his shoulder brushed hers. He moved away, enough to save him contact, even if he still felt her heat. "That was one of my favorite days."

He watched as Amalie studied the photo. There Julian was, grinning with his dad, arms around each other.

"It was an early birthday gift from my parents," he continued. It was good to talk about his dad, but at the same time it felt like a knife had slammed into his gut. "I remember being scared about flying."

Amalie turned her gaze onto him. "It was worth it, wasn't it?" she asked, her words calm and sweet.

The tenderness Julian found in her eyes and voice held him momentarily captive. He blinked, returning his attention to the picture. "To see Sampas play? Absolutely. And when we got to New York I thought I was hot shit, you know? I was just a Georgia boy who loved tennis, but that trip changed everything. I told my dad..." He paused, and Amalie wrapped her fingers around his. He wanted to shake off her touch, but he couldn't deny that it felt nice, especially with what this next bit would cost him. "I told him that night after the match that I wanted to play in the US Open more than anything. So, you see, this isn't just about me. I know I'm an arrogant ass, but it's not about me being the king of the court anymore. I'm a different man now. This is about making up for my mistakes and not only making myself proud but finally making my father proud."

His vision grew watery. He used one hand to wipe his eyes, the other not ready to let Amalie go yet.

"And make him proud you will, Julian." Her words were hushed, her eyes glassy. "Thank you for sharing this with me."

He nodded, his throat tight.

Amalie rested her head on his shoulder and wrapped her arms around him. "If you tell anyone I hugged you, I'll kill you."

Much needed laughter sprung from Julian. "Noted."

They sat there for a while, him in her arms, her head on his shoulder, as his dead and unfeeling heart slowly came back to life.

THE NEXT DAY, AFTER PRACTICE, AMALIE STOPPED BY JULIAN'S BENCH AS HE packed up his racket. "So, we need a Write Night."

Julian stilled. "A what?"

"A Write Night, a night where we work together on this novel. I'm putting my foot down. It's happening."

Julian rubbed the back of his neck and sighed. "Fine. When?"

Amalie perked up like he'd just offered her a million dollars.

"Really?" Her eyes were bright, and that smile…

He gave her a chin nod and returned his attention to his tennis bag. "Name the time and place."

"Your apartment? In about an hour? I can bring dinner."

The first thing he wanted to do was tell her no. He didn't want her in his space. He was already struggling with having her in his mind all the damn time.

"Yeah, sounds good," he said around a hard swallow. "I'll see you then." Julian pulled his bag over his shoulder and watched her disappear through the gate with a small wave.

After rushing home to shower and clean his apartment, Julian got the place looking decent. It was a bachelor pad to its core, with no decorations, just a few pictures of him with his parents. Should he try to find something else to put out? He looked around his living room with its recliner and sofa and large television and shook his head. There wasn't anything else to put out. Anticipation and excitement moved through his veins, something he hadn't felt off the tennis court in a long time.

A knock at the door drew his attention. He didn't even look through the peephole because he knew without a doubt that it was Amalie. When he opened the door, there she was, all pretty and perfect in those tight yoga pants he loved with a cropped gray sweatshirt that fell off one shoulder, showcasing her creamy skin and a black sports bra. He couldn't look away.

"I brought food!" She lifted two large white bags into the air. "Tacos, nachos, and enchiladas. I hope you're hungry!" She paused, staring into his eyes as her face pinked. "For food, I mean. Hungry for food. Not me. Why would I even say me? Anyway."

He hadn't tried to blink away the carnal thoughts clouding his mind, and Amalie had obviously read them with ease. He couldn't say he cared.

He wanted her to know how she made him feel. Still, her rambling was adorable. He had to tease just a little.

"You look a little flustered." He held the door open. "Why don't you come in? I'm definitely hungry."

She stepped past him, headed toward his kitchen table, bringing that familiar wave of vanilla, the smell that pretty much lived in his thoughts now.

He watched her bend over and start arranging things on his kitchen table, her eyes tracking between the food and his apartment. "Nice place," she said, her voice a little shaky.

The curve of her ass and a sliver of milky skin at her waist caught his eye. "Yeah. I like it." Julian swallowed hard and joined her, his voice thick. "A lot."

Amalie looked up at him, reading his eyes again, and took a deep breath before turning her attention back to the food. "So, I thought since this is Write Night, we should get started as soon as possible. We have a lot to cover and not a lot of time."

"What do you mean not a lot of time? We've got all night." Julian grabbed one of the boxes of nachos she'd set aside. He absolutely meant to brush his chest against her back as he did it, his breath at her neck. If she turned her head just slightly, their lips would almost touch.

Amalie stiffened, her strangled laugh finally snapping Julian out of his lust-filled haze.

"Funny, but"—she cleared her throat—"we *don't* have all night. We have to get plenty of sleep so we're rested for our run."

Julian should've moved away without touching her again, but his body liked to act of its own volition. He dropped the nachos and leaned forward again, his hands blocking her between him and the table. He leaned close and spoke against her ear. "You sure?"

His gaze dropped to her mouth. She bit her lower lip before she finally spoke. "Could you make it worth my while?" Her voice was a throaty whisper he'd only heard in his dreams.

What? *That* was not what he expected.

Julian fumbled for words. It didn't matter that she got on his nerves like nobody else and they still kind of...sometimes...disliked each other.

He'd wanted to know what she tasted like since that very first night at the bar—all fiery and full of life.

His eyes zeroed in on her lips and then skimmed down her body. A dumb move considering he needed to keep distance between them because he wasn't sure he could survive another encounter like they'd had in the locker room. Flirting was one thing. Intimacy and knowing and sharing and revealing his true self was entirely something else. Something he needed to avoid.

When he didn't reply, Amalie turned around slowly, making sure every part of her brushed every part of him. It was agony and bliss all at once when his cock stirred. But the smirk on her lips tipped him off to reality before she even opened her mouth.

She rolled her eyes and smacked his chest lightly. "Come on, Casanova, put away your sexy-time moves and work with me on this novel."

She moved away from him, scooping up her box of enchiladas, and plopped down into one of his chairs. She seemed unaffected, and he would've believed that if it weren't for the way she refused to meet his eyes, her food suddenly the most interesting thing in the world. The crimson blush that spread across her throat and chest was another dead giveaway. He felt a tiny victory knowing that at least he'd gotten to her, because she'd certainly gotten to him.

He cleared his throat, grabbed his food, and sat down across from her.

"Fine. First question?" he asked in an effort to calm himself.

"I need to know why you quit tennis. Writers need to understand their character's past. Their wounds. The things that make them do something like let go of a dream."

It felt like the room was closing in. He pushed his food around in the box, his appetite disappearing. "I can't go there, Amalie."

When he glanced up, he was met with those beautiful eyes, only they'd gone cold as ice.

"Are you serious right now, Julian? I asked you about your dad. You said no. I asked you about Fox. Nope. And now this? Another freaking no?" Amalie looked like she might stab him with her fork.

"Listen, I haven't talked to anyone about my dad. It's a big deal for me. I will tell you about him, but I need it to be on my own time. Can we agree to that?"

She sat down her fork and exhaled, a softness to her eyes where there was once an inferno. "Yes. If you swear you'll really try. Novels aren't written overnight. I need to understand you so that I understand Jax. I know that might sound strange, but it's how my writer brain works. I need to know *you*, Julian. *Really* know you and not just the fact that your ass makes tennis shorts look good."

Julian wanted to make a quip about ways she could really get to know him but decided not to push his luck. He scooped a chip into the queso, chewed, and then answered. "For now, I can help you write the tennis match scenes. Like Paul said, those need to be realistic. I can help you lay it out so it makes sense and is easy for readers who don't follow the sport to understand."

Amalie sat back in her seat, outwardly relieved. "That's a start. Thank you."

"You're welcome." Unable to take it anymore, Julian had to ask, "So you think I'm hot, huh? And you like this ass in tennis shorts? Which pair? The black ones? Or the white ones because you can kind of see the outline of my boxers?" He raised a brow to accent his point.

Her mouth crooked. "You're impossible."

His gaze swept over her body. "And apparently hot."

Three hours later, Julian had edited two tennis match scenes. He felt quite proud. Who knew he was even capable? Amalie had moved to the coffee table while he laid back on the sofa, hands behind his head, answering her questions as she fired them, fast as his serves.

"So what I need to remember when writing those match scenes is the power of the game." Amalie tapped her chin with her pen.

Julian nodded. "That's one of the most important things because, to be a tennis player, a successful one, you've got to be mentally and physically strong. You've got to have the stamina to keep going as long as it takes to finish, no matter how hard it is."

Yeah, for the first time in his life he hadn't meant a comment to sound sexual, but man, did that ever. Amalie's pen stilled and her eyebrows inched up to her hairline. Her mind was totally in the gutter and the thing was, he knew she needed this night, so he decided not to call her on it... this time.

"Well, I think that just about covers it," Amalie spoke up as she shut her notebook. "And wow. You have no idea how much all of this helps! I feel like I know what drives Jax now. To a point anyway. And these scenes!" She leaned an elbow on the couch, grazing his bare knee. "You really showed up for me tonight. I know this isn't your thing, but thanks."

He sat up, tapping her on the nose. "Only for you, princess."

Her skin flushed red, one of his favorite things about her. He helped her gather her stuff and then walked her outside. Out of nowhere, she stumbled over her own two feet, arms flailing. He reached out to steady her, inadvertently bringing her closer to him. Her eyes dilated, her chest brushing against his as her breathing picked up. He squeezed his eyes shut and willed himself not to do anything stupid. When he opened them, any previous thoughts of avoiding intimacy evaporated from his brain.

"God, you're beautiful." His voice was thick; the desire woven through those three words was unmistakable.

Amalie blinked, her lashes kissing her cheeks as her beautiful mouth parted on a gasp, her hands tightening around his biceps. His hand had caught her on the bare skin at her waist, right where her sweatshirt was cut, her skin hot beneath his touch. He wanted to pull her closer and kiss her. It was driving him wild not knowing what she tasted like.

"You are too." Her voice was so low that Julian almost thought he'd imagined her words.

She reached up, fingers trembling like they might move into his hair, but then her hand came crashing back down to her side, her body pulling away from his. He loosened his hold on her, hating how empty it felt without her in his arms.

She pushed her hair away from her face and quickly put distance between them. "Well thanks again."

"No problem. Any time." Julian lifted a hand in a wave, although he really just wanted her in his arms again.

She waved back, a ghost of a smile on her lips, before getting inside of her car. Just as she started to back her car out to leave, Amalie rolled down the window, shouting into the chilly night air. "For the record, I definitely like the white shorts best!"

Chapter Ten

AMALIE

The day before Valentine's Day, Amalie was about to leave one of Julian's practices when he stopped her, his hand on her shoulder.

"Hey, you know, if you need a date for Valentine's Day, I'm available," he said with a wolfish grin. He even had the audacity to wink at her.

Walking backward, Amalie let loose a wry laugh. "I bet you are."

Ever since Julian's admission in the locker room and Write Night at his apartment, Amalie noticed things had become...easier between them. Julian had been happier.

"Listen, I was just kidding," he said. "I've got options, you know."

She slipped through the gate with a derisive snort. She bet he did, or could if he wanted, but she imagined both of them would be spending Lover's Day dreadfully alone.

The following night, after spending hours struggling to write an intense scene between Penelope and Jax, followed by another several hours avoiding 101 Romantic Comedy marathons on TV, Amalie dragged herself to one of Julian's evening practices. A cool breeze caused a chill to rush up her spine as she pulled her blue and white plaid fleece jacket tighter. Georgia weather was notorious for being drunk—one day it was in the eighties and then the next day it was in the fifties. It was obvious which part they were cycling through now, but of course Paul and Julian were unaffected. She watched as Paul directed Julian through a few solo drills before really getting into the night's workout, and then he ambled over.

"How's my girl doing?" Paul asked as he sat down next to Amalie.

"Good. Happy Valentine's Day, by the way. I'm sure you have some hot date tonight, huh?" She playfully elbowed the older man.

"Nah." He waved off her question. "I bet you got some big plans, though."

She snorted, her gaze flicking to Julian. His hard work showing in the firm lines beneath his shirt. "Usually Romina and I binge watch *The Office* or *Parks and Rec*, but this year she has a date…and I have my television."

Paul shifted slightly. "Now I don't believe that for one second."

Amalie's eyes were still glued to Julian, admiring how he moved like a well-oiled machine.

"Amalie, can I ask why you're here?"

Her brows knitted together, confused. "I'm writing a book. You know that."

Paul studied her intently. "I know that, but is it really necessary for you to be at *all* the practices? Don't get me wrong—" He patted her knee. "I'm fine with it, but if I had to guess, I think you're paying more attention to him"—he tilted his head toward where Julian was still warming up at the far end of the court—"than to tennis."

Her pen tapped out a nervous rhythm. "What do you mean?"

He gave her a knowing look, which only made her fidget even more. "I'm just saying that I think you might like him."

Amalie immediately shook her head, her words coming out shrill and rushed. "What? No. Absolutely not. I'm just here for the book. That's all I'm here for."

Paul stood, that wise-guy expression still etched across his face. "And all I'm saying is I'm pretty sure he might have some feelings for you, too."

The air whooshed right out of Amalie's lungs as she leaned forward with a shocked, hushed, "What?"

She and Julian sparred. Teased. Flirted. And *that* she could do. But nobody said anything about *feelings*.

Paul nodded as he pulled out two sticks of Juicy Fruit and pushed them into his mouth. As he worked on chewing them, he said, "Well, the way he complains about you, I'm just saying. It's how I was with the love of my life. My first wife."

"Your *first* wife?" Amalie asked, desperate to get the attention off her and her frenzied thoughts.

He nodded, unfazed. "Yep, I used to complain about her all the time, but that's neither here nor there. What I'm getting at is that I'm curious about your intentions with my athlete. Now don't get the wrong idea—I'm not trying to say what should be. *But*, I figured you might want to take stock of your own feelings, see where you stand."

Without thinking, she lifted her notebook and fanned her face. "Look, Paul, it's really sweet of you to talk to me about this, but…no. I don't have any sort of *feelings*," she spat the word out as if it were rotten, "for Julian. Unless wanting to stab him in the eye counts? I've definitely wanted to do that."

Paul chuckled. "You're just lying to yourself now, girl." And with that, he headed toward Julian. "Twenty sprints, no stopping, or I'll make you do them all over again from the beginning," he called out.

Amalie pressed her lips together as Paul turned back and winked while Julian shot him a bird behind his back.

Once Julian started his drills, her mind returned to Paul's earlier comment. She didn't think of Julian as…*more*, did she? She agreed he was gorgeous, and yeah, sex with him would most likely be stellar, but they weren't compatible, not to mention just how moody and unpredictable he could be. But it was true that when he tried, she found herself completely drawn into his universe.

Paul called an end to practice, snapping her out of her musings. *Oh.* She hadn't noticed that a fourth person had joined them. Where Julian leaned over his bag, a twiggy brunette stood, dressed in a form-fitting red dress, her lips painted to match. The girl giggled at something Julian said, and it only increased her beauty. Julian straightened, his expression more animated than she'd ever seen, topped off by a beautiful smile. He spoke in a low murmur, causing the girl to laugh again. When had Julian become so charming? And why did it piss her off so much that he'd never bothered to show Amalie this side of his personality?

She shouldered her tote as Julian headed toward her, the brunette now swinging her hips as she sashayed toward the exit. Amalie kept her eyes straight ahead as she walked past him, her jaw clenched so tight it hurt. Once she made it past Julian without even an acknowledgment, she felt undone, and she didn't—*couldn't*—understand. She wasn't some teenage girl pining over an unrequited crush. As a matter of fact, this entire thing was ludicrous. She would just go home and binge-watch *Parks and Recreation* while shoveling pizza in her face. That would make her forget this weird day.

Julian's arm snaked out, wrapping around her bicep and gently pulling her back to him. He gave a quick shake of his head, his lips thinned out. "Hey." That one word sounded more like a question, his voice ragged and rough.

Amalie wrenched from his grip, careful not to dissect how that simple touch electrified her in ways Max's never had. *It's been a while,* she reminded herself. Anybody would make her feel something at this point.

"Yes?" she asked, her voice icy.

"I wanted to tell you happy Valentine's Day." He pushed his bag farther up on his shoulder, his eyes sincere. And that's what killed her.

"Well, now you've told me. Same to you. Enjoy your date!" Her words were brittle and dripping with sarcasm, but she kept her head high as she headed for the gate.

Even though Romina had a date for the evening, that didn't stop her from texting Amalie for the hundredth time, asking if she wanted to be a third wheel.

Amalie lay on her couch, suffering from one hell of a downer mood. She groaned and grabbed her phone off the floor, declining yet again. Earlier, she'd given her friend the condensed details about Julian having a date. A freaking *gorgeous* date. The thing that really ate at her was how bothered she was by the whole thing. All she'd thought about since seeing him with the girl at the court was why anything about Julian's romantic life got to her. Why did she care about who he dated *or* his engagement to Nadine Merriweather? Why did thoughts of that woman fill her with a sinking feeling, something hot in her veins?

The answer glimmered like a star in her mind. With as distant as Julian was, she couldn't imagine how he ever grew close enough to someone to date, let alone get engaged. Worse, though it killed her to admit, it hurt that he gave himself to women who seemed shallow and empty. It had been a feat for Julian to allow her, the woman he spent hours with every day, even a glimpse of the real him, when she wanted so much more.

With a sigh, she pulled her laptop out of its case and propped it on her lap. She owed Stella some pages. After staring at the blank screen for what felt like hours, the words started to come at a slow drip and then finally began to flow. Her hands flew across the keyboard, her heart soaring with each stroke. *This.* She missed *this*. Writing a story transported her to another world, a world where she controlled the outcomes and gave all her beloved characters the happily-ever-afters they deserved. A sense of freedom accompanied each word she typed. She could actually be herself and not be judged or have her last name hanging over her head. With this story in particular, it moved her one step closer to the bestseller she needed, the one that would be her ticket out of what Julian once called her gilded cage.

That magic, the sheer joy of writing, continued to flow for several more pages before she called it a day. Satisfied with her progress, she emailed everything to Stella and slumped back onto the couch.

A knock at her door brought her senses to high alert. Her dad was out of the country and wouldn't be back until the following week, and Simone was out with Damien, enjoying a child-free night, so...that only left ax murderers. She got up slowly, careful not to make any noise even though she was sure a serial killer wouldn't outright knock on the door before killing her. Right? *Right?*

She looked through the peephole. Holy cannoli. Julian stood there, all dressed up. The only thing she could see was his top half, but it was more than enough. He wore a light-blue dress shirt that made his eyes look sultrier than usual, set off by a skinny navy tie with tiny pink polka dots, and...*sigh.* He held a pink bakery box in his lovely hands.

Amalie glanced down at her old, ratty Agnes Scott T-shirt and her skull print leggings in a panic. Her hair sat on top of her head in what was essentially a rat's nest, and she had no makeup on.

After another knock, she opened the door slowly, registering a flicker of surprise across Julian's face. She searched behind him, looking for the woman in the red dress.

As if reading her mind, Julian slid his hands in his pockets and leaned against the door frame, his eyes locked with hers. "I'm alone. Mind if I come in?"

She swallowed back the knot in her throat and moved aside, motioning for him to enter.

He pushed off the doorframe and stepped past her, then turned to meet her eyes again, but not before she caught him scanning her from head to toe. A grin twisted his lips. "Nice outfit."

Amalie crossed her arms over her chest with an impatient snort. That dress shirt was doing amazing things for him, for his eyes, his body, everything. The sleeves were rolled to his elbows, revealing muscular, tanned forearms brushed with brown hair. Then there were the dress pants hugging those fantastic thighs that somehow hadn't lost their touch over the years.

With a lift of an eyebrow she asked, her voice completely flat, "Terrible date? Did your general douchey demeanor scare her off?"

Julian took a step closer, the scent of his woodsy cologne and his distinct, hot, sexy man smell wrapping Amalie's senses in a heady blanket of *it's not a good idea*. "I couldn't get through dinner with her."

She blinked, feeling bewildered. "Really? How…awful."

"Yeah, I couldn't do it." He scrubbed a hand through his hair and let out a breath. "I took her home and came here. But not before making a special stop." He held the pink box out to her. "For you."

She accepted the gift, but just like when he'd asked to come inside, she had no words. Julian ditched his date with Ms. Gorgeous, and when he could've done anything else, he didn't. He came here. To Amalie.

Her heart swelled as her fingers traced the box before opening it to reveal a dozen heart-shaped donuts. A *you're-totally-forgiven* smile split her face. "Thank you," she said as she led him to the couch. He nodded as he sat next to her, so close their shoulders brushed. She thought about moving or scooting down, but that would just draw attention to her awkwardness.

She reached for a donut, but then turned to him, nose scrunched. "Why did you buy me donuts?"

Julian's hand traced an outline of a skull on her knee, his voice rough. "Because I wanted to tell you happy Valentine's Day."

She was held captive by the movement of his fingers, her body growing hot as she remained frozen, donut in hand. "But you told me that at the tennis court," she said dazedly.

He dragged his gaze to hers, a thousand different emotions flitting through his eyes like the fluttering pages of a book. "I didn't do it properly." He moved to trace a skull on the top part of her thigh, slowly moving up, up, and up.

Was Write Night Seducer Julian about to make an appearance? If so, Amalie didn't know if she could resist him again.

Then suddenly, as if jolting awake, Julian pulled his hand from her leg, blinking several times. Amalie bit down on her disappointment, careful to stop the groan that wanted to come rolling out. Once recovered, Julian reached for a donut too, stuffing it into his mouth.

"Hey!" Amalie pulled the box to her chest, cradling it protectively, desperately trying to erase the memory of his touch.

He shrugged. "You snooze, you lose."

How quickly they returned to their normal banter.

"But you bought these for *me*," she said.

"I figured we could share."

"Ha, think again! I don't share sweets."

Julian grinned as he ran his hand over his perfectly fitting pants. "So why aren't you out tonight? I figured you'd have a date—one of those rich boys from the country club or something."

She pursed her lips and then extended a hand to the television where *Parks and Recreation* played. "Meet my date. We're horribly busy, as you can see."

Julian looked at the screen and back to her. "It's actually kind of perfect. Mind if I join?"

She took a bite of her donut, saying with her mouth full (her debutante mother would be absolutely appalled), "Well, seeing as you *did* bring the donuts, I guess I kind of have to say yeah."

Julian's lips tilted in a lopsided smile as he settled deeper into the couch, kicking off his square-toed dress shoes. "I'm keeping that up here for future use." He tapped his temple with his finger.

"What? That it's easy to bribe me with food?" Her voice was light as she set the box on the coffee table and stood.

"You bet," he called after her as she went to wash her hands in the kitchen.

When she returned, Julian was in the process of removing his tie—his throat, oh that sexy throat of his, constricting with the movement. The tie made a *swish* sound as it slid from his neck, and her mind ventured into all kinds of daydreams that involved various ways he could use that tie…on her. He made matters worse when he began unbuttoning his shirt a little, revealing the hollow of his neck. It was basically begging to be licked. She wet her lips as she gawked, thankful that he hadn't even realized she was standing there. He sank into the couch and kicked his feet up on the coffee table, effectively waking her from her stupor.

Awkwardness settled in her bones, and her heart rate kicked up as she wondered if she should sit back down beside him or sit in the other chair? Julian was the hardest person to read, and she still didn't fully understand what he was doing at her house, but it was impossible to deny she was glad he was there.

As though sensing her dilemma, he patted the spot where she'd been sitting. "Come back. I won't bite." She raised a brow, and he added, "Unless you want me to."

Amalie sighed dramatically in an attempt to hide how affected she was. With a huff, she bravely plopped down next to him. Julian swung his arm around her, pulling her close to his chest. "You know you like it."

Like it? If he had any clue to the thoughts racing through her mind, he would be shocked. The temptation was way too much, actually touching him and sitting there on the couch like a couple, all cuddled up, especially since her risqué daydreams still sat at the forefront of her mind. Julian smelled so good, his sandalwood cologne mixing with his skin, giving her a smell that was so uniquely him that ignited her senses. On top of that, he looked so damn good all undone and rumpled. Her hands itched to run up his thigh, to explore, and her lips trembled with that leftover thought from earlier, to press against the tanned sliver of skin that was visible from his unbuttoned shirt.

Her thighs clamped together as she contemplated climbing into his lap and just saying to hell with inhibitions. She needed to move away from him for a second or else their entire arrangement was going to unravel. Julian propped his head on hers, his voice low, and said, "You know, Paul recommended I go out on that date tonight."

Taking a deep breath that did nothing to calm her hormones, Amalie moved under the pretense that she was trying to meet his stare. His arm fell away and she tried not to think about how much she missed it. "What?" Her voice was a little too shrill.

Julian nodded as he scratched his freshly shaven chin. She missed the scruff—it added a level of sexy roughness. "Yeah, he told me I deserve a break, a chance to blow off steam, but I couldn't get into it. Alexis was hot…"

Amalie's lips flattened, her body instantly cooling down with those words, but Julian continued on undeterred. "But she was boring as hell and giggled at everything I said."

"And we both know you're not that funny." Amalie winked and stretched her feet out. She pushed one foot onto the coffee table, knocking off a familiar ecru square painstakingly embossed in silver and black. It fell toward Julian, and he leaned forward to pick it up.

"What's this?" he asked.

She snatched it from his hand, her gaze darting down to the classic stationery that screamed money. "It's an invitation to my sister's party next month."

Julian studied her. "The one Romina mentioned a while ago?"

Shocked he remembered it, she fought to hide her surprise and answered, "That would be the one."

"And Maxwell will be there?" he asked, Maxwell's name coming out between gritted teeth.

"Of course. He runs in the same circles, and I'm sure he'll bring his perfect fiancée." The words sounded bitter even to her ears, but not for the reasons one would think.

"Do you still love him?" Julian asked, leaning forward, his elbows on his knees, his muscles tight.

"*God* no. I hate him. I just…I go to these things…and you know what? Never mind. Let's just watch TV or talk about something else, anything else. Even tennis." She turned her attention back to the screen, carefully avoiding his eyes.

Julian grabbed the remote, clicking off the TV before settling the full force of his stare on her. Something in his eyes made her lightheaded.

"No. I want to talk about this, Amalie. You always make such a fuss about me being shut off, but you're not any better. I feel like even though we spend all this time together, I don't know much about you at all, but I know I want to."

A lump formed in Amalie's throat. His words were tiny little sinews stringing pieces of her heart together. So often she was overlooked, pushed aside. It was rare that anyone cared to know exactly what made her tick.

Thrown off-balance, she shook her head as she put the invite on top of the box of donuts. She tapped it with a few fingers, making an offbeat rhythm. "You know I like donuts," she offered weakly.

"I know. I know you drink sweet tea like it's crack too, and that you love to write but lost yourself along the way, and that we're a lot more alike than we think, but this personal stuff? I feel it's only fair that if I have to share, so do you. You've even met my mom, but I've only seen your family in sad-looking photographs." He gestured to her mantle.

"You're not missing much." Amalie sighed as she ran a hand over her messy bun. "Well, you'd like Simone and her daughter, but my parents?" She shook her head, not finishing her sentence.

"Are they home?"

"No. My mom took off with the guy she was having an affair with when I was nineteen. I only get postcards and guilt gifts from her. My dad? Well, he's been gone since the end of January and will be back sometime next week." At Julian's questioning look, she added, "He's traveling overseas, checking on our international hotels." She pulled in a breath and added, "But the truth is, I don't miss either of them, as horrible as that may sound. I feel less suffocated, less pressured without them hovering nearby."

"Why?" Julian angled his body to fully face her, sincerity lacing his tone.

"Because for my whole life, Simone has been their world and that's fine. You'll be shocked to hear that we actually have a good relationship, but she stays busy with her family and social stuff. She's the heiress, you know? But their attention shifted just slightly when my book hit it big. They realized I was worth something, if that makes any sense?"

Julian nodded. "It does."

"Yet they still didn't care about my actions, my running off to New York"—she gave her head a little shake—"at least not until I failed. Then they said they weren't really surprised. My dad said I wasn't cut out for success, and that's why Simone was next in line."

Julian's face had gone red. "He said that to you?"

She nodded, her jaw tight. "Yes. He's always tried to force me into this mold, like when he shoved tennis down my throat. But the thing is, I just don't…fit. Now you see why this book is so important to me? I've got to get out of here"—she gestured to the four walls surrounding them—"and get away from this life."

Julian moved her hand so that it was palm up, and then gently, and excruciatingly slowly, laced his fingers through hers and squeezed. "I'm going to try my hardest, not only for me but for you. Got it?"

His voice was thick with emotion, his touch waking parts of her soul that had long been asleep, and she had to fight back tears that suddenly threatened to fall. Julian was a lot of things, but he had her back. He'd promised to fight for her, *with* her for this preposterous idea of theirs to succeed.

"Thank you." Her voice hushed as his thumb stroked her wrist, and her body shook with the touch.

"So, what were you going to say earlier? About the parties?" he asked.

She squirmed, suddenly realizing why Julian had fought so hard when she questioned him about personal things. Revealing oneself was a lot harder than she'd made it seem.

She released a pent-up breath. "When I go to those stupid events, I feel like a loser." She frowned. "They all treat me like one. Except for Simone, of course. She faces a ton of pressure from our dad, but she handles it with so much ease and grace."

"I can imagine, but hey"—he lifted their joined hands—"you're not a loser. When is this thing?" He leaned forward, perusing the details on the invitation. "March twelfth, right after the Island Open. I'm going with you."

The way he said it brooked no argument, but Amalie didn't roll like that. She didn't think anyone should be subjected to her family's dysfunction. But there was something else wiggling around in her mind.

What if, after seeing her in that environment, her insecurities and awkwardness would show, and Julian would finally see what a failure she was? What if he saw her the same way everyone else did? That alone would break her heart. She couldn't risk it.

She moved away from him, taking her hand from his. "No, you don't have to. Actually, trust me, you don't *want* to do that."

His eyes crinkled at the corners. "Trust me, I do. I'm going as your date, so go ahead and let your sister know to expect me. No arguments."

She tried to ignore the sudden lightness in her chest, how it felt to have someone truly on her team. "Fine, but don't say I didn't warn you."

"Babe, I think I can handle a few rich, stuck-up assholes. You forget what sport I play," he teased, his comment drawing a soft laugh from her.

Julian grabbed the donuts and pointed the remote at the TV, turning *Parks and Recreation* back on. "Can we start from the beginning? I've never watched this show."

"What?" Amalie gaped at him. "Never?"

He shook his head and bit into a donut. "Never."

"Then yes, we can totally watch from the beginning."

They sat side by side, shoulder to shoulder, thigh to thigh as hilarity unfolded onscreen. But at some point, Amalie's eyes grew heavy, and before she knew it, she was startled awake by the feel of a gently calloused hand running up her arm.

When she opened her eyes, Julian stared back at her, his beautiful face mere inches from her own. She was nestled against his side, held against his body in an even more intimate way than before. The backs of his fingers played along her jawbone, and she couldn't help but inhale the scent of his cologne that lingered on his wrists.

She had to be dreaming.

But then Julian leaned forward and pressed a delicate kiss to her cheek. The warmth of his lips seared her skin and heated her from within. She closed her eyes, hardly able to think. If she just turned her head, their mouths would meet, and it would be over. Any restraint she'd had before would be no more than a memory.

Her heart pounded like a drum as desire stirred through her like a living thing. She ran her hand up his arm and twisted her fingers in the fabric of his shirt.

Julian pulled back, staring her in the eyes again. "It's almost midnight, princess. I couldn't let Valentine's Day pass without you getting a kiss. Even if it was from a jerk like me."

The corner of his mouth curled, and she tried desperately to mirror the action, her mind swirling back to the reality that this night wasn't going to go any further, which was for the best. She knew that, even if her body hated her for it.

Julian slipped from her grasp, grabbed his tie, and slipped on his shoes. He snatched one last donut, then Amalie walked him to the door. Even still she ached to feel him against her one more time, which seemed wild now that she was waking up.

"See you tomorrow, princess," he said, "and happy Valentine's Day." He leaned forward in the doorway, kissing her on top of her head. "Don't say I never gave you anything." He winked and gestured with his donut, and then he was gone.

Amalie pressed a hand to her chest to steady her fluttering heart, thinking he'd given her more than he knew, and it terrified her.

Chapter Eleven

JULIAN

March blew in quicker than Julian expected, but it didn't matter—he felt ready. His body hummed with anticipation as he waited for Amalie to pick him up. This weekend was the Men's Island Open at Jekyll Island, off the coast of Georgia, and if he did well, he'd get enough points to play the sectionals at Stone Mountain, the tournament to get into qualifying for the US Open.

He replayed Paul's words in his mind as he paced. "You should win it. Mainly weekend warriors playing, but there will be some good players from around Jacksonville and Atlanta. This is good for you to learn how to win again."

Now that last part stung because Julian heard the part that went unsaid —that he hadn't won in a very long time. Paul wasn't being hurtful, it was just the cold, hard truth.

But that wasn't the only thing that had him pacing. Wesley Walker, a young tour professional, would be playing. Lots of young players had done this in the past but rarely at Jekyll Island, so it was kind of a big deal.

Paul had left early for Jekyll Island to get things settled, leaving Julian and Amalie to make the almost five-and-a-half-hour trek together. Amalie had been brimming with excitement, and she'd booked their rooms at her favorite place in the state of Georgia, the historic Jekyll Island Club Hotel. But Julian was on edge. Tomorrow he'd be playing to see if he was good enough, to see if he had what it took to be a champion.

And then there was this *thing* with Amalie that he couldn't quite figure out. Something had shifted between them on Valentine's Day. Something he wanted to explore, even though he had no business even thinking about it.

"Get your head in the game, man," he reminded himself as he adjusted his headphones around his neck. A text from Amalie alerted him that she was downstairs.

With a deep breath, he headed to her shiny silver Audi. The first hints of an early spring blew through the air, although there was still a winter chill that refused to give way.

Amalie rolled down the window, and he tried not to pay attention to how gorgeous she looked—flushed, her lips wet with some sort of gloss. "Just throw your stuff in the back," she said by way of greeting as she popped the trunk. Julian nodded and placed his overnight and tennis bags on top of her luggage.

Damn, it was a small car, and he was not a small guy. He would be a whopping six inches away from Amalie, and today was not the day for that, not with his adrenaline rushing and her, well, looking like a snack.

He opened the door to the back seat and slid over the cool, supple leather. This probably wasn't going to go over well.

Amalie met his eyes in the rearview mirror. "Um, why are you sitting in the back?" Her eyes darted to the empty passenger seat and back to him. She turned to actually make eye contact instead of talking to his reflection.

God almighty, she really did look edible. She wore a V-neck T-shirt that revealed a tempting line of cleavage now that she was twisted to face him. The back seat looked like an even better idea now.

Julian's mind raced, searching for an excuse that wasn't *I ache for you, and I can't ache today.* The best thing he could come up with was his usual barbarity.

He raised his chin. "I'm the athlete. Does Roger Federer sit up front with his driver? This is a big tournament. Sitting in the back makes me feel like a pro again. Amps me up."

Without missing a beat, Amalie shot back, "Well, consider this, you're not Roger Federer, so get your butt up here, please. I hate not talking on long car rides, and I need you to DJ."

Julian pushed his sunglasses over his face. "You know I can't resist you, especially when you say please." Against his better judgment, he switched seats.

"Thank you." Her smile was genuine as she handed over her phone.

"I guess this means I can play whatever I want on repeat then?" He smiled, finger hovering over said jam.

Amalie laughed and shook her head. "Only if I get to play nineties pop."

It was going to be a long drive indeed.

THEY ARRIVED AT THE JEKYLL ISLAND CLUB HOTEL AT THAT HAZY PART OF THE day when the sky turned pink and red before melting into black. The hotel was beautiful, a place full of history and purported ghosts. The turret with the club flag stood against the fading sky, looking more like a postcard than real life.

Julian and Amalie's rooms were in a building separate from the main hotel. Amalie gushed that she preferred to stay in Sans Souci, the dark green structure that oozed old money, rather than the main building because there was more privacy. They had side-by-side deluxe rooms right next to Paul, all facing the wharf, with a shared balcony complete with white rocking chairs—Southern charm at its finest. Each room was spacious, with a table and four chairs tucked into the bay window alcove, along with a humongous bathroom.

Julian turned to say something to Amalie, but she had already disappeared into her room without so much as a *good night* or *screw you*.

Suddenly antsy, his mind racing once again, Julian stepped out onto the balcony, enjoying the cool breeze coming in off the wharf. People were milling about in the dying twilight—but even among the quiet hive of activity, a flash of red caught Julian's eye. Amalie was on one of the coquina footpaths headed toward a set of benches facing the marsh, her hands tucked into her hoodie.

He hastily threw on his sneakers and headed out. He almost went after her empty-handed, but he knew she liked food gifts, and he'd do anything to brighten her day. He swung by the Pantry, a small café overlooking the hotel's courtyard framed by vibrant pink flowers, chairs, and a fountain. He picked up the largest cup of sweet tea they sold.

He didn't have to walk far to find her sitting on a bench surrounded by trees, the view of the spidery Sidney Lanier bridge pretty epic from her spot. Leaves crunched under his feet, causing Amalie to jump, her head whipping around to skewer him with a death stare that she quickly schooled into a bored expression.

"Can't get enough of me, huh?" she deadpanned.

Julian pressed his lips together, not wanting to confirm the truth of her words. He held out the cup, his Southern olive branch. "I brought you crack."

Her face lit up, making her even more beautiful—the rare light blue of her eyes, the haze of the sunset making her hair look like a halo. He wanted to look away, to not notice these things, but he'd have to be blind for that to ever happen.

She moved her bag to the ground, wordlessly giving him permission to sit. "You know the way to my heart." Her head tilted to the side before taking a sip of the tea, her eyes closing in ecstasy as a moan escaped from her mouth. "That's so good," she added, her voice low and sultry.

Julian normally would've made a joke, but he was mesmerized by the show Amalie had no idea she was putting on. Suddenly wildly uncomfortable in more ways than one, he cleared his throat, trying to erase the thoughts of Amalie naked and moaning that flew through his mind.

"It's beautiful here, isn't it?" Her eyes locked on something across the marsh.

Enthralled, Julian kept his gaze on her as he said, "Yeah, it is." It was a dangerous slip, but he meant it, and he didn't care if she knew.

Amalie slowly turned to face him, her expression as soft as her voice. "Why aren't you in the room? Shouldn't you at least be *trying* to rest?"

He sighed as he brought his arm up along the back of the bench, stretching it behind her shoulders. He felt her stiffen as his thumb brushed over her shoulder blade, but she eventually relaxed once he began making circles there. "Yeah, but my mind won't stop racing, and I wanted to be with you because sometimes that's the only time it quiets. Is that okay?"

Her lips parted in surprise, but she quickly recovered. "Oh, sure. Of course that's okay."

His thumb did another sweep across Amalie's shoulder, running a featherlight touch back and forth. "You make me feel calm, princess, and right now that's what I need more than anything."

She studied him for a second, the intensity of her gaze forcing him to look away. "It's funny you say that," she said, "since you actually have the opposite effect on me. Shows how one-sided this friendship is if you ask me." She punctuated it with a playful shoulder nudge.

Julian's hand found the tip of her hair and, testing his limits, wound his fingers through the mess of curls, his movements unhurried and relaxed. "So you admit that we're friends? It's finally official, huh?"

Her breathing picked up. "Might as well be, I guess. We have four more months together."

Four months sounded like a long time, but Julian feared it might not be enough. Would he ever see her after the US Open or after her book was finished? Would they still text and go for morning runs?

He shook his head, trying to focus on the present instead. They sat there together, his hand wrapped around Amalie's delicate curls, talking about everything and nothing at the same time. He decided to call it a night when Amalie's head fell on his shoulder, her eyes fluttering closed. A part of him wanted to stay that way, to revel in the feel of her, to memorize the peaceful expression on her face, her sweet scent that enveloped them, but he had to wake her for his own self-preservation. This thing with Amalie was spiraling, and he couldn't afford to screw it up. As much as he hated it, he pushed her hair away from her starlit face and whispered, "Hey, sleeping beauty, those snores of yours are starting to scare the children...and a few animals."

She woke with a mumbled start. "Haha. So funny."

The walk back to Sans Souci was a quiet one, the sounds of a true Southern night wrapping them in a weird sort of haze as the frogs croaked and the ocean lapped lazily against the shore of the marsh.

It wasn't until they stood at the doors outside their rooms that Amalie spoke, her voice thick with sleep, her eyes heavy. "I know I'm no replacement for your dad, but I want you to know I believe in you. I wouldn't be here if I didn't."

What she did next surprised him even more than her words. She stood on her tiptoes and kissed his cheek, the touch so featherlight that when she wordlessly slipped into her room, Julian questioned whether or not the whole thing had been a dream.

Chapter Twelve

JULIAN

ADRENALINE PULSED IN JULIAN'S VEINS ONCE HE ARRIVED AT THE JEKYLL Island Tennis Center.

"Any pre-match rituals this morning?" Amalie asked as they walked to the end of the first court. He tried not to notice how her lavender sweater brought out her eyes or how spectacular her ass looked in those jeans.

Things between them appeared normal, at least on the outside. On the inside, though, Julian's emotions were all over the place. He'd gone to sleep with the scent of her on his shirt, on his skin, and he dreamed about the things that had flashed through his brain when she'd moaned while drinking that stupid tea of hers.

"Actually, yeah." He cleared his throat as he adjusted his headphones for the second part of his ritual.

"I have to watch one of the *Rocky* movies before every single match, and I come on court with "Eye of the Tiger" blaring in my headphones."

Amalie nodded, eyes alight with interest as she asked, "Do your rituals usually work?"

He sobered instantly. "They did until I stopped caring." The admission shocked him. It was the first time he'd said that out loud to anyone aside from Paul.

"But things are different this time. You got this, Smoke." She gave him a little wave before making her way into the small section of stands to the side of the court. Julian caught himself shaking his head and smiling, enjoying the way her hips swayed with each step. Of course, Paul came over and interrupted that, offering a few last-minute tips about his opponent, and then it was go time.

When Julian's feet hit the court, the thrill of the game came rushing back. He pictured his dad behind the green fence, his nod of encouragement, that hideous golden tennis racket necklace he always wore sparkling in the sun. Julian used to joke that the necklace, a gift from Julian's mom, made his dad look like a '70s mobster. His throat constricted at the memory, but he hoped that maybe, just maybe he could make his old man proud.

Better late than never.

The day went by in a sports-movie montage kind of way. Julian beat every opponent put in front of him, finally getting a feel for winning again, and damn if it didn't feel good. He rode that high to the championship match later that afternoon.

As he stood across from Wesley Walker, the seventeen-year-old baby-faced pro, all he could hear was the sound of his pulse beating a heavy bassline as they waited for the coin toss. Up into the air the coin went, glinting in the late-afternoon light, with Wesley winning the toss and calling for Julian to serve first.

Julian rolled his shoulders and neck as he did a zigzag jog back to the baseline. Fine. The kid wanted him to serve first? He could do that. As a matter of fact, he lived for it.

Looking up, he zeroed in, everything else fading away, that undeniable *something* that had been missing burning through his veins.

After dropping the first set, the intensity picked up for both players as Julian put pressure on Walker. He made him run more, his shoes squeaking on the asphalt as he tried to run down each ball. Julian's heart felt like it was about to beat out of his chest by the time he finally hit an ace to win the second set in a tie break.

"Come on!" Julian yelled with a fist pump, trying desperately to keep himself hyped up. This kid was no joke.

Julian knew he'd have to bring something extra in the third set but wasn't sure if he had it, despite Paul and Amalie's encouragement from the sideline. The sound of each player grunting with every shot echoed through the court, followed by feet shuffling across the asphalt in an attempt to put everything they had into each ball. It was razor tight down the stretch, and Julian found himself trailing 5–4 and match point in the final set.

Sweat cut across his face as he understood the utter importance of this point. He'd trained for this. He knew what to do.

Without hesitation, he lunged into the serve, sending it right into Walker's body, and in return was given an easy ball in the middle of the court. As he moved toward the ball, knowing what weighed on this shot, he tightened his grip. He had it, he *knew* he had it as he released his racket through the ball, the power of the Julian Smoke forehand rippling through his body as he crushed it up the line to save match point.

There was no doubt in his mind that shot would be a winner.

His eyes frantically tracked the ball only to see it just miss the line. He sank to his knees in disbelief, his head in his hands as denial and shock coursed through his veins.

The match was right there in his grasp, and he let it slip away.

Drinking in a shaky breath, he pulled himself up off the court despite the chill in his veins, the slump in his shoulders. His feet moved toward the net on autopilot and he offered a mumbled *congratulations*. Years from now, when he looked back on this memory, he'd only be able to recall that final moment on court, the moment where he choked.

He had blinders on, not hearing or seeing a damn thing. He shoved his racket into the bag with enough force to punish it for not serving him well during that match, and then he walked off court without looking for Paul or Amalie.

But his coach met him outside the court, looking like they'd just won the tournament. He clapped Julian on the shoulder. "Man, that was awesome!"

"What the hell are you talking about? I *lost*," Julian spat out.

Paul then channeled the Cheshire cat. "Yeah, I know. It was fantastic."

Julian pinched the bridge of his nose. "What?"

"Man, you would've been unbearable if you won that match."

Wait. This was his *coach*, right?

Julian's frown deepened. "What do you mean *unbearable*?"

"You love the *Rocky* movies, yeah? Well, then you know he doesn't win the first match." Paul punctuated his words by waving his hands around, like that explained everything.

"Yeah, and…?" Julian drawled, still not following.

"You need some adversity, especially for an arrogant kid like yourself."

"Thanks, Coach?" Julian managed, confusion and sarcasm mixing through his tone.

Turning away, he saw Amalie's fiery red hair moving toward them. Her entire face was lit up, her eyes trained on him like he was the only thing in the world. If he hadn't just lost, it would've been intoxicating. As it were, it was just flat-out embarrassing.

He didn't have time to think about much else because as soon as she reached him, Amalie threw her arms around his neck with a little squeal. His hands found the dip of her hips, itching to keep her there against him, but she stepped back and did a little excited dance, bouncing on the balls of her feet, beaming.

"I'm so proud of you! You played your heart out. When you did whatever this move is called," she mimicked him hitting a drop shot, "I got chills, I tell you. Chills!"

Julian dipped his chin in acknowledgment, feeling like a kid who had just been handed a participation trophy, and headed in the direction of the car. Yeah, he'd played his heart out, but it still hadn't been enough. He heard Paul and Amalie's footsteps behind him.

"She's not wrong you know," Paul called out.

Julian didn't say anything until they reached Amalie's car. She popped the trunk and he started shoving his equipment in, trying to wrap his head around the loss. He could sense Paul and Amalie doing this weird telepathic conversation with their eyes, so even though they weren't speaking out loud, he was desperate to get their focus off of him, more specifically, worrying about him.

"When do we play next?" he asked, leaning against the car. Amalie put her hands in the pockets of her jeans and Paul shoveled gum into his mouth.

"We don't," his coach spoke up. "You've got enough points to be entered into the lottery for sectionals. Now's the time to just train and get ourselves right. I don't need you out there with your brittle psyche losing matches."

A sound came from Amalie, drawing Julian's attention. "What are *you* laughing at?" He had a good idea, but he wanted to hear her say it.

She just shook her head, studying her shoes, her hand covering her trembling lips. "Nothing. Nothing at all."

Julian knew, unlike in the past, that he needed to dust himself off and keep moving. After all, he was one step closer to the US Open. That realization caused his pulse to hum in his ears. "Well, I guess we better get to training, then."

Chapter Thirteen

AMALIE

Romina smiled as she put the finishing touches on Amalie's winged liner. "You look *hot*."

"I feel like I'm going to throw up."

"It was those chili cheese fries I told you not to eat. Serves you right."

Amalie stared at her reflection. Somehow her best friend had transformed her into Rita Hayworth, complete with soft, cascading curls and super glam red lips. The black dress she'd chosen for the occasion was a sleek, simple number with a trapeze-cut neck and an open-back design. The dark, shimmery material sparkled when the light hit it just right, making it look like a blanket of twinkling stars.

"Oh, don't forget these!" Romina rushed forward with a small blue box.

The large diamond drop earrings inside had been a Christmas gift from Amalie's mother, purchased with her alimony payment. They *were* stunning.

As Amalie fastened the second earring, a knock sounded at the door.

"Oh, God." She took one last glance in the mirror, her trembling hands fussing over imaginary wrinkles in her dress. She was famously overthinking everything, like the fact that she was about to walk into a party with Julian Smoke on her arm.

Romina put her hands on Amalie's shoulders, looking at her head-on, her expression serious but calming. "Listen to me. You're going to slay this party. Just breathe."

Amalie nodded, standing up straighter. Her chaotic thoughts fell away as soon as she opened the door. She choked on a gasp as her eyes unabashedly drank in the sight of Julian, dressed in a tux that had been perfectly tailored. His hair was combed neatly, the natural wave of it still rebelling over his dark eyebrows. And those damn eyes. They got her every time.

"Uh, oh, hi, hello, hey." *Smooth.* Her cheeks reddened, but she took a deep breath and managed to say, "You clean up nice." Her gaze dropped to a bouquet of perfect pink orchids clutched in Julian's grip, her heart doing a little somersault.

Julian's eyes flared as he studied her from head to toe until his gaze landed on her lips. Amalie tried to school her features, but Julian looked at her like he wanted to eat her up, and honestly, at this point, she was totally on board with that idea.

"God, Amalie, you look"—he let out a ragged breath, his hands clenching briefly and then relaxing—"you look incredible. Wow."

"Why, thank you." Her limbs tingled, a sense of empowerment rushing through her at making someone like Julian stumble with his words.

Julian shot her a panty-dropping look and shook his head. "Damn stunning."

"Indeed she is." Romina piped up, hand on her hip. "Are those flowers for her?"

Julian startled and extended the bouquet to Amalie. "Oh, hey, Ro. And yeah, these are for you, Amalie." He gave his head a little shake and added, "I can't think straight with you dressed like that."

She smiled. It was impossible not to, even though her heart was in her throat. "Thank you for the flowers *and* the compliment. These are my favorite."

"I'll put them in water," Romina said. "You kids get out of here. I don't want you back before midnight." She grabbed the flowers and disappeared into the kitchen.

"I know those are your favorite," Julian responded as he took a step closer, his glance falling to her mouth once more.

Amalie's breath caught in her throat. He wanted to kiss her; she could see it written all over his face, in his eyes, in the way he slowly licked his lips.

Julian reached for a strand of her hair and slipped it between his fingers before offering his arm like a gentleman. "Ready to go?"

She accepted, and for a moment, they just stood there, staring into one another's eyes. This couldn't be. A couple months ago, they'd hated each other.

Hate. Hate. Hate. Anything else had seemed so impossible.

Yet here they were, arm in arm, stepping into the night with enough electricity between them to light the world.

AMALIE AND JULIAN STOOD OUTSIDE SIMONE'S MASSIVE HOME IN ANSLEY Park, a neighborhood nestled right in the middle of downtown Atlanta. Edison bulbs had been carefully strung from tree to tree, illuminating the immaculately landscaped yard. March nights in Georgia had a tendency to be chilly, so no one was out roaming around. Knowing her sister, always the planner, Simone had probably rented a tent with heaters for the backyard. Amalie anxiously twisted a bracelet around her wrist, her palms growing damp as she scanned rows of luxury cars.

"You all right there, princess?" Julian asked, breaking her from her silent freak-out as he leaned closer.

Amalie exhaled and shook her head. "Honestly? No. I'm freaking out a little bit."

Julian gave her a quick nod of understanding as he lifted her chin so that their eyes met. Her pulse went completely mad at his touch.

"Screw these people, Amalie," he said. "You're a force to be reckoned with. If they can't appreciate you, then they can screw off."

She straightened at that, smoothing her dress down. "You know what? You're right. Let's do this," she said, hooking her arm through Julian's, heading straight into the lion's den.

Thankfully, Simone was their first encounter, waiting with a little squeal and a tight hug for Amalie.

"Simone, you look stunning." Amalie brightened as they broke apart, her eyes scanning her sister's lithe frame clad in a gorgeous red dress with a lace bodice.

Simone flapped a hand at her. "Not next to you. Oh, Maxwell is going to eat his little shriveled-up heart out tonight."

This earned a startled laugh from Julian, and Simone's attention zeroed in on him like a hawk. She raised an eyebrow at Amalie and then beamed at Julian as she extended her hand. "I'm Simone, Amalie's extremely rude and boorish sister. Forgive me for unintentionally ignoring you, but as you can see, my sister is quite the goddess and I was distracted."

Julian shook Simone's hand with a smile that took Amalie's breath away. It wasn't fair for someone to look that good. Almost as if she knew what was going on inside Amalie's head, Simone shot her a quick wink.

"Julian Smoke. Nice to meet you, Simone. I've heard a lot about Amalie's infamous sister, so it's nice to finally meet you in the flesh." Amalie turned to him, awestruck. Sometimes she forgot he wasn't always a caveman and that he'd had to schmooze during his days on the pro tennis circuit.

"Likewise, Julian. My sister talks about you all the time, and I have to tell you that we both think what you're doing is incredible." Simone's voice was soft.

Julian hitched his shoulders in a quick shrug, and his mouth kicked up as he said, "Thank you," although his eyes never left Amalie's. She knew she should look away, but she just *couldn't*.

"So Julian, I simply *must* ask, don't you think Amalie is the most gorgeous girl at this party?" Simone spun her hand in an airy motion about the room.

Amalie did everything she could to suppress her groan while telepathically willing Simone to shut her mouth. Julian's gaze raked up and down her body in a sensual caress, hovering in certain places a little longer than others, setting her flesh ablaze. His lips twisted in that sexy grin that often signaled he was up to something. "Amalie's *always* the most beautiful woman in the room."

While Simone looked entirely too pleased with herself, Amalie's heart thrummed in a quick, thunderous beat that echoed all the way into her ears. The pull between her and Julian was strung so tightly that she could almost reach her hand out and strum it with her fingers.

Simone's sudden laugh broke the tension. "Oh, I like this guy, Amalie."

Just as she was about to say something else, one of the caterers approached, stress lining his brow. "Mrs. Lennox? There seems to be a bit of an emergency regarding the crab puffs. Could we perhaps get your approval on something else?"

Simone nodded good-naturedly. "Of course. I'll be there in just a moment." After the caterer disappeared, Simone turned back to Amalie and Julian. "There are bigger issues in the world, yet this is considered an emergency." She shook her head. "I hope to catch you both again tonight, and Julian, it was wonderful to meet you."

"Likewise," Julian answered smoothly.

With that, Simone kissed Amalie on the cheek and disappeared into a sea of glittering diamonds.

"Well now, there's not much else for us to do besides hit the dance floor," Amalie said. "Tell me, Smoke, do you dance?" She playfully hip-checked him.

His gaze darkened instantly. He watched her with a predatory, hot-blooded stare that should've sent her running. Instead, it woke places that had lain dormant for far too long. She felt alive for the first time in years. The revelation had her fingers itching to reach out and touch him.

"I dance as well as I play tennis," he answered, his voice huskier than before.

Julian extended his elbow, and her stomach swooped as she linked her arm through his. She felt all kinds of eyes on them as they made their way through the crowd. Julian was a beautiful specimen of a man, and she wasn't surprised people were studying him like a walking piece of art.

The dance floor was exactly where she'd anticipated—housed in a white tent in the backyard, filled with fancy heaters to offset the early spring chill. It felt like they were making the climb to Everest with how long it was taking them to reach it. Just as Amalie saw the band and tasted sweet victory, Satan's spawn and his over-enunciated words caused her to freeze in her tracks.

"Amalie? Is that *you*?" Maxwell asked, derision obvious in his tone.

Julian's hand tightened at her waist, his body moving closer to hers almost as if to shield her from a threat.

Maxwell's voice was so completely opposite of Julian's. There was nothing decadent or sexy about it.

Amalie tensed, hearing the words he'd hurled at her the night she realized just how toxic he really was—that she'd only made the bestseller list because of who her daddy was, that she was a nobody and wasn't cut out for writing. Slowly she and Julian faced Maxwell the third, or as they both had started referring to him, Maxwell the Douche.

Julian's lips tipped into a wry grin. Maxwell wasn't an ugly guy, but standing next to Julian he looked like a hobbit. He had muddy brown eyes that rarely expressed an emotion other than greed. His wheat-colored hair was short and spiked up all over the place, doing nothing to hide his receding hairline. His lips were too thin, his face too babyish, his body too beanpole. On Maxwell's arm was an orange girl with platinum blonde hair that was so big—like 1980's beauty queen contestant big—that Amalie was in awe of whatever brand of hairspray the girl used. But Amalie's eyes didn't linger there for long as her gaze dropped to the girl's perfectly manicured talons that were digging into Maxwell's arm.

"Who else would it be?" Amalie asked.

Julian drew her even closer. Being this near to him was intoxicating. To make matters worse, his thumb began brushing soft circles on her waist. She had never loved a backless dress more than she did right then.

Call it temporary insanity, but she gave in to the charade. She swung her arm around Julian's narrow waist and gripped his jacket.

Maxwell watched their interaction with disdain, his lip curled into a sneer. Of course, he did the insecure posturing thing and ran his eyes over Julian, sizing him up before speaking again. "This must be the tennis player who can't cut it and needs your dad to float him, just like Andrew did for you all those years ago."

He might as well have said, "This is the dog shit on my shoe." It would've sounded the same.

Julian, despite his extreme ego, let it roll right off him. But Amalie was not about to do the same. "Not that it's any of your business," she said, "but he's a legit contender for the US Open. I'm writing a book about his comeback." She shot Julian a winning smile to punctuate her point.

Maxwell, who always did have a low-key tendency to be smarmy, coughed out a little mirthless laugh into his fist. "Oh, right. This is that last little project that I've been hearing about at the country club. The one that's going to be your wake-up call to join the rest of us in the real world."

Oh hell no. Amalie was about to let him have it, but Julian shifted the slightest bit, his touch becoming more possessive. "*This* is the clown you wasted all those years on?" He gave Maxwell a *go to hell* look and then squeezed her hip. "You are way too good for him, Amalie. Come on, babe. Let's dance."

The astonished expression on Maxwell's face was absolutely priceless.

As she let Julian lead her toward the dance floor, Amalie touched her lips, surprised at the smile she found stretched there. It had been so long since she had someone on her side, and it felt good.

The dance floor was dimly lit, and a band played in the far corner. As if on cue, a stunning instrumental version of one of Amalie's favorite songs, "The Very Thought of You" by Billie Holiday, began to play. It was a weird movie-moment coincidence, but then her eyes darted to the band in time to see Simone wink and then disappear. That explained it.

"Thank you for having my back," Amalie whispered as Julian wrapped his arms around her, pulling her close.

"I'm willing to have your front, too, if you're ever interested." The left side of his sulky lips tipped higher, revealing his dimple, making him look even more sinful.

"Julian!" she squeaked before resting her head on his chest to hide her flaming face. His words stirred something inside her, and she was dangerously close to just letting him have at it. *So, so close.* Somehow, she managed to say, "That is *not* what friends do."

She lifted her head in time to see Julian's lips tilt as he swallowed. "Some do." His eyes smoldered, his pupils wide and full of desire. "That Maxwell guy?" he said by way of subject change as he shook his head. "You have no idea how badly I wanted to knock the shit out of him. What did you ever see in that guy? You're, well, you're *you*, and he's an asshole who wouldn't even begin to know how to make you happy."

She worried her bottom lip between her teeth as she tightened her grip around his neck in an effort to keep her hands from running through his hair. She wanted to blurt out, "Would *you* know how to make me happy?" Instead, she asked him, "What do you mean I'm *me*?"

His fingers gently traced a line down her cheek. "I think you know what I meant by that," he said, the hand still around her waist pressing deeper, trembling. Something inside of her came undone as she realized he was nervous.

"Julian." His name was breathy as she spoke it. She wasn't sure what her next words were going to be, but she felt certain that at the end of them he would kiss her senseless. She could feel it in the way his eyes caressed her skin, in the tightly coiled tension of his body.

Just as she was about to speak, not caring about the consequences, she saw movement out of the corner of her eye. It took everything she had not to unleash a string of curses that would make a sailor blush.

Andrew Warner tapped Julian on the shoulder. "Mind if I cut in?" His Savannah drawl sliced the moment to ribbons.

Amalie and Julian jumped apart like guilty teenagers. Irritation pricked at her as she gave her father a bored look, her tone matching as she said, "Dad." Seeing that he wasn't going anywhere, she released a heavy sigh. "Maybe we ought to talk *off* the dance floor."

Not waiting for either man to follow, she deftly maneuvered through the crowd, but not before grabbing a glass of champagne from a passing waiter. Then she stupidly showed her cards as she came to a halt, taking a long, loud gulp.

"I had to come over and meet my investment," Andrew said, sizing Julian up before shoving a hand toward him. "Andrew Warner. Nice to finally meet you, my boy."

Amalie nearly choked on her drink. She wasn't offended that he hadn't come over to see *her*. No, she was used to being an afterthought. It was the fact that he'd belittled Julian. An *investment*? *Boy*? Her blood boiled as she watched the two. She wanted to snap, but somehow she held herself together, and God bless Julian for being more collected than she could ever be.

Andrew clapped Julian on the back and added, "You were great at Georgia. *Three* national championships? Unheard of."

Julian muttered an embarrassed, "Thanks."

"You know I'm an alumnus there. I've been paying for you for a while. You know I always contribute—obviously, I still am."

Amalie couldn't even make herself look at Julian. No wonder he'd called her "rich girl" with such venom.

"Um, that's an inappropriate thing to say, Dad." The words were awkward and stilted, but they were out there.

Andrew's shrewd gaze zeroed in on her. "Oh, Amalie, come now and grow up. Everything boils down to money, and if I recall, you wouldn't be on this little adventure if it weren't for *my* money."

The mortification from earlier grew while Julian's discomfort showed as he shifted his weight from foot to foot, his shoulders taut.

"My daughter here is different, Julian. I tried to tell her to get a real job and quit this silly writing thing. If she was writing the great American novel, fine. But let's face it, she's not. All I want is for her to be taken care of, to have security like her sister. My Simone"—he lifted his hand to where Simone stood, chatting up an old couple in the corner—"travels the world doing advertising for Warner Hotels."

Knife to the heart, twist, and turn. It was almost an audible sound, the squelch of her heart being ripped to shreds by the man who was supposed to always protect it, to protect *her*.

Hot tears stung behind Amalie's eyes, but she refused to cry. Julian's hand suddenly wrapped around hers, his fingers easily lacing through her own, his touch calming the dizzying nausea washing over her. When she dragged her humiliated stare to meet his, she recoiled before drawing closer. The anger in his eyes was beyond anything she'd ever seen on or off the court.

His voice came out just short of a polite growl. "With all due respect, Mr. Warner, you're being an asshole, not only to me but most importantly to your daughter." He squeezed Amalie's hand in emphasis.

Her lips parted in surprise. No one ever spoke back to Andrew Warner, inside or outside of the board room.

"She's a brilliant writer and an even better person," Julian continued, "and I expect her to be treated as such. Oh, and by the way, I'm not your fucking investment, and I'm not your boy. Come on, Amalie." Julian led her around her father without a backward glance, maneuvering them through the tent and outside to the brick pathway that led to the front yard. They didn't stop until they reached the sidewalk, where Julian's car was parked.

Moonlight painted the hardened angles of his face in an ethereal silver glow. Amalie honestly would've studied him the entire evening, cataloging his striking features in her memory, the twitch and pop of his steely jaw, the pull of his dark, arched brows over eyes that begged for something—a word, a glance, *anything* from her. Then the reality of what just happened and what it could've cost them doused her like a bucket of ice water, her earlier lust replaced by her blood crackling in her ears. Andrew Warner was a force to be reckoned with, and he was their meal ticket.

A meal ticket Julian just pissed off.

"What did you just do?" She disentangled herself from Julian's reassuring touch, ignoring how cold and alone she suddenly felt without it. He'd gotten in her head tonight—the magic of the party, his body in a tux, his overwhelming good looks—everything had her all messed up and beyond confused. "You probably just cost us everything."

A grim laugh tumbled from his mouth as he cocked an eyebrow. "So you wanted me to stand there and *let* your father degrade you? Better yet, why didn't *you* stand up to him? You're fiery as hell with everyone else."

She straightened her spine, shocked it was still a firm row of bones given that he was right. "You don't know what you're talking about."

"I think I do."

Amalie lifted her chin. "How could you know? You, the man who's afraid to talk about his past? It's like you're so busy being weighed down by it that you can't even look toward your future, something that could bring us both down if you're not careful."

Julian reeled and Amalie wanted to cram those words back into her mouth, but it was too late. Besides, she'd meant them, hadn't she?

"So, that's what this all boils down to, huh? Always coming back to what I can do for you?"

"Which isn't much."

Julian shook his head in disbelief and narrowed his eyes at her, as though he didn't know the woman standing before him. "You know that's not true," he said. "But maybe if you stood up to your father, you wouldn't have to do this in the first place."

Oh, how wrong he was. It didn't matter what she did, it would always lead to this push of working for the family business, because what else did she have?

"Again, you don't know what you're talking about."

He jabbed his fists into his pants pockets. "It doesn't matter. Don't worry about me ever speaking up or defending you again. Come on, let me take you home."

She stiffened. Was he for real? What he couldn't even begin to fathom was that if she made a move against her father, she would lose her world—her house, food, inheritance, you name it. The only things that truly belonged to her were the clothes in her closet and her car, which she purchased with her book royalties. She didn't even know where she'd go if she didn't play by her father's rules.

Shame wrapped her in a suffocating embrace as she kept reminding herself that she was a grown woman who shouldn't be afraid of retribution from her father. But she was.

However, this thing with Julian was an area of her life she *could* control.

With straightened shoulders and head held high, she bared her teeth. "I don't need you to defend me, and I sure as hell don't need you to take me home."

She reached down and pulled off her high-heeled shoes and ran, those early morning runs with Julian actually paying off. She disappeared into the house, into the throng of people, pretending she didn't hear Julian calling her name, pretending she hadn't fallen a little bit in love with the jerk for standing up to her dad when no one else would.

AMALIE THANKED THE UBER DRIVER AND FUMBLED WITH HER KEYS AS SHE made her way around her father's house, avoiding going inside. When she reached the pool house, her hand went to the door to find that it was already unlocked. She knew exactly who awaited her. Part of her yearned to turn and run, but another part, the fiery part that Julian referenced earlier, became an inferno which forced her to open the door.

Her father sat perched on her couch, his hands steepled as his icy glare speared her. Judge, jury, and executioner. "Amalie."

"What are you doing here? You can't just barge into my place," she said, anger and indignation rising in her veins.

Her father stood, his hands sliding into his pockets. "You forget that it's not yours. It could be though, if you'd just let me take care of you. Think of it, you could stay here, and we could be a family. I know I was absent most of your childhood and then your mother left—"

She dropped the heels dangling from her fingertips, the sound deafening as the shoes clattered to the floor. "Whatever it is you're about to say, *don't*. I'm so tired of your excuses."

Her father lifted an eyebrow, although it was a struggle for him to show any type of expression. "In that case, let's cut to the chase. You need to know that I won't stand for you and that tennis player—"

"Julian. His name is *Julian*."

"Fine, I won't stand for you and *Julian* treating me as you did. I've been thinking that maybe I made a mistake backing this venture. I thought this would be a good wake-up call for you, but—" Her father shook his head, derision oozing from his tone when he spoke. "It's time for you to give up this charade." Andrew's mouth twisted, a sour expression slipping across his face as he continued. "You'll take over Simone's job in advertising. I'm moving her into the CEO position because she wants to be home more and because I'd like more time to play golf. Doesn't that sound wonderful? You'd get to travel the world, on my dime."

Amalie sucked in a breath. He wasn't even going to let her see this through. In her father's eyes, she'd failed before she'd even started. It was what he wanted all along, to keep her under his control. Her heart had already been torn to shreds by this man and now it felt completely obliterated, nothing left except for a gaping black hole.

Writing was everything. She lived for the smooth sailing of her fingers over her laptop keys, the satisfaction of writing the perfect line, of feeling that hum of magic in her veins as a story came to life right before her eyes. There would be no time for writing if her father had his way. Working for him would suck away every ounce of creativity from her life.

Her mind raced, trying to figure out if there was a way to do this without him. There had to be. There was no way she was going to go work for him, to have her soul slowly siphoned away every single day.

Pulling in shallow breaths, she said, "And if I refuse?"

Her father's expression faltered slightly but quickly righted itself. "Then you'll need to find somewhere to live."

It was the answer she'd anticipated, one last attempt to keep her under his thumb.

"Fine. I'll leave," she responded flatly. Had she really just said that? *Holy shit.*

Her father blinked slowly and then shook his head, and with that, everything was back in place. "Then you'd better start packing."

"Yeah, guess so." She stormed off, leaving her father standing alone as she disappeared into her bedroom, where she moved on autopilot, grabbing a suitcase and throwing clothes inside.

Her entire world had just been submerged into a fishbowl. *Oh my God, what have I done?* She could stay with Romina for the night, but after that where would she go? Where would she work?

Acid burned the back of her throat as she hastily pulled designer clothes off hangers and shoved them into her suitcase. "Amalie," her father's cold voice came from the doorway.

"What, *Father*?" Fury ignited her tone. She'd moved on to shoes.

"You can't be serious. You have no means. You can't do anything, can't survive without me."

"That's where you're wrong!" She stuffed what would have to be the last of her belongings into her suitcase, not even looking at him as she strode from the room and tore the key off her key ring, slamming it down on the kitchen table. She was in her car and squealing down their gravel driveway before she even realized it.

Only when she got to the main road did she completely fall apart.

Chapter Fourteen

JULIAN

Julian hadn't seen Amalie in over a week, not since the party. He'd even gone by the pool house, only to find out from a maid that she'd left. He knew one person who'd know where she was, however.

"You know I can't tell you." Romina sat behind her desk, arms crossed, ponytail swinging as she shook her head.

"But I need to see her, Romina." He sat down in the chair across from her. "I'm worried. I know what I did might've messed things up, but me and Amalie...we can figure it out. I feel like shit, and look, I don't... I'm not good at any of this. Never have been. But damn it, I'm going to start trying."

Romina's face softened. "For her. You're going to start trying for her, aren't you?"

His hands curled over his knees. That's what he was saying, wasn't it? Even if he hadn't realized it. Otherwise, why did it bother him so much that he hadn't heard one of her wisecracks or seen that gorgeous face?

A strange feeling pierced his heart.

Romina waved him off. "You don't have to say anything. It's all over your face. Don't worry, your secret's safe with me, especially since you two are business partners, or whatever." Her eye roll told him she didn't exactly believe that. "I'll tell you where she is, but I'm also going to make sure you hear what I have to say first, 'kay?"

She tightened her ponytail as if to punctuate her words, and all Julian could think was, *Oh shit*. In his experience, when girls tightened their ponytails things were about to go down. He braced himself.

"You're going to be nice to her. Y'all can keep on with that hot banter, but no more talk about her being a rich girl, because as of a week ago, she's dead-ass broke. And I have you to thank for that."

Bile rose in his throat. Seeing his expression, Romina shook her head. "No, you don't understand what I'm saying—it's a good thing. Her dad is toxic, and honestly, I have no idea how she survived in that environment for as long as she did."

"Because she's tough," Julian interrupted.

Romina nodded. "Damn right, she is. So for her to get out of that, thank you, because now maybe she'll be able to breathe and write that second bestseller that's eluded her. But you're going to treat her like the Queen of England, do you understand? She's low right now and trying to figure out her life, and she doesn't need you stomping all over her heart on top of everything else. When you see her, you better remove whatever issue there is between you two and help Amalie—and yourself—move forward. If you don't, I'll have your balls in a vise grip so fast, your head will spin."

Julian choked back a laugh. This girl was scary as hell, but he had mad respect. She had her best friend's back, and since that best friend was Amalie, well, he was glad she was on her team.

After promising Romina that he understood, he headed to her apartment to face Amalie. Each step leading to the second floor made his pulse pound harder, the sound of his sneakers on the concrete like the soundtrack to a final showdown. God, he prayed that it wouldn't be the end. The thought of losing Amalie scared the shit out of him. And he wasn't ready to give up on the US Open, either.

The door swung open before he even had a chance to knock, and there she was, like a ray of sunshine. Seven days felt like years now that he was standing there speechless and drinking in every little thing about her.

It was two in the afternoon, and she was in her palm leaf-print pajamas that were cute as hell, and her hair was a tangled, frizzy mess on top of her head, but she was still the most beautiful damn thing he'd ever laid eyes on. He wanted to open his mouth and let those words come spilling out, but then she narrowed red-rimmed eyes at him, sizing him up. It was obvious the wisest thing to do was let her speak first.

"Romina called to give me a heads-up. What do you want?" Her voice had lost that lyrical lilt. Instead, it was flat and lifeless.

"I wanted to see you. I missed you." His voice cracked. Could she hear how much he meant it? His hand came up to rest on the doorjamb while he silently prayed she wouldn't slam the door on his fingers.

Amalie rubbed her arms absently, her mask of indifference slipping. "Missed me?" She sounded like a child who couldn't fathom that someone would feel that way about her.

Man, he was one lucky bastard to even know her. How could she not see her own worth every time she looked in the mirror? From here on out he would do everything in his power to make sure she knew how important she was, how fucking amazing she was.

"I did. I *do*. I'm here to apologize and to pay you back." He leaned close enough to smell her intoxicating perfume.

Her face screwed up in confusion. "Pay me back?"

"Let me in and I'll explain."

He could see her weighing her options as she nibbled at her bottom lip, and he had to force himself to look away because all he could think about was how those lips would taste. Sadly, he hadn't thought of much else since he'd held her in his arms on the dance floor.

"Fine." She moved back from the door and opened it wider so that he could come in.

His focus immediately snagged on the couch, where pillows and blankets were haphazardly piled at the end. On the coffee table were scattered pages and her old, trusty gray journal, along with her laptop.

She made a sweeping gesture, her voice acidic. "Welcome to my home. A couch and a coffee table." She crossed her arms over her chest, her lip trembling as she looked away.

A crack like an electric charge shot through his heart. In two steps he was standing in front of her, arms wrapped around her shaking frame, his lips kissing her hair. "I'm so sorry," he murmured.

Her hands gripped him tighter in response, like she needed this.

"You're the toughest person I know, princess. If you want to fall apart right now, I'm here. I'll help put you back together, okay?"

Amalie nodded against his chest, a few stray sniffles escaping, and then she moved away from him so fast it was like the moment had been a figment of his imagination.

She wiped her face with the back of her hand, straightened her shoulders, and just like that, he watched Amalie's defenses snap right back into place.

"So, are you sorry that I'm here sleeping on Romina's couch, or are you sorry that I don't have the money to help you now? I figure Romina told you my father cut his funding."

Julian hadn't fully thought through the implications of her choice to move out and how that affected him. Yeah, there'd been those annoying sneaking doubts that failure was already happening, especially after he got his ass kicked by a seventeen-year-old kid, but he sure as hell wasn't ready to throw in the towel yet. He shook his head as a thought crashed through his mind, knocking something loose and sending an epiphany shooting forward.

"You want the truth? The truth is that I'm sorry for all of it, but even though we're down, we're not out. Here, sit." He motioned to the sofa scattered with papers, and he chose a chair next to it, leaning forward, hands clasped. Reluctantly, Amalie sat down.

"I'm not sorry for taking up for you. I'll never apologize for that, but I am sorry for how I went about it," he began.

Amalie inched forward, placing a hand on his. "No. Don't apologize for that. I've replayed that night on a loop, and I'm mortified by how I acted. That's why I haven't tried to contact you. I should've reached out to you sooner and apologized. I was awful and I'm sorry."

Julian shook his head. "Apology not needed."

She remained silent for several heartbeats, picking at the sofa. "So what are you going to do about...stuff?"

Julian knew what she wasn't saying, could still feel her walls up a mile high. He also realized that what he was about to do would change everything between them, and would hopefully prove to Amalie that he was all in.

"I've got to do this tennis thing whether you help me or not." His hands gripped the arms of the chair as he took a deep breath and then let the truth slide out. "My dad was my first coach when I started playing at five. He was amazing and had tennis in his DNA."

Amalie gasped, her hand moving to her neck. "Like you," she spoke gently.

He shook his head. "Not like me."

"You can say whatever you want to downplay your talent," she said fiercely, "but you don't get that kind of skill by training, Julian. It's something that comes naturally."

Her words wrapped around his heart, meaning way more than they should. He inclined his head slightly, his "Thank you" hushed. "Anyway, I went pro at twenty-one. It got off to a good start, but then I started to fade."

Amalie nodded. "Now *that* I did know. That and Nadine, but that's for another time."

Nadine. His jaw clenched. He'd rather have a prostate exam than ever talk about that woman.

Julian swallowed the lump in his throat—he had to get this out. "My dad was everything good in my life, but I got lost somewhere along the way despite everything he instilled in me." The words were becoming harder to say. After all, this is what had been eating away at him, bit by bit, for the last nine years. Hell, even before his dad died.

Amalie placed a hand on his forearm, her touch soothing and steadying. He tried to overlook the way his heart sped up. He was thirty years old, for crying out loud. One single touch should not undo him, but Amalie wasn't your average woman, either.

"When I started to suck, my dad wanted me to go back on the Challenger Series to find my way again. I refused. Quitting the pro circuit and going back down to the Challenger world would be embarrassing, not to mention a huge blow to my ego."

"And then Anthony approached you when you were weak?"

He nodded, anger flooding his veins at the thought of that vulture. "Yeah, when he approached me, I didn't hesitate. I jumped at the chance to remain pro with all of the perks, without even discussing it with my father. I thought I knew everything."

"And that's changed?" Amalie asked sarcastically, throwing a pointed glance at him. She was attempting to lighten the mood, and the fact that she cared enough to do that caused his breath to bottle up inside his chest.

His first instinct was to blurt out some smart-ass comment in reply, but Amalie, completely oblivious of the effect she had on him, added, "So tell me, what was it about having Anthony as your agent that enticed you so much?"

He ran a hand through his hair, his eyes focused on the beige carpet, careful to avoid her gaze even though he could feel it boring into the side of his face. "It was his talk of fame and endorsements and girls that had me intrigued. I wanted all of those things, Amalie, and I didn't care how I got them, even if it meant losing my love for the sport or firing my dad after... after everything he'd given up for me, everything he'd done for me."

"Julian..." Her voice was soft, but it still echoed through the quiet of the apartment. "We don't have to—"

"No. I need to. I owe it to you." He met her wide eyes. "You're the only person I've ever talked about this with, and if I just get it out, then maybe I won't always feel like I'm suffocating."

She gave him a reassuring nod. "Tell me everything, then."

Julian focused on just how easy it was to do that with this girl. He'd been engaged to Nadine for six months, and they'd never talked about anything other than sex, money, or parties.

"When I was a kid, my dad worked two jobs so that my mom could stay home with me. What he didn't tell me, what my mom let slip later on, was that he had a third job on the weekends. He worked so that I could have the best tennis equipment and gear."

"I wish I could've met him," Amalie interrupted, her voice sad. "He sounds like a great man and a great dad."

"He would've loved you," Julian said, trying to somehow loosen the clenching fist that gripped his heart.

Amalie laughed, a soft tinkling sound. "We could've double-teamed you with the ball busting."

Julian snorted. "Yeah, I could totally see that going down."

Amalie's voice turned serious again. "So what did your dad say about Anthony?"

It was suddenly too hot. Julian pulled at the neck of his shirt, feeling strangled by it. These memories were the tough ones, but they were the ones he pulled out and shuffled through at night as he tried to drift to sleep. They consisted of moments where he asked, "What if?" What if he'd actually kept his dad as his coach during his pro months? Where would he be now? Would his dad still be alive? Would he be proud of Julian?

"He said Anthony was scum and that I needed to get out of my contract." His foot bounced with the words, his hands twisting in his lap. He wanted to close his eyes, to breathe deeply, but this was like pulling off a band-aid, the quicker, the better.

His dad was wearing his favorite blue tennis shirt, his hair thinning a lot more than it had in recent years, his eyes, the unusual green that were exact replicas of Julian's, were tired and drawn.

"This is a huge mistake, Julian. Anthony will ruin you and move on, but not before he sucks the life out of you," Oliver Smoke warned, his mouth set in a grim line as he watched his son with a mixture of worry and disappointment. "He only cares about the money and fame."

A mirthless laugh broke free from Julian. "Is there really anything else, Dad?"

They were the words that a punk kid would say, one who didn't know anything about the world and how it operated.

He'd never forget the way his father looked at him then, the way he'd averted his eyes as if he didn't recognize his own son anymore. "Yes, son," he'd said. "There's tennis, a love for the game, something you've lost sight of, and it shows on the court. You're distracted by your desire for those other things, things that don't matter when you're doing what you love."

Julian had never been much of a hothead. His parents had taught him to keep his head down and set a good example. But in those days leading up to finalizing his contract with Fox and the fallout afterward, Julian found himself turning into someone he didn't want to be. He grew angrier quicker, said things he didn't mean just because he knew they'd sting. And that's what he'd done to his father on that awful, terrible day.

He still remembered the way the anger snaked through his veins, the snarl in his voice as he slung barbs at his father, knowing he didn't mean a single word that came out of his mouth.

"Maybe you're just jealous that I'm doing what you never could." His father, a proud and tall man, hunched over in defeat, as if Julian's words had been a physical blow.

"Julian, if you believe that, I'm sorry. You know everything your mother and I have ever done was for you. But I see it's time we step back and let you make your own decisions." Oliver clapped him on the shoulder, his eyes sad. "But no matter what, we'll always love you and be proud to call you our son."

Even now Julian felt sick as fresh pain and regret shrouded those memories. That had not been the last time he'd seen or talked to his dad. He eventually apologized, but things never felt the same after that. Then a few months later his father died of a heart attack while mowing the grass. Julian carried the burden of that guilt and sorrow with him every day and wondered if it would ever get better.

Amalie sat in silence as Julian finished his story, her eyes glassy. "I know 'I'm sorry' isn't really enough," she finally spoke, "but it's a start. I'm sorry about your dad, but I can tell you that he'd be so proud of you right now."

Julian nodded, surprised at the emotion in her voice, the protectiveness that encased her words.

Desperate for a subject change, his eyes flicked to the pages scattered on the couch, reaching out for a few of them. He caught Pen and Jax's name across them. "I see you're not done writing Jax and Penelope's story, which makes me happier than you'll ever know."

Amalie scrunched her nose as she made a face, taking the pages from his hands. "Actually, I've given up on the story. Not writing. I plan to start a new story soon, but I, uh, I realized I couldn't write this one without you, so I decided to be done with it."

It felt like a fist held Julian's heart in a vise grip. "But are you done with me?"

Amalie's already intense stare brightened. Those blue-gray eyes, always so wild. He couldn't help but wonder if they ever calmed, if there was ever a time when Amalie didn't carry the pressures of the world on her shoulders. Damn if he wouldn't like to be the man to help shoulder some of that pain, to be the reason she felt whole again.

"Julian..." He could feel Amalie studying him as she fidgeted. "Honestly, before you showed up, I was done with you, not because I was angry but because I didn't feel like you took this seriously, like it meant as much to you. You always held something back, but now..." She shook her head. "Now you've told me everything. You've given me that last piece of yourself that you've been holding back and well, it's changed things. You know when I first met you, I felt a spark, and tonight, I felt it again. But..." Her posture slumped. "What about the money?"

He touched her skin, unable to help himself. "Amalie, it's not about the money. It was nice while it lasted, but I don't think for a minute that you and I can't make things happen on our own. I just need to know if we're still...a team."

Excitement danced across her face as Amalie sat ramrod straight, and it took all he had not to let his eyes drop to her braless chest. She took a deep breath, which didn't help his gaze-aversion difficulties, and then said, "You know what? I'm *not* done with this. I'm not done with *you*, not by a long shot. Hell yes, we're still a team. I can offer my credit card, which I happen to pay the bill for, along with what I have left from book royalties. I've applied for some freelance writing positions, too, which can help."

The passion in her voice was a living, breathing thing that held the power to completely unravel him. She was still in this, even though she didn't owe him a damn thing. It felt like Julian was able to take his first full breath in days as a weight lifted from his shoulders.

"Hey, don't worry. We'll talk to Paul and figure it out. I can sell my drugs—"

Amalie's breath hitched, which caused him to chuckle. "Pharmaceuticals, princess. You know, my day job? Besides, I have a ton of vacation days saved up since I never had a life aside from eating, drinking, working, fu—" At Amalie's pointed look, he redirected that last line. "Dating."

Her eyes were downcast as she smoothed out her pajamas, her reply quick as she muttered under her breath, "You wouldn't even know how to date."

He moved nearer, studying the freckles across her nose just as she lifted her face. His voice dipped low. "Jealous? We can remedy that if you want." He wiggled his eyebrows so she could take it as a joke or read between the lines and find the truth hidden somewhere in there. Because it was there, all right.

Amalie rolled her eyes. "Dream on."

Julian couldn't help himself, his grin widening so much that his cheeks hurt. "Stardust, I know you're developing feelings for me, which is perfectly normal. I totally understand that. I mean, I am a supreme athlete, after all."

Amalie scoffed even though she refused to meet his stare. "Umm, no. That's, ah, no."

Huh. Very interesting.

"And why Stardust? Like David Bowie or...?"

"No." His fingers gently traced the freckles high on her cheeks and across the bridge of her nose before leaning back. "Like the freckles across your face. They make these patterns that remind me of constellations, so they're basically stardust."

Amalie licked her lips, and the movement had Julian completely entranced. "I like that."

They may have lost Andrew Warner and his financial backing, but it looked like they still had each other, and that had to count for something.

Chapter Fifteen

JULIAN

Breaking the news of Andrew Warner's financial exit to Paul went a lot better than expected. Apparently, Andrew had everything paid up until the end of the month, but after that, Paul agreed to coach Julian for free. He said he "felt Julian had the right stuff and wasn't a complete waste of time" after seeing him hang with that kid, Wesley Walker, in the Jekyll tournament. Paul wasn't the biggest fan of Andrew Warner anyway, so yeah, that helped, too. Romina was united in the "I Hate Andrew Warner" tour and was also training Julian for free.

Training tripled in intensity, but Julian didn't mind. The more Paul kept him busy, the less opportunity he had to think about Amalie and how protective she was of him and how that pretty much softened his Grinch heart.

March bled into April, and April blew through to May. June arrived before he knew it. It was amazing how time passed so quickly when you were busy being a damn adult. Julian was exhausted from having to schmooze and kiss ass all day at work and then practicing for hours on end at night. He hardly recognized the interior of his own apartment, rarely there for more than a few hours at a time, and those hours were pretty much spent with his eyes closed. Amalie stayed busy taking on as many freelance jobs as she could, even stepping in as a secretary for Romina, a position they all knew Ro made up just for Amalie. He admired Ro for that.

Since it was the weekend, Julian had an early morning training with Paul, even though he wanted to hit the snooze button when his alarm went off. He gulped down the rest of what Amalie called his "plant vomit" smoothie and then made his way onto the court, already tired, and Paul hadn't even made him run yet.

He'd already started sweating on the short walk, the humidity enough to strangle him. When he arrived, Amalie was there, sitting on the bleachers, notebook in hand, and stifling a yawn. Julian hated not getting to see her as much as he used to. It was probably for the best, though, because if things were the way they used to be, he would've already kissed her and told her exactly how much he thought about her (which was entirely too much to be considered healthy). Better not to shit where you eat and all those platitudes.

They had managed to find time for a few Write Nights, where they worked on chapters of her novel, all while he fought his animal instincts like a boss. She'd also made decent progress on her own, though Jax was a little too much like Julian for his liking, but he'd known that would be the case when he signed up for this. He also found it kind of flattering.

Paul, of course, looked fresh as a daisy, smacking on his gum. "All right, kids, gather 'round." Amalie offered a sleepy nod as she met them at the net. Julian's eyes scanned her bare legs, enjoying the fact that the weather was hot enough for shorts because, damn, her legs were something else. She wore a black tank that had little brown buttons, a few of the top ones undone, just enough to hint at her cleavage beneath the fabric. Although all of that was sexy, he enjoyed her mind even more, which he reminded himself as he dragged his gaze away from her pale skin and back to her face.

Of course she caught him. One eyebrow raised, the ghost of a smile lingering over her lips.

He winked as he waited to hear what his coach had to say.

Paul cleared his throat. "Amalie, you know I like having you around here, but for the next month or so it's gonna be just me and Julian. It's the only way I can get him to stop staring at you."

Julian jerked his head back. "I'm not looking at her." He totally *was* looking at her. He was always looking at her. He slid a quick side-eyed glance at Amalie, who seemed to be enjoying this a little too much.

Paul, God bless him, continued as if Julian wasn't even there. "It makes sense anyways that you're not gonna be here. You gotta work now." Hooking a thumb toward Julian, he added, "He's working, too, so we ain't got time to play relationship."

Julian and Amalie stared at one another, that familiar tension between them still taut and alive as ever.

The thought of seeing her even less than he already did made Julian question his sanity. He was letting their steam-roller connection sputter in neutral while he chased this tennis dream that might not even amount to anything. Was he a fool? Nothing promised him that Amalie would be around forever. There was no guarantee that some other man, one who could give her the attention she needed, wouldn't come along and sweep her right out of Julian's reach.

Before he could protest, Amalie smiled, a tight, false expression that didn't touch her eyes. She looked sad, but Julian couldn't tell if that was just his wishful thinking reading more into her response than really existed. "No problem," she said to Paul, but her eyes—those stunning eyes —stayed locked on Julian. "Consider me as good as gone."

Paul looked between them, as though he could see their chemistry humming in the air. "It's just temporary, you two."

At the same time, Julian and Amalie came to life, nodding with crumpled brows, saying things like, *Oh, we know, it's fine, really. It's no big deal. Not a problem.*

But it *wasn't* fine. It *was* a big deal. It *was* a problem. At least to Julian, anyway.

Paul patted them both on the shoulder. "Now that we got that over with," he said, "let's get on with practice. Better make it a good one Julian, since Amalie here won't be seeing you until sectionals."

He glanced at Amalie, who speared him with a look he was fairly certain had been forged from her own panic, a look she was trying very hard to make appear as something else. He knew the feeling, only he wasn't so good at hiding it.

As they followed Paul, walking side by side, Julian let his fingers tangle with Amalie's. She didn't pull away. Instead, she looked up at him and said, "It's only a month. It'll be fine." Then, as though covering her tracks, she added, "We'll be back to Write Nights in no time."

He squeezed her fingers, hoping she was right.

Julian and Paul trained harder than ever during the month of June. After each practice, as soon as Julian got home, he couldn't help but text Amalie.

Julian: Hey. Whatcha doing?

Amalie: Working on the book. Oh! I need to send you a picture of this lizard-shaped cheese puff I just found.

Julian snorted. She always knew how to cheer him up. Practice had been rough, and he needed a pick-me-up.

Julian: Send a pic. Do you have any questions for me?

Amalie: I do, actually. I'll call.

Before he could finish reading the text, his phone rang.

"Hey, you," she said by way of greeting. Her voice felt like sunshine, and it hit him in the gut at how much he missed her.

"Hey. Practice isn't the same without you."

"You miss my face, don't you?"

"Actually, I do."

A pause, a throat clearing. He regretted nothing.

"Well, I didn't realize I was such a distraction that I needed to give you some space," she joked—there was no malice in her words, just honesty. He could almost envision her smile.

"You have no idea. Kinda hard not to notice the beautiful redhead sitting in the bleachers every day."

She laughed at that. "Well then maybe this is a good thing. I don't want to divert your attention away from the game. That's what's important right now."

Julian wasted no time, since it was the perfect segue. "Speaking of what's important, I have to know, are you just sitting around eating cheese puffs in your underwear?"

Amalie snorted, and he noticed it sounded a little freer than her usual laughter. "Actually, I'm in my underwear and nightshirt, but close enough.

And it's not just cheese puffs. I've thrown some wine in there too. Romina's staying over with her boy toy, so I have the apartment to myself."

Julian tried not to choke on the water he'd just taken a sip of. Images of Amalie in a nightshirt and sexy little lacy undies ran rampant through his mind. What he wouldn't give to take her clothes off, explore her until she was about to fall apart, and then put her back together again.

He tried to control his breathing, to calm the heat rushing through his body. Before he could even come up with a response, to make some provocative remark, Amalie acted as if she hadn't just dropped a bomb on him.

"Ugh, this sofa is just not...comfortable." Her words were strained as he heard her moving around.

"Well, I sleep in a king-size bed that you're welcome to share anytime."

Now *that* would be a sight to see. He imagined her writhing beneath him, could almost hear the sounds she'd make. His dick hardened at the thought.

Completely oblivious to Julian's struggle, Amalie continued. "We'll see. Anyway, let me ask you about this tennis match I'm working on. I'm trying to figure out what it feels like to win. I know how *I'd* feel, but for a person like Jax, like you, to win something you've wanted for so long...what does that feel like? I want to make sure that I write it perfectly."

Julian readjusted himself on his bed, naked Amalie images still emblazoned on his mind. He needed to focus. This was important. He blew out a breath and tried his best. "What match did he win?"

"The sectionals tournament you're about to play in." She sounded almost guilty.

"Some would consider that a jinx."

"Some would consider it good luck and good vibes."

"Fine. It's probably the same feeling *you'd* get if *you* won something. Or you know, the feeling you get when you've written the perfect scene, like the one where Penelope and Jax make out?" He waited.

"You only like that scene because of the sex."

Oh, if only she knew. If only she knew what was going on in his head, how he was straining against his boxer briefs. "I like everything because of the sex, but really, that scene was perfect. I felt their emotions, and it was killing me that they weren't together. When they finally hooked up, I might've shouted. So yeah, winning feels like writing something along those lines."

"Aww. I didn't know you loved it like that. But, flattering as that is, I imagine winning feels a little more intense than simply writing the perfect scene."

"Well, what about when you found out *Breaking the Fall* was on the bestseller's list? You were overjoyed, your heart probably felt like it was about to flutter out of your rib cage, your breathing staggered, tears coming to your eyes, all because you'd worked so hard for so long and it was overwhelming that you finally got what you wanted."

There was silence on the other end of the line, and Julian thought maybe he'd said too much. She wanted an answer, and that was the best he could give.

"Julian," her voice was soft. "That was beautiful and perfect, and I was trying to write down every single word that came out of your mouth. Maybe *you* should be the writer."

He brushed it off, but inside he glowed under her praise. And because he was done talking about all of this and had more pressing questions, he decided to deflect and get to the heart of the matter.

His voice dropped an octave, the sound hoarse and unfamiliar to his own ears. "So, nightshirt, huh? You don't sleep with your shirt off?"

Her familiar giggle came through the phone. "Hmmm…depends on what mood I'm in."

"What kind of mood you in tonight?" God, she was killing him.

"This wine is making me feel pretty hot. As a matter of fact…"

He heard rustling on her end, and he swore it sounded like material against skin. "I just had to take my shirt off because I felt flushed," she said. "Hey, I imagine a guy like you sleeps with *nothing* on."

He brought his fist to his mouth. She was sitting there talking to him in nothing more than her underwear and acted like it was no big deal. "How did you know?"

"Just a feeling."

"I can give you some feelings." There was no mistaking the pain in his voice as he throbbed in misery.

"Well, how would you do that?" There was a sexy, teasing lilt to her voice now, more rustling on her end of the line, and he imagined her getting beneath the sheets on the couch. Where were her hands? What were they doing?

Oh shit. His brain short-circuited for a minute since the blood was flowing elsewhere.

"Hey, Julian," she said, but he hadn't taken the phone away from his ear.

"Yes," he answered, trying to stifle the desperate pant of his breathing, but he knew she'd already noticed it.

A small laugh trilled from her throat, a sound that was low and sexy, completely devilish and utterly tantalizing. "Enjoy your night. Think of me," she finally said, then the line went silent.

With a groan, Julian dropped the phone on his bed and scrubbed his fingers through his hair before sliding a hand beneath the sheets and giving in to her command.

Chapter Sixteen

JULIAN

THE DAY BEFORE SECTIONALS, PAUL PULLED UP THE DRAW. THIS TOURNAMENT was on a different level than the Jekyll tournament. Sectionals would be filled with guys itching to play the US Open. This was real competition, and one particular name garnered Julian's interest.

Taylor Pratt was a nineteen-year-old American player who had just turned pro in February and had already played a couple of futures events and one pro level, where he won two rounds at the Memphis Open. In other words, the kid was a force to be reckoned with. According to the draw, the only way Julian would play him was if they both made it to the finals—a more realistic situation for Taylor than for himself.

Paul rubbed his hands together and said, "Hey man, this is great. This kid's legit. If you get to play him, we can get a better idea of where you're at."

On the first day of the three-day tournament, Julian, Amalie, and Paul agreed to meet at the Stone Mountain Tennis Center, which was thirty minutes from Julian's apartment in Dunwoody, just outside Atlanta. That morning, when Julian jogged down to his car, he noticed a tiny white box on his seat, a note on top with his name scrawled in his mom's familiar handwriting. Even though his fingers itched to open the box first, he went for the envelope. A messy add-on at the top read, *"What have I told you about locking your car doors?"* It made him grin, and then he started reading.

Julian,

There aren't enough words to tell you just how proud I am of you. What you'll find in the box is something you'll recognize instantly. I hope it brings you luck and makes you feel like your Daddy is right there with you the entire time.

I love you,
Mama

With shaky hands, he opened the box. Staring back at him was his father's gold tennis racket necklace. It was an ugly, gaudy thing, but Oliver Smoke wore it every single day and swore it brought him luck on the court.

Julian's fist clenched over the metal, feeling the cool bite of it in his palm. This was the best gift anyone could have given him.

He didn't waste any time securing it around his neck, admiring it in the rearview mirror. With a quick glance at the time, he backed out of his apartment complex, dialing his mom.

"Hey, honey," his mom's Southern accent drawled.

"Hey, Mom. I got the necklace. Thank you."

He could hear the smile in her voice. "You're welcome. I figured you'd like it, like having a piece of your family there with you on the court."

His hand traced over the intricate design, the other hand on the wheel. "I love it." There was a brief pause. "So, you coming to the tournament?"

His mom sighed. "You know, I don't think I will. I thought I could break the superstition, but I can't, not yet anyway. That's part of the reason I wanted you to have the necklace. That way you'd have your father and me there with you in spirit."

He wasn't surprised. The superstition his mom concocted while he was in college was something she clung to tightly—she absolutely refused to watch his matches live, instead only watching the recorded versions.

"That's cool. I figured you wouldn't, and the necklace more than makes up for it. But listen, if I make it to New York, you'll have to come then."

"I wouldn't miss it for the world, honey. But I think we need to change the wording there. I think you should be saying *when* you make it to New York, not *if*."

"Mom, New York is a pretty fucking big *if*."

"Julian! You watch your mouth. I hope you don't talk like this around Amalie. Speaking of Amalie—"

Damn, she probably already had their wedding china picked out.

"Pulling into the parking lot now, Mom. Gotta go. Love you!"

"I see what you're doing, but I love you too! Good luck!"

When he got out of his car, the first thing he noticed was the smell of asphalt burning. It was July in Georgia, which meant it was hotter than seven hells. The second thing he noticed was Amalie standing outside of her car, nervously adjusting the strap of her writing bag.

God, she was beautiful, waiting there with the morning sun reflecting in her hair like fire dancing in the breeze.

A stronger wind blew the strap of her white tank off her shoulder, making her laugh as she swiped a hand along her sun-pinked skin to correct the fallen fabric. Julian's breath caught. Seeing her in person after a month was almost too much, but seeing her there without some other guy on her arm was even better. He'd worried that during their time apart someone else would catch her eye, someone who actually deserved her. Things had kind of died since their racy phone call...the one that he replayed over and over in his mind. He still couldn't shake that low, throaty tone her voice had taken, the image he'd had in his mind. He'd wanted more of those phone calls. Hell, he'd wanted all of that in person, but Amalie told him she didn't want to be a distraction, so she'd taken a step back.

In an attempt at failed self-preservation, he zeroed in on her downturned mouth, her nose scrunched as she studied her phone. She looked up at the sound of his feet on the pavement. Was it his imagination or did her eyes light up when she saw him? She shoved her phone in her back pocket and rushed over to him, her arms wrapping around his neck. He picked her up, feeling her body press against his. He breathed in her heady perfume, his nose brushing her skin, and all he could think about was pressing his lips to her pulse.

"Miss me, Stardust?" He pulled away, admiring those eyes, those lips, everything about her overwhelming his senses as his hands tightened on her waist, relief flooding his words.

"Of course I did." She grinned back, that very relief he felt mirrored in her own stare. She pushed his hair from his eyes, her fingertips brushing his skin, leaving a trail of heat in their wake. "And I know the feeling's mutual, right?" She stood up on her tiptoes in an attempt to better see him eye to eye, and all he could think about was kissing her.

"You know it is. I thought about you every day…and every night." He couldn't help himself.

Her cheeks flushed, painting a crimson sky beneath her freckles. She plopped back down on her feet, and even though he hated to do it, Julian released her from his embrace as she tucked her hair behind her ears. A small smile played across her lips.

Deciding to help her out and not be a complete dick, he changed the subject, although all he wanted was for her to tell him the same—that she thought about that night on the phone way more than she should. "Hey, when I walked up, you looked upset. Everything good?" he asked.

She sucked in a breath before meeting his eyes. "I'm going to tell you, but you have to promise that it won't affect your game and you won't freak out."

Dread trickled through him as he tried to appear chill and unaffected even as his mind ran through all the things that could mess with his game, and that list was *long*.

"Helloooo? Yoohoo!" Amalie called as she waved a hand in front of his face, bringing him back from his worst-case-scenario daydreams. When she seemed content with his attention level, she said slowly, her eyes wide, "Julian, do you promise?"

"Yeah, fine, I promise. What is it?" he snapped, a little sharper than intended. His mind was about to jump off the deep end, and the sooner he could reel it back in, the better.

Amalie didn't even flinch or cock an eyebrow—that's how he knew whatever she had to tell him was bad. She *always* gave him hell and kept him in line.

She unleashed a shaky exhale. "So, Paul can't come this weekend." She winced, one eye open as she waited for Julian's reaction.

Of all the worst-case scenarios that flitted through his mind, that was definitely not one of them. Paul was his coach, his rock, his *guy* who was always there. No, this was worse than he could've imagined.

He glanced around the parking lot without really seeing anything.

Amalie reached a tentative hand out toward him, her words soft. "Hey, you okay?"

He gave her a curt nod as he leaned back against her car, away from her, away from her comfort. "Why can't he be here?" he grated out, his voice all hard edges as he fought against the free-for-all now raging in his brain.

Amalie took a step back, her hand dropping to the top of her writing bag. "He's sick," she said simply, as if that explained everything when in reality it explained nothing at all.

Julian's eyes flicked up to her face, looking for signs of how bad it was, worry instantly slamming into him.

His words were crowded, falling out on top of each other as he straightened. "How sick is he? Are we talking a cold or terminal?" Because in his mind there was no in-between.

His eyes must've given away his anxiety, because Amalie stepped forward again, determination etched across her face as she placed a gentle hand on his arm. Her touch steadied him instantly, anchoring his wild mind. She was the only person in the world able to do that.

"He's got pneumonia, and you know the older you are when you get it, the rougher it is. Luckily, Paul caught it early and he'll be fine. His doctor wanted him to rest for a few days. He was going to come here anyway, but I talked him out of it." A tiny laugh slipped out of her, and it was the cutest thing he'd ever heard.

"But he'll be okay, right?" he repeated dumbly. Somewhere along the way the unpredictable bastard had become more than just a coach to him.

Amalie nodded, her entire countenance completely changed now that she didn't have the burden of Paul's news on her shoulders. "He'll be fine, Julian. I promise." Then she changed gears, turning into a little Paul Jr., her voice gruff like his, her fake Brooklyn accent atrocious as she said, "Now

let's go kick some ass, son." She bounced on her toes as she raised a fist for
him to bump.

Julian was surprised to hear laughter filtering out of his own mouth as
they fist-bumped. Amalie's happiness was contagious, a powerful drug
that chased away the worries that plagued him.

His eyes swept over her, loving the light in her eyes, the curve of her
mouth, and the happy flush of her cheeks. She was so free, so different
from the uptight girl he first met. This version of her was dangerous in the
best possible way.

JULIAN WAS RIDING A HIGH ON SUNDAY MORNING, HIS CONFIDENCE SOARING
after two days of strong play. He'd won his first match Friday evening and
the same with two matches Saturday. He easily dismantled his semifinals
opponent and was all set for the finals, where he'd play none other than
Taylor Pratt, the kid from California he and Paul had talked about.
Honestly, he was more surprised by how well he was holding up
physically; it looked like Romina's torture and training had paid off. He'd
hardly felt winded, and he'd played more these past three days than he
had in years. If he won this tournament, he'd earn a spot in the qualifying
tournament, which was one step away from the main draw of the US
Open. It was wild to even think he was so damn close.

As Julian and Taylor did a brief warm-up, Julian tried to take stock of
what he had going for him. His forehand and serve were working really
well, but he knew things would be different with Taylor. The kid had fire in
his eyes, in his stance, as he called heads for first serve—a ballsy move
since most guys liked their opponent to serve first. The kid wanted it.
Badly. And Julian was the final obstacle in his way.

What the kid didn't know was that the feeling was mutual.

As Julian walked back to the baseline, he pulled out the cold chain that
settled against his heart, brought it to his lips and kissed it, holding it up to
the sky, and then pushed it back beneath his shirt. He could almost feel his
father there with him on the court. He tightened his blue headband, and he
was ready. Better yet, he was hungry.

Julian quickly realized this kid was a beast. He played left-handed, and that really tested Julian's backhand. Not only that, but Pratt played with a lot of spin and splice, making it difficult for Julian to find a comfortable rhythm, forcing him to play a variety of different shots, and keeping him continuously on his toes.

With each bounce of the ball, Julian sensed his mental game being torn to shreds. He was letting this kid get to him, ruffle him, and it was hard to come back from that. The other players challenged him physically but not mentally. Taylor Pratt was dangerous because he did both. As a matter of fact, he did it so well, he beat Julian in the first set.

Pratt called for a restroom break when the first set ended. The chair umpire asked Julian if he needed to go, too. For a minute Julian zoned out, thinking to himself, *Damn it all if I've got to piss, but I don't deserve it after that. I should just piss my pants since I'm playing like a toddler.*

"Julian? Do you need to use the restroom?" the chair asked again, breaking through Julian's self-loathing. He almost said no, just to punish himself, but instead, he nodded wordlessly.

He'd barely made it off-court before Amalie fell in step with him, the sound of her sandals echoing against the asphalt. He didn't meet her gaze because he didn't want to see the pity that was probably written all over her pretty face. That last set was embarrassing, and he hated that she had seen him play like that.

Aggravated, he bit out, "I don't need to talk to anyone right now. I just need to think."

Amalie was undeterred and continued walking with him, her shoulder brushing his. "But Paul has a message for you."

That got his attention, his head whipping around. To his surprise, there was no pity in her expression. Oh no, not at all. Her jaw was set, her lips pressed together, determination radiating from her.

"What?" he asked, not sure if he'd heard her correctly.

"Paul has a message for you," she repeated, her voice tight.

Julian sighed, feeling his shoulders hunch with the effort. He turned to look at the restroom door. "Fine. Just give me a minute." And without waiting for a response, he disappeared into the men's room. He headed into the stall and locked it, desperate for the privacy, the quiet.

He clenched his fist and glared at the wall, the urge to punch it strong. He wished he had his racket with him. He needed to hit something, to scream, hell, anything to get rid of the shitty feeling running through him. Losing wasn't the end of the world, he knew that, but losing here? That meant the end of the road, and he wasn't ready to walk away yet.

The sound of the restroom door flying open and slamming into the wall scared the shit out of him. He stopped pissing for a minute, waiting to see if he was about to get murdered.

"Hey, Taylor, is that you man?" Julian called out.

"I'm washing my hands. It's a redhead. I think she's here to see you."

Silence, followed by the sound of Taylor grabbing paper towels and the door shutting again.

"Paul says you need to get the ball to the backhand side," Amalie's voice echoed through the room.

Julian shook his head, biting back laughter. This girl was too much.

"I'm trying to piss, Stardust," he admitted, then, "Wait, Paul said what?"

"By all means, finish taking a piss. I'll just read off these messages as you do." He could almost imagine her waving her phone around as she said that.

So he did, and she continued. "He said you need to get the ball to his backhand side and take more chances there. Oh, and you need to go more to the body with your serve."

Julian stepped out of the stall and washed his hands, meeting Amalie's gaze in the mirror. "How? How's he even watching this?"

Amalie typed a quick text and got a response almost instantly, her ringtone echoing throughout the bathroom. "He said he's got it streaming live through a webcam he hooked up." She scrunched her nose as she re-read the message. "Probably illegal, especially if Paul's involved." She gave a little shrug and then tucked her phone into the back pocket of her shorts. "But hey, do what he says, okay? Smoke?"

At the sound of his nickname, he turned and caught her eye. Everything about Amalie in that moment dared him to trifle with her as she stepped closer, placing herself directly in front of him. His fingers itched to feel the satiny fabric of her white tank, to feel her skin.

She reached out a finger and poked him in the chest. "Now's not the time to play like you're afraid, do you hear me? You're better than this, and you're letting a nineteen-year-old intimidate you. Go back out there and take care of this pubescent punk like I know you can." To punctuate her words, she grabbed two sticks of Juicy Fruit out of her purse, shoved them into her mouth, and began to punish them just like Paul.

Julian burst out laughing. "Did Paul put you up to this, too?"

"No, he didn't. This is all me, and it's what you need to hear. Now get out there and do what you came here to do," she all but growled, sticking a fist out for him to bump. He stared at it for a minute, his lips still tilted in a smile.

She slung out her hip, aggravation flaring in her eyes. "So help me God, Smoke, if you don't fist bump me…"

He lifted his hand to his chin pretending to think about it, loving how hot she was when she was mad. She narrowed her eyes at him and then he finally bumped her small fist. Afterward, she gave him a nod and then led the way back to the court. His mind cycled through Paul's advice, realizing his coach wasn't wrong.

But it wasn't Paul's guidance that made him feel better, stronger, like he actually had a shot. No, it was Amalie who had done that. Hell, she'd followed him to the bathroom just to get him pumped up about the remainder of the match. He liked that, liked having her in his corner.

When he got on the court, Pratt was already there, hopping back and forth, keeping his legs warm. He gave Julian a nod, and then they retreated to the baseline. Just as Pratt was about to serve, a familiar whimsical ringtone rang out, causing lots of grumbling and eyes searching for the culprit.

He suppressed a smile as he heard Amalie's flustered, "Ah! Sorry!" and then there was silence.

Everything changed after the pep talk in the bathroom. The poor young gun didn't stand a chance. The match went three sets with Julian winning. The kid looked just as stunned as Julian did at the outcome.

Julian wasted no time scanning the crowd for a familiar head of red hair, and he felt a sudden flare of joy once he found her. She was on her feet, cheering and doing some sort of godawful dance—all of that was for *him*, because he did it. *He actually fucking did it.*

He shook his head in disbelief as he walked over to shake Taylor's hand. Later, as he packed up his stuff, Julian realized he was still shaking, still amped from the win. He was on to the qualifying tournament, his dream that much closer to becoming a reality.

Out of nowhere, Amalie's soft little body came crashing into him with enough force to almost knock him backward. Her arms wrapped around him and squeezed, not caring that he was soaked with sweat. Her excitement was contagious, causing him to bark out a laugh. Damn, he'd missed her.

"You did it! I knew you could do it!" she squealed.

Those words were so familiar—they were the words his dad would say after every win. He'd clap Julian on the back and pull him in for a hug, his eyes smiling so much they wrinkled at the corners like rays of the sun. It wasn't fair that the man who taught him to love the sport couldn't share this moment with him, his so-called comeback.

Tears burned at the back of his throat as he swallowed the emotions clawing their way up. Instead, he focused on the people who were still here.

A look of understanding crossed Amalie's face as she squeezed his biceps a little tighter. When she spoke, her voice was bright enough to chase away any darkness. "You're going to New York! To qualifiers— you're *so* close to the Open! We should go see Paul, right? Maybe celebrate with him?"

Julian's immediate answer, the silent one in his head was a big fat *Not yet*, because the truth was that he wanted her all to himself for a while. Who knew what inane "relationship" rule Paul would throw down next, now that Julian was on to the big leagues.

He gave Amalie's hand a quick squeeze, then wrapped his arms around her waist and pulled her close. It was a brave move, but then again, his adrenaline was set on high.

"Or we could go somewhere," he said, staring down into her grey eyes. "Just me and you. I haven't seen you in so long, and I'm so pumped right now. I have you to thank for this."

Something flashed across her face, something a little like tempered panic. Her hands rested on his biceps, and he watched as her throat moved on a swallow. "Julian."

The friction of her body against his, his words, he realized that all of it suggested something a little deeper than its surface-level meaning. He meant what he said, and he wanted nothing more than to have hours to explore every dip and curve of her body. But that invisible boundary between them, that working relationship? Yeah, he'd crossed that, judging from Amalie's reaction.

"You know what? You probably wouldn't be able to keep your hands off of me if we were alone, so we should go see Paul," Julian deflected with a shrug. "I just need to take a shower first."

Amalie's relief was palpable as she took a step back, her expression filled with unspoken gratitude. "Please do, because you stink," she joked as she waved a hand in front of her nose.

"You know you love it," he shot back as he headed toward the locker room, walking backward, his eyes not leaving Amalie's.

"In your dreams, Smoke, in your dreams." She laughed as she turned on her heel and headed to the parking lot, leaving him beaming like an idiot in her wake.

Chapter Seventeen

AMALIE

AMALIE STRETCHED WITH A YAWN, THE WARMTH OF EARLY MORNING SUNLIGHT falling across her as it filtered through the blinds. She sat up slowly from the couch, kicking the sheets and blankets off, smiling down at her freshly painted toenails that had little tennis balls painted on the big toes. Her fingernails even matched.

The last few days had been a whirlwind as she prepped for their trip to New York for qualifiers. She knew that everyone would be in their own separate hotel rooms, but that didn't mean that she couldn't look her best. Her hair was freshly trimmed and blown out, and yeah, she might've gotten a bikini wax, a few new pairs of lacy underwear, and maybe even another thong, along with some sexy little skimpy pajamas that also made it look like she wasn't trying too hard. Who knew if Julian would ask for her company to watch a movie or something…in his room. Paul had already said he'd be scarce, aside from the tournament. Either way, it didn't mean anything would happen, but she'd be damned if she didn't make Julian want her as much as she'd been dreaming of him. Butterflies danced in her stomach as her excitement about the day grew.

The sound of her phone dinging with an email brought her back down to earth. She snatched it off the table lightning fast—she was expecting to hear from Stella, who she'd sent pages to last night. It was the best thing she'd written in a while. She'd enjoyed every minute of writing it, too, and felt a strong connection with the characters...probably because the characters were her and Julian. Her hands trembled as she clicked on the email. Then she read the words, any hope she'd had now completely dashed.

She clutched the arm of the sofa, an attempt to ground herself as her head floated on a wave of dizziness. She looked down at the phone again, wanting to throw it through the damn window, anything to get it the hell away from her.

As she re-read that email for the third time, her eyes pricked with tears that she refused to let fall. The email was the final nail in the coffin. Her hopes of repairing her reputation, of being published again, shattered around her.

HI AMALIE,

I regret writing this email, but I've been reading the pages and I just can't seem to connect to the characters or the storyline. In the current publishing world, I don't think I could sell this, much less an idea I'm not one hundred percent sold on. Your beginning pages had promise but along the way seemed to grow false, losing much of that heart I'd enjoyed so much in your writing in Breaking the Fall. I do wish you success in your future endeavors and hope you know that this opinion is subjective. Thank you for giving me the opportunity to read your work. It's truly been a pleasure.

Best,

Stella

AMALIE STOOD UP STRAIGHT, TRYING TO CATCH HER BREATH AS EVERYTHING went sideways. Once she was finally able to gulp oxygen, she released a grating scream of frustration.

It was over. All over. No one would take her now. Stella was the one person who still seemed to believe in her, who was willing to take a chance on her and now...

Amalie clutched her stomach as it roiled, her morning coffee threatening to make a reappearance. Her cell phone dinged again. It was a text from Julian. He'd made it to the airport already because Paul insisted they get there a good three hours before their flight. Normally that would've cheered her up, but she slumped as she darkened the screen.

Julian. She had to keep going for Julian. Just because she was destined to remain a failure didn't mean that he was.

Maxwell's harsh words echoed through her brain, her father's adding to them. Both had been clear that she didn't have what it took to be a writer, that she'd only made it this far because of her stupid last name. Part of her wanted to march up to the courthouse when they got back from New York and change it to something else, anything else but Warner.

Even though her heart was breaking, even though she knew her dream had just died a fiery death and she was left with nothing but a hole in her heart to show for it, she packed up her stuff, threw her bag over her shoulder, and shot a bird at nothing in particular, before slamming the door behind her.

THE DRIVE TO THE AIRPORT WAS FILLED WITH MORE ANGRY, ANGSTY MUSIC than she'd listened to since her teen years. Her eyes watered, ruining her mascara, but with a sniff, she sucked those tears right back in. A quick check in the mirror confirmed that her nose rivaled Rudolph's, and her hair—she'd meant to put dry shampoo in it before she left but completely forgot—practically stood up on its own. She haphazardly twisted it into a messy bun. Screw it.

She made it through security without any trouble, aside from a few sideways glances from both the agents and fellow flyers. One sweet older woman with white hair even asked her if she was all right, to which Amalie honestly answered, "No," feeling her eyes water again.

How could she be all right when everything was falling apart? What was she going to do with her life? She didn't enjoy freelance writing like she thought she would, so that was out. Maybe her father had been right. Maybe he'd just seen what was staring back at her in the mirror all along.

As she made it to the gate where Julian and Paul waited, a few rogue tears slipped down her face, followed by a burning in her nose and that god-awful crying headache she always got. Her traveling companions were easy to spot because they were standing while everyone else was sitting, something that didn't surprise her, since they were naturally a little fidgety.

Their gazes swung to her, expressions pinched with worry as they took her in. She looked down at herself, having forgotten what she was even wearing: an oversize raggedy gray shirt over black tennis shorts. It wasn't...it wasn't the worst thing, she supposed. But God, the rest of her was a hot mess.

Julian made the first move, meeting her before she could join them, but Paul wasn't too far behind. Normally she would've checked out Julian's ass or noticed how his clothes clung to him perfectly, highlighting the muscles he'd worked so hard for, or those green and gold lightning-strike eyes of his...but today, today there was none of that. All she could focus on was how terrible it was going to feel to admit to him, someone she cared for, someone she wanted to be proud of her, that she had once again *failed*.

"Stardust?" Julian moved forward to take her duffle from her shaking hands. His voice was soothing, his entire countenance protective, and it nearly broke her. She tried to keep her face from crumpling as she shook' her head. Moving even closer, Julian softly touched her chin to get her to look at him. When their eyes met, she saw that his face was a study in well-worn concern, those adorable little eleven lines of his creased. "What's wrong? Did someone hurt you? I'll kill..."

"Easy there, Romeo," Paul cut in with his usual dry self. "Amalie, you wanna talk about it?"

Amalie spoke while desperately trying to keep the tears at bay. "Not really, but you guys should know..." She sucked in a few quick, shallow breaths. "Stella dropped me."

Julian grabbed her hand, squeezing it, bringing it to his mouth for the gentlest of kisses. A lifeline if there ever was one.

"She dropped me because she didn't think the pages I sent could sell, that the book...that I—" She was winding up for a long trip down self-deprecation lane, but Julian interrupted her, leaning in even closer. Paul closed in on the other side.

"I know where you're going with that train of thought," Julian said, folding her into a hug, "and it's not going to lead you anywhere good."

For a minute, she was distracted as the comforting scent of spice and musk, of Julian wrapped around her. He was warm, and his touch was electric, but tears still raged behind her eyelids.

She stiffened in Julian's arms as she tried to keep herself together. She was so used to maintaining appearances because a Warner "never shows weakness" and a Warner "doesn't cry." Such toxic statements. She knew that now.

And maybe that's why, with Julian rubbing her back in soothing circles in the middle of a busy airport, his low timbre murmuring and coaxing reassuring truths in her ears, she finally, finally allowed herself to fall to pieces.

AS AMALIE EXITED THE PLANE, SHE FLEXED HER HAND, THE PHANTOM TOUCH of Julian's still there. Apparently, he was terrified of flying and had spent the entire trip grasping her hand in a death grip. Being near him was, however, almost enough to temporarily distract her from her worries. For right now, she'd focus on Julian and the possibility that maybe later tonight she'd knock on his door to see if he wanted to hang out and she'd catch a glimpse of him in a towel with water beading on his muscles...

Whew, that part alone sent her imagination into overdrive.

Once outside the airport, Julian shot her a smile, one that lit up every stone-cut angle of his face. "Thank you for that back there. You made me almost forget I was on a plane. *Almost.*" And then he winked, sending his cuteness factor over the ledge and into the abyss of her dirty mind.

"I aim to please," she joked as she playfully bumped his shoulder. The simple touch made her world spin.

"Do you now?" Julian's voice pitched deep in a wicked bedroom voice, one she hadn't heard from him before.

To play off how affected she was, she stopped, making a show of looking for Paul. It wasn't a total lie—they had actually lost sight of him. He was known to get sidetracked by an Auntie Anne's or two.

Her eyes flashed up to meet Julian's stare. The air between them thickened, snapping taut as he studied her. His eyes twinkled, the golden specks glinting in the fluorescent light as he crooked one corner of his lip into that trademark Julian Smoke smirk Amalie once loathed. Now?

Now she found it absurdly sexy.

"You look nervous, Stardust. Since when do I make you nervous?" He took a step closer, his tongue sneaking out to wet his lips, his eyes dropping to her mouth, then back up again.

Amalie fidgeted under his perusal and right on cue, her cheeks felt terribly hot, the tattoo twining its way down her neck and chest. Curse her porcelain skin (fine, ghostly pale skin) and its penchant for showing every single emotion.

She gave Julian a toothy smile, one that fought to grow wider because bantering with him would always be one of her favorite pastimes. "You don't make me nervous, thank you very much. If I look nervous it's because my blood is practically pure caffeine right now. I drank several sodas on the plane," she answered nonchalantly.

Julian shook his head as he turned around to see Paul waving two large bags of Auntie Anne's pretzels in the air, beaming so brightly that his lips disappeared beneath his white mustache.

"Snacks for later," Paul explained.

Amalie's mouth watered at the scent of melted butter, salt, and dough.

"Let's get this show on the road, then," Julian announced as he grabbed her luggage. "You ready for this?" he directed just to her, his voice dipping so low it made her toes curl as he led them out front where a taxi van waited.

Ready for what? For a late-night rendezvous with him? Because, yes. For qualifiers? Because, yes again.

Not sure how to answer, she just shrugged in a yes/no, noncommittal way.

They all crawled into the van, Paul taking one of the middle solo seats. Amalie moved to the bench seat in the back, thinking Julian would probably take the other solo seat, but nope. Instead, he ducked in after her, his big body making the back seat suddenly seem very small and cramped. His entire right side pressed against Amalie. Each time their knees bumped, it sent a frenzied spark to her stomach, waking the slumbering butterflies.

After a few minutes of silence, Julian turned to her, placing a gentle calloused hand on her knee as though it belonged there. And maybe it did. It felt amazing. An anchor. A tether.

Comfort.

"This can be the last time we discuss it," he said, "but I want you to know that I read every single page you emailed me. I thought your pages were magic, that *you're* magic, and I just…" He ran a hand through his hair. "I can't sit back and let you give up, knowing the amount of talent you have. There are other ways we can get the book out there, but please, please don't give up. For me."

Words that were on the tip of her tongue melted away. It was hard to say or do anything because Julian's hand, his perfect hand, was *still* on her knee, on her bare skin, and his thumb was rubbing lazy circles back and forth, causing her nerve endings to stir. Then…then there was the fact of what he'd just said. Her pages were magic. He believed in her. How long had it been since someone actually really and truly believed in her besides Ro?

His words wrapped around her like an embrace, and in a moment of absolute bravery, she placed her hand atop Julian's and squeezed, ignoring her fluttering heart, the want settling low in her belly, the unabashed longing racing through her veins. "We'll see, but Julian? This is about you. We're here in New York for *you,* and before things get too hectic, I want you to know that I'm going to be right by your side the entire way, no matter what happens with my writing. I don't know if I've ever believed in anything more than I believe in you—I've never doubted you." Julian gave her a pointed look, and she quickly added, "Aside from when I found you mumbling incoherent garbage at the bar back in January?" She hoped he could see in her gaze all that she couldn't say. She needed him to know how deeply she believed in him so that he could believe in himself.

His forehead wrinkled with a slight shake of his head as he turned toward the window. He looked so boyish and uncertain. "I can't believe we actually made it this far. It's weird, but I feel like we might jinx it if we discuss it, so you want to talk about something else?"

"Yes, please do before you two make me vomit on my brand-new polo," Paul groused while watching the hustle and bustle of the city go by.

Amalie laughed. One thing was for certain, this trip wouldn't be dull, not by a long shot.

WHEN THEY ARRIVED AT THE HOTEL, PAUL CHECKED IN FIRST AND THEN disappeared to find his room. Amalie felt strange checking into a hotel that wasn't a Warner Hotel, but she didn't want anything to do with her father. That thought alone caused her to stand up a little straighter as she stepped up to the counter.

The receptionist gave her a friendly smile. "Welcome to New York City. Name please?"

"Thanks. It's Amalie Warner." Julian shifted at her side, his gaze taking in the city through the lobby windows.

The woman's brows furrowed as her typing on the keyboard sounded more panicked. "Warner, correct?" she asked, her voice thin.

Amalie's heart rate picked up as dread filled her veins. She'd been around the hotel business enough to recognize the look on the woman's face. "Is there a problem?" She made sure her voice was polite—it wasn't this person's fault if what she feared had actually happened.

The woman stopped typing and looked up apologetically just as Julian leaned in closer, suddenly one hundred percent invested in this conversation. "Actually, it looks like we've overbooked and somehow your reservation got lost in the shuffle. With the tennis qualifiers and several conventions going on right now, every major hotel is full."

Amalie brought her hand to her temple wondering what in the hell she was going to do when Julian stepped even closer. He tapped on the counter and then shot the woman one of his smiles. "Hi. My name is Julian Smoke. Is my reservation still in the computer?"

The woman looked down at her screen and relief shuddered through her as she answered, "Yes, thank goodness."

"Then she'll," he hooked a thumb at Amalie, whose stomach just pitched to her knees, "stay with me. Will that work, Amalie? We don't have to tell Paul. He'll pitch a fit."

"I can always try to find something else, like a private rental, and pray they don't have bed bugs," she said to Julian, but he shook his head.

"Last minute in New York?" He nudged her with a playful look in his eyes. "Besides, I think you might be my good luck charm. I'd kinda like to keep you close."

Trying to act unaffected, she smiled, her stomach flip-flopping like mad. "All right. That would be great, thanks."

As Julian finished checking in, all Amalie could think was at least she'd prepared for this situation. She couldn't see where sharing a room with Julian *wouldn't* lead to some type of sexy adventure.

Needless to say, the trek to the room was quiet and somewhat awkward, at least on her end.

"Didn't think I'd get you alone in a room so soon." Julian shot her a wolfish grin as he leaned forward, brushing her shoulder with his chest.

Amalie rolled her eyes, even if the words settled deep in her veins, causing a pleasant little shiver to dance along her spine. Julian scanned their room key, then held the door open for her.

Her nerves were overwrought as she stepped inside with the man who'd dominated her daydreams for the past seven months. And good God, some of those dreams... They woke her in the middle of the night in a sweat with the sheets twisted. Those dreams alone made her body chaotic with need; what would an actual touch from Julian do to her?

Annihilate her. Most definitely. If a steamy phone call or Valentine's Day kiss on the cheek could make her feel so alive, so turned on...

Focus on the room, Amalie. Just focus on the room. As she tried to do that, she noticed their room had been decorated in mostly white with touches of beige here and there. It smelled like lemon Lysol, which at least let her know it was clean. She immediately made her way to the windows, doing the awkward slide thing with the blinds and then looking at their view of an alleyway behind the hotel.

Sunlight streamed onto the bed.

Wait. The bed. *Bed.* Singular.

She bit the inside of her cheek. Julian was cracking jokes as he fought with getting his tennis bag and other luggage through the door and hadn't realized she'd fallen silent.

Once he threw his stuff onto the petri dish—er, the hotel room carpet— he met her stare as she fought to appear calm and collected. "You look like you're up to no good," he teased, his voice gruff.

Amalie looked at the bed. "There's one bed and two of us."

Julian smirked, and it wasn't his usual kind—this was a dangerous, predatory thing that threatened to eat her right up. And the messed-up thing? She wanted to be eaten. Yep.

"Is that a problem, Stardust? You afraid to share a bed with me?"

Playing it cool, she lifted her chin. "*You* should be afraid. I toss and turn and flop around like a fish. You won't get any rest."

Julian took another step closer, a slight swagger in his hips. "Is that so? Maybe I don't want any rest."

Her heart tripped over itself at the images that conjured. "Julian." She poked his chest, his hand reaching out to encompass hers, holding it there against his heart. "This is serious. I want you to win." She left out the part about how she wanted him in general.

Sobering, Julian squeezed her hand. "I'll be plenty rested, so no need to worry. The bed has plenty of space for both of us, and if you toss and turn into me, I'll just nudge you back to your side."

Amalie nodded. She was a grown-ass woman who could share a bed with a man she had a crush on. Wasn't she?

"Yeah, sure. That works for me. Thank you again for letting me share your room."

"Of course. I wouldn't have it any other way."

With that, Julian kissed her knuckles and started unpacking his stuff. With the way Amalie's heart stuttered at the feel of his lips, she knew she'd made the right decision.

Chapter Eighteen

JULIAN

JULIAN FELT CONTENT AS HE WALKED DOWN BROADWAY WITH AMALIE NEXT TO him, every once in a while, her body twisting into his, or his hand going to the small of her back as they navigated the crowds. They'd just had dinner with Paul at Bond 45 near Times Square but left him waiting for a lady friend as they headed toward the theatre district. The heat of the day had subsided, so it was actually pleasant to be out on the streets.

Amalie's fingers brushed his forearm, drawing his attention from the lights and the sounds of the city at night. "Hey, there's one thing I haven't talked to you about, and it's something I really want to know, and I feel like if I don't ask it now, I'll combust."

Julian scratched his eyebrow, lips curving. "Okay, shoot."

"What happened with Nadine?"

All of the air left his lungs as his body tensed. He turned to look at Amalie, who'd shoved her hands in the pockets of her black sundress, her attention on her feet as they strolled.

"I'm an idiot," she said. "Ignore that. It's just…I'm curious about her, you know? She seemed to be your last serious girlfriend, fiancée, or whatever, or am I wrong? Did I not put all of the pieces together correctly?"

"No, you're right. Nadine…Nadine and I were a mess. I was desperate for her and proposed to her two and a half months in, when everything started falling apart. Definitely not my brightest idea."

She pursed her lips and then with a nod threaded her arm through his in a movement that appeared as natural as breathing. People were laughing in the night air, car horns were honking, trains were clattering along the tracks, but all he could see was Amalie.

He forged ahead. "Nadine was the one to leave me, even though it should've been the other way around. She actually justified having an affair with another tennis player. Can you believe that?"

Amalie gasped. "What?"

Julian nodded slowly. "According to her, it was my fault she slept with someone else, said I didn't make time to actually engage with her. She ended up marrying the guy, an up and coming German player, Lorentz Schaaf. That wasn't the only reason she cheated on me though. I sucked on the court, and she thought that was an embarrassment," Julian admitted as he picked at invisible lint on his shirt.

"But she knew you had a schedule to keep, that you were an athlete. If she really loved you…"

Julian shrugged. "I don't think she really loved me."

Amalie drew them to a stop in the middle of the sidewalk, just outside the Richard Rogers theater, drawing a few comments and glares. Julian watched as she swallowed and studied her freshly painted nails before asking, "Do you still love her? Or miss her?"

He moved them away from the chaotic crowd and lines beneath the lit awning. "God, no." He paused then, taking her in. "Wow. Amalie Warner. I'd swear I see jealousy on that beautiful face of yours." A hopeful spark moved through him at the thought.

She shook her head as they started walking again, the hotel just in sight. "Of course not," she answered, her words tinged with a sardonic, disbelieving edge. She even went the extra mile to scrunch up her face like the idea was preposterous.

Julian cocked his head to the side, studying her, hoping she felt the intensity of his gaze because suddenly things between them felt like they were nearing combustion…or maybe it was just him? Either way, she shifted her eyes away from him, but he saw a ghost of a smile on her face as her fingers tightened on his bicep.

They kept conversation light as they made their way back to the room, but that underlying current of tension had only thickened. Julian fumbled with the key card a few times before it finally swiped green. Once inside, he swore the room had shrunk in size.

Just as he took a step forward, Amalie stopped in her tracks, causing Julian to bump right into her ass. His hands steadied her by latching onto her waist, which put them in a really tantalizing position. "You good?" he asked against her hair, letting her go even though he didn't want to.

After a heartbeat, she spun around, face pink. "Oh, sorry. Didn't know you were right there... I was just going to, ah, get something out of my suitcase."

Julian raised a brow. Her suitcase was by the bed, in the opposite direction. It was like as soon as they stepped inside the room they'd forgotten how to act around each other. They were alone and there was one bed and they'd had all this undeniable sexual tension brimming between them for *months*. Tonight it would either boil over or somehow manage to simmer. He wasn't betting on the latter.

"It's cool. I'm going to, ah..." Julian looked around the room and perked up. "Grab a book and read, maybe? Or watch SportsCenter? Or maybe a cold shower." Anything to calm himself and dim the thoughts of what he wanted to do with Amalie. *To* Amalie.

They moved at exactly the same time, bumping into each other again. Amalie's hand accidentally brushed against Julian's cock which was doing its damnedest to be half-hard, causing her to jump back. "God, sorry. I—"

He couldn't help but smile. "Just trying to feel me up. I got it."

Amalie brought her hands to her cheeks. "I swear I wasn't. But hey, how about you go take that shower? Give us each some time to..." Her words trailed off, but he knew exactly what she meant.

"Yeah, that's a good idea. I'm a little sweaty anyway." He didn't waste any time gathering his stuff and heading to the bathroom. As soon as the door clicked shut, he took his first deep breath since they'd made it back to the room.

He stepped in the shower, the cool water running over his body. A single door was all that separated them now, unlike the distance between them when they shared that one, mind-blowing phone call.

He placed his hand flat against the shower wall as water poured over his face, imagining Amalie as he had that night. His breath came fast and he grew hard, a temptation, but he didn't want to be spent should things escalate tonight, and he prayed they did.

He'd noticed that her nails were done, and he'd smiled when he caught sight of the little yellow tennis balls on two of them. She also wasn't normally a dress girl, but she'd busted one out tonight. What she didn't know was that she didn't have to do anything extra to get his attention— she'd been bringing that A-game ever since he met her.

He towel-dried his hair but decided to leave it damp and to forego a shirt. After a quick perusal of his reflection, he knew Amalie wouldn't miss the abs that had fully come in, his hips dipping into a V he'd thought he might never see again. He was counting on her eyes following that trail to the icing on the cake—he was still half-hard, and he wore his white tennis shorts, the exact pair Amalie had admitted she loved. It was an obvious effort, but he tamped down any expression as he swaggered out of the bathroom.

Amalie was bent over her duffle, gathering things to her chest, and he couldn't help but scan the view. Damn. Her legs always looked fantastic, but they looked extra smooth and a little sun kissed. Something about the way she stood on her toes had his eyes drifting upward to the curve of her ass...

He grabbed Pete Sampras' *A Champion's Mind* from his bag and made his way to the bed. Just as she turned around, an article of clothing dropped from her arms onto the edge of the duffle. A black thong that had his mind conjuring all sorts of dirty thoughts.

"Bathroom's all yours," he said.

"Oh," she gasped, looking up. "Ohhh."

Yeah, she was totally soaking him in, and as he moved to tuck in with his book, he caught her glancing at his ass a few times. And he loved it. Loved knowing that—if that look on her face was any indication—she wanted him.

Amalie's mouth hung half-open, her eyes dark with lust as her gaze skated over his shirtless chest before dipping down, down, *down*. Her tongue darted out to wet her lips.

Julian cleared his throat, trying very hard not to let the satisfaction filling him translate to his face. "Eyes up here, Stardust."

She blinked once, twice, and then, with a reddened face, turned back to pick up the panties she dropped. She was seriously adorable when she blushed.

"You're going to give me a complex." He settled into the bed, careful to make sure the sheets didn't hide what Amalie had been checking out. "I was really hoping you'd like me naked."

No woman had ever captured his attention the way Amalie did. Damn if she didn't make him jittery, make him feel like he was about to step foot on the tennis court. He loved the spark in her gray eyes when he pushed the boundaries, the way desire consumed her irises, darkening them to ash.

"You're ridiculous." Amalie rolled her eyes and pretended to be aggravated, but she wore a half-smile that quivered at the corner. "I'm just gonna…gonna…go." She pointed toward the bathroom, stretching *go* into three syllables that sounded more like a question. She didn't even give him time to nod or make a comment before he heard the door shut.

As soon as the shower cut on, his focus was completely shot. He re-read the same page ten times while trying not to imagine Amalie's body all wet and slick. What was going to go down once she got out of that shower? Was he finally going to make his move? He couldn't quite read her one hundred percent, and earlier she was nervous about sharing the room. He released a shuddering breath and decided all he could do was wait.

After what felt like forever, the shower shut off. Amalie came out, her hair wet and curly, but that's not what held his attention. Hot damn. The woman was dangerous in those black pajamas. Her bottoms were short, showing off the curves of her thighs and causing Julian's imagination to run wild with what was hidden under that silky fabric. Her tank top dipped into a V, showing off her cleavage. But that wasn't the only thing on display. Her hardened nipples shone like little pearls beneath the material.

Julian's mouth went dry, his skin went hot, his hands flexing at his side.

Amalie must've felt his stare as she dropped her dirty clothes in a pile next to her bag. She turned around, lust still lighting her eyes. "You okay there, Smoke? I kinda hoped you'd like me naked."

He nodded wordlessly while readjusting the blankets. He had to get himself under control.

Everything moved in slow motion until she bumped into the chair that held his bag, knocking a book onto the floor. She bent to pick it up, holding a very worn copy of *Breaking the Fall*. She tilted her head in question.

"It's a good book." He tucked one arm behind his head. "You should read it."

The laugh that came out of her was deep and throaty, full-on seductress as she placed the novel on the nightstand. "Julian Smoke. I thought you didn't like reading."

"I'll do anything when it comes to you," he said, realizing how serious he sounded, but he couldn't help it. "Don't you know that?"

And then she was next to him, moving under the covers, her smooth legs grazing his, her body facing his. He could smell her sweet vanilla perfume, the detergent from her clothes, feel the heat from her skin, and it was almost unbearable.

As he turned to face her, he stared into her eyes, and damn if he didn't see the invitation written there. "You're awful close, princess."

She took a deep breath, as though summoning her courage. "I meant to be."

Julian swallowed back the knot in his throat, and even though he was in sensory overload, he leaned forward, tucking Amalie's hair behind her ear, a finger moving down her chin...

Chapter Nineteen

AMALIE

AMALIE'S BREATH CAUGHT AT THE FEEL OF JULIAN'S TOUCH, SO SIMPLE YET explosive.

His leg brushed hers, his knee coming to rest between her thighs...not as close as she wanted, but just close enough. She could hardly think, not even about all the things she wanted to do to him, because this Julian was overwhelming. She could keep sarcastic Julian at arm's length, friend-zone Julian at wrist length, although it was tough, but this guy melted every last defense she had.

She wasn't a palm reader or a psychic, but Amalie was willing to bet that tonight would be the night she made an epic mistake or would say something about how her once-silly crush had evolved into something much more complicated. She could feel all of that simmering below the surface, and with Julian's body pressed against hers, his hands tracing soft paths over her hand, wrist, forearm, and dipping to curve along her hips, it would be oh so easy.

Julian was focused on her skin, and he bit his lip as if he liked what he saw. That look, on a man like Julian, could make a woman's body scream *DANGER! DANGER!*

Anxiety clenched Amalie's gut as she thought back to their earlier conversation about Nadine. He was *desperate* for her. What did it feel like to have someone absolutely desperate for you? It was something she wanted to know. More importantly, it was how she wanted Julian to feel for *her*. Not for Nadine. And the thing was, by the way he was staring at her now, she had to wonder if they weren't already there, at that place of sheer agony and deepest desire.

Any worry fell away, and all thoughts of Nadine vanished, the look in Julian's eyes enough to spur her forward. Her breath hitched and picked up under Julian's intense stare, her body trembling with his soft friction on her inner thigh.

Julian put on the smolder, and she realized what he'd attempted drunkenly at the bar all those months ago didn't hold a candle to this. His eyes were heated, his jaw prominent, his mouth hooked into her favorite lopsided smile, his dimple popping. "Stardust, there's so much that I want to do to you." Each word that came out of that sensual mouth of his dripped with sex. The lyrics from "Hot in Here" drifted through her head, and she almost had to physically stop herself from fanning her face.

Amalie's breathing grew heavy as the space between them grew electric, a tangible thing holding them in place. She looked at him, and not from beneath her lashes. No, she met his stare head-on, because she owned her feelings this time, just this once not caring about the consequences. All she could think about since they stepped foot in that hotel room was Julian and how much she needed him, how he was the only one who could fill the void in her chest.

"Why don't you show me?" she challenged, her voice a sultry whisper.

Julian moved, his eyes flashing a deep green, the color of the forest during a thunderstorm. He was slow, achingly slow, as his hand reached forward to hold the back of her head, his hand digging deep into her hair. The feel of his fingers fisting in her locks threatened to completely unravel her.

"This is a terrible idea." Julian's voice had taken on that deep, husky timbre, a tone that promised hours, hell, even *days* of endless pleasure and tangled limbs beneath the sheets.

His thumb came up to rub a gentle path over her lips. She wanted to know how he kissed, how he did…other things. Was he rough or was he gentle?

It didn't matter, not when she wanted it all from him.

A tiny gasp escaped her as she reacted to his touch, his scent, his *everything*.

"It's a terrible idea, yes," she finally murmured against his thumb.

He stilled, a slow-building grin tilting his lips. His eyes blazing as they flitted from her mouth to her eyes and back again. "Tell me we shouldn't do this then." He moved closer, his hand running a line up and down her neck, featherlight, and Amalie found herself arching into his touch, the reaction immediate and natural. *"Tell me,"* he coaxed, even though his tightening grip in her hair and his fevered touch screamed the absolute opposite.

"I can't. Not this time," she answered, her voice stronger now, which was surprising given the fact that white-hot lust lit her up like the Fourth of July.

She slipped her hands around the back of Julian's neck, finally burying her fingers into his unruly hair, and then Julian's mouth brushed over hers in the most torturous almost-kiss of her entire life. It was barely a whisper, but it was already hotter than any full-on kiss she'd ever experienced.

"You're going to ruin me, Amalie."

Her hand clasped around his wrist, stilling his movements. "Shut up and kiss me already."

He moved, rolling her to her back as he hovered above her, his biceps flexing with the effort of keeping his body weight off her, but that effort was in vain as she arched into him, pressing against his hardness.

Her hands flitted over his arms, her nails digging into his shoulders before raking down his firm chest. A noise erupted from Julian, a cross between a moan and the sexy sounds he made on the tennis court. His head slanted, and his breath danced over her skin, her heart beating a crazed, frantic rhythm as a shiver skittered up and down her arms. Were they really doing this?

Then his mouth came crashing down on hers, lips working to part her own, his tongue gaining entry on a wet slide. It was not a gentle kiss. It was the type of kiss that threatened to end Amalie, to devour her and leave her senseless. It was months of foreplay that finally came to a head, and it was heaven, complete with fireworks and wobbly legs, and absolute *wanting*.

Amalie touched the curly hairs at the nape of Julian's neck and tugged him even closer, pressing their chests together, earning her a delicious, approving growl.

Julian pulled back slightly and edged the thin strap of her tank off her shoulder, then leaned down to bite the curve of her breast before licking her skin.

Her entire body bowed upward with the movement, muttered words of nonsense streaming from her lips as she grabbed his head and held him there, allowing him to pull her tank down further, fully exposing her.

"My God, I might not survive this night," he said, his tone full of reverence as he pressed his weight into her a little more, the feeling of being so fully enveloped by him nothing short of deliriously delicious.

He bent his head and flicked his tongue over her nipple, and she nearly levitated. Her hands frantically came to his waist, edging down, first grabbing his ass, sighing at how perfectly firm it was, her head in the clouds with what his mouth was doing to her breasts.

He moved back up to her neck, kissing along her jaw as his hand slid down and fingered the hem of her shorts. He hesitated, looking to her for consent.

"Yessss," she hissed between her teeth as her hand finally snaked between them, feeling his arousal against her palm.

Julian growled into her neck, pushing himself into her hand, from fingertip to wrist. "Fuck, Amalie," he whispered against her throat before nipping her earlobe. It was the hottest thing she'd ever heard or felt, and all she wanted was for him to finally touch her between her legs. Like *yesterday*, damn it.

As if reading her thoughts, he touched her there, over the thin fabric of her night shorts and skimpy underwear. He rubbed and teased and moved back and forth. "Damn, you're wet."

"Because I'm dying." Her words came out all breathy. All she wanted was to see him, sweat-slicked and working hard for her, for him, for whatever this was between them. She wanted all of her daydreams and fantasies to manifest in this moment.

She grabbed his taut arms and with an evil smile, flipped herself on top of him, allowing full access to his hardness where she needed it most. She gasped at the feel of him and couldn't stop herself from moaning when he took her nipple into his mouth.

He tugged at the waistband of her shorts. "Get these off."

She lifted up, about to rip them off her body because she wanted him inside her, now, but a knock—no, actually a loud *boom*—came from the door. They stared at one another before turning toward the sound.

Amalie couldn't think straight, her skin stretched too tight over her bones, her blood boiling in her veins. All that existed was Julian and his mouth. Did she take her birth control? Because those lips gave the types of kisses to knock you right up.

"Were you expecting anyone?" She jumped off of Julian, breathless, and began nervously smoothing her hands over her hair, pulling the strap of her tank over her shoulder.

God. Raw, vulnerable Julian plus hot almost-have-your-way-with-me Julian was like a freaking unicorn. Who knew when she'd stumble upon that again?

Julian blinked slowly, completely dazed as he gave a quick shake of his head. "Are you?" he asked, darkly.

"No," she hissed. The knocking continued.

Amalie was beyond pissed at having what could've probably been the single hottest night of her life ripped away.

Julian, however, seemed to be slowly recovering as a devious grin brightened his face. He rose on an elbow, slipped his hand up the inside of Amalie's thigh and yelled, "Go away. We're naked in here!"

"Julian!" she mouthed, brows raised. Seriously though, they were about 2.4 seconds away from stripping off clothes, so it wasn't a complete lie.

The knocking stopped, and just as Amalie was about to suggest they pick up where they left off, a voice they both knew *exceedingly* well thundered behind the door.

"If that's the case, I'll have both your hides. I specifically told Julian no hanky panky before matches!" Paul called back.

"What the hell?" Julian slid from the bed.

Amalie followed with a shrug as she pulled a cardigan over her PJ's and tossed Julian a sweatshirt.

His brows furrowed in confusion. "What am I supposed to do with this?"

Amalie tried not to laugh, grabbing the shirt. "You wrap it around your waist to hide your erection, dummy. You could poke someone's eye out with that thing." Julian chuckled and ran his hands over his face. "Stand still and let me do it," Amalie said as she wrapped the sweatshirt around him and tied the sleeves together in the back. It looked ridiculous and only kind of helped, but there wasn't much else to be done.

Still shirtless, Julian made his way to the door, Amalie scurrying behind him. Her plan was to basically be invisible.

Julian opened the door a crack, keeping the lower half of his body hidden from view. "What do you need, Paul?"

Amalie couldn't see Paul from where she stood behind the door, but she could only imagine his reaction. He'd definitely said *no sex*, and yet here they were about to sex it up.

"Well, I didn't think I'd be barging in on *this* when I got the news," Paul admitted. "Can't say I'm surprised though."

Julian straightened, the door opening the slightest bit. "What news?"

Amalie even peered out from behind him, pulling her cardigan tight across her body. Paul didn't notice her as he was laser-focused on his athlete.

"The USTA just called me and"—Paul made direct eye contact with Julian as he continued, one hand moving over his beard—"they're giving you a wild card into the US Open. You're in, son! You're *in* the US Open!"

Amalie jumped up with a squeal, launching herself at the back of a very shocked Julian, wrapping her arms around him. Julian squeezed her hands before looking back at his coach.

"Are you serious?" Julian asked, his voice choked, hesitant.

"I'm serious! You did it!" Paul nodded emphatically.

Julian, still holding the door cracked, held a hand out to fist bump Paul. "I'd hug ya but…"

Paul grimaced and quickly bumped Julian's fist. "Yeah, I don't wanna be on the other side of that door. We're good, kid."

Julian laughed, the sound husky and deep. He lifted an arm and tugged Amalie to his side. Tears clouded his pretty eyes as he pressed his dad's necklace reverently to his lips.

"As soon as I got the call, I ran up here as fast as I could," Paul said, giving Amalie a wink and a nod.

Julian's eyes flashed to Amalie's, her heart soaring at seeing him so happy. A small voice in the back of her mind cooed, *That's what love is*, but she pushed it down, way down.

With the biggest smile Amalie had ever seen on the man, Paul gave Julian a mock punch to the chin. "This is perfect. Now we don't have to worry about you playing in that qualifying tournament and getting injured. We get more time to train at home."

Julian shook his head as he ran a hand through his hair. "I just...I can't believe it."

"Well, believe it. I already contacted the airline, and we leave for Atlanta in the morning. Don't worry, I sweet-talked the hotel into refunding the nights we aren't staying. And, son, you better rest while you can because we're about to begin the next level of your training."

Both Amalie and Julian's eyes widened. Paul's training was already pretty brutal. She shuddered at the idea of what another level would entail. Of course, Paul was completely oblivious and kept talking. "So, like I said, I need you kids to get some *rest*, got it?"

"We hear you, Paul," Amalie answered, with only the slightest bit of snark.

"You got it, Coach," Julian added with a mock salute.

Paul gave Julian a wild-west stare down. "Come on, Julian, you've watched *Rocky*, you know Mick's rules. Same as mine. No messing around until after the Open."

Heat rushed up her neck, the images from earlier still fresh on her mind. When neither she nor Julian spoke, Paul made a big show of pointing to his eyes with two fingers and then back at Julian before he turned and disappeared down the hall.

Julian shut the door, rubbing the back of his neck, shock still etched across his expression. "This is unreal. A guy like me doesn't get wild cards. I'm waiting for them to call and say they've made a mistake." He moved back to the bed, sitting down. He looked completely stunned.

Amalie went to him, hands resting on his shoulders. "It's not a mistake. You earned it."

Julian looked up at her. As soon as their eyes met, he reached for her hands. "Amalie." His voice was soft and serious.

She put up no fight as he pulled her down on the bed beside him. She tried to calm her frenzied heart as they turned on their sides, each propped up on an elbow, their bodies only inches apart. Would they finish what they started? She needed some sort of release. She'd die without it.

She tried to gather herself as she watched Julian's lashes fan across his dark cheeks each time he blinked, the soft caress of his fingers trailing over her arms, his gaze pinning her to the bed. She opened her mouth to crack a joke, to deflect, because suddenly she felt everything to her very core, and it was almost too much.

Julian's slow movement cut off her joke, his hand shifting beneath her chin, tilting it, his thumb rubbing over her bottom lip, his eyes tracking the movement. She wanted that hand elsewhere.

Her mouth went dry at the spark in his eyes, and then Julian made his move, dipping his head and crushing his mouth to hers in a kiss that made her toes curl as a soft moan escaped her lips. After what felt like forever, yet still not long enough, Julian pulled back, running his fingers over her cheekbones.

"Stardust," he whispered as he finally laced their fingers together, laying their hands between their bodies. "I've got something to say to you, and I just need to get it out, okay?"

She nodded, her nerves raw because of his nearness, his mesmerizing touch, and the fact that she now knew what his lips tasted like.

When he spoke again, she noticed that he made sure to meet her eyes. "I don't know if you can tell, but I care about you, Amalie. More than I've ever cared about any woman. No one else is like you—a smart-ass, witty, beautiful writer with a heart of gold. No one else can put up with my shit, either."

Oh, this beautiful man was irresistible. His words had her feeling things she'd never felt before.

"If I kiss you again, put my mouth on you, I'll never want to stop. I had no plans of stopping before Paul barged in. But now that, um, some of the blood has rushed back to my brain, I realize that I want to take you out on dates, do things right with you. But I can't yet. Tonight, that drunken dream from the bar, it turned into reality, and for the first time in my life, I'm going to chase after it. And to do that, I've got to focus." He sighed, released a ragged breath, then brought a hand up to cup the back of her head, his fingers splayed and tangled in her hair. "I won't be able to focus if I don't follow Paul's rules tonight." He pressed his forehead against hers. "I want everything to be perfect the first time I make love to you. I don't want any distractions. Once I'm inside you, Amalie, I have a feeling I'm never going to want to come out. I want you to be mine, but I also want to be able to give you all of me, and right now I can't." He drew back then, eyes dark, his words leaving her in a heady yet disappointed haze. "I guess I just needed you to know why, much as I want to, I can't go any further," he continued. "At least not yet." His fingers tightened in her hair, a pleasant pressure sending sparks all the way down to her toes. "Does that make sense?" His gaze dipped to her lips for a minute and then returned to her eyes.

A weight had been lifted from her heart as she allowed his words to sink in, the meaning cementing itself deep within her mind as she stroked his cheek. She loved the feeling of her fingers quietly skating over his dark stubble. How often had she daydreamed of doing that?

"I get it, Julian, I do, because I want this for you more than I've ever wanted anything," she said softly.

Julian's eyes dilated, the black of his pupils eating up the color, leaving only a look of undiluted hunger and want.

Prompted by that look and the recent good news, she blurted, "I like you way too damn much, Julian Smoke, and I can't wait to see you win." She smiled. "I also can't wait for you to make love to me. But I'll do my best to be patient."

With a groan, Julian brushed his lips over her knuckles once more. "With you saying things like that, looking like you do, it makes me want to say fuck the consequences. It makes me want to worship every single inch of you the way you deserve to be worshipped."

Her skin tingled at his words, at the look on his face. Even though her body was aflame with all that hot-as-hell imagery coupled with the phantom touch of his lips on hers, she knew what he said earlier was right. Although it went against everything she wanted, everything she felt, she said, "Then you better get to your side of the bed, Smoke." She slid away from him and used her foot to nudge him.

"Fine, I'm going." He held up one hand in surrender, playfulness stretching across his handsome features as he scooted over, but his other hand still held hers between them in what felt like complete and utter reverence. "Good night, Amalie," he said in that low, rumbly voice of his just before closing those beautiful eyes.

Amalie sighed as she desperately tried to cool herself. She'd wait until he was asleep, and then she'd slip into the bathroom to get relief because as it was, she was a throbbing mess.

As Julian's scent enveloped her, she answered with a soft smile, "Good night."

Chapter Twenty

JULIAN

THE NEXT MORNING JULIAN'S ALARM WOKE HIM HOURS BEFORE THEY HAD TO catch their return flight. His first thought was of Amalie, but she was nowhere to be found. Her side of the bed was rumpled, and he figured she'd gone to find something to eat.

When he told her last night that he liked her, he'd been lying...sort of. He more than liked her. He had the scary, sneaking suspicion his feelings were verging on something much bigger, but he didn't exactly want to put it all out there the first time they kissed, even though they were well on their way to more than that before Paul barged in.

Julian had been strung so tightly that he woke in the middle of the night, sweating, with Amalie's ass pressed into his groin. With a hushed groan, he extracted her from that position and then disappeared into the bathroom to take a cold shower and finish what Amalie started. Had she gotten any relief? He'd heard her go to the bathroom in the night as well, and he clamped his teeth on his pillow when a gentle moan sifted under the door. He hoped she'd been doing what he imagined. That was half the reason he had to take care of himself.

His thoughts were interrupted by the ringing of the room phone.

"Hello?" All kinds of uncertainty filled his voice because everyone he talked to used his cell number.

"This is Marleen from the front desk. May I speak to Miss Warner?"

"She's out right now."

"When she returns will you have her bring an alternate method of payment to the front desk? This morning she dropped off her credit card to replace your method of payment and it's showing up as declined. Or perhaps you could bring your card down? It was accidentally deleted in the process. I apologize for that."

Leave it to Amalie to be sneaky about paying. Julian shuffled for his own wallet on the nightstand. "Sure, it's no problem. I'll bring one right away."

He dressed and headed downstairs, making a mental note to ask Amalie about her credit card. They'd been splitting everything because she was hell-bent on helping, but that phone call had him worried.

As soon as he stepped from the elevator on the first floor, he passed a sitting area near the entrance. Standing there saying goodbye was none other than Amalie and Andrew Warner, the latter dressed in a crisp beige suit with Ray-Bans tucked into the lapel, his salt-and-pepper hair parted and combed to the side.

What the hell?

Julian couldn't make out Amalie's expression since her back was to him, but she slipped out the door while Andrew hung back.

Julian continued to the desk, hoping that maybe he hadn't been spotted.

"Julian," Andrew called, causing Julian's entire body to tense as he turned around.

Andrew walked with an eerie grace as he met Julian halfway. He looked slightly aggravated. At least Julian *thought* Andrew was aggravated. It was nearly impossible to tell, since the man's face never wrinkled, just like his clothes.

"Is there a reason you're here?" Julian asked without preamble.

Andrew's lips pursed in dry amusement. "I came to see my daughter. We had business to discuss."

Julian shifted from foot to foot as he crossed his arms in the universal "back off" gesture. "I can't imagine what business you have to discuss, since we're doing this thing without *your* help."

"Son—" Andrew started.

Wrong.

Julian stiffened immediately. "No one calls me that except for my dad and Paul, and seeing as my father is dead, I suggest you choose another rich-boy nickname. Preferably not one you've used before, like *investment.*"

Andrew flinched, the movement nearly imperceptible. Julian gathered there wasn't much in this world that could surprise the man, so he took it as a victory. "Fine, *Julian.* Before I leave, I should ask what you thought about your wild card?" Andrew adjusted the bright green silk tie around his neck.

Dread trickled into Julian's veins like poison. "How do you know about my wild card?"

"Technically it's *my* wild card, since I had everything to do with it," Andrew challenged.

Julian felt his nostrils flare, his jaw tightening as he pointed a finger directly in Andrew Warner's face. "You're a sick bastard, Andrew. You know that? That wild card?" He thumped his chest. "It's mine. Not yours. *Mine.*"

People in the lobby stopped and turned their heads, some lingering, others going about their business, but Julian didn't give a shit. He couldn't believe this. Despite the words coming out of his mouth, he knew that wild card didn't belong to him. No, the whole fucking thing felt tainted now. This was something he'd wanted to do on his own, but Amalie's father swooped in and somehow "saved the day."

Did Amalie know about this? Of course she didn't. She knew how important it was for Julian to do this on his own. She wouldn't do that to him.

"Amalie's going to be pissed when I tell her about this," Julian added. "Or is that why you're here? To gloat. Or maybe you're trying to win back your daughter. You know, the one you left out in the cold like a fucking stranger."

The corner of Andrew Warner's lips kicked up, an air of annoying confidence pouring off his tailored suit. "Who's to say she doesn't already know, that it was her idea? That she's given up on this foolish dream of hers?"

Julian clenched his fist so tightly that he could feel crescent moons being carved into his palm.

Andrew cocked his head, his face arranged in an expression that was clearly meant to radiate superiority. "Is that a spark of doubt I see? Not so sure that Amalie didn't have something to do with it? Talk to her or don't, it doesn't matter to me. Either way, I'm viewing this as an *investment*." Oh, he was sure to put the emphasis on that word. "Besides, you'll look good out there on that blue court wearing my hotel's logo."

"I'm not wearing your damn anything," Julian bit out, the words chopped short by his teeth.

"You will unless you want me to call the USTA and pull my funding. Looks like the Warner logo will be on your shirt, on the sides of the courts, maybe even on the cups the fans drink from. Worthwhile *investment*, if you ask me."

Julian seethed, everything around him turning red. It was Anthony Fox all over again, and there was no way he believed that Amalie brought Andrew into the fold. Andrew Warner was the most manipulative bastard he'd ever met, and he refused to accept anything that came out of that man's mouth.

"Fuck off," Julian spat, and without another word he stormed out of the sitting area, his head throbbing.

He needed a minute to breathe, but first he needed to settle the bill. With his shoulders hitched high, tension flickering down every muscle in his body, he made his way to the front desk.

"Hi, may I help you?" a chirpy brunette asked.

It took everything Julian had to keep his calm, but he managed to grit out, "Marleen called and said that our payment was declined. I came to settle up."

"Name?"

"Julian Smoke and Amalie Warner." God, saying those names together was something he loved, but he couldn't suppress the angry thoughts swirling in his mind, Andrew's shark-like grin at the forefront.

"Oh, those charges have already been covered."

That call was less than ten minutes ago. Unless...

"Could you tell me who covered them?" The air constricted in his lungs as he begged for it not to be who he thought.

The clerk nodded. "Of course. It was Andrew Warner. He covered everything in full just a moment ago."

Julian's feet were glued to the spot as he stared down at the marble pattern on the desk. Pieces were clicking into place: Amalie and her dad, the wild card, paying for the room. He didn't want to believe it, didn't want to believe that asshole Andrew, but the truth rang inside him.

She'd gone back to her father. There was no other explanation.

"Sir? Are you all right?" The voice sounded like it was underwater, but Julian broke out of his rage-filled haze long enough to nod and stride away from the counter to the elevator bank where he waited. Why would Amalie do this? It was all too convenient to not be connected.

He needed to find her, needed answers.

Desperate for some type of distraction, he pulled his phone from his shorts and opened Twitter, shocked to see his name trending. Wait, how could that be? He clicked on his hashtagged name and saw the headline, the one that had everyone in an uproar: "Smoke Beats Garner for Wild Card."

Ethan Garner was a beloved tennis player, although he hadn't been performing well lately, which explained his recent retirement announcement. Wild cards were often controversial, but hell, people were roasting the shit out of Julian. One person said he was trash, another called him a has-been, but the one that really stuck was the one that said, "Well, he better live up to it. It would suck if he lost in the first round."

He was burdened again by those very expectations he'd talked to Amalie about. Now they weren't his, they were the fucking world's.

He hadn't asked for this. He wanted to do this on his own because he'd always taken the easy road. This was his chance to prove himself, and it'd been snatched away. Rich assholes were always taking shit from him—the country club tennis pro, Anthony, Nadine, and now Andrew…and maybe Amalie. God, he hoped he didn't have to add her to that list. It'd kill him.

Shoving his phone back into his pocket, he tried to tamp down the building nausea and decided not to look at anything else until he talked to Amalie. Thankfully, he didn't have to wait long. She returned to the room about twenty minutes later, bagels in hand, a stunning smile illuminating her face. She wore an olive dress that showed off her sexy legs, but he was not to be deterred.

"Sorry I left without waking you. I got hungry and couldn't wait."

"Hey, I need to talk to you about a few things." Julian stood from the desk chair.

Her expression was blank as she set the bagels down next to him. "Sure, what's up?"

His mind was spinning, but he tried to tackle one thing at a time. "Why didn't you tell me you were having money trouble? That you'd maxed out your credit card?"

Horror washed over her face as she took a step back. "How would you even know that?"

"The front desk called and wanted one of us to bring a different card to pay for the room. Why didn't you tell me you were having money issues?"

Amalie squinted. "Because I'm handling it. I don't need your help."

Her tone was defensive as hell. But that was the thing, wasn't it? It told him everything he needed to know.

He decided to play stupid for just another minute, curious as to what she'd say, what lies she might tell even though the thought made him want to hurl.

"Well, let me know if you need help. I told you I don't mind—"

Amalie sliced a hand through the air. "Oh my God, I got it. I hear you."

He held his hands up in surrender. "Fine, fine. But I have to ask, how's your dad?"

Her body flinched, and her eyes snapped to meet his as a shadow passed over her face. "What?"

Anger rolled around inside him like a storm. "Yeah, I saw him in the lobby, that smug son of a bitch. Looks like he paid for our room charge. Is that what you meant when you said you had it covered? Asking Andrew for help?"

Amalie stared at him without blinking as her lips worked for a reply.

Julian's stomach clenched. It was true then.

Biting off her response, he continued, "He told me *he's* the reason I got the wild card. And that you knew about it." Julian took a step forward, his body vibrating. "I told him there was no way you knew, that you wouldn't betray me that way."

Her hands came together, wringing. "He...he told you about the wild card?"

Everything stopped. His heart pounded feverishly, the thumping so loud it roared in his ears. What was she saying? It sounded as if…

"So, you *did* have something to do with it? You mean to tell me that for once he wasn't lying?" He was praying that this was a nightmare or some sort of joke.

Amalie waved her hands in front of her body. "Wait, you don't understand—" Her words stumbled over themselves.

An intense heat slithered through his veins. Why would she do this? After all he'd shared with her? Betrayal was something he simply couldn't forgive, not after Nadine, not after Anthony, not after what he'd done to his father.

His teeth clenched so tightly it felt like his jaw was about to snap as he ran his hands through his hair, his feet pacing, staying far away from Amalie, the girl he thought he was falling in love with. "No, Amalie, I think I understand perfectly."

Her sharp intake of breath echoed through the room. But before she could say anything else, Julian said, "I'm so angry I can't even look at you right now."

Without another word, he tore out of the room, slamming the door on any future he might've had with Amalie Warner.

JULIAN SAT NEXT TO PAUL ON THE FLIGHT HOME, DOING EVERYTHING HE COULD to avoid Amalie, who was a row over. He leaned closer to his coach, his words hushed, "Andrew Warner bought me the wild card. Did you know?"

Paul nodded and Julian felt his earlier anger appear, threatening to snarl and bite. Before he could say anything, Paul held out a hand toward him. "I know it's not how you wanted to get into the US Open, but it's the best thing that could've happened."

Julian made a noise in the back of his throat. "I think I should refuse it, turn it down."

Paul's head jerked back. "And you'd be the biggest fool to walk this earth, son. You don't turn something like that down. It is what it is, and now we focus on not wasting this chance."

Julian opened his mouth to argue, seething at the idea of being indebted to Andrew Warner, knowing that man's gaudy-ass logo would cover his tennis gear. Paul cut off any response with a shake of his head.

"I don't want to hear any arguments. Case closed on that front. Now that you've got me in crisis mode with your lover's spat, I've got a new practice partner to keep you occupied, to keep your head in the game."

That was the last thing Julian had on his mind. All he could think about was Amalie and how he already missed her even though she was on the same flight as him. There was an ache in his chest, like a piece of his heart was missing, despite how absurd it sounded.

"You listening to me?" Paul asked with a nudge of Julian's shoulder.

"Yeah, yeah. New practice partner to keep my mind off of Amalie and this shitstorm. Who is it?"

"Austin Johnson, a top-fifty player and an Atlanta boy just like yourself. I think y'all will get along well."

Julian nodded as he let his head rest back against the seat. He wanted to look around Paul and across the row, to get Amalie's attention. Instead, he curled his hands into fists and closed his eyes. He'd finally given her everything, every piece of him that he had, and she'd thrown it all away. He knew that in the coming days he'd miss her even more. He'd miss her smile, her wit, the way she held her pen between her teeth during a nail-biter rally, the way she peppered him with questions so she could get her character, get *him* just right and real. He hoped she didn't give up on her writing, because it would be a damn shame if she did. She'd put talk of all that on the back burner while they were in New York, and he wished she hadn't.

Regardless of any of that, she'd betrayed him. Everything between them was ruined and he would have to learn to live his life without her in it.

Chapter Twenty-One

AMALIE

"WE COULD ALWAYS SLASH HIS TIRES," ROMINA POINTED OUT, HER FORK waving through the air like a sword. The idea had her eyes sparkling.

Amalie shrugged as she pushed her pancakes around her plate. It'd been two weeks since Julian accused her of going behind his back, working with her dad. He hadn't even given her a chance to explain, and that upset her more than anything. He should've known her better than that, should've let her explain the truth about what he thought he saw. Julian's stubbornness fueled her own, because now she refused to even try to reach out to him. What good would it do? He'd already made up his mind and wouldn't believe her. Besides, if he thought the worst of her so easily, then what they had probably wasn't real anyway.

She accepted that this was her life now: a failed writer sleeping on her best friend's couch while trying to make ends meet with an asshole father somehow thrown into the mix and a nonexistent love life. Thankfully, Romina and Simone had been amazing supports—Simone was more of the PJ's, ice cream, and Netflix sort, where Romina ventured into Carrie Underwood "Before He Cheats" territory. This was all new to Amalie, of course. Her breakup with Maxwell hadn't left her feeling this bereft, and yet she and Julian weren't even really technically a *thing*.

Her lungs constricted as she thought about the way he'd looked at her that morning in New York, his lip curled in disgust as he laid out how she'd wounded him, betrayed him. Then he up and left without allowing her any further say. She wanted to despise him, but she just couldn't bring herself to do it. That didn't mean she wasn't pissed, though. She'd had no idea her father was in town.

No, he'd tracked her down that morning in New York, catching her on the street and leading her back into the hotel lobby, telling her that he'd pulled some strings to get Julian a wild card. Apparently, he'd heard that Julian really had a shot, that people were talking about him, and he couldn't pass up the chance to use Julian as a means of garnering attention for Warner Hotels.

Amalie had been mortified to hear that, knowing it would hurt Julian's pride. She'd resigned herself to tell Julian once she got back from getting breakfast, to let him know she had absolutely nothing to do with it. From there she thought they could figure out the next step together—to refuse the wild card, perhaps? Hell, she didn't know what exactly, just as long as it had nothing to do with Andrew Warner and his toxic parenting.

And now she realized that her father most likely staged the entire thing just so Julian would witness it. He didn't want them together, not with how Julian supported her, believed in her, not with how he didn't fit into the country club set or bow down to the great Andrew Warner. And how the hell did her father know her credit card had been declined? She would never have asked him to pay the bill. Just thinking about it made her blood boil.

"Hellooo. Earth to Amalie. Did you hear what I said?" Romina waved a hand in front of Amalie's face as she scooted her chair back.

The sound pulled Amalie out of her pit of loathing, and her eyes snapped up to Romina. "I'm sorry, Ro. What?"

Romina threw her purse over her shoulder and then put her hands on her hips. Crap. It was serious if she had her hands on her hips.

"I asked if you've heard from Julian yet, or at least Paul?"

Amalie swallowed the lump in her throat, tucking her hair behind her ears as she shook her head in response. "Not a word."

She stood from the kitchen table and, after washing her plate, moved to the couch that had become her unofficial office.

Romina's mouth tightened into a disapproving line. "I already told you that he hasn't missed a training session, and that I've made it my personal mission to torture the hell out of him, but yesterday I brought your name up and he refused to talk about you. He looked miserable."

Amalie hoped in some sick, sadistic way that he was hurting just as much as she was. She missed his irritating ways, his inappropriate jokes, his knowing eyes. She missed *him*, and he hated her. *Abhorred* was a better word for it.

With a sigh, she stabbed at invisible lint on her pajama pants. She hadn't worn real clothes in a few days. "Can we just agree to a temporary ban on discussing him?"

Her friend studied her for a beat, her brown eyes like laser beams shooting straight into Amalie's soul. Ro's expression softened once she found what she was looking for. "You really liked him, huh?"

Amalie's body stiffened. Romina had hit the mark, though it wasn't like Amalie had been particularly careful to hide it. As soon as she'd returned from New York, she'd given her friend the Cliff's Notes version of her hot-hot-hot make-out session with Julian. That night played on a loop in her thoughts, and she couldn't help but think if he was that incredibly skilled with his mouth, with *anticipation*, then the sex would be mind-blowing. She bit the inside of her cheek at the thought. No other man had sent her senses into overdrive, awakening every single inch of her, igniting that greedy spark deep down in her belly.

Her cheeks reddened as she pictured Julian's toned, naked chest and the sounds he made when he hit a tennis ball. Gruncillating (yes, there was a technical term for those dead-sexy noises).

And yeah, sex would've been great, but she couldn't deny that what burned between them was so much more than that. At least for her. Her heart was in the game now, getting battered.

Romina cleared her throat, a knowing look on her face. "Stop daydreaming about that asshole."

"I can't help it, Ro."

Romina wagged her pointer finger back and forth. "Nope. No. No, ma'am. Don't you dare wallow in this." She motioned to where Amalie sat on the couch with greasy hair and day-old pajamas. "You pick yourself up, dust off your fine behind, and write. Channel this into that novel and write the best damn thing this world has ever seen. You don't need him to finish it—not anymore. You got this. In the meantime, I'll be here to help you get over that bastard."

Amalie's eyes flicked up. "He's not a bastard. He's…he's…"

"A bastard."

"He's not, but I see you're in Mama Bear mode, so no use in arguing."

"Nope, you know it's pointless. Now, you gonna write?"

Amalie exhaled the biggest sigh known to humankind and sank deeper into the couch. "I don't even know how to finish the book. I've got this guy who's finishing his journey, but what about the girl, the love interest? I don't know where to go with her story." The parallel was not completely lost on Amalie.

"Why don't you write the love story *you'd* want?"

Wouldn't that hurt too much? she wanted to ask. Instead, she just nodded. When Ro was like this it was just easier to agree and move on.

"Look, I gotta head to work, but call me if you need me, okay? Now open that laptop and work those little fingers to the bone," Romina said as she bent down to kiss Amalie on top of her head. She waved as she slipped out the door, leaving Amalie alone with her thoughts and her unfinished manuscript.

Since Stella's devastating email, Amalie had sought out other agents, some with cold queries, others with referrals from authors she knew, but over half had already come back as form rejections. With a sigh, she opened her email browser and went through all the fresh rejection letters. Would anyone ever want this damn story? Was it a waste of time? But no one wanted her story. What sucked even more was the fact that this story was something she believed in. It was one she wanted the world to read. Thanks to Julian, the tennis parts were realistic, and also thanks to Julian, she had a pretty amazing male lead in Jax. It was the most connected she'd felt to a character she'd written. And then there was Penelope, the character she'd loosely modeled after herself and Ro. That girl was badass and snarky and didn't give up. *She didn't give up.*

Amalie looked around the apartment. She'd moved out from under her father's tyranny, took the harder path, all because she believed in herself. She'd sacrificed so much to follow her heart, and it didn't seem fair to tap out now.

Julian's words came back to her. *I thought your pages were magic, that you're magic…but please, please don't give up. For me.*

The truth was, she'd felt the same about him, thought he was magic. After all, *he* hadn't given up. He'd gotten to the US Open, well, with her dad's help, but damn it, he'd still worked his ass off to make his dream a reality, to place himself in the realm of possibility and opportunity. Why shouldn't she do the same?

She took one last look through her rejections and then grabbed her phone, pulling up her favorite writing music. If no one would take her, she would do this on her own. She'd self-publish the novel. She'd work herself to the bone to reach out to bloggers and reviewers. She'd blitz her social media pages. She'd do everything she could if it meant keeping the dream alive. Julian started at the bottom. So would she—although this wasn't really the bottom, it was just a different path than she originally wanted to take.

Feeling lighter than she had in days, she wrote her heart out, taking Romina's advice. She wrote the love story she wanted, wrote the grand romantic gesture that would steal her heart, and before she knew it, she had a story she was proud of.

Well, it didn't happen that quickly. She still lacked an ending and then the remaining tennis scenes which would have to be written with the internet's help. Her heart literally hurt as she thought of Julian, but she pushed through.

As a distraction, she pulled up another search and found a book cover designer who could create a beautiful cover on a budget, as well as an affordable book formatter. She'd take on a few more freelance jobs to buffer her finances, revise the novel, probably rewrite it one or two more times before finding an editor, and then, well, she'd release it to the world.

But…the cover designer and the formatter needed a title. Amalie pressed her hand to her forehead. She'd been struggling with that for a while and nothing had stuck. Her mind wandered to Julian and the way he played tennis now, painting the lines, as he and Paul had called it. That term had always seemed beautiful. With a gasp, Amalie shot up from the couch, hands over her mouth. That was it! *Painting the Lines.*

Her heart sped up at the thought. It was almost enough to make her forget that her and Julian's love story wasn't the one she'd written.

Chapter Twenty-Two

JULIAN

A WEEK AND A HALF HAD PASSED, AND IT WAS THE FRIDAY BEFORE THE US Open, just three days until the tournament started. Julian had just finished practicing with Austin at the USTA Billie Jean King National Tennis Center. Paul thought practice would help Julian calm some of his worries about the draw, which was set to release any second. Thankfully his coach was right, since all he could think about was getting out of his sweat-soaked clothes. He thought he'd get a reprieve from the Big Apple's humidity, but not so much.

When he and Paul headed to the locker room, Julian couldn't help but think of how Amalie would be loving every minute of this, taking pictures and talking to all of the tennis players. The other night he almost signed up for Instagram and Facebook just so he could see if she was on there, just to get a glimpse. But deep down there was still so much anger. He wondered if she'd be at his first match, and if so, what would they even say to each other? He thought about that way more than he should, but as usual, those feelings were quickly doused by the image of the Warner logo everywhere he looked.

So much for learning to live without her.

Just as he put his tennis bag down on an empty bench, his phone buzzed with a notification. He looked at Paul.

"Might as well check it so you can get in the right mindset," Paul answered in a grizzled voice.

And with one click, the world felt like it was tumbling down around him. He would be playing Dominic Meklau, the number four player in the world.

He barely registered Paul taking the phone from his hand, his coach's voice barely coming through the roar of Julian's pulse in his ears. "Dominic Meklau?" Paul said. "We can handle that."

The Austrian was set to be the next generation of tennis. This was the same guy who bumped Alexander Becker from his number four spot. The twenty-three-year-old was coming off a win at Wimbledon and was a major force in the tennis world. Hell, there was talk he could very well win the US Open. Veteran players on the tour actually said in their interviews that they were afraid to play Meklau. Yeah, and that's what Julian was up against, first thing.

Julian finally snapped out of it when Paul handed his phone back to him. He sat on the bench with a loud thud, his shoulders slumped, foot bouncing. "I worked this hard to get this far only to play the number four player in the damn world during the *first* round? I know I'm good enough to beat some of these guys, but we're talking about top players now, more specifically a recent Wimbledon champ." His hand rubbed incessantly at his forehead. "What was I even thinking? I can't do this. I don't even belong here. Hell, Andrew Warner bought my way in, so this is probably a big *fuck you* from karma."

He wished he'd never even gotten the wild card. All it did was make him feel like a fraud. He'd even made the mistake of looking on social media again, of searching his name and seeing what everyone was saying about him—that he had no right to be in the US Open because he didn't earn it. The worst part was that he had those same thoughts. All he could do now was play like he deserved it and silence those doubts, which was made even more difficult by the fact that his first opponent was a beast.

Paul struck the back of Julian's head with a solid *thwap*.

"What the hell?" Julian's hand flew to the offended spot.

"Snap out of it, kid. You're going down a dangerous road with those kinds of thoughts, and now's not the time for them. Guess what? You made it here. If you weren't capable of playing with the big boys, you wouldn't be here. *You*"—he poked Julian's chest with a stubby finger covered in gray hair—"deserve to be here. This is your chance to live the dream, to not get discouraged and give up before you've even had a chance to prove who you are."

Without conviction, Julian replied, "I know. You're right."

Paul cocked an eyebrow as he continued. "Damn straight I'm right. So what that you're playing Meklau. You're just as good as he is, and remember this: he had to start somewhere and now look where he is. Who says that can't be you? That it *won't* be you? But if you start with all this woe-is-me talk first thing, then yeah, you'll lose. You can't go in there with this kind of attitude. It's not what's in your heart, but what's in your head that's holding you back. You got tons of heart and you'll show the world that on Monday." With a dismissive hand, Paul looked down at his watch, then back at Julian. "Let's go. Your mom should be at the hotel by now. I didn't spend all that time convincing her to break her superstitious live-match ban to come to New York for you to lose your nerve. We'll have a nice dinner and not think or talk about any of this until Sunday."

Julian agreed, but what he didn't say, what he was afraid to voice, was the fact that if he failed at this, he couldn't go back to selling pharmaceuticals. He couldn't go back to living a normal, mundane life. After these last few months, he realized that he wanted more, and damn it, he was going to go out there and get it.

By the time Sunday rolled around, Julian's nerves were in tatters. He tried to shake out his arms and stretch his neck as Paul led the way to the locker rooms at the Billie Jean King Tennis Center, but he was still a mess. As soon as they stepped inside, the melody of different languages and the sight of other players getting ready to leave for the night engulfed Julian.

Paul and Julian headed to a row of benches in the corner—the farther away from everyone the better, at least for right now. It was then that Julian understood he'd finally made it. This was his childhood dream, to play on Arthur Ashe Court, and now he was actually here—it was a reality.

The realization had his stomach dipping and twisting, and goosebumps slid along his arms. That feeling was quickly overtaken by something else the moment Andrew Warner swaggered his vampire-looking ass into the locker room, a rectangular white box in hand.

The air sparked, suddenly charged with tension. Paul edged closer to Julian, a protective dad gesture if he'd ever seen one. Julian on the other hand, didn't budge, only giving Andrew the slightest tip of the chin.

"I've got something for you." Warner's gaze skated over the locker room and then returned to the box he set down on the bench.

Julian held his breath as Warner opened the box, moved aside white tissue paper, and then pulled out a sleek black headband, black socks, and shorts to match. The court shirt was the last thing he revealed.

Paul raised his eyebrows and gave an approving nod. Maybe it wouldn't be so bad to let Andrew Warner pay for his tennis gear.

That thought lasted all of a second because Warner turned the shirt to the side, where a gaudy, oversized Warner Hotels logo had been stitched onto each arm. Not just one arm, but *both* of them.

"I'm not wearing this," Julian growled, eyeing the tennis shirt with obvious disgust.

Paul sighed and was about to speak when Warner said, "You have to. I got you here."

"Andrew, you and I both know the boy got himself here on his own merit," Paul interrupted. "He would've been here one way or another, you just expedited the process." Paul's words gritted between his teeth. Julian had never seen his coach coiled so tight, like a cobra ready to strike.

Warner lifted an eyebrow—it took a lot of effort, but he did it. "I see we beg to differ on that point."

Julian snarled at the logo again and then met Paul's indignant glare. "That bastard branded me. That's what this bullshit is."

Normally tennis players got to choose their sponsors and the logos were tasteful and didn't make them look like a walking billboard. Most players had a sportswear brand and then a tiny sponsor patch on their sleeve. This was over the top; the patches were the largest size the ATP allowed and obviously done to make a point.

Julian's fingers curled around the embroidered patch, poised to rip it off.

"Do it and I'll forfeit the match." Warner's eyes were cold. To add further insult to injury, he all but sneered. "Besides, my hotel stamp will look good on you." Without another word, he left, knowing that he didn't leave Julian with a choice.

Paul didn't waste any time stepping forward. "What I said to him was true. But you know this is a rich man's game and sometimes you just gotta play. You got yourself here, no matter what he says. Now go get dressed and forget about those gaudy-ass logos on your shirt. Let your tennis speak for itself."

One by one, players started filtering out of the locker room, eventually leaving just Julian and Dominic, along with their teams. Julian felt his body tense, nerves from earlier having returned. With trembling hands, he tied his headband around his head, while Paul shot him looks that wordlessly asked, "You okay, kid?" Julian gave him a nod as he sat back listening to his music, jiggling his knee, and willing himself to keep his shit together.

He surreptitiously sized up Dominic from across the room. The guy was the real deal. His shoes had his name on them, and he sported a killer state-of-the-art racket. Like that wasn't enough to mess with his brain, Dominic's tall frame had muscles on top of muscles.

Thankfully, Paul nudged Julian's shoulder, rescuing him from his own stupid thoughts. "It's almost time."

Vibrations shook the stadium, a familiar bassline echoing into the locker room. As was the custom at the US Open, the first-night match opened with fanfare and a concert.

"Smoke! Meklau! You're up!" a security guard called into the room. Dominic started gathering his bags like the professional tennis player he was, while Julian remained sitting, head bowed, foot bouncing.

"Hey, Julian, time to get up," Paul said as he tapped his leg, stopping the movement.

Julian nodded wordlessly, feeling the bile rise up in his throat as his shaky hands gathered his stuff.

Paul clapped him on the shoulder and looked him in the eyes. "Just remember this is a game where heart is everything. And you've got all the heart in the world, Julian Smoke. Now go show these bastards how to play some tennis."

Julian fist-bumped his coach with all the smile he could muster and followed the event director down the revered hall where pictures of US

Open legends watched him pass. Chills rose on his arms, and he paused a second to live in the moment. But then he kept moving, drawing closer to the court entrance. Security guards and members of the press awaited, the click-click-click of cameras a symphony echoing down the hall.

He cast a quick glance over his shoulder and watched Dominic. The man was cool, calm, and completely unaffected by any of this. Julian tried to push down his anxiety and attempted to mimic his opponent. He stood up straight and slapped on his game face, even though he felt like he was going to puke or shit himself—it really was a toss-up between the two.

He reached up to make sure his headband was tight enough and found his hair slick against his skin. *Damn.* He was already sweating buckets and hadn't even noticed.

In an attempt to calm himself, he looked ahead only to find Charles Avery, former tennis player and coach turned analyst, waiting for him in front of ESPN's camera. Was he going to have to talk in front of the camera? Paul hadn't prepared him for this, other than a grouchy, "Just don't say anything stupid."

As Julian moved closer, Charles turned and gave him an easy grin, the camera following his every move. "Now, Smoke, this is your first time on this big of a stage. You've been out of the game for a long time. What are you feeling?" Charles held the microphone so that Julian could answer.

His heart raced. He had to look like a deer in headlights, but the longer he took to respond, the stranger he seemed, so he attempted to speak. "Ner —" His voice cracked like a pubescent boy. He cleared his throat and his face felt like it was ablaze. "Nerves," he said again, this time sounding somewhat like the thirty-year-old man he was.

Charles didn't even bat an eye. "You're already sweating, man. You've been getting pumped up in the locker room?"

Julian's face burned hotter. "Yeah, yeah, that's what it is."

Not the fact that he was scared out of his mind.

Charles nodded knowingly and then wished him luck. Charles Freaking Avery wished him luck. He was living a dream, a sweaty but amazing dream.

The fans' cheers rumbled beneath his feet as he and Dominic stood at the mouth of the tunnel—the stadium and all its packed glory in full view.

Holy. Shit. Center Court was mostly dark, save for a few roaming spotlights that bathed the crowds and court in blue. A white spotlight was aimed at the players' entrance.

Then he heard it, the announcer's deep voice. "Welcome to Nighttime Primetime in the first match of the US Open. From the United States of America, Julian Smoke!"

The stadium erupted in cheers and chants, a bass-heavy song playing to highlight his entry, and he froze, totally and completely in awe.

"Go ahead, Mr. Smoke," one of the ushers at the mouth of the tunnel prodded, but Julian didn't want to go anywhere.

This was beyond incredible, and he reached for his dad's chain. He kissed the golden racket, then tucked it back inside his shirt, memories of the man who taught him to love the sport playing through his mind on a highlight reel. "It's all for you, Dad," he whispered to himself as he made his legs carry him forward onto hallowed ground.

The lights were blinding against the night sky, the roof open to let in the breeze. The crowd was rowdy and loud, the energy unlike anything he'd ever experience again. He knew that with a striking certainty. The atmosphere was electric; it was a living, breathing thing, pulsing around him.

And he fed off it.

Julian lifted a hand in a wave like he'd seen other players do, and the crowd grew louder, wilder. The sound sunk deep into his bones, adrenaline pumping and tangling with his nerves.

He stopped at the first player's seat setup—two director's chairs with blue backs and white outlines, his hands shaking as he dropped his bag from his shoulder, pulling out energy gels and sports water. A tap on the shoulder broke him from his pre-match ritual, and he looked up to see his opponent with an amused expression on his face. Julian hadn't even heard his arrival on court announced, that's how in his head he was.

"Hey, man. That's not your seat," Dominic said, leaning in to be heard over the crowd.

"Oh shit. Sorry, sorry," Julian stammered as he hastily gathered his stuff and carried it to the second chair.

He should've been embarrassed and could probably imagine what the commentators were saying about him as they called the match, but he didn't care. He was here. *At the US Open.*

He turned toward his end of the court, toward his box. There was his mom, all teary-eyed and beaming, along with Paul, but no brilliant red hair in sight. Deep down he thought she'd show up because, well, she'd gotten him this far, whether she realized it or not.

Paul caught his attention and mouthed, "Paint the lines."

Julian's mind went into competitor mode, shutting down everything else as he moved to the net for photographs with Dominic, followed by the coin toss. Julian ended up winning the toss and elected to serve first.

He and Dominic moved to their respective sides of the court, warming up for a minute before the match actually began. He stepped up to the line to serve and took a deep breath. And as his first serve went across the net, it came back just as fast and hit the line.

Damn, this was for real.

It shouldn't have taken him by surprise, but somehow it did, the sheer power Meklau demonstrated overwhelming him. Julian's mind whirled, and he struggled to gain his composure. To make matters worse, to really screw with his head, his serve was broken twice as he lost the first set 6–2.

By the second set, Julian felt a shift in the crowd as they started getting behind him. He felt the pulse in the stands and knew this was his chance, that he needed to get this set. At 6-5 Meklau served to him, and Julian nailed a shot right on the line.

Meklau had trouble getting to it and, once he finally did, he hit a high lob over the net. From some deep reserve, Julian channeled Pete Sampras as he jumped up and smashed the hell out of the ball, letting out a roar.

That move? Yeah, that move was huge. Not only had he taken the second set, but he also stole the momentum of the match, something that could make or break a tennis player.

His mind raced, his body thrumming with electricity, the adrenaline pounding in his ears. If he could just hold his own serve, he could take the match in two tie breaks. *Two* tie breaks. He could manage that, not necessarily *easily*, but he could manage it.

No matter what happened out on the court, he desperately wanted to avoid five sets. A five-setter would crush him, especially since he wasn't accustomed to playing that long.

Shaking it out, he tightened his grip on the racket, letting it ground him to the here and now. He leaned forward at the hips, moving back and forth on the baseline, determined to finish the drill.

After winning the third set, Julian felt more confident than ever, especially when he saw a chink in Meklau's armor in what would hopefully be their fourth and final set. His opponent was starting to doubt himself, the most dangerous thing a tennis player can do. How many times had Paul reiterated to him that tennis was more mental than physical?

His heart began to thunder as he realized that victory was close, so close he could taste it. And damn if it didn't taste good.

With everything he had, Julian hit his eighth ace, effectively closing out the match with his first US Open victory.

The feeling was more than he was prepared for as he fell to his knees, completely wrought with emotion. Unbidden tears fell from his eyes, one after another, his heart both happy and sad at the same time.

He kissed his father's necklace, held it fisted in his hand as he raised his eyes heavenward. *We did it, Dad.*

He could've stayed on his knees in tears for who knows how long, but if his father had taught him one thing, it was to be a good sport, and in tennis, you didn't celebrate too long before shaking your opponent's hand.

Afterward was another story, of course.

So Julian pulled himself together, piece by piece, as he lifted his body and walked to the net where Meklau waited. His opponent gave him a hug and a pat on the back, along with a muffled, "Good game, good game," and then he was off to pack his bag.

After Julian did a quick wave to the stadium and applauded the fans for their support by doing a clap against his racket, he quickly realized that this was only one match. Now he needed to focus on the next opponent, just like his dad would've told him if he were still there.

JULIAN BRUSHED HIS HANDS THROUGH HIS WET HAIR, HAVING HAD PLENTY OF time to think in the shower. He'd won. He'd beaten the number four player in the world. It was enough to make his legs shake. But even with that win, even knowing that he'd made his father proud, that he was well on his road to redemption, he couldn't help but wonder about the missing redhead.

"Hey, Paul?" Julian called as he stuffed his sweaty clothes back into his tennis bag.

Paul had been jubilant, and that excited twinkle was still in his eye, but it became shaded, almost like he knew what he was about to ask. It was enough to make Julian wince.

"Have you heard from Amalie? Do you know if she's here somewhere?"

Paul cocked an eyebrow. "Why would she be?"

Julian shrugged. "I don't know, I just thought maybe—"

Paul removed his battered RF hat and rubbed what hair he had left, sending it this way and that as he cut Julian off. "Why would she come when you accused her of being in cahoots with her father?"

Julian stood up straight and lifted his chin. "It was no accusation. I saw them. Hell, Andrew told me the truth, even though I didn't want to hear it," he shot back.

Paul gave him a scalding look. "Andrew Warner lies, son. Amalie had no idea that her daddy got you into the US Open."

"What about Andrew paying for our room? What about seeing them talking that morning?"

"Andrew is a master manipulator, and he got what he wanted, like usual. You walked out before even hearing Amalie's side. She was set up just like you were."

Guilt slithered through him as everything started piecing together. Any response he might have had disappeared.

Paul let loose a beleaguered sigh that heaved his entire frame. "It's time for you to stop living in the past. You're bogged down there, and it's clouding your judgment. That girl is part of the reason you're here, and it's because she truly believed in you. It's not because she asked her father for help. Amalie hasn't talked to him since she moved out, at least not until that morning in New York."

Julian shook his head, everything Paul had said fully registering. "Wait. How do you know all this?"

Paul lifted a shoulder. "Amalie told me."

Julian shook his head again. "But why didn't you tell me sooner?"

"Because Amalie asked me not to. She said you'd believe whatever you wanted to believe and that the truth wouldn't matter if you already had your mind made up."

Punch to the damn gut. But she was right, and suddenly he understood why, his mind reeling with more clarity than he'd had in days. Years, even. He hadn't trusted her. He hadn't trusted her because he'd yet to learn to trust himself. He'd gotten so used to betrayal that it was the first thing he expected out of people, even people he loved. Because why not? He was capable of hurting those he loved. He'd hurt his dad so much with the greatest betrayal of all. He didn't deserve anyone's loyalty, or at least that's how he'd felt until about sixty seconds ago. Now he saw that belief for the damaging lie it was.

"Paul, I've been an ass, haven't I?" Julian plopped down onto the bench, his head in his hands.

Paul clapped him on his shoulder. "Don't worry. Just like this tournament, you and Amalie ain't over. I just needed you to understand why she wasn't here, so that maybe you could concentrate on tennis. You have one of the easiest draws left in the tournament. You've got an unbelievable chance to do something special here if you keep your focus."

What Paul said was true. Julian had an incredible opportunity. The higher ranked a player, the less ranked opponents they had to play until the semifinals. The draw just opened, and with the level of game Julian was currently playing, it should be a breeze.

"Gotcha, Coach," he answered with a nod.

Paul shifted his feet. "You have a strong chance to get to the final, hell, to win the whole thing. This isn't the same as all those years ago, got it?"

Julian hooked his bag over his shoulder. "Got it."

He knew it wasn't the same, not by a long shot. He was actually enjoying the sport, not the money this time. Even as he thought about those things, Amalie kept moving to the forefront of his mind like a flashing neon light, her absence a gaping hole in his chest. How was he supposed to get her back when he never felt like he had her in the first place?

And just like that, he knew what he had to do.

Chapter Twenty-Three

JULIAN

JULIAN WALTZED UP TO THE FRONT DESK AT THE WARNER HOTEL, THE VERY same place Andrew had put him and Paul up for the duration of the US Open. The clerks had to know how to contact their boss.

"Excuse me," Julian asked as he leaned forward on the ornate counter. Everything about this place was sleek lines and screamed money. It made his skin crawl.

The older woman behind the check-in desk squinted, adjusted her glasses, and then offered him a genuine smile. "I know you!"

"Ah, geez," Paul muttered at his side.

Julian braced himself. He wasn't really sure what to expect. In tennis, only big players were recognized unless they were a Cinderella story…

Well, hell.

As Julian's mind struggled to formulate a response, the woman continued. "You're the Employee of the Month!"

His brows inched closer together as he leaned over the desk, certain he'd misheard her. Trying to channel his Southern boy manners, he cocked a grin. "I'm sorry, ma'am, I thought you said, 'Employee of the Month'?"

"I did! See?" The woman was downright giddy as she spun around and pointed to a picture behind her.

Inside a gilded frame, more decadent than anything he'd ever owned in his life, was a photo. Of him. It was a press junket photo he'd taken for the US Open. Below it was a fancy plaque that read Employee of the Month.

Paul dissolved into a fit of laughter as the realization struck. Julian, on the other hand, felt fumes burning his nose.

He ignored both Paul and the woman's confused expression as he tapped one, two, three beats on the counter. "Could you please get Andrew Warner down here? Tell him—"

"His Employee of the Month is here," Paul interrupted, still chuckling.

The woman looked to Julian for confirmation and he just nodded.

She picked up the phone and spoke in a hushed tone. After a minute, she hung up, a smile pasted on her face. "If you'll follow me, please."

She didn't wait to see if they'd actually follow, but instead hustled across the marble floor, her heels making a *clickety-clack* echo through the cavernous lobby. They took a right down an Employees Only hallway and then stopped outside the third unmarked door.

"Please go on in," the woman said. "And congratulations again, Mr. Smoke, for being named Employee of the Month."

Julian held his hand up, not even turning to look at his coach. "*Don't.*"

Paul laughed anyway, even as they entered what appeared to be Andrew Warner's lair.

It was well appointed, everything immaculate and in its place. An unassuming glass desk sat in the center, juxtaposed by Andrew Warner, who glared at them from behind a tumbler of whiskey.

"Figured you'd still be here," Julian said without preamble, moving farther inside the room.

Without waiting for an invitation, he sat in one of the two cushy leather chairs placed strategically in front of the desk. He knew it was late but had taken a gamble that Andrew would be celebrating the win of his *investment.*

"Congratulations are in order." Andrew took a sip of his drink and sucked his teeth.

Paul sat down, making an *oomph* sound.

"For being Employee of the Month or for winning my match?"

Andrew couldn't even try to fight the curl of his lips on that one as he swirled the remaining liquor in his glass. "I thought it was rather clever."

Paul made a show of looking at his watch and then spoke up. "Look,

Julian has something to say to you, so we need to get on with it. My athlete needs to rest up, not waste time shooting the breeze with you. Julian, go ahead and ask him about Amalie."

Andrew appeared to malfunction momentarily but quickly recovered at the mention of his daughter's name.

"Have you heard from Amalie?" Julian started.

"No. You?" There was a new tone there, a thread of vulnerability woven through his words.

Julian shook his head. "Not since that shit you pulled. I turned on Amalie, accused her of things she didn't do, things that were all *your* doing."

Andrew placed his tumbler on the desk.

Realizing he wasn't going to add anything to the conversation, Julian continued. "And that's why I'm here. I'm here for *her*. I'm here because even though I want to call her or fly to Georgia and get on my hands and knees and beg forgiveness, I can't. So this is the next best thing since you and I both messed up. I'm going to have to work on things on my end, but you? You need to work on things, too. You're her father and you're supposed to have her back, to cheer for her, to pick her up when she's down, not kick her."

Andrew rested the fingertips of both hands on his desk, then leaned forward, his eyes cold. "Don't presume to know anything about my relationship with my daughter."

Julian stiffened, refusing to back down. "I'll presume all I want because I know the truth. I've seen it play out in front of my face. What father does what you did that day at the hotel?"

"A father that wants the best for his daughter, who wants her to have options, who wants her to have a future, and not with the likes of you."

"Because I'm not some stuck up rich hotel mogul? Fine. But the truth is you can't let her live her own life because once she's gone, you have no one. Simone is there, sure, and she's doing exactly what you want by helping run Warner Hotels, but she went out and got a family of her own before you thought to stop it, didn't she? Amalie, though, had no one after Maxwell. No one but daddy. And guess what? Daddy had no one either because he ran his wife off by being an asshole. And now Amalie is pulling free of your grip and you can't live with the thought of losing her. Not to a writing career, not to me, not to anything. But her life is not your life, and I'll be damned if I sit back and let you hurt her any more than you already have. Amalie is the most wonderful person in the world, and you're going to lose her if you don't fucking wake up, old man."

Paul's stare bore into the side of Julian's face, but he kept eye contact with Amalie's father, not backing down.

"You truly think I'll lose her?" Andrew finally spoke after a beat.

"I do. I think she'll cut you out of her life forever if you don't make a move now. Support her dreams. She wants to be a writer—accept that. Accept that Amalie's different in the best possible way. Accept that not everyone in your family wants to be a part of the hotel business. Be a father. Love her no matter what. Just…just don't be yourself."

Paul beamed at that, and with a loud thump on the chair's armrests, stood. "Well, I think this has been enlightening. Let me wrap it up for y'all real quick. Julian, get your head out of your ass and focus on tennis and not being an idiot when it comes to Amalie. Andrew, stop being a prick to pretty much everyone and treat your daughter with some respect. If I had a daughter like her, I'd be proud." Tilting his head toward the door, he looked over at Julian, "Let's go."

"I think Paul just earned Employee of the Month." Julian laughed as he rose from his chair, leaving a stunned Andrew Warner in his wake.

Chapter Twenty-Four

AMALIE

AMALIE'S NERVES WERE A JUMBLED MESS AS SHE SAT ON THE EDGE OF ROMINA'S couch, waiting for Julian's post-match press conference to come on the television. Her heart had been lodged in her throat throughout the match, her body sweaty and wired, her stomach on the verge of expelling all those cheese puffs she ate earlier.

Even though she and Julian were no longer whatever they were before, she still wanted him to win, to go all the way. Once he hit the court, she knew it would happen. The camera zoomed in on his beautiful face, and even though it made her heart ache to see him, she was proud of the ferocity that shone in his eyes. The man prowled the court like he owned it, and in the final nail-biter rally, he proved that he did.

Of course, after he won, the crowd completely lost it. Tennis was a sport that loved an underdog. With the wild card debacle with Garner long forgotten, Julian had quickly become America's sweetheart. He already knew how to work the crowd, and by the end of the match, he had them eating out of his hand, cheering for *him* instead of for the world's beloved number four.

The longer she sat there staring at the replays, the commentators talking about Julian, the harder it became not to think about exactly how she felt. This, what she felt for him, was more than a crush. Yep, three words balanced on a tightrope, begging to be spoken that morning she got him breakfast at the hotel.

I love you.

It wasn't like she could turn that off, even though she realized she hadn't meant nearly as much to him.

Suddenly, Julian emerged on screen, taking a seat in front of a set of microphones and looking every bit the tennis star she always knew he was. His hair was slick from the shower, a sleek, black training jacket and shorts combo hugging his athletic frame. At least her father's logo was nowhere to be seen on the jacket...for now. She knew he'd remedy that soon, especially with Julian's success.

All thoughts were forgotten with one glance at Julian, so at ease. She took in the slight tilt of his lips, lips that she had touched and tasted, lips that she dreamed of kissing way too often.

"You've got this, Smoke." Tears blurred her vision, and her chin trembled as her hands fisted, nails biting into her skin.

Blowing out a steadying breath, she looked down at her laptop. She'd been putting the finishing touches on her story but found that she still needed a lot of help with the tennis portions. The *Julian* aspect. Some things simply couldn't be found online.

The announcers filled the silence as they waited for the conference to be called into session. Pressing a hand to her chest, she wondered how in the hell she was supposed to make it through listening to him talk. His low, gravelly voice still did magical things to her body, and even more devastating things to her heart. Just as she was debating whether or not to turn off the TV to stop this torture, her phone rang.

Paul's name flashed across the screen. Leave it to Paul to call her during Julian's first-ever press conference.

"Paul, shouldn't you be watching your athlete and making sure he doesn't say anything stupid?" she said as soon as she answered.

Her eyes flicked up at Julian. He looked so handsome with that roguish grin and infectious laugh. The media loved him.

Paul chuckled. "They'll save the tough questions for later. Right now it's all fluff, so I'm not worried. I *am* worried about you, though. I knew you weren't coming to this match, but what about the next one?"

She sighed. "I can't. Not after what happened, Paul. There's no point in me being there."

"There's every point in you being here. You're part of the reason that boy is here. You kept him believing in himself, and I know he did the same for you. I think you should be here, Amalie."

"I...I can't."

"You could use it for your book. It'd be great research." There was a brief pause before he spoke again, this time a little sheepishly. "Besides, I've already bought you a plane ticket and everything."

Amalie was stunned. He *what*?

"Oh, Paul. Thank you, but no. I can't accept." The words tasted vile on her tongue, completely at odds with the way her heart raced at the chance to see Julian again.

"I'm sending it anyway. Amalie, I know you still care about him—that's why this hurts like it does—and I'm telling you he cares for you, too. He needs you. He needs all of us. You can't come this far and then step back behind the curtain. I'll see you in New York. Gotta go."

The phone disconnected. *Darn it, Paul.* He seemed mighty sure of himself.

She looked back at the TV. They were now talking with Meklau. She'd missed it. She'd missed Julian, but she was still hurting and...she just wasn't ready yet.

She kept telling herself that as she curled up on the couch, pulling the blanket over her body. She kept telling herself that as tears fell from her eyes. She kept telling herself that as she replayed Paul's words over and over.

Julian needed her.

Julian cared for her.

Julian...

AMALIE FOUND HERSELF THINKING ABOUT PAUL'S OFFER, ESPECIALLY AFTER THE plane ticket arrived on Romina's doorstep the next day. On top of that, Paul was trying his hardest to keep her in the loop, to make her feel like she was still part of the team.

He even sent her a picture of Julian after he won his second-round match in straight sets. The thought of Julian actually winning the entire tournament was less of a dream and more of a reality. Amalie had watched that match, even though it pained her to do so. It was bittersweet. On the one hand, she was desperate to see him succeed, on the other, with each swing of his racket, her heart took a beating. Though the match had been pretty easy, she noticed there was something different about him, something…hollow about his play, about his press conference. He was still well-loved, but he seemed more uncomfortable now, more awkward.

Julian Smoke was *never* awkward.

It tugged at her heart, and she looked at the plane ticket again. She shook her head and got back to work on emailing her book cover designer with some input on the final cover.

Then came the third-round match, and holy crap—that was one for YouTube. His opponent, Gaspard Durrand from France, had an infamous unpredictable streak. The guy was wild. He threw his racket, broke it over his head, and threatened the chair umpire and, eventually, Julian, too.

Finally, the chair had enough and disqualified the out-of-control son of a bitch even though Julian was easily winning. In the end, even Amalie knew it was a good thing. Julian didn't have to expend any extra energy and he wasn't drawn into the bizarre head games. Julian was clearly in the zone, turning into a beast on the court.

August bled into September and Julian's fourth-round match came and went without any particular fanfare. He breezed through it, defeating his opponent in straight sets. That difference Amalie noticed in Julian during the second round intensified after the win of his fifth match, the Quarterfinals. He won in straight sets again, but seemed tighter, shoulders hunched. This wasn't the Julian she was familiar with.

She leaned forward on the couch, listening to the announcers as they awaited the press conference. They showed highlights from the match and then showed pictures of Julian—pictures of him and his father, him and Nadine. Her heart dropped as her foot tapped out a frantic beat.

"Even though the media loves Julian Smoke," an announcer said, "it's apparent the feeling isn't mutual. According to multiple sources, he refuses any interviews aside from the USTA-mandated post-match conferences. He even turned down several sports networks. One wonders if it has something to do with his fall from grace nine years ago. Oliver Smoke coached his son until Julian made it to the pros and snagged the attention of then super-agent Anthony Fox. A lot of things happened following that change, none of them good, and I'm certain a lot of reporters are digging to find out exactly what went wrong."

It was clear to Amalie that Julian was still fighting those demons, and if they were to ask him... Bile rose at the thought.

The camera shifted, and there was Julian taking his seat at the press conference table, back in his black gear, and just like Amalie predicted, a big old, ugly Warner Hotels logo sewn onto the sleeve of the jacket. She bet he loved that. But when her eyes scanned the face of the man she couldn't help but love, she noticed small blue half-moons beneath his eyes. He looked drained and, with the vampire media essentially digging into his past, Amalie got worried.

The usual post-match questions came first: *Did you ever imagine you'd be here? Tell us about your father and the huge role he played in your life. How are you feeling after that last match?* With surprising patience, Julian answered every single question as if he were hearing it for the first time.

"Julian, you were once engaged to Lorentz Schaaf's wife. Will that factor into your game at all? You've got to admit it's pretty distracting for a semifinal match."

What the what? The next opponent Julian would face was his freaking *ex-fiancée's husband*?

Amalie's mind rushed to those pictures of Julian and Nadine on the internet. She was stunning and sophisticated and...married, thank God, although according to Julian she didn't have much care for fidelity. But Amalie couldn't help but be irrationally apprehensive. Would he see Nadine? Would he fall for her again? He'd said he was over her, but he admitted that he'd loved her at one time.

Thankfully, he cleared his throat and schooled his expression into one of polite disinterest. "I can assure you that it won't factor into the semis. This has been my dream ever since my dad brought me to this very court to watch Pete Sampras play. I won't let anything get in the way at this point." He gave the reporter a nod and then began to answer another question, this one about how he would prepare to take on Schaaf.

"Thank you, Jesus." Amalie exhaled, not even realizing she had been holding her breath.

Just when she thought he was out of the woods with stressful questions, the reporters flipped the script and asked Julian another question that was completely brand new.

"So, Julian, we've asked you about your father's influence on your tennis career, but do you ever regret letting your dad go as your coach? Do you think things would've been different if you'd kept him instead of letting Anthony Fox hire your new coach?"

Amalie flinched, bringing her curled knuckles to her mouth. She watched this proud, swaggering man reduced to a twenty-one-year-old all over again. His shoulders curled forward, fear and guilt and self-loathing filled his eyes as his mouth flattened into a grim line. Her heart broke as she leaned forward so much that she stumbled over the edge of the couch, her hand reaching out to catch her fall.

She moved closer to the television on her knees, her hand still covering her mouth.

"I…" Julian started, his voice a cracked mess. "I…"

"Come on, Julian. I'm here," she said under her breath as she watched him struggle to answer what would seemingly be an easy question for anyone else.

But she *wasn't* really there, was she? She was in Georgia while he was in New York getting hounded by the media after the biggest win of his life.

"I'd rather not talk about it," he finally gritted out.

Amalie released a breath, relieved he hadn't put himself through that.

Buzzing filled her ears, erasing the sounds of the rest of the conference. She staggered to her feet like a zombie, stumbling a little, then straightened herself. She closed her laptop and then packed as quickly as she could.

"Hold on, Smoke. I'm coming," she said softly as soon as she closed the apartment door.

Chapter Twenty-Five

AMALIE

NERVES AND THREE SODAS DID NOT MESH WELL. AMALIE WAS A HOT MESS AS she spilled herself into a taxi once her flight landed in New York. Her heart pushed her toward Julian—and she definitely wanted to go there, even though they had some work ahead of them—but there was somewhere else she needed to go first.

As her foot jiggled restlessly, she reminded herself that this was all for Julian.

When the car pulled to a stop in front of the imposing gray building, Amalie felt her stomach tumble. This was the olive branch she'd extend to Julian. She just didn't think she'd have to ask her father for a favor so soon, especially one he didn't stand to benefit from.

Paying the driver, she stepped onto the sidewalk, the city lights twinkling overhead. The evening breeze ruffled her hair as she adjusted her purse. Placing one foot in front of the other, she found herself being personally greeted by the doormen inside, along with the front desk staff. Knowing her father, he probably gave them pictures of his family to memorize—though it was shocking that he'd included her.

Drawing in a deep breath, she made her way to the elevators. Just before entering, her phone rang. Thankful for one last distraction before facing the inevitable, she stepped into an alcove in the lobby before answering it.

"Hello?"

"Amalie?" a voice asked.

"This is she."

"Hi! This is Lily. You emailed me your book to format this morning."

"Hey, Lily. I'm really excited about working with you."

"Well…" Lily drawled, "that's what I'm calling about. You see, I like to run through the novels I'm formatting to make sure I choose the right elements, and I got caught up in yours. It's pretty freaking amazing."

Amalie's lips stretched so wide her face hurt. "That's awesome to hear. Thank you so much."

"That's not why I'm calling, though. I'm calling because I have a friend who's an agent with the Prynne Company. I really think this is something she'd be interested in and wanted to see if you'd be all right with me forwarding this to her?"

Amalie's hand flew to her mouth, tears pooling behind her eyes. Suddenly all the hard work and heartache seemed like it might actually have been worth it.

"Oh wow. Yes, that's totally fine. I, wow, I can't thank you enough." Her voice was a watery quiver.

"It's no problem at all. Her name is Brynn Monroe, and if she likes it, she'll be the one to contact you. If not, I'll move forward on formatting, but…well, not to get your hopes up or anything, but I really think she's going to love it. We'll talk soon."

"Absolutely. Again, thank you so much." Amalie hung up and released a shaky breath. "Yes! Yes, yes, yes, yes! *Hell* yes!" She fist-pumped and danced and squealed as happy tears slid down her face, not caring who saw her. To think that a few weeks ago she'd considered giving up, deleting all her novels from her computer, and saying to hell with it. But Julian had stopped her, had encouraged her in both his words and his actions. He was going after the US Open full throttle, and it made her determined to take a step out on her own. *She* did this—not her last name.

That phone call gave her the needed strength to push forward. She no longer cared about what her father had done to make Julian think she betrayed him. She didn't want to live in anger, always trying to win battles. Now all she cared about was Julian and this dream they shared.

With haste, she made it to the elevator, pressing in the penthouse code. When the elevator came to a stop, the doors opened to reveal her father, hands in his pockets, looking effortlessly cool as always.

Amalie quickly wiped away her tears and stood ramrod straight, no expression on her face as she met her father's questioning stare.

"Happy tears or sad tears?" he asked casually, giving her room to step off the elevator and into the opulent foyer.

"Weren't you going somewhere?" she asked, her voice flat.

"I heard the elevator and knew that only two other people had the code, and Simone's still at her conference. I hoped it was you," he said with a shrug, surprising her. "So happy tears or sad tears?"

She sucked in a breath, readying herself for the inevitable argument or insults once she shared her news. But this was what she'd dreamed of for so long, what she'd worked so hard for over these last few months, so she had absolutely no intention of hiding it, least of all from her father.

"Happy tears," she answered, proud of how strong her voice sounded. Her father nodded but said nothing, so she continued. "The person I hired to format my book is sending it to her friend who's an agent. She thinks she'll like it."

Andrew Warner nodded and then offered her a genuine smile, not one of the fake ones she was used to from him. "I always knew you'd do it again, Amalie. You've got a God-given talent, and I knew it was only a matter of time."

Her expression went slack. "Say what?"

Who was this man and what had he done with her father?

He inclined his head toward the living room and said, "Let's sit and talk."

Shaking her head, she followed him to the living room where he wasted no time sitting down on uncomfortable furniture that was more for design than functionality. She chose to remain standing, arms crossed in an act of protection. To his credit, her father didn't say anything, just leaned forward, studying her.

"Amalie, I haven't done right by you all these years, and I know I hit a low point by driving you and Julian apart with a lie. I thought I was helping you, but I realized I was just trying to control you. Julian made me see that."

Her heart fluttered. "*Julian* talked to you?"

"Among other things, but yes, he told me that if I wasn't careful I was going to lose you. I wonder if I haven't already?" His voice cracked a little, causing Amalie to do a double-take.

This was most definitely information overload, and she didn't know what to focus on first. The fact that Julian had cared enough to talk to her father or that her father was about two seconds away from crying.

While she stood there wrestling with her thoughts, he continued. "I see the contempt in your eyes when you look at me, and even though it kills me, even though it reminds me of your mother, I find that I can't change who I am."

"And why is that? Why can't you change?" she interrupted, digging in her heels.

Her father shook his head. "I should have changed when your mother tried to get my attention, but I didn't, and she found someone else. I'm set in my old bastard ways, liking control. But I need you to know that I've been hard on you only because I love you so much, and I just don't want you to fail or be hurt in any way. I didn't realize that in doing so, I was the one who hurt you the most." He rubbed his forehead and avoided her eyes. "It took me years to build what I've built, and if I can make your life easier by involving you in the family business, then why shouldn't I push that instead of encouraging you to chase a dream that has the propensity to crush you?" He sat back in the chair, suddenly looking very tired.

"Wow," she said, totally unsure of what was happening. "Well, I know it's hard for you to sit on the sidelines, holding your breath and wondering if I'll fail again, but if I fail, then at least I tried. Writing is like breathing for me, and to cut that out of my life would be like suffocating. I'm putting myself out there, which isn't the safe thing to do, I know, but safe does not always equal happy, Dad. I've got to make my own path in the world."

Amalie's father stood, his hands outstretched. "Can you forgive your dad for being such a selfish bastard?"

Confusion and hope warred within her heart. She'd never seen her father like this, *ever*. He'd never apologized, never looked so *human*. Amalie's breath felt like it was bottled up in her throat.

"I'm almost terrified of what's going on in that head of yours." Her father cocked his head to the side.

"This is just…it's a lot to get used to is all. It's not bad, I promise."

In one swift movement, her dad embraced her, then pulled back just enough so that his earnest stare met her own. "Amalie, I'm so sorry, and I'll do everything I can to make up for what I've done, for the things I've said. But I love you, kid, and I'm proud of you."

At first Amalie was stiff in his embrace, this being their first true hug in years. Forgiveness settled into her heart, tears clouding her vision as she finally hugged her father back.

"Thank you, Dad." She sniffled as they finally pulled apart. She quickly brushed at the wet spots her tears left on his suit jacket. "Just as long as you never make me work for you and you let me do me."

A chuckle escaped her dad as he nodded. "I think I can learn to do that. I guess Julian had some good advice after all."

"Oh really? What else did he say that was so life-enriching?"

Her father shrugged. "He made me see what I was missing out on and pretty much told me that I'd been the world's biggest jerk." Apparently, Julian knew the truth behind what went down a few weeks ago, and her father actually felt remorse over it.

A thousand thoughts flew through her mind, but she forced herself to work through one thing at a time.

Her face scrunched in confusion. "Okay…you're not off the hook yet, but if Julian knew the truth, then why didn't he reach out to me?" She fought to tamp down the anger surging in her veins.

Her father shook his head. "Believe it or not, this was the best he felt he could do. He felt what needed to be said should be done in person, and I've got to tell you, he feels like a right idiot for what he did. He showed remorse and not to mention bravado by showing up at my office unannounced."

Huh. Her father was never Julian's biggest fan, so that was saying something. Maybe all was not lost. Maybe Julian had been thinking of her just as much as she'd been thinking of him.

Amalie's lips quirked, but then her face smoothed out as she thought about the real reason she'd shown up to the last place on earth that she wanted to be. "Dad, I actually came here to talk to you…"

"About Julian, I assume?"

"Yeah, about Julian, and about those ugly-ass hotel patches you've got that poor guy wearing." She giggled.

And then her father did something she couldn't ever remember witnessing—he laughed. Like really and truly laughed. "Those patches are hideous, aren't they?"

She couldn't help but nod emphatically. "So, will you do me a solid and get rid of them? Let him play for *himself*, not for Warner Hotels?"

Her father stilled and then turned to face her fully. "I'm going to have to be nice to this boy, aren't I?"

Amalie laughed with a nod.

"If it's that important to you, then of course."

"It's very important to me." The unspoken was still heard loud and clear. *Julian is very important to me.*

"Consider it done, then," her father said without hesitation. "Say, what do you think about hitting up that old burger joint you used to like when you were younger?"

"I'm down for that." She was always down for food, and now that she was on her own, it'd be pretty awesome if her dad was paying, too.

As they strolled into the balmy night, Amalie felt her heart slowly stitching itself up, one suture at a time, one kind word from her father at a time—all thanks to Julian. He was the only missing piece, and of course, she wondered what he could've possibly said to get through to Andrew Warner.

She'd find out soon enough. because come tomorrow she'd be in his box, rooting for him the same way he'd secretly rooted for her.

Chapter Twenty-Six

JULIAN

"Where are the patches?" Julian asked as he flipped the shirt over in his hands and then turned it inside out. They had to be there somewhere because Andrew Warner had been pretty hell-bent on Julian being his little advertising bitch.

"Don't tell me you miss them," Andrew cracked as they all stood huddled around a bench in the locker room.

Julian and Paul shared a wide-eyed look, but it was Julian who ultimately spoke. "Did Andrew Warner just make a joke? Holy shit, I think he did."

Paul guffawed, but Andrew simply shrugged. "Just do me a favor, kid. Make sure you deserve her, because if you don't, well, let's just say I do have an impressive weaponry collection." And with that, Andrew strode out of the locker room.

Julian turned to Paul. "What the hell did he mean by that? Did Amalie have something to do with this?" He lifted the patchless shirt in question, heart racing. Was she here? Did she know how much he needed her? How much he missed her?

Paul's eyes crinkled. "You know she did."

"Why would she do that?"

"You know why, you idiot. You've just been too dense to see what's been there all along. It's why you talked to Andrew and told him to stop treating his daughter like trash. You love each other."

Damn. Paul was right, like always. Amalie deserved better from Julian. He vowed that she would get it, and soon. He had a lot of groveling and apologizing to do, but he'd do it...on his knees if he had to. He'd do whatever the woman wanted because the truth was right there in front of his face, a truth he'd known for a while but had been too damn scared to admit it: *he loved her.*

"Hey," Paul's gruff voice broke through Julian's little zone-out.

"Yeah?"

"You know I'm all about an Amalie and Julian reunion, especially when you've been the biggest dickhead known to man—"

"Hey!"

Paul steamrolled right over him and said, "But I need you to focus on this match, on the semifinal, for right now. After you win this, after you win the US Open, you go get the girl, but right now you've got Schaaf out there waiting to beat you on court."

Schaaf. Amalie had made Julian completely forget about his ex-fiancée's husband, the guy she'd latched onto because she thought he'd eventually be a tennis star. Typical toxic Nadine.

He shuddered at the thought. There was absolutely no love lost there. He'd *thought* he'd been in love, but given the intensity of his feelings for Amalie, what he'd felt for Nadine had been a sick impersonation of love, an infatuation maybe, lust definitely. Amalie was the sun, the moon, the stars, everything bright, whereas Nadine was everything that strangled the light and suffocated hope. He'd go out there and beat Schaaf, not because he was looking for revenge but because he wanted to prove himself to the girl he loved.

He straightened his shoulders, lengthening his body as he gripped his racket and stood facing Paul. Determination laced his voice as he said, "I'm ready. Let's paint the lines."

As Julian walked onto the court, his attention was glued to his box. He caught sight of her red hair standing out in a sea of black and white, or at least that's what it looked like to him because everyone else just faded to the background when Amalie was around. She was an explosion of color in his dull, dark world. She was watching him, too, and he couldn't help but wonder if he looked like a man starved, because that's what he felt like. She was stunning as always in a white blazer, with a black lace top half-tucked into jeans with rips along the legs.

Amalie gave him a small grin and wave before Paul pulled her attention away, probably on purpose. As much as Julian tried to dismiss the stupid flip-flopping thing his heart did, he couldn't, not when it came to *her*.

Pride surged through him, the unmistakable need to show off, to do well for himself, for his father, but also for Amalie.

Slowly his gaze swung over to his mom who looked teary-eyed and happy. This was the freaking semifinals of the US Open. He was doing the damn thing.

Once he got his stuff set up, Julian made his way to the net. When Schaaf joined him there for the coin flip, Julian shook his hand and noticed the guy wouldn't even make eye contact. Julian felt his lips curl. He was already under Schaaf's skin, and they hadn't even started the match yet.

After winning the toss, Julian didn't hesitate to announce that he'd serve first, and then he started the match like a man on fire. He served multiple aces in the first set and couldn't help but notice that Schaaf looked totally lost on the court.

The sound of cheers and thunderous applause from the stands helped Julian move through that first set. He was thankful Paul made him study Schaaf's matches, and he'd noticed that, against unknowns, the crowd usually pulled for Schaaf.

Definitely not the case here. Julian felt relaxed out there on the court, the most relaxed he'd been in a while, like a weight had been lifted off his shoulders, a weight he was sure had to do with the stunning redhead in his box.

During the changeover, as Julian was headed to his seat, Schaaf muttered, "I saw you brought me another woman." He motioned toward Amalie with his chin. "Heard her daddy got you into this tournament."

Red. That's all Julian saw as anger ignited his veins.

His relaxed, easygoing confidence went to hell. It took everything he had not to beat the shit out of Schaaf right then and there.

Of course, after that little mind game, Schaaf started out strong in the second set, breaking Julian's serve. In a flash of utter fury, Julian smashed his racket against the net post.

Never, *not once*, had he ever lost his composure on court. It was something his dad was big on, and it was something Julian wasn't exactly proud of. Schaaf—the prick—had him exactly where he wanted him. That pissed Julian off even more, which then made him feel like he was slowly unraveling, especially when the umpire gave him his first-ever warning for racket abuse.

The unraveling continued for the next fifteen minutes and resulted in Julian easily losing the set 6–1. When the third set rolled around he regained his composure, eventually leading to a tie break.

Tension engulfed the stadium, the crowd humming with it because they knew what Julian knew: the outcome of this set was crucial to the match. He couldn't let Schaaf get into his head again. He didn't come this far to lose to an egotistical asshole.

At seven–all in the tie break, with Schaaf serving, Julian felt more tuned in and delivered a strong return that left Schaaf scrambling. Julian took advantage of that and made his way to the net to put away a high volley. The crowd roared, and that energy gave him the power behind his next serve, which was a 130-mile-per-hour ace down the middle. He had Schaaf on the ropes, doubting himself. Just as Paul said, the mental game was even more important than the physical.

Surprisingly, the fourth set offered no real drama as Julian marched to a 6–3 closing set victory. In the end, he collapsed to the ground in complete and total awe.

Holy shit. He'd done it.

He gripped his dad's necklace as he shared the moment with the man who'd taught him what it was to love tennis.

The crowd chanted his name as he stood. His lips curled into a smile, but there was only one other thing that would make this perfect. His gaze swung to his box, and there was his mom clapping like a wild woman alongside Paul, but it was Amalie he wanted to see. And there she was in all her beauty. She radiated joy, and just like that, every missing puzzle piece to Julian's heart clicked into place.

"Hey," he mouthed to her, trying to keep his cool. But damn, it was hard to have any type of swagger when he'd just made it to the US Open finals and Amalie was here, the one person who meant more to him than anyone in the entire world.

He watched as she laughed, as it reached all the way up to those unusually bright, gray eyes. "Hey," she mouthed back. Then she shooed him to the net, her eyes still sparkling.

As he walked to the net for the customary handshake, which was indicative of your respect for your opponent, although Julian had none for Schaaf, he felt like he was walking on freaking air. Then he noticed that Schaaf wasn't at the net. Nah, Schaaf had already packed up his bag, and all Julian was left with was the sight of his opponent walking off the court to a chorus of boos.

The child in him wanted to call out something asinine, but he kept himself in check as he waited for Charles Avery to approach for the on-court interview.

Julian's mind was a jumble of excitement and flashes of images, his body vibrating like a damn livewire ready to pop and explode. He wanted nothing more than to run to Amalie, to apologize for being the world's biggest dick, but he knew he had to play the media game first, even though it'd been slowly siphoning his soul these last few days. Those personal questions hurt, and even though Paul said it was best to be transparent with the press, there were some lines Julian thought shouldn't be crossed, some questions that he would never answer.

Thankfully Charles never stooped to that level. A former tennis player himself, he had kept it all about tennis, and thank God for that.

Charles motioned to the crowd and then swung his attention back to Julian. "First of all, congratulations are in order."

Julian tried to be humble, bow his head, all the things he should've been the first time around. "Thanks, Charles."

"So, Julian, what do you think about the lack of handshake after the match? You know that's pretty uncommon."

Uncommon was an understatement, but Julian figured if he was married to Nadine he'd be pretty miserable, too. Poor asshole. He shook his head. "I don't waste my thoughts on people who don't matter."

Charles gave him a nod and followed up by asking, "What are your thoughts as you head into the finals?"

That was so surreal. *Finals.* Julian pretty much doubted himself the entire way until this very moment. It was surreal to think that one drunken declaration to a beautiful stranger could be the reason he was standing here on the blue asphalt of Arthur Ashe Court.

He ran a hand through his sweaty hair as he responded. "Honestly, I can't think beyond the fact that I'm talking to Charles Avery after the semifinals of the US Open." The crowd laughed.

Charles even fought back a grin before he asked, "What do you do between now and the final? How do you prepare for Javier Rodriguez?"

With a shrug, Julian jokingly answered, "I reckon my coach and I should be asking you. We weren't supposed to make it this far."

As Julian walked off court after his interview, he didn't feel like Cinderella anymore. He felt like he belonged.

Chapter Twenty-Seven

AMALIE

"WHAT IS THAT EVIL...WOMAN DOING HERE?" CHARLOTTE HISSED.

Amalie turned to see who prompted Charlotte's wrath. Ah, Nadine. Beautiful, perfect Nadine with her waves of honey-colored hair, her pale skin and pale eyes, her humongous boobs nearly spilling out of her designer top. Instead of consoling her husband after his loss, she'd chosen to creep around backstage at Julian's press conference. As a matter of fact, she'd positioned herself so that she would be the first thing Julian saw as he stepped out of the long hallway leading from the locker room.

Amalie's hackles rose as she watched Nadine take out a tube of lipstick, carefully apply it, and then fluff her hair. Anger and jealousy sliced through her as she contemplated walking over and cursing the woman out. It made her hug the blazer she'd shed tighter to her chest—but she wasn't a slob in her sexy lace tank that she'd bought just for this occasion.

Then Julian emerged, thick hair still wet from the shower, and her mind instantly went to the gutter, imagining that water sliding down those chiseled abs she knew he was rocking.

Seeing him up close again felt like being on the highest point of a roller coaster. Her heart pounded frantically, both terrified and excited at the same time. What would she say to him? Would he go to Nadine? She twisted her hands together, hating the feeling of uncertainty.

The security official herding Julian to the stage moved through the crowd with ease, letting everyone know there was no time to stop and chat, that they had to get on with the press conference since the match ran later than expected.

"Juli!" Nadine called out in a nasally, run-your-nails-across-a-chalkboard voice.

Amalie and Charlotte both winced. Amalie's nails bit into her palms when she saw dread overtake his features. Paul was right behind him, and the look Paul shot the woman could've turned her stone.

"Juli, it's me!"

Juli? Not once had Amalie ever heard anyone call him that. Is that what she screamed out when...

Nope, don't go there, don't even think about it.

Julian shook his head and kept walking, his eyes searching. Was he... could it be that he was looking for her?

"That's my boy." Charlotte playfully bumped Amalie's arm.

Amalie's heart skipped at the snub. He'd literally given Nadine the cold shoulder and instead was *definitely* looking for her. How did she know? Because as soon as his beautiful green eyes landed on her, his entire countenance changed. His shoulders straightened and his smile grew bigger and more carefree than she'd ever seen it. He nearly ran over the security official in his attempt to get to her.

Just as he reached for her, the cockblock, er, guard, said, "We have to keep moving, sir."

"Amalie, we need to talk. Wait for me?" Julian asked in that husky voice of his.

It took everything she had to suppress a shiver at the glorious sound, the sound that she never thought would be directed her way again.

"Of course." Amalie nodded.

Julian didn't realize that all he had to do was ask and she'd give him anything he wanted.

He inched around the guard and squeezed her hand in promise, electricity sparking through her arm as he did, and then he was ushered onto the platform.

Unable to help herself, Amalie's eyes darted to Nadine who stood openmouthed and fuming. Realizing that she'd been seen, the woman turned and made a run for it.

"That's right, run, honey," Charlotte taunted, causing Paul to choke on a laugh.

Amalie quickly turned back to Julian, who was settling in. His back was straight, his entire face lit with pure joy. If his dad could see him now, he'd be so proud.

Noticing where Amalie's attention had strayed, Charlotte was all smiles. "He's been doing so well with these conferences, hasn't he? Honestly, with the mouth on that boy I thought for sure he'd just flub it." She then shrugged almost as if to say, "What can you do?"

Just as Amalie opened her mouth to respond, the first question was asked.

"So, Julian, what is Amalie Warner, Warner heiress, doing in your box?"

Amalie's mouth fell open as she blinked slowly, her eyes trained on Julian. She felt both Charlotte and Paul's stares, but she ignored them. She didn't know why she was surprised that someone had noticed her. No, what had her hanging on, waiting with bated breath, was his response.

Julian looked visibly stunned for a split second, but he recovered quickly, his expression softening. What that look did to her ovaries was downright sinful.

"Amalie?" he asked, her name, those three syllables, a caress across her skin.

She drew her hand up to her face, covering her mouth. God, what was he going to say?

"Frankly I wouldn't be here without her. She believed in me from day one, and she's more than an heiress. She's an amazing woman and a brilliant writer." Butterflies in her stomach tumbled over themselves making her dizzy. Now *that* she hadn't expected.

Everything else fell away as Julian turned toward her, smiling that lopsided grin she loved so much. Loved. Loved. *Loved*.

She had to tell him, didn't she? Or did he already know? A poker face was never her strong suit, especially when her resting face was *à la* serial killer.

"So, you're not dating her?" the reporter continued, obviously unsatisfied with his answer.

Julian's lips tipped even higher as he slowly turned back to answer. "Not yet. I plan to talk to her about that as soon as we wrap this up, so can we get a move on?"

Chuckles erupted around the room as Julian kicked back on his chair, looking at her again and winking. Flirt.

"Well, I called that," Charlotte said with a knowing grin.

"Betcha I called it first," Paul added.

"How about we all just chill a minute?" Amalie held up her hands, her face on fire.

Thankfully, Julian wrapped up the conference and headed toward them with all the swagger and arrogance Amalie had grown to love.

As she stood watching him, that beautiful soft look on the hard angles of his face, the more difficult it became *not* to think about what she wanted from Julian. After this was over, win or lose, she wanted him in her life.

Time stood still, her heart and soul free-falling through oblivion with that admission. The possibility of them together was no longer a fantasy. It was real.

Pure joy trickled through her entire being, and then anything and everything she'd thought to say incinerated with one glance at Julian, because his gaze was primal. Her first instinct was to shrink back, that's how strong it was.

His muscles bunched like a lion ready to pounce, and then in one, two, three long strides, his arms were wrapped around her in an embrace, her feet literally floating off the ground, her blazer shoved off to Charlotte.

"Stardust," he said breathlessly, and her insides ignited and danced.

"Missed me, did you?" she joked as she squeezed him back, reveling in the muscled cord of his arms, inhaling his cologne, committing every bit of their encounter to memory.

"You have no idea," he whispered, giving her one more solid squeeze before slowly releasing her, her body brushing against every single part of his, chest to chest, liquid heat pooling in her belly, making her breathless at the intimate contact.

A tremor rocked through Julian's body, proving he was just as affected. *She* was the one who caused him to tremble like that, and it made her feel invincible.

There was so much she wanted to say, so much they needed to discuss, but it fell away as she allowed her fingers to play with the damp curls at his neck. Moving her mouth to his ear, she said, "I always knew you could do it."

Julian pulled away, just enough to see her face, and the edge of his lips quirked up. "We have a lot to talk about. You're coming back to the hotel with me." Then that smile melted away, replaced by a look that threatened to completely unravel her. His finger slid up to her shoulder beneath the strap of her tank top, teasing the skin there. Goosebumps followed in the wake of his touch.

"Oh, is that right?" Amalie teased, cocking her hip, in an attempt to play off how overwhelmed she was by this man.

He bit down on his lip, and damn it all to hell, it was the hottest thing she'd ever witnessed. She wanted to suggest they get out of there right freaking now, but by some miracle she didn't say a word.

Paul's throat clearing totally killed the vibe she and Julian had going on.

"Yes, Paul?" She turned to find him with his arms crossed over his chest, amusement plastered across his features.

"Don't even, Coach," Julian said with humor in his voice.

Paul held up his hands defensively. "Look. You two go celebrate tonight, but my rules remain the same. I'm not gonna lay them out here in front of your mother, though."

Charlotte raised her hands in the air, her floral kimono fluttering. "And thank the Lord for that." Amalie tried not to melt into a puddle of humiliation, while Paul, completely undeterred, grabbed Julian's shoulder and kept talking.

"Go have fun," he said. "Tomorrow is a big day, and after training with Austin and all the press junkets, you'll be completely sequestered from everyone. Tonight's it before the final, so enjoy yourselves, but not *too* much. Got it, kids?"

"Damn, I think we got it two minutes ago," Julian said as he wrapped an arm around Amalie's waist. His touch seared her skin through her shirt, making her mind slip back to what felt like ages ago when they were at Simone's party. Back then this was all just a fevered dream, and now it was their reality. "And with that, we're out. Good night." Julian tipped his head toward Paul and then kissed his mom on the cheek.

After a chorus of goodbyes, Amalie and Julian were led out back and ushered into an idling Mercedes.

"Feeling like Roger Federer now, huh?" Amalie teased, her nerves all over the place. Julian's leg was pressed against hers, the air crackling with awareness.

Julian said nothing as he studied her, taking her hand in his. "Amalie," he said softly. "God, I've missed you."

She took a deep breath and turned toward him. There were things she had to say, had to get out even though the anger had long since evaporated once she'd realized exactly why she was so hurt by him.

"You were a real asshole to me, to even think that I would ever go behind your back on anything, to think that I'd hurt you like that." The pain she'd pushed down for weeks laced her every word.

Julian's face crumpled, his hands moving up her arms and across her shoulders until they buried in her hair, his thumbs tracing her cheekbones. He looked haunted as he leaned his forehead against hers.

Her heart raced, completely at odds with the words she'd spoken. Even after all this time he still made her feel like a teenager in the throes of first love.

"I was the biggest asshole," he said. "And I...I can't tell you how many times I've wanted to call, to apologize, but I worried that I'd lost you forever, and the possibility that you'd tell me we didn't stand a chance was worse than anything, so I just...waited and hoped and prayed that we'd find our way back to each other." He inhaled and looked her in the eye, his expression pained. "Can you ever forgive me? I know it was you who had your dad remove the patches, and knowing that gave me reason to hope."

Amalie's heart filled to nearly breaking. "And you talked to my dad and reminded him he had a heart. I guess you could say we're even."

Julian shook his head. "We're in no way even. I've got a lot of groveling and making up to do, and I plan on starting tonight."

Shivers danced along Amalie's spine as a response struggled to find purchase on her tongue. As if on cue, the car rolled to a stop in front of none other than the Warner Hotel. "I thought we were going back to your hotel?" Major disappointment settled in her belly.

Julian cocked his head. "I'm staying here. Didn't your dad tell you? He put us up here for the tournament."

Of course, he did. *Thanks, Dad.*

"Wild coincidence. I'm staying in the penthouse." Amalie held out a hand as they stepped from the car. "Wait. That totally sounded like a little rich girl thing to say, but I'm only saying it because I'm too broke to stay anywhere else." She laughed nervously.

"No penthouse for you tonight, I'm afraid," Julian said with a wink as he laced his fingers through hers. "Let's go, Stardust."

The trip to Julian's room was perfectly awkward, her body humming with anticipation of what lay ahead. She was fully aware that Paul had rules, but her body cried out that rules were meant to be broken.

Thankfully the elevator was quick, and Julian shot her a sexy grin as they stepped out. There were no inappropriate quips, which had Amalie's legs shaking even more.

Julian opened the door to his room, and the sound of it clicking shut echoed around them, locking them away in their own little world.

"So…" Amalie began, her heart about to take flight as she found her courage. "About Paul's rule… How serious are you about sticking to it?"

Julian quirked a brow, his expression dangerous. "Not serious at all. I'll be damned if I waste this night."

With that alluring swagger, he prowled toward her and threaded his hands into her hair, thumbs tracing her cheekbones, his eyes so dilated they were mostly black. Amalie fisted his shirt, pulling him closer, his body completely flush with hers.

That was the consent he needed. Without wasting another second, his mouth slanted over hers, swallowing her pent-up sigh as her knees threatened to give way.

Julian let out a groan, and she tugged his hair at the nape of his neck, desperate to take the kiss deeper, wanting more. Another groan, and then his hands were sliding down her ass to her thighs and hoisting her up, her legs wrapped tightly around his waist. Their kiss, so desperate and impatient, was a far cry from sweet now.

It was a race to see who could devour the other first as Julian carried her to the bed, falling down over her and propping up on his strong forearms. Every touch ignited a fire on her skin, and she knew when this was over, she would be completely consumed.

"Amalie." His voice was rough as he released her mouth, taking a quick pull at her lip before raining kisses down her throat. He hovered at her collarbone, licking and nipping as his fingers toyed with the strap of her tank.

Her breath came out in pants as she sat up and tugged off her shirt.

"Holy shit," Julian croaked, his stare sliding over every curve of her body, his tongue darting out to wet his lips. Suddenly, her phone rang, the sound momentarily jarring them from their lust-filled haze.

"Do you need to get that?" Julian asked, his voice a low, husky drawl, his possessive stare having never left her body.

"Hell no." This was something she'd dreamed of for months and nothing was getting in the way of it. Not again.

Julian exhaled a sigh of relief and then yanked off his tee. "Oh, thank God."

Her mouth went dry, her lips longing to map the lines of his body. The phone continued to ring, increasing the radiating sense of urgency as he brought his mouth to her chest, biting and sucking the curve of her breast, his tongue tracing the cups of her bra. She wanted to scream at him to rip it off.

As if reading her mind, Julian's fingers went to work. "Let's see about getting rid of this."

With a flick, the bra was unhooked and flung across the room. At the sight of her bare skin, Julian's eyes flared, and his breathing quickened. The intensity of his study sent a shudder down Amalie's spine.

"Like what you see?" she asked, using one of his favorite lines.

He dragged his gaze to meet her eyes and held himself over her again, their bodies aligning, causing Amalie to squirm with need. He pressed his hard chest against her breasts, his skin molten lava against hers, his rigid length pressing against her thigh. His mouth hovered just inches away from her lips, but then he leaned in and wrenched a kiss from her that felt like she'd given up her soul.

Amalie gasped, her heart colliding wildly against her ribs as he pulled back just a little and looked her deep in the eyes. "If we do this, Stardust, no more bullshit. It's you and me. Is that something you're cool with?"

God, yes. She'd never wanted anything more. She wanted him to mark her as his.

She opened her mouth to speak, momentarily failing. Her senses were short-circuiting in overload—the feel of Julian, his smell, every single thing about him wrapping around her heart and squeezing.

"Make me yours," she whispered on a throaty exhale.

And with the sexiest growl, he lowered his head to her nipple, his mouth devouring her like their last glorious night in New York. There would be no interruptions this time. Amalie would make sure of it.

The heat of Julian's tongue sucking and flicking caused a breathy moan to escape her, her body acting on its own accord as she writhed against him, everything hot and firm, causing him to press his cock against her harder in response.

She brought her nails to his back, dragging light scratches down his skin. He groaned at the feel and captured one of her hands in his, holding it captive against the bed as he dragged his wicked tongue down the valley between her breasts. Each moan that drifted from her lips made him smile against her body.

He caught her gaze. "Can I taste you?" His hand drifted down her waist and settled between her legs. With firm pressure, he teased her clit through her jeans. "Right here?"

She almost shattered just hearing those words, just feeling that touch. After so many months of denying her desires, the ache that bundled there felt dangerous, ready to explode. She wasn't sure she would live through what he was about to do to her, but she nodded, breathless.

His stubble pricked her skin as he descended, sending every single nerve ending into overload. Amalie sucked in a breath and held it as his deft fingers removed her jeans with ease. He looked up at her, eyes bright, and then her underwear followed her jeans to the floor.

Julian sat back on his knees, between her legs, his calloused hands caressing her from knee to hip, over and over, until he paused, spreading her wide as his eyes drank her in.

"Beautiful," he whispered, and then he slid his long body flat on the bed, his mouth replacing his hands, trailing kisses up the inside of her thigh.

Amalie could hardly breathe, watching his dark head inch closer, every muscle in his broad shoulders and back rippling as he hooked his arms under her hips. He shot her a look that made her nervous, in a good way, because he looked hungry, the erotic glimmer in his eyes speaking volumes.

His kisses were slow and tortuous, his tongue working her clit with steady, slow pressure at first, the intensity increasing to a fever pitch as the mumbled sounds he made against her sent shivers through her body.

"Julian," she called out as she began to throb. "Julian, I want you. Inside me."

His eyes flicked up, and the corner of his mouth lifted. "Patience, Stardust. We've got a long night ahead."

His tongue slid inside her, and she fisted the sheets, her eyes closing as another moan left her. He'd given her what she asked for, but it wasn't enough. She couldn't stop her hips from grinding against his mouth, searching for *more, bigger, deeper.*

"Please," she begged, threading her fingers into his hair. "More."

He groaned, his grip on her tightening as he trailed his tongue up again and nibbled her, bringing her to the precipice of an orgasm she needed more than air.

But then, with their gazes locked, he slid a finger inside her, then another, his thrusts matching the relentless rhythm of his magnificent tongue.

Amalie rose on her elbows, overtaken, gasping as mind-numbing pleasure coursed through her, her sex clenching around Julian's fingers through the spasms of release. "Julian! Fuck!"

After she'd ridden out the orgasm, Julian dipped his tongue inside her again, tasting her as she slowly returned to her senses. With a provocative smile painted on his face, he gave her one last, long lick, eliciting an impatient whimper from the depths of her soul as he moved for the condom in his bag.

"Here, let me," Amalie shot up, not wanting to miss a chance to touch him, to hold him, to *see* him. She'd imagined him naked. Dreamed of it. She couldn't wait any longer.

Julian stood at the side of the bed, the expression on his face filled with lust and adoration. Wordlessly, he shucked his jeans, leaving only black boxer briefs that clung to his thick muscled legs, his firm, rounded butt, and a cock that strained against the fabric.

Amalie's mouth watered. Oh, yes. She was in for a night of delicious fun.

She half expected Julian to make a joke or quirk a brow, but this Julian was laser-focused as he stepped out of his underwear, allowing her to see him completely bare for the very first time, to see exactly where that sexy trail of hair led to.

Her lady parts clenched and tingled at the sight of him, the sheer size and perfection of his entire body.

He touched her chin, making her look at him. "Touch me," he said, and Amalie thought she might melt.

She didn't hesitate, closing her hand around him, watching his stomach muscles flinch in response. God, he felt wonderful, like steel wrapped in silk.

Julian made a strangled sound as she stroked him, admiring. "Condom, Stardust. I can't bear much more."

She bit her lip, feeling his eyes watching her every movement as she rolled the rubber down his cock. She kissed his stomach, and then, he lay her back onto the bed, gently, his mouth capturing hers.

She reveled in the feeling of his skin against hers, in the thought of finally having him inside her, after all of those months.

"You feel so good," she mumbled against his lips.

"You ain't seen nothing yet." A grin quirked his lips, making her smile. Slowly, he filled her, eliciting a little gasp. In that moment she felt absolutely complete, especially when her eyes met his and she saw a new emotion flickering behind the depths of his lightning-strike stare. It sent a bolt of longing straight to her heart.

"You're perfect," he bit out as he moved, the rhythm deliberate, hitting her exactly where she needed.

"Let me get that in writing," she said, trying to make a joke, but then he reached his hand down between them, touching and teasing, and her eyes fluttered shut on a sigh.

"I'll give you anything you want."

"Then give me everything," she panted.

As if a switch flipped, Julian picked up the pace, leaning back just a little, creating friction at a new angle that threatened to make her come apart at the seams. A soft sheen glistened over his body as he pumped harder, going deeper. Damn if the sight of him, all sweaty and naked and carnal, wasn't the hottest thing she'd ever seen. She bent up to bite his shoulder, causing him to groan. He leaned down, his lips pressed to the pulse of her neck, biting and soothing with long kisses.

A shudder rolled through her. She was close again, oh so close. Her grip on his shoulders tightened as she moved with him, her heart pounding in her ears. "Julian," she called out… "Please don't stop."

"No way in hell." His voice was ragged as he gave her one long thrust that sent her over the edge.

Starbursts built from technicolor dreams burst behind her eyelids, muffled cries floating between them as she buried her head in his shoulder. She'd never felt so undone, every fiber of her being unraveled.

His hands gripped the back of her head, his mouth on hers, a sexy tennis grunt erupting from him. She felt his body tighten in the wake of her orgasm, her hands running over the tension in his shoulders as he found his own release.

The world had changed. Everything was brighter—almost like she'd been living a half-life until then.

Julian pressed soft kisses to her temple, his breath still coming in struggled gasps, the feel of it sending another shiver down her spine, despite what just happened.

He looked her in the eyes, and with the sweetest smile said, "You have no idea how long I've wanted to do that."

Amalie's fingers brushed his hair from his eyes as she reached up to kiss his lips. "Me too. How long before we can do it again?"

"Paul's going to be so pissed." Amalie smiled into Julian's chest, her fingertips trailing along his ribs. They were tangled in the sheets, the last few hours having been more than she could've ever dreamed.

"What he doesn't know won't hurt him. It was worth it, every time." Julian kissed the top of her head. His other hand stroked up and down her side.

She wished he'd move that hand over just a few inches, and she was about to tell him so when the movement stopped.

"Hey, did you ever check to see who was calling you?"

Her mind tried to work through the sex-fueled haze and finally, it clicked. "Oh, crap. No, I didn't. Can you hand me my phone?"

She admired Julian's body, every muscle flexing as he reached for her cell on the nightstand and handed it back to her. His thumb moved to the corner of her mouth. "Got a little drool there, Stardust," he teased.

She was about to tell him to shut up when she began listening to the first part of the voicemail. It was Brynn Monroe. *Holy shit.*

Amalie sat up even straighter, the sheet falling from around her body. Julian's eyes tracked her movements as she listened to the voicemail a second time.

"It was Brynn Monroe, and she wants me to call her back as soon as possible." The words stumbled out of Amalie's mouth, her heart racing.

Confusion flickered across Julian's face. "Who's that?"

Realizing that she hadn't even told him about Brynn because she'd been too busy trying to get in his pants, she quickly explained who the woman was and what this meant. As soon as she finished, Julian's face lit up.

"Call her back."

Amalie giggled. "I am, I am. Hey, hand me a shirt so I'm not talking to my potential agent naked."

Julian groaned in protest but still tossed her his shirt. She wanted to sniff it like a freak, but it wasn't exactly cool to do that with the shirt's owner watching her like a hawk. After throwing the shirt on, she dialed the number.

"Hello?" A clear, crisp voice answered the phone.

"Hi, this is Amalie Warner. I'm calling for Brynn Monroe."

"Hi, Amalie. This is Brynn speaking. Listen, I'm calling about your novel, *Painting the Lines.* I know Lily mentioned that it's loosely based on Julian Smoke's current Cinderella run at the US Open?"

"It is. He helped me write the tennis scenes so it would be more realistic. You'll notice that some of the remaining tennis scenes still need a little polishing, but otherwise it's finished."

"And we'll work on those scenes, absolutely. But I loved the story. I loved every single thing about it and finished it in one night. Look, Julian is really popular right now, and the entire country is talking about him. I think we can definitely sell this story, but also, I talked to a contact of mine who said a director is interested in making it into a movie, you know jump on this whole thing while it's still hot. Here's the only issue. The director's leaving for Europe for six months and would need to meet with you tomorrow and Sunday for negotiations. I've already purchased a red-eye ticket to LA and left it at the airline desk if you're interested."

Interested? A movie deal? A book deal? All of it in one go? It was everything Amalie had been dreaming of since her first book made the bestseller list.

Her head was fuzzy, like she wasn't getting enough oxygen to the brain, so she took a deep breath to steady herself. This was it. It was finally happening. But...

"Did you say you'd need me to fly out tonight and be there for the next two days?" She felt Julian studying her, but she turned, avoiding the question she knew she'd find in his eyes. She'd just gotten *here,* in New York. The US Open final was in two days. She wanted to be here for that, to watch Julian follow his dream, but this was her dream, and didn't it deserve a chance, too?

"I did. Would you rather think about it and call me back? I can give you about fifteen minutes before I need to be in a meeting. Call me back at this number, and Amalie?"

"Yes?"

"It's worth it, I promise. This will shoot you even farther than *Breaking the Fall* did. I can guarantee it."

But at what cost, especially after everything she and Julian had just shared?

"Brynn, I can't thank you enough for your kind words and for taking the time to even read my manuscript. I'll definitely be calling you back in just a few. Thank you again."

"No, thank *you* for giving me the opportunity to read it. I look forward to hearing from you. Talk to you soon, Amalie."

And with that, the line went dead, and Amalie was left sitting there, sputtering and completely in a daze.

"Everything okay?" Julian broke through her reverie, concern lacing his voice. He smoothed her hair back from her face and tucked it behind her ear. And just like that, her heart was torn.

With a slow nod, she took Julian's hand. "Brynn wants to represent me. She thinks the book could sell and has a director interested in optioning it. They want me to fly to LA *tonight*."

His face brightened as he crushed her to him in a hug, his mouth at her ear. "Baby! Baby, that's fucking amazing! I knew this would happen. Didn't I tell you? I told you you'd kick ass!"

She knew he'd always believed in her, and without his encouragement she never would have moved on to the next phase of her writing. When Stella dropped her, she wanted to give up, but it'd been Julian who kept her going, who taught her to keep fighting and to believe in herself.

Amalie slowly moved away from the hug. "But I wouldn't be there for your match on Sunday. They need me in LA the next two days to talk to the director."

She was sure he'd already heard that part but just wanted to make certain he understood. God, the conflict inside was threatening to tear her apart. How could she have one of the happiest moments of her life and yet feel so awful?

"And then, you know, tonight we kinda"—Amalie coughed, her face heating into what had to be ten shades of red—"took a big step, er, several big steps…"

Julian took her hands in his. "Now's not the time to worry about that. I'm not going anywhere."

"I feel bad about not being at your match…"

Julian shook his head. "This is your dream, Amalie, and more than anything I want you to have it because you deserve it. You've followed me for months and have watched me get my moments, now it's time for you to step into the sun and get yours."

"But—"

And then Julian leaned in and kissed her forehead, making sure she met his eyes as he scooted away. "But nothing. You're going to get on that plane tonight, and you're going to make us proud, okay?"

"You…you won't be upset that I won't be at the final?" This was all so different than how Maxwell acted when she sold that first book. He had been jealous of her success, had sabotaged it, but then again, Julian was not Maxwell. She could see it in his eyes that he truly wanted what was best for her.

He shook his head. "How could I ever be mad when you're chasing your dream? Come on, let's go to the penthouse and get your things. I'll ride with you to the airport." He grabbed his room key while slipping on his clothes and shoes.

Standing from the bed, Amalie wordlessly did the same and then made her way over to him. She placed a light hand on his arm, her heart melting at the tenderness in his stare, in his words, in everything about this man she wholeheartedly *loved*.

"You should stay here," she said. "Rest and get ready. You and I both know the media will mob you if they see you out and about. I'll be fine, I promise. We'll talk when I get back, because I have a feeling Paul will have that phone of yours on lockdown." She gave him a smile, confidence and excitement lighting up her heart. This was it. This was her time.

Julian looked uncertain, like he wanted to argue with her about accompanying her to the airport, but she stood on her tiptoes, and kissed him, effectively silencing him. "No arguments." She pulled back, her voice filled with pride. "You're going to win. I know it."

Julian nodded, his eyes crinkled at the corners, his lips tilted up. "You be safe, Stardust. I want you to know how proud I am of you."

"I know. Right back atcha."

She turned toward the door, but Julian grabbed her wrist and pulled her against him.

"Amalie..." He looked so serious, his eyes a little damp, his voice cracked around the edges.

She slid her hands up his arms and laced her fingers behind his neck. "Yes?"

"I..." His gaze fell and his brow crumpled as he swallowed back the words that were clearly difficult to say. "I...I just want you to know that this," he nodded toward the bed, "was everything." He kissed her softly. Sweetly. "*Everything*."

Her eyes watered, but she quickly blinked back the tears. "For me, too. One hundred percent for me, too." She pulled him in for one more tight hug, careful not to kiss him again. If she did, she'd stay. She'd stay and tell him that she loved him...and then straddle him on the desk chair. "Goodnight, Smoke. And good luck, even though you don't need it. I'll see you soon."

With that, she got the hell out of his room, making a run for the penthouse.

Something Julian said stuck with her—that she'd been with him for his moments and now it was her turn. She couldn't help but worry that their dreams were taking them in two different directions, but the feelings between them were obviously real and strong, no longer crush territory but something far more powerful, powerful enough to withstand any storm. As she dialed Brynn's number, she realized she had to believe in Julian and what they shared and the fact that all of this was meant to be.

Bigger still, she had to believe in herself.

Chapter Twenty-Eight

JULIAN

WHEN THE MORNING OF THE FINAL CAME AROUND, JULIAN WAS WELL-RESTED, but everything he ate or drank threatened to reappear and he couldn't stop bouncing his legs, his hands tapping out offbeat rhythms on his knees.

His mind went to Amalie, as it often did, along with his latest revelation when it came to her. He'd decided that the next time he saw her, he was going to tell her he loved her. He'd wanted so badly to tell her right before she left for LA, but the words just wouldn't come. Well, no more playing it safe. Wherever life took her, he was going to be right there at her side.

"What's that about?" Paul asked, voice gruff and all-business as he motioned to Julian's face.

Julian ran both hands through his hair. "Don't worry. When I get on the court, I'll be one-hundred-percent focused on tennis. I can promise you that. But I can't help but think about Amalie. I love her, man. I love her more than I've ever loved anyone, and that scares the hell out of me, just like all of this"—he spun in a circle, his arms out to gesture to his surroundings—"scares the hell out of me."

Suddenly the doubt he'd been doing a pretty good job at pushing down rose to the surface.

Shit. Not now. *Not now.*

Paul furrowed the white caterpillars above his eyes. "What do you mean?"

Julian shrugged. "I mean I'm scared I'll fail today. What happens then? This is all I've wanted for years."

"Even if you lose, which I don't think you will," Paul responded, "it wouldn't be the end of the world. But *if* by some fluke you do lose, the USTA wants you on tour, *permanently*. Apparently, you've finally appeased the tennis gods."

Andrew had already told Julian as much, which actually added to his mounting worries. "And that's just it, Paul. I don't know if that's what I want, because that would mean I wouldn't see Amalie as much. Whatever I decide, it'll be with her by my side because I'm not half-assing this thing with her. That woman is everything to me."

The sound of clapping rang through the locker room, and then Andrew Warner surfaced, looking more relaxed than Julian had ever seen him. "Well said, my boy. Well said. You just might deserve my daughter after all."

Julian smiled, still shocked they were even on speaking terms.

"I just came to give you this," Andrew said as he dug a small, folded square of paper from his perfectly pressed navy suit. "From Amalie. She gave it to me before she left for LA. I'm to let you know she's here in spirit."

Julian reached for the note as his heart swelled. That girl.

"Good luck, Julian. We're all rooting for you." Andrew gave him a quick pat on the shoulder before disappearing through the locker room doors.

Julian looked at Paul, then at the note in his hand. Paul nodded his chin toward it. "Well? What are ya waiting for?"

Julian unwrapped the note, his eyes greedily taking in every dainty scrawled letter and loopy *Y*.

JULIAN,

   You can do this. I've believed in you since day one, although sometimes I hated to admit it. Go out and play the match your dad always knew you could play.
   —Love, Amalie

· · ·

HE GULPED AS HE READ IT ONE MORE TIME. SHE WAS RIGHT. HE COULD DO this, not only for himself, but for his father and for her.

Folding the note reverently, he tucked it in his bag. Just as he zipped it closed, security called for him and Javier to start their walk. Julian tried not to study his opponent too much, but it was hard not to. Javier Rodriguez was a Spaniard the tennis world had nicknamed "The Dog," because he could and would chase down any ball and efficiently send it right back over the net. This fact alone made him one of the toughest competitors on the tour. He'd already racked up three French Opens and one US Open and was looking to add another win to that list. If all of that wasn't enough, the guy was 6'1" with a sturdy build, legs like tree trunks, and a physique that screamed he could beat your ass.

As Julian walked down the hallway in front of Rodriguez, his ears began to ring, his body tingling with the urgency and knowledge of exactly what was at stake.

As usual, Charles Avery waited at the mouth of the tunnel, microphone in hand.

After pleasantries, Charles got right down to it. "What's your mindset going into the match?"

While most players offer a generic answer, like "I just want to play each point," Julian was completely honest. "I really don't know."

Normally Charles would ask a follow-up question, but thankfully, it was like the man could sense that no other questions needed to be asked, because he extended his knuckles, giving Julian a fist bump. "Go get him."

As Julian walked on court to a packed house, the crowd erupted, flinging their support fully behind him. He tried to soak it in, hoping the momentum would carry him through the match.

He looked over at his box and his gaze flicked over Paul, Romina, Austin, his mom, Andrew…

His stomach dropped, that flicker turning into a full-blown flame as he locked eyes with Amalie.

Shock trickled through his veins because she was there when she should've been in LA. He stumbled a little as he found his way to his chair, not taking his eyes off her once.

"Hey," he mouthed, his brows scrunched in confusion. He felt a niggle of worry that she might have done something reckless, like walk away from her chance because she felt the need to support him. If that were the case, he'd stop this match right now just to put her on a plane back to California.

Her smile grew even wider, reaching all the way up to her eyes as she tilted her head. "Hey."

He saw movement out of the corner of his eyes and saw Paul flapping at the end of the row. "Everything is fine. She did great in LA!" he yelled above the noise.

Relief eased some of the tension in his shoulders as his eyes flicked back to Amalie, who was laughing. She gave him a thumbs up to reiterate Paul's announcement.

"I'm proud of you," he mouthed, placing a hand over his heart, before turning to the chair umpire.

When he and Rodriguez made their way to the net for the coin toss, he could see that his opponent's face mirrored his own, etched with unwavering steely resolve. Julian lost the toss, and Rodriguez elected to serve. As the match started, Julian struggled with the speed and power of Javier's serve. Damn it. He couldn't let this guy run him all over the court, but he moved like he was in mud, his footwork sluggish. Of course, Rodriguez was anything but sluggish. That guy was tuned in, and he pounced right away to break Julian's first service game. The crowd was silent, and there was no real energy in the stadium, which sucked because Julian so desperately needed it, needed something, *anything* at that point.

The set went by and looked more like an exhibition match, with Rodriguez easily winning 6–1. Julian's mind was spiraling, those old doubts slowly twining themselves through his brain and reaching down to twist around his heart. At the beginning of the second set, Julian had the opportunity to start off serving but ended up double-faulting to give the first game away. His nerves were total and utter shit. He was playing scared, and as hard as he tried to claw his way out of the pit he'd tripped into, it was too late. He gave the set away, 6–4.

Get it together, man. Get your shit together.

Toward the beginning of the third set, the temperature changed drastically as clouds darkened the stadium. As they were locked in an intense first game of the set, Rodriguez held serve, and once they headed for the changeover, rain pelted the court.

Julian lifted his eyes to the sky, big heavy drops hitting his face. Within less than a minute, the umpire announced that play had been suspended while the roof was being closed and directed Julian and Rodriguez to go off court into separate locker rooms.

Julian slumped over as soon as he sat down in the locker room, his soaked hair in his hands. He was fucking up big-time out there.

A sound at the door had him looking up to find Paul headed toward him. Just as his coach opened his mouth to speak, Amalie's voice came right behind, feistier than ever. "What the hell? You got your head in your hands like you're just giving up?"

Julian turned, drinking her in like the mirage he thought she was. She was just so damn beautiful.

Storm clouds rolled in her eyes as she slammed his locker shut in utter frustration. Damn, he'd forgotten how hot she was when she was mad. "Get your ass up! You've come this far and now's not the time to let your mental game suck. I could tell in that last game you were hesitating. Well, you know what? Julian Smoke doesn't hesitate! He goes after each ball and he paints the damn lines! When this roof gets closed, there are no more timeouts for you. This is it. Now go out and win this thing. Your dad didn't waste all those years training you just for you to get to the final of the US Open and to give up without a fight." She blew a wayward strand of hair from her eyes as Julian's hand itched to touch it, to touch her. She turned her fierce angry eyes to Paul. "Now Paul, you can go ahead."

Paul's lips twitched beneath his mustache as he shook his head. "Nah, I think I'm good."

Energy thrummed through Julian's body as he realized that this moment was something he didn't even know he desperately needed. It felt like he was able to take his first full breath since the match started.

He caught Amalie's eye, her chest heaving, her breath coming in quick gasps. Suddenly appearing nervous, she smoothed her hands down over her striped sundress. "Oh, well, good then. I'm going to head back up there before I get in trouble for being here. So, you know what to do now, right?"

Julian's grin grew so wide it felt like it swallowed his face. "Yeah, I know exactly what to do."

Amalie pushed her hair behind her ears and gave him and Paul one last glance before nodding curtly, and then moved toward the door.

"Hey," Julian called, his voice thick as he gently grasped her hand as she passed the bench where he sat.

A tiny gasp escaped her pouty lips as he tightened his grip on hers, attempting to channel some of the emotion he felt into that single touch. "Thank you, Amalie. Really, I mean it." He stood up from the bench, wrapping his other hand around her waist and pulling her toward him. "None of this would be happening without my Stardust."

Amalie's lips parted, eyes bright as she brought a hand to his face, rising on her tiptoes to plant a kiss on his lips. "I could say the same about you."

"And I could say we have a tennis match going on and save all of this for afterward," Paul said with a cough.

Julian and Amalie both laughed and shook their heads. He bent down giving her one more kiss, this time on the forehead, before she slipped out of the locker room.

As soon as the door closed gently behind her, Paul turned toward Julian, lips still twitching. "So, now what?"

Feeling like a new man, free from his fears of failure, Julian pulled his dad's necklace out from beneath his shirt and ran his fingers over the ugly gold racket. "I'm going to win, and then I'm going to get the girl."

Chapter Twenty-Nine

AMALIE

BY THE TIME AMALIE SAT BACK DOWN IN THE BOX THE ROOF WAS FULLY CLOSED and they were preparing to bring the players back out. She could still feel Julian's touch on her skin, see that crooked grin of his. A smile crept upon her lips, her fingers brushing over it to check if it was really real.

"Someone's happy." Romina gently bumped Amalie's shoulder.

"Let's just say it's been a really good few days."

And it had. She'd signed on with Brynn as her agent and negotiated a contract for *Painting the Lines* to be made into a film, a combination of events that was almost unheard of, especially with how fast everything had happened. On top of that, she was about to watch the man she loved win the US Open. It was wild to think how far they'd come from that night in the bar.

"You really do love that boy, don't you?" Ro said with a grin.

Amalie nodded, her earlier smile stretching even wider across her face as she watched the crowd settle into their seats, the chair umpire heading back onto the court.

"I can't believe I'm going to say this," her friend continued, "but you're perfect for each other."

Just as Amalie was about to reply, the players came out to thunderous applause. Her heart thumped wildly, frantic and barely contained as she took in Julian's strong form, his cocky smile. He looked over and winked.

Romina leaned in and added, "And he's madly in love with you."

Amalie couldn't help but gently shove her best friend's shoulder with her own and roll her eyes. "Oh, please…"

But she hoped it was true.

Chapter Thirty

JULIAN

JULIAN WAS DOWN 0–1 IN THE THIRD SET, AND HE KNEW THERE WAS NO MORE
margin for error.

With that thought, he held serve easily without losing a point. He
channeled Andy Murray, roaring after winning the game, signaling not
only to himself but to his box, to the crowd, to Rodriguez, that he was all in
and wasn't going down without a fight.

Julian centered himself, letting his breath come in and out in controlled
pants, focusing on the task at hand, which was dismantling the toughest
opponent he'd ever faced.

As the set reached the tie break, Javier served first, and Julian smoked
the ball right past his opponent, painting the line. He fist-pumped the air,
his adrenaline electric.

Now was the time. He could hear Amalie encouraging him not to give
up, could hear Paul telling him that was exactly the shot he'd been looking
for the entire match. If he could just get through this tie break, then he had
a shot at victory. He felt the strength to win deep down in his bones.

And that he did. He won the third and fourth set with surprising ease,
evening out the match with the fifth set deciding who would take home
the title.

Julian wiped his sweaty hands on his shorts, narrowing his gaze on

Rodriguez as he watched him walk to the chair umpire. His opponent asked for a bathroom break, but Julian chose to stay on court. If he left now, his momentum would be all screwed up.

As he waited, he took a sip of water and then made a point to stay loose by doing a light boxer shuffle. His mind was focused, zeroed in, but then the crowd, that wonderful, fantastic New York crowd, drew his attention. The fans started off by doing the wave, and then they broke into a chant— "Smoke, Smoke"—they shouted over and over again. Julian couldn't suppress the smile that lit his face. The fans believed in him; they believed he could win this thing. If he did, he'd be the first American to become the men's US Open champion since 2003.

When Javier returned, he looked dead at Julian as he knocked into his shoulder, throwing him off course, turning the crowd into a booing horde. Julian felt the anger lick at his veins, but he fought down any response to react. He'd react during the next set, Rodriguez could bet on that.

The next set began with Julian ready to serve. He let the steady bounce of the ball on the asphalt calm his temper, at least long enough so that he could channel it into a killer serve. Even with all of that intensity, the fifth set was grueling, lasting over an hour before he and Rodriguez arrived at a tiebreaker. The US Open, unlike every other major, has a fifth-set tiebreaker, making it that much more intense. It was do-or-die.

Julian started out behind in the tie break and it looked like Rodriguez was getting his second wind. Even with Julian hitting two screaming aces, both over 135 mph, it didn't faze the man. If Julian didn't do something, his dream would be over and he wasn't ready for that, not yet, not when he was so close.

With several deep steadying breaths, Julian hit two winners that put him behind Rodriguez by only one point.

The next rally was the longest of the tournament, of Julian's career. He and Rodriguez were locked in opposite corners in a forehand, cross-court battle. Julian's heart thundered, his pulse resounding in his head. On the forty-eighth shot of the rally, Julian sent a forehand down the line to get his first chance to take the lead in the tie break, evening the match at 5-all.

On the next point, Julian struck a forehand crosscourt, out of reach of his opponent. The crowd erupted as match point was called. Julian could win. *He could win.*

Julian's hands shook, but one glance at the stands, one look at *her*, and he was centered.

Amalie beamed at him, genuine and full of hope and pride.

Julian brought his eyes back to the court as he moved to the baseline to serve. With a shaky exhale, Julian stepped to the line for the biggest point of his life. As he tossed the ball in the air and started his lunge toward the shot, he let out a massive grunt and struck an ace up the middle, winning the match in a stunner.

Emotion crashed over him, the roar of the crowd thundering in his ears as he fell to the court, his hands covering his face as tears overtook him. He felt his dad looking down on him, patting him on the shoulder and saying, "Good job, son. I'm proud of you."

Julian drew his necklace out of his shirt, brought it to his lips, and kissed it. When he stood, he pointed toward the heavens. This was everything he'd worked for, everything he'd wanted for so long. He'd done it.

Now it was time to get the girl.

Chapter Thirty-One

AMALIE

Julian climbed the stands, people patting him on the back as he wove his way through the crowd. He was coming for *her*, his eyes locked on her the entire time.

Amalie held her breath and held onto Romina's shoulder, because she felt like she just might float up and away. Each step that brought him closer made her smile grow wider, her heart racing with the unknown.

As the crowd's cheers swelled to a crescendo, Julian reached the box. His eyes were still locked on her, as though she were the only thing that existed, the intensity smoldering in his gaze enough to set her soul ablaze.

She opened her mouth to say something. What? *Congratulations*? *Great match*? But before she could find the words, Julian grabbed her around the waist, pulled her body to his, and his lips crashed down on hers. Frantic. Wild. Desperate.

Perfect.

Fireworks went off behind her eyelids, every single part of her in flames. She kissed him with reckless abandon, throwing everything she felt into that kiss, her hands twined in his sweaty hair, his hands tangled in her wild waves.

Nothing else existed in that moment. Well, until the announcer said, with way too much cheek, "Well, folks, I guess Smoke succeeded in dating Miss Warner after all."

Cheers and whoops from the crowd brought them back to the real world. Amalie felt the reluctance in Julian's muscles as he slowly pulled away and looked down into her eyes. "I love you, Amalie Warner. I've been holding that in all this time, and I'm tired of it. All I want is you, Stardust, just you. Can you give me that?" His tone was earnest and unsure despite his expression.

Amalie's heart fluttered, tears misting her eyes. "I think I can do that," she teased. Then, laughing and crying at the same time, she finally uttered the words she'd been dying to say for so long. "I love you, too, Julian Smoke. So much."

Epilogue

AMALIE

ONE YEAR LATER

"You ready?" Julian asked as he bent down to kiss Amalie's temple.

"Let's do this." She grinned, rearranging the books on the table one more time. This signing was the biggest one by far, one at The Strand in none other than New York City. For years this had been Amalie's dream to host an event at this very bookstore. As a gift for the finalized casting of the *Painting the Lines* film, her publisher made it happen.

She caught a glimpse of the line outside, and when Julian came in, he'd confirmed that people were wrapped around the building and down the street, everyone giddily holding copies of her book. What a surreal thing to hear.

As she took a deep breath, happiness filtering deep down into her lungs, she realized she didn't fully appreciate the success of *Breaking the Fall*. She felt like a debut author all over again, and this time she was determined to do things right. As a matter of fact, she'd already written her next novel and it was in the process of going through its final edits with her amazing editor.

The door opened again, her head snapping up to see Paul and Charlotte piling inside. "Me and my girl here are ready to celebrate!" Paul guffawed as he leaned down and pulled Amalie into an embrace as Julian's mom gave her a floral-scented peck on the cheek.

"Paul, we've discussed this—" Julian griped even as a smile struggled to break free across his beautiful face.

"And I've told you love is love and can't be helped when it strikes, son. When you know, you know." Paul clapped his former athlete on the shoulder.

A lot had happened in the last year. Paul was engaged to Julian's mom, after many good-natured complaints from Julian of course. Julian quit tennis to open the Oliver Smoke Tennis Center, his very own center built with the earnings from his wild run at the US Open a year ago. He wrangled Paul into the adventure despite the fact that after the US Open, practically every tennis player wanted Mercado as their coach.

With all of his success, Julian had been right by Amalie's side during hers...as her husband. Yep, they'd gotten hitched a few months after the Open because, like Paul said, when you know, you know.

"Hey! You didn't start the party without us, did you?" Andrew Warner called from somewhere in the shelves—of course, he'd found a side door to enter because he was extra like that. Simone and Tallulah were in tow, everyone all smiles.

"Amwee!" Tallulah, her three-year-old niece, squealed as she rushed toward Amalie, wrapping her in a sticky hug.

"Of course not, Pops," Julian smirked. Oh yeah. He'd taken to calling her dad *Pops* because it rankled like a mother. But Andrew Warner, having undergone some sort of major soul reconstruction, would only flinch and squeeze his eyes shut for a brief moment. It was safe to say that he'd finally stepped up and done everything he could to make up for all those lost years.

Simone reached into her suitcase-sized purse and pulled out a copy of *Painting the Lines* and slid it across the table.

"What's this?" Amalie picked it up, noting the worn corners.

"It's from us!" Romina called out from the doorway, coming in with a bottle of champagne in one hand and a bag of plastic champagne flutes in the other.

"We all signed it and made sure to get a couple of people from your other signings around the country to sign it as well," Simone explained softly.

Amalie's eyes watered as she opened it, her fingers tracing over the inked words of so many who loved her, who supported her, who believed in her.

"Hey, Stardust," Julian said as he bent down so he was eye level with her, his fingers pressing softly into her cheek. "Have I told you how proud I am of you? How proud I am to be your husband? Just how much I love you?" His voice cracked with emotion, his eyes glassy.

"Only every day." Amalie smiled back, placing the book on the signing table so that she could move her hands over the scruff on his face. "I love you too, Smoke."

"Get a room!" Paul interrupted playfully.

Amalie turned. "We have several as a matter of fact."

"And have christened each extremely well, I must say," Julian added without missing a beat.

"Oh, God." Andrew covered his ears while everyone else laughed and started to get settled.

"Are you ready, Mrs. Smoke?" the manager asked as she motioned to the door where fans were peeking in at the curious assembling of all the people that Amalie loved most.

"I'm ready." Amalie grinned back. She'd always be ready, ready to live her dreams, ready to love to the fullest, ready to give the world hell.

Thank you for reading! Did you enjoy? Please add your review because nothing helps an author more and encourages readers to take a chance on a book than a review.

Also be sure to sign up for the City Owl Press newsletter to receive notice of all book releases!

And don't miss book two of the Ace of Hearts series with THE WILDE CARD available now. Turn the page for a sneak peek!

Sneak Peek of The Wilde Card

The last thing Simone Warner expected when she walked into the Victoria ballroom at the Fairmont Chateau in Lake Louise was to have the wildest night of her life.

She stepped into the crowded room—replete with a rented disco light spinning over a parquet dance floor, a free bar, and thumping music—and read the sign near the main doors. *Welcome to The Tennis Ball, hosted by Alex Wilde.*

Simone rolled her eyes, hard, and glared down at Amalie, the beloved little sister who'd convinced her that a vacation out of the country was exactly what she needed. Amalie hadn't been wrong. So far, the trip to Canada had been a relaxing break from Simone's busy life as Tallulah's worn-out mom and Warner Hotels' hanging-by-a-thread CEO. But attending this party? That had taken a lot more convincing on Amalie's part. Yet somehow, as always, Simone gave in.

"The Tennis Ball?" She couldn't help but laugh, shouting over the music. "Really?"

Who knew Alex Wilde had a thing for puns?

Simone glanced around the ballroom. Was he even here?

Though she'd watched Wilde's tennis game devolve over the last few years, she had to admit that she found his whole persona intriguing. He was passionate, gorgeous, and didn't seem to care what anyone thought of him. Still. Being that they were at one of Alberta's most elegant resorts, she'd expected more from the French-Canadian tennis star than a college-style kegger, though she wasn't sure why. Wilde was a legendary lothario and not even thirty yet. She supposed a kegger with fangirls bouncing around everywhere fit him perfectly.

"Don't start." Amalie strained her voice over the music. "It's the perfect place for you to mingle and get your single on." Donned in a stunning black cocktail dress, she made an elegant, sweeping gesture toward the gyrating masses of tennis players, agents, coaches, and one too many admirers.

If Simone glared at her sister any harder, laser beams were going to shoot out of her eye sockets. She and Damien divorced a year ago, after one hell of a public scandal. With his cheating exposed, and what felt like the whole world scrutinizing their lives, Simone withdrew. It wasn't easy going from the working mom and wife life to single mom. Being a party of one had yet to become her new skin.

And dating? That was totally out of the question. At this point, even walking across a dance floor in a ballroom packed with hot tennis players made her want to melt into the wall.

She shrugged. "I'm not really feeling it. I think I'll stick with you for now."

The truth? She'd been there less than five minutes and already wanted to leave.

Simone clutched her bag under her arm, turned on her stiletto heel, and took one step toward the exit.

"Oh no you don't!" Amalie dragged Simone away from the door. "No one knows who you are here, and they don't give a damn about what Damien did. Besides, you haven't had a fun night out in forever. Just promise me this *one* night. Pretty please?"

Simone was defenseless when it came to her little sister.

"Fine," she groaned. "But I'm not dancing."

Amalie beamed, thoroughly pleased with her methods of persuasion, and looked out over the party. She motioned to the far side of the ballroom where her husband, Julian Smoke, and his former coach and business partner, Paul Mercado, stood chatting up some guy who looked vaguely familiar.

Amalie wiggled her brows. "Now *he's* cute. Let's see if his personality matches his pretty face." She grabbed Simone's wrist and hauled her across the crowded space, just missing Paul as an older gentleman whisked him away.

Amalie was determined to help Simone get out of her funk, and that meant letting loose and being open to whatever the universe brought

Simone's way—including men. But Simone hadn't come to Canada to husband-shop or even *fling*-shop. Romance equaled complications, as did sex, and she wasn't up for any of that in her life. After her divorce she'd tried to be as low-key as possible, for her and for her daughter.

"Bastien, this is my wife, Amalie, and my sister-in-law, Simone," Julian said as they arrived, slipping an arm around Amalie's waist. He seemed tense, a rarity for him. "Ladies, Bastien Demers is a top ten player from Canada with his sights on his first US Open title."

Simone realized why he looked familiar—he was Alex Wilde's stepbrother. She'd seen him on television once or twice.

Julian and Paul were well known for their dream run at the US Open six years ago. Julian, a Cinderella story, won the Open even though he was an underdog. Now he owned the Oliver Smoke Tennis Center, named after his dad, back in Atlanta. He had a big meeting with someone at the chateau, which happened to be the current location of the US Open series kickoff party *and* this after-party, but everything was all very hush-hush. Was Bastien the focus of all the secrecy? Amalie had been tight-lipped on the subject as well, which had Simone doubly intrigued given that Julian and Paul had been hounded with offers over the last few years to coach players, including some of the biggest names in the sport. Still, the two always turned them down flat, so Simone knew without a doubt that the meeting didn't have anything to do with coaching. Maybe some sort of sponsorship? Whatever it was, they were afraid to jinx it.

"Pleasure to meet you both." Bastien seemed chill when he shook Amalie's hand, but when he took Simone's, his demeanor shifted like the wind. His fingers danced over her bare ring finger, and his mouth ticked up into a smirk.

Sure, she supposed Bastien could be deemed attractive, if one liked overly clean-cut—and *young*—preppy types, but that sleazy leer that suddenly took over his face, complete with narrowed eyes and puckered lips, made Simone want to roll her eyes. Again.

Bastien's gaze dropped to her chest. Granted, her cleavage was on display to the world thanks to Amalie's insistence on this particularly low-cut dress. Simone loved the emerald green satin, but she did *not* like being ogled. No one had seen this much of her body since...

Damn. It had been a really long time.

Bastien bent to kiss Simone's hand, but before he could bring his mouth to her skin, she jerked away from his grasp. He could've been as gorgeous as Alex Wilde himself and that look still would've made her want to run the other way.

His eyes roved over her, from head to toe, and not in a welcome, seductive way. "Simone, you're quite stunning, aren't you?" He was still talking to her boobs.

Julian elbowed Bastien, giving him a dangerous scowl, his voice menacing even over the music. "Easy, man."

Simone shot her brother-in-law a grateful look but would fight this battle herself. "Bastien," she almost purred as she sidled closer, "tell me how you feel about women nearing forty with an eight-year-old child? You look like the paternal type."

When he paled, her lips tilted in a wicked smirk.

"Um, a kid?" he croaked. "And forty? That's amazing." He glanced away and lifted his beer, aiming the bottle at a cluster of men who hadn't acknowledged him in the least. "Tom!" he cried. "My man!"

And just like that, he disappeared.

Amalie nudged Simone in the side. "Do you pull that trick on all the hot guys who come on to you?"

"It usually works on the younger ones. Besides, he wasn't my type." Simone looked at Julian. "No more introductions tonight. Please." She eyed the exits again, wishing she was in her room reading a book.

Julian held up his hands. "Hey, I had no idea Bastien would be such a douche when he approached us to ask about coaching. Trust me. I learned what kind of guy he was quick. You don't have to worry about any more introductions from me."

Suddenly, Paul returned with an older man at his side. "Julian! Amalie! I want you to meet someone!"

Amalie pointed at Simone. "Don't leave. It's still early."

The moment Amalie turned her back, Simone took her chance. She grabbed a glass of champagne off a nearby tray and slinked toward the exit that led to the balcony. She wouldn't leave the party completely. She'd promised her little sister, and she never broke promises to Amalie. But fresh air and less noise and fewer people?

Yes, please. Now maybe she could hear herself think. What better spot to do a little introspection about one's life than somewhere beautiful like this?

She stepped onto the chateau's miraculously empty terrace. The light from the party spilled outside, and string bulbs hung above like twinkling stars. She released a sigh that made her entire body deflate before lifting the drink she'd pilfered to her lips, clutching her purse in her other hand. She was so glad to be alone. Coming to this party had obviously been a mistake.

Simone strolled toward the stone-cobbled edge overlooking Lake Louise, admiring the way the moon reflected on the water. Along the way, her heel caught on a nick in the concrete, causing her to stumble and spill some of the champagne on her dress.

"Shit!" She wiped frantically at the fabric. It was no use. It looked like she'd wet herself.

Just wonderful.

"Pardon, but I think if I go any longer without speaking, I'll scare you," a deep, rumbly, velvet voice spoke up—a voice with a strong French lilt.

She turned and squinted into the darkness but couldn't make anything out aside from a long silhouette leaning against the side of the chateau.

"Fleeing the masses?" the lovely voice asked.

Simone straightened, that voice sending a trail of soft chills along her arms. "Yeah, you could say that." She studied her hidden companion, hoping for a better look. "Not really my scene."

"Mine either."

Finally. Someone who agreed with her.

She grinned at the shadow. "It's really awful in there, right? I mean, The Tennis Ball? Come on." She rolled her eyes playfully before taking another sip from her glass. She might be wearing most of the alcohol, but she was determined to at least drink the last drop.

A husky laugh, decadent and warm, emanated from the darkness before a man stepped into the light. "I don't think the host is much of a party planner."

Simone choked on the champagne, spitting it out…

…and onto the very expensive-looking shoes of Alex Wilde, aka "The Wilde Card."

Of course, she'd just insulted him *and* spit on his shoes. It was on par for her night.

Simone looked up at him, and her mouth went dry. Holy hell, he was close. She could even smell the woodsy scent of his cologne. To be honest, she felt a little overwhelmed, because this man was *a lot* to behold.

He tilted his head, such a subtle movement, savage beauty sharpening the planes of his face. It should be illegal to look like that.

He scrubbed a hand over a neatly kept beard that was a shade darker than his shoulder-length, sandy blond hair. Simone might've had a slight beard fetish, which made this moment even more awkward. And those eyes. Were they brown? Or black as the night itself? She couldn't tell in the light, but she felt absorbed by his gaze, felt its heat caress her skin. But unlike with Bastien, the moment wasn't uncomfortable. It made her...*hot*. Was her heart beating faster?

She drew in a deep breath to steady herself. She was not interested in men right now. Nope. None of them.

Not even Alex Wilde.

Alex studied her a moment longer, and then a slow, heart-stopping grin unfurled across his face. He glanced down at his feet. "It's all right, *chérie*. I didn't like these shoes anyway." He shifted, and the golden glow from the string bulbs accented the rich, tawny color of his skin.

Simone cleared her throat, even though it still burned from coughing. Her cheeks threatened to do the same, and she fought the urge to squirm, to do anything aside from standing there blushing like a schoolgirl.

Unable to stifle said urge, she brought her clutch under her arm and toyed with its clasps. "Oh, ah, no. I actually like your shoes. Very...shiny."

Brilliant words there, Simone. She turned, placed her champagne flute on one of the tables, and let out a huge but very silent exhale, trying to get herself together.

Feeling slightly better, she twisted back around and shot him a nervous smile.

Alex held out a hand, his handsome face still illuminated with mischief. "I'm Alex Wilde, and I swear, I had nothing to do with that train wreck inside. The party planner is the one to blame for that."

Simone hesitated but finally took his hand, trying to ignore how good his skin felt when his long fingers folded around hers. "It's so nice to meet you. Sorry about what I said. About the party. It's really great, I'm just...a little too old for this kind of thing."

After a long beat, their hands fell apart. Alex slipped his fists in his pockets, the corners of his mouth quirking. "You? You can't be a day over twenty-five."

She shot him a smirk, knowing full well he was flattering her. "I'm many days over twenty-five, actually. Enough that *that*—" She pointed at the party. "—gives me a headache."

He laughed, the skin around his eyes crinkling. "Age is just a number. Hasn't anyone told you?"

Simone's voice was bone-dry when she volleyed back. "Says the twenty-nine-year-old tennis star."

Oh geez. She wanted to yank those words back inside her mouth.

His eyebrows shot up. "You know how old I am?"

Saving her from further embarrassment, Simone's phone buzzed. Normally, she wouldn't scan her messages in front of someone, but with Tallulah being at camp, she wanted to make sure it wasn't her.

"Sorry, I need to look at this." She pulled her phone from her clutch.

Alex nodded, and then her eyes were on the screen.

Not Lula. It was a text from her father. *Again.*

Simone clenched her jaw, as she shoved her cell back into her clutch. Her father hadn't noticed that Simone had been less enthused lately with her work as Warner Hotels' CEO. Everyone still looked at her with pity, asking how she was handling Damien's indiscretions rather than asking about the latest business deal she just closed. Besides, the CEO life wasn't exactly something she'd chosen for herself. She wanted out but hadn't figured out how to handle disappointing her father in such a massive way.

"Is everything okay?" Alex asked.

Simone lifted her head and shoulders, realizing she probably looked as adrift as she felt. "Yes, thank you. It's nothing that won't eventually work itself out."

"Want to talk about it? I've been told I'm an excellent listener." He propped against the wall and crossed his legs, his slim black pants hugging muscular thighs.

She scanned him from head to toe, her focus quickly traveling back to his face. She didn't doubt that he was an excellent listener—*among other things*. Things she really didn't need to be concerned with.

She fought the urge to smack her forehead. "In all honesty, I came outside because it was stifling in there, and I wanted to have a moment to process some things going on in my life, but now I find myself not wanting to think about any of it at all."

He folded his arms over his gray dress shirt, black tattoos dancing along his forearms. "I can absolutely distract you if needed. But before I can do that, I think I should know the name of who I'm distracting, *non*?" He angled his upper body toward her, his eyes glinting, a small smile playing on his full lips. Warmth radiated from him, the smoky scent of his vetiver and amber cologne mixed with musk tickling the air between them.

Being distracted by the enigma otherwise known as The Wilde Card was the absolute last thing Simone had expected out of this night.

"I'm Simone." It was funny. Just moments ago, all she wanted was to leave this party, and now she wasn't sure if anything could drag her away, which surprised her to no end.

Alex dipped his head. "*Enchanté*, Simone." Her name rolled off his tongue, drenched in an accent that made her toes curl.

She gripped her clutch, grounding herself. Her confidence had wavered the past year—something about a husband of ten years cheating on you will do that. Throw in the fact that she was only three years away from forty? Yeah, it had been rough. Turning forty wasn't precisely the issue, but for someone whose life had always been planned to the letter, she was approaching the milestone less sure of herself than she'd like.

"Now that we've properly met, may I ask why you're not inside? This is your party, after all, and you're out here lurking instead of mingling."

Yikes, did she really just say that?

Alex laughed, a sweet, honeyed sound that reminded her of the summer nights of her youth, filled with lightning bugs, stolen kisses, and broken curfews.

He kicked off the wall, looking completely roguish as he fully faced her. "*Lurking*? That makes me sound like some kind of stalker, *non*? Besides, aren't you the one who knew my age?" He shrugged playfully. "I'd rather like to think I was brooding."

She couldn't contain the surprised laughter that burst from her lips, happy to gloss over the part where her brain had saved tiny little factoids about this man.

"*Brooding*? Is that what you'd call it?"

Alex shifted his shoulders, still smiling. "Why not? Maybe I grew tired of talking about tennis and wanted some air." His voice was lighthearted, but she sensed a tightness stretching out his words.

Simone knew he'd been struggling with his game lately, but she didn't know why, exactly. He had a killer serve, but there was still something...*off*.

He spoke again, looking out toward the lake. "Or maybe I'm avoiding someone."

Of course. "Ah. An ex?"

"*Non*. I don't have exes. It would be my stepbrother, Bastien."

Simone put away that first part for later but scrunched her nose at the mention of the guy who'd ogled her. "Oh, yes. I met him earlier. He's…" Well, really what was there to say? He was horrid.

"Trust me, I know." Alex rubbed his bearded chin and leveled her with his stare. "Simone, may I ask you something? Why did you come to this party?"

That was a loaded question, yet suddenly, she found herself more comfortable with Alex Wilde than she had any right to be. Besides, it wasn't as if she'd ever see him again after this *tête-à-tête*.

"My sister made me." Her lips formed a small smile at that. "But also, I came out of curiosity I suppose."

His captivating eyes sparkled. "What do you mean?"

"It's hard to explain," she confessed, "but I feel like I've done everything I'm supposed to do, and yet I still ended up in the wrong place. Now I wish I would've taken a few chances along the way, maybe even made a few bad choices." She lifted a shoulder. "I thought this party could get me out of a rut."

A breeze blew in off the lake, ruffling her hair. Alex reached out and tucked a flyaway strand behind her ear, his fingers dancing over her skin so delicately, yet electricity sparked between them. It wasn't hard to see how Mr. Wilde attained his playboy status.

He was bewitching.

With a quick sweep beneath her chin, he drew back to catch her eye. "Perhaps we can help each other, if only for a night. What do you think about that?" His hand fell back to his side, but he was still close enough that she felt fully enveloped by him.

Her body swayed toward his, of its own volition, a coquettish answer on her tongue. "I think you have my attention."

But was that all that came out? No, of course not. She also *yawned*—the kind that made her eyes water and her mouth stretch wide enough to pop her jaw. She shielded Alex from most of that, but still. Without question, she felt a thousand years old.

"Sorry." The apology was part yawn. Could she possibly get any sexier? Yeesh.

He chuckled, not bothered in the least. "Listen, if bad choices are what you're looking for, I can spend the rest of the night sharing my terrible advice. Trust me, I have plenty, with experience too. And then you can make all kinds of poor choices."

She arched her brow and bit back a grin. "And what do you get out of it?"

"Maybe you'll rub off on me, and I'll never make another bad choice." He tilted his head. "Maybe it will help get my awful tennis under control."

Simone liked that idea...*a lot*. Suddenly, she wanted to get messy and make mistakes.

Alex continued before she could reply. "As a matter of fact, I can be your first bad choice." His words were pitched low, and he punctuated them with the sexiest wink she'd ever witnessed. Good God, this man had skill.

Emboldened, she brazenly held his stare when she spoke. "And what exactly do you suggest?"

"Tennis. Do you play?"

The confidence in Simone's shoulders faded a little. "Hold on, is that your move?"

Maybe she'd misread him. Maybe she was *that* old, old enough that she couldn't even recognize flirting anymore.

But then the corners of his mouth curved, and his voice was nothing more than a dark melody. "I have other moves, *chérie*, but you might not be ready for those yet."

She smirked, somehow bolstered by the innuendo. "You're not the only one with moves. I used to play, and I was really good."

Alex lifted his chin, a challenge glittering in his eyes. "Show me."

Show him?

"There's a court on the grounds," he continued. "Just waiting for us."

"Wait." She blinked, her breath coming out in a rush. "You want to play with me? Now? Tonight?" God, that sounded way more sexual than she intended. "I mean, tennis. Play *against* me. In tennis."

He laughed, clearly catching her faux pas, but then he moved closer, his voice a little quieter, a little more serious. "Yes," he said. "I want to play with you. Very much."

She could barely breathe. She was definitely skirting her comfort zone here, but something told her she'd regret it if she walked away now. She shouldn't be so intrigued by Alex Wilde. Her ex had a thing for the ladies too—any and all of them. But it seemed that, for tonight at least, tennis-playing men with sandy blond hair, fuck-me eyes, and a slightly wicked reputation were Simone's catnip, despite the fact that she'd been staunchly against any sort of romantic entanglements approximately ten minutes ago.

Funny how things change.

"Sure," she finally said. "I'll just go up to my room to change my clothes. Meet you down there in half an hour?"

Alex dipped his chin, and when she turned to walk away, a light touch grazed her hand. It was the barest whisper, a few fingertips, and then it was gone.

"See you soon, Simone."

She offered a small wave, her entire body vibrating. After all, she had a feeling Alex Wilde might be the best bad decision she'd ever make.

Don't stop now. Keep reading with your copy of THE WILDE CARD available now.

And sign up for Ashley R. King's newsletter to get all the news, giveaways, excerpts, and more!

Don't miss book two of the Ace of Hearts series with THE WILDE CARD available now and find more from Ashley R. King at ashleyrking.weebly.com

Simone Warner is a mom, a perfectionist, and former CEO. She's spent her life living up to the expectations of others—which is why she decides to have a one-night stand with a gorgeous tennis player eight years her junior. One wild night of reckless abandon, right?

Not exactly.

After she quits her job as CEO of Warner Hotels, Simone agrees to help notorious tennis player Julian Smoke coach a new top-secret player. Tennis has always been her passion, and Simone eagerly takes the plunge. What she doesn't expect is for her steamy one-night stand to waltz through the doors with a smirk on his face and a racket in hand.

Alex Wilde can't seem to get a handle on his game. Obsessed with besting his vile tennis star step-brother, he turns to Julian Smoke and his training center for help. That's when he sees *her*—the only woman who has ever left his bed without a goodbye. Simone Warner is his new assistant coach…and his only hope at getting back into the game.

The problem? Alex can't stop thinking about the woman who holds his future in her hands. And now, he has to play a very different kind of game, one where he has to win the girl.

Everyone knows to never underestimate a wild card—on or off the court.

Please sign up for the City Owl Press newsletter for chances to win special subscriber-only contests and giveaways as well as receiving information on upcoming releases and special excerpts.

All reviews are **welcome** and **appreciated**. Please consider leaving one on your favorite social media and book buying sites.

For books in the world of romance and speculative fiction that embody Innovation, Creativity, and Affordability, check out City Owl Press at www.cityowlpress.com.

Acknowledgments

First and foremost, I want to thank God for all He's done for me. Writing is a gift and I thank Him for it every day. I'm grateful for His love, unending glory, and grace, and for dreams that come true. None of this would be possible without Him.

To Jared, my whole universe— I struggle to find the words because they simply aren't enough to express the depths of my love and gratitude for you. You've always been my biggest supporter and have never doubted me, even when things looked bleak. It's one hundred percent accurate to say that I wouldn't have made it this far without your love and unending enthusiasm for not just this story, but for each of them. When I didn't think I could do it, thank you for playing *Runnin* from Creed II to pump me up, for the clips from *Rocky*, for always making me laugh so hard my stomach hurt, for always being down for period piece binge watches, for loving *Pride & Prejudice* as much as I do, for letting me bounce ideas off of you, for helping to create characters (hello, Paul Mercado lol). I am grateful for the hours spent helping me craft the perfect tennis scenes, for making sure that I got Julian Smoke just right. Gah, I'm thankful that I have a hot (inside and out) tennis player of my own with incredible calves haha— I love you more than words, boo. Thank you for sharing this beautiful life with me. To our adorable cat child, Cleo, thank you for the cuddles and keeping me company while I write. I love you, you cute, rotten thing.

Without Charissa Weaks, my amazing, supportive, and brilliant editor, none of this would exist. Words cannot express my gratitude for everything you've done— for taking a chance on me, for making my dream come true, for believing in Julian and Amalie's story. I am grateful for your boss level editing skills, for making this story stronger and tighter, as well as for everything you've taught me along the way. Your patience and kindness have meant so much and have made this entire process the greatest joy. You are a rock star!

To Tina Moss and Yelena Casale, as well as the entire City Owl team, you'll never know how grateful I am that you took a chance on me, for being so kind and patient, always willing to help or answer questions. I am so proud to be a part of the Owl Squad. Thank you to Marianne Hull for your copy edits, as well as to Miblart for the beautiful cover design.

Bill and Carol, my parents, both of whom are no longer on this earth. My love of writing stems from both of you. I'm thankful for my Mom who cultivated a love of reading in me, for taking me to the public library so that I could check out stacks of books bigger than I was, for encouraging me to read to her every night. To my Dad, who cheered me on, who believed in me always, who told me I could become a writer if I wanted to. I miss and love you both and wish you could be here to share this moment with me. Thank you for your love.

To my second parents, Phil and TK, thank you for your constant encouragement, for always believing in me and praying for me. I am so glad that I not only have Jared, but I have you both as well. You never gave up on me or laughed at me when I said I wanted to be a writer. TK, thank you for always being so willing to read my novels— even those from the early years that were definitely not good haha. Phil, thank you for always being so excited whenever I have writing news, for always checking in on how things are going, and for not doubting that I could do this thing. I love you both more than you know!

Ginger, thank you for being the best sister I could ask for, for fueling my love of reading, for introducing me to *Anne of Green Gables,* period dramas, and for the countless *Babysitter Club* books you bought for me when I was younger. Lee, thank you for the Stephen King novels, for helping me figure out my writing style, for never doubting me. Aaron, thank you for being you. I'm so proud to be your aunt. Also, thank you for helping me navigate this process with your knowledge and expertise. I love each of you more than you know. Thank you for your love and support— it means so much. I am so lucky to have you as my family.

Brent, thank you for everything you've done to help me these past twelve years as I worked to become a published author. You stopped what you were doing countless times to help me work through synopses, query letters, even chapters. God knows I need help with commas and you helped me with those too. I wouldn't have made it without you bro. I appreciate you more than you know. Melissa, thank you for your encouragement, cards, and excitement for this chapter of my life. Ryan, thank you for always believing in me during this writing adventure. Haley, thank you for your encouragement and support for this adventure, as well as for being my book cover model for *Letters*. A shout out to my precious nieces and nephews, Mazie, Graham, Claire, Seth, and Sofia. Kristen, I can't thank you enough for being my beta reader, for your enthusiasm, kindness, and honesty. Will, thank you for helping me with this dream since day one, for the writing advice and edits of other works. I love each of you and am so grateful that we are family.

Karen Grove, you were the first person in the industry to make me stop and think, "Hey, maybe my writing isn't total trash!" Thank you for believing in Amalie and Julian from day one and helping me work the monstrosity that it was into something that I could submit to publishing houses and agents. You taught me so much and I will always be so grateful for you, your amazing editing skills, and your encouragement. It means more than you know. Victoria Loder, who crafted my Twitter pitch for #PitMad, which led me to my fabulous editor, Charissa. Your pitch was perfect and catchy and is one of the reasons I landed the book deal. I am so grateful for your brilliant mind.

Bonnie, thank you for being my ride or die, for reading my stuff (and bless it, helping with those dang commas) even though you don't like to read lol. I feel privileged and am thankful to have you as my friend. Erin, I am so grateful for you as one of my dearest friends, for the hilarious videos and memes you send me, for not doubting that I could do this for one second. To Candace, thank you for being my very first fan outside my fam from day one, for always being so kind and supportive and never hesitating to read over my novels. Lori, thank you for reading the very first draft of PTL even right after surgery, as well as for your love and support. Michelle, thank you for your encouragement and always making me laugh with funny memes in the group text. Erin, I am so grateful for you as one of my dearest friends, for the hilarious videos and memes you send me, for not doubting that I could do this for one second. Beth, you've believed in me since day one and have always been so excited and supportive of me each step of the way. Thank you for not only being a friend, but for being a photographic genius. Your photography skills are unparalleled and I'm thankful for your time, as well as for your inspired book photos and author shots. Vicki, you're one of my favorite people at work. Thank you for always being so pumped about this adventure and for always being so kind to offer help if needed. Hillary, thank you for being another one of my favorites, for your card that brightened my day, and for always being so wonderful. Shelly, thank you for your precious card, as well as for never hesitating to look over a query letter or a chapter for me. Lindsey T., I am grateful for your kind heart, for always being so willing to read over my novels and for offering honest insight. I love each of you and everything you've done to get me here means more than you'll know.

Jennifer L. Armentrout, one of my favorite authors. Thank you for encouraging me to keep writing all those years ago. You have no idea how much you help the writing world and that it is a better place thanks to you.

To my social media friends, fellow 2020 debuts and City Owl sisters, bookstagrammers, book bloggers, Inkslinger PR, and readers, I am indebted to you. Thank you for the support throughout this entire process as well as getting the word out about *Painting the Lines*, as well as for taking the time to read it. My heart is full.

About the Author

Ashley R. King is a middle school English teacher whose love of the written word began when her mom took her to the public library, letting her check out stacks of books taller than she was. She's the least athletic person you'll ever meet, but that doesn't decrease her love for her favorite sport, tennis. She loves swoony romances and is addicted to sweet tea. When she's not teaching or writing happily ever afters, she can be found snuggled up with a book, traveling, or quoting obscure lines from her favorite movies and tv shows. She lives in a small town in Georgia  with her favorite person in the world—her husband, and their sweet and chatty spoiled cat, Cleo.

ashleyrking.weebly.com

 facebook.com/ashleyrkingwrites
 twitter.com/ashleyk628
instagram.com/ashleyrkingwrites

About the Publisher

City Owl Press is a cutting edge indie publishing company, bringing the world of romance and speculative fiction to discerning readers.

Escape Your World. Get Lost in Ours!

www.cityowlpress.com

 facebook.com/CityOwlPress

 twitter.com/cityowlpress

 instagram.com/cityowlbooks

 pinterest.com/cityowlpress

 tiktok.com/@cityowlpress

Made in United States
North Haven, CT
01 August 2023

39816842R00164